about grace

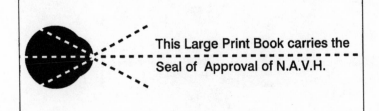

about grace

ANTHONY DOERR

Copyright © 2004 by Anthony Doerr

Published in 2005 by arrangement with Scribner, an imprint of Simon & Schuster, Inc.

Wheeler Large Print Hardcover.

The text of this Large Print edition is unabridged.
Other aspects of the book may vary from the original edition.

Set in 16 pt. Plantin by Carleen Stearns.

Printed in the United States on permanent paper.

Library of Congress Cataloging-in-Publication Data

Doerr, Anthony, 1973–
    About Grace : a novel / Anthony Doerr.
        p. cm.
    ISBN 1-58724-779-8 (lg. print : hc : alk. paper)
    1. Separation (Psychology) — Fiction.   2. Fathers and daughters — Fiction.   3. Runaway husbands — Fiction.
    4. Caribbean Area — Fiction.   5. Precognition —
Fiction.   6. Alaska — Fiction.   7. Dreams — Fiction.
    8. Large type books.   I. Title.
    PS3604.O34A63 2005
    813′.54—dc22   2004058386

for my mother and father

As the Founder/CEO of NAVH, the only national health agency solely devoted to those who, although not totally blind, have an eye disease which could lead to serious visual impairment, I am pleased to recognize Thorndike Press★ as one of the leading publishers in the large print field.

Founded in 1954 in San Francisco to prepare large print textbooks for partially seeing children, NAVH became the pioneer and standard setting agency in the preparation of large type.

Today, those publishers who meet our standards carry the prestigious "Seal of Approval" indicating high quality large print. We are delighted that Thorndike Press is one of the publishers whose titles meet these standards. We are also pleased to recognize the significant contribution Thorndike Press is making in this important and growing field.

Lorraine H. Marchi, L.H.D.
Founder/CEO
NAVH

★ Thorndike Press encompasses the following imprints: Thorndike, Wheeler, Walker and Large Print Press.

There must be some definite cause why, whenever snow begins to fall, its initial formation invariably displays the shape of a six-cornered starlet. For if it happens by chance, why do they not fall just as well with five corners or with seven? . . . Who carved the nucleus, before it fell, into six horns of ice?

— *From "On the Six-Cornered Snowflake," by Johannes Kepler, 1610*

Book One

Book One

1

He made his way through the concourse and stopped by a window to watch a man with two orange wands wave a jet into its gate. Above the tarmac the sky was faultless, that relentless tropic blue he had never quite gotten used to. At the horizon, clouds had piled up: *cumulus congestus,* a sign of some disturbance traveling along out there, over the sea.

The slim frame of a metal detector awaited its line of tourists. In the lounge: duty-free rum, birds of paradise sleeved in cellophane, necklaces made from shells. From his shirt pocket he produced a notepad and a pen.

The human brain, he wrote, *is seventy-five percent water. Our cells are little more than sacs in which to carry water. When we die it spills from us into the ground and air and into the stomachs of animals and is contained again in something else. The properties of liquid water are this: it holds its temperature longer than air; it is adhering and elastic; it is perpetually in motion. These are the tenets of hydrology; these are the things one should know if one is to know oneself.*

He passed through the gate. On the boarding stairs, almost to the jet, a feeling like choking rose in his throat. He clenched his duffel and clung to the rail. A line of birds — ground doves, perhaps — were landing one by one in a patch of mown grass on the far side of the runway. The passengers behind him shifted restlessly. A flight attendant wrung her hands, reached for him, and escorted him into the cabin.

The sensation of the plane accelerating and rising was like entering a vivid and perilous dream. He braced his forehead against the window. The ocean widened below the wing; the horizon tilted, then plunged. The plane banked and the island reemerged, lush and sudden, fringed by reef. For an instant, in the crater of Soufrière, he could see a pearly green sheet of water. Then the clouds closed, and the island was gone.

The woman in the seat next to him had produced a novel and was beginning to read. The airplane climbed the troposphere. Tiny fronds of frost were growing on the inner pane of the window. Behind them the sky was dazzling and cold. He blinked and wiped his glasses with his sleeve. They were climbing into the sun.

2

His name was David Winkler and he was fifty-nine years old. This would be his first trip home in twenty-five years — if home was what he could still call it. He had been a father, a husband, and a hydrologist. He was not sure if he was any of those things now.

His ticket was from Kingstown, St. Vincent, to Cleveland, Ohio, with a stopover in Miami. The first officer was relaying airspeed and altitude through loudspeakers in the ceiling. Weather over Puerto Rico. The captain would keep the seat belt sign illuminated.

From his window seat, Winkler glanced around the cabin. Passengers — Americans, mostly — were reading, sleeping, speaking quietly to one another. The woman beside Winkler held the hand of a blond man in the aisle seat.

He closed his eyes, rested his head against the window, and gradually slipped into something like sleep. He woke sweating. The woman in the seat beside him was

14

shaking his shoulder. "You were dreaming," she said. "Your legs were shaking. And your hands. You pressed them against the window."

"I'm all right." Far below the wing scrolled reefs of cumuli. He mopped his face with a cuff.

Her gaze lingered on him before she took up her novel again. He sat awhile and studied the clouds. Finally, with a resigned voice, he said, "The compartment above you isn't latched properly. In the turbulence it'll open and the bag inside will fall out."

She looked up. "What?"

"The compartment. The bin." He motioned with his eyes toward the space above them. "It must not be completely closed."

She leaned across the blond man beside her, into the aisle. "Really?" She nudged the blond man and said something and he looked over and up and said the bin was fine and latched tight.

"Are you sure?"

"Quite."

The woman turned to Winkler. "It's fine. Thank you." She went back to her book. Two or three minutes later the plane began to buck, and the entire cabin

15

plunged for a long second. The bin above them rattled, the door clicked open, and a bag dropped into the aisle. From inside came the muffled crunch of breaking glass.

The blond man lifted the bag and peered inside and swore. The plane leveled off. The bag was straw and printed with an image of a sailboat. The man began taking out pieces of what looked like souvenir martini glasses and shaking his head at them. A flight attendant squatted in the aisle and collected fragments in an airsickness bag.

The woman in the middle seat stared at Winkler with a hand over her mouth.

He kept his gaze out the window. The frost between the panes was growing, making tiny connections, a square inch of delicate feathers, a two-dimensional wonderland of ice.

3

He called them dreams. Not auguries or visions exactly, or presentiments or premonitions. Calling them dreams let him edge as close as he could to what they were: sensations — experiences, even — that visited him as he slept and faded after he woke, only to reemerge in the minutes or hours or days to come.

It had taken years before he was able to recognize the moment as it approached — something in the odor of a room (a smell like cedar shingles, or smoke, or hot milk and rice), or the sound of a diesel bus shaking along below an apartment, and he would realize this was an event he had experienced before, that what was about to happen — his father slicing his finger on a can of sardines, a gull alighting on the sill — was something that had already happened, in the past, in a dream.

He had standard dreams, too, of course, the types of dreams everyone has, the film reels of paradoxical sleep, all the improbable narratives concocted by a cerebral cortex working to organize its memories. But occasionally, rarely, what he saw when he slept (rain overwhelmed the gutters; the plumber offered half his turkey sandwich; a coin disappeared, inexplicably, from his pocket) was different — sharper, truer, and premonitory.

All his life it had been like this. His dreams predicted crazy, impossible things: stalactites grew out of the ceiling; he opened a door to find the bathroom stuffed with melting ice. And they predicted everyday things: a woman dropped a magazine; a cat delivered a broken sparrow to the back door; a bag fell from an overhead bin and its contents broke in the aisle. Like dreams these apparitions ambushed him in the troubled fringes of sleep, and once they were finished, they were almost always lost, disbanding into fragments he could not reassemble later.

But a few times in his life he had fuller visions: the experience of them fine-edged and hyperreal — like waking to find himself atop a barely frozen lake, the deep cracking sounding beneath his feet — and those dreams remained long after he woke, reminding themselves to him throughout the days to come, as if the imminent could not wait to become the past, or the present lunged at the future, eager for what would be. Here most of all the word failed: These were dreams deeper than dreaming, beyond remembering. These dreams were knowing.

He shifted in his seat and watched phalanxes of clouds pass below the wing. Memories scudded toward him, as distinct as the fibers in the seat-back in front of him: he saw the blue glow of a welding arc flicker in a window; he saw rain washing over the windshield of his old Chrysler. He was seven and his mother bought him his first pair of eyeglasses; he hurried through the apartment examining everything: the structure of frost in the icebox, a spattering of rain on the parlor window. What a marvel it had been to see the particulars of the world — rainbows of oil floating in puddles; columns of gnats spiraling over Ship Creek; the crisp, scalloped edges of clouds.

4

He was on an airplane, fifty-nine years old, but he could be simultaneously — in the folds of memory — a quarter century younger, in bed, in Ohio, falling asleep. The house was still and going dark. Beside him his wife slept on top of the comforter, legs splayed, her body giving off heat as it always did. Their infant daughter was quiet across the hall. It was midnight, March, rain at the windows, and he had to be up at five the next morning. He listened to the click and patter of drops against the panes. His eyelids fell.

In his dream, water swirled three feet deep in the street. From the upstairs window — he was standing at it, palms against the glass — the neighborhood houses looked like a fleet of foundered arks: floodwater past the first-floor sills, fences swallowed, saplings up to their necks.

His daughter was crying somewhere. Behind him the bed was empty and neatly made — where had his wife gone? Boxes of cereal and a few dishes stood on the dresser; a pair of gum boots waited atop the stairs. He hurried from room to room calling for his daughter. She was not in her crib or the bathroom or anywhere upstairs. He pulled on the boots and descended to the front hall. Two feet of water covered the entire first floor, silent and cold, a color like milky coffee. When he stood on the hall carpet, the water was past his knees. His daughter's whimpering echoed strangely through the rooms, as if she were present in every corner. "Grace?"

Outside more water muttered and pressed at the walls. He waded forward. Pale spangles of reflected light swung back and forth over the ceiling. Three magazines turned idly in his wake; a bloated roll of paper towels bumped his knee and drifted off.

He opened the pantry and sent a wave rolling through the kitchen, jostling the stools. A group of half-submerged lightbulbs like the caps of tiny drifting skulls sailed toward the refrigerator. He paused. He could no longer hear her. "Grace?"

From outside came the sound of a motorboat passing. Each breath hung in front of him a moment before dispersing. The light was failing. The hairs on his arms

21

stood up. He picked up the phone — the cord floating beneath it — but there was no dial tone. Something sour and thin was beginning to rise from his gut.

He forced open the basement door and found the stairwell entirely submerged, lost beneath a foamy brown rectangle of water. A page from a calendar floated there, something of his wife's, a photo of a candy-striped lighthouse, darkening and turning in the froth.

He panicked. He searched for her beneath the hall table, behind the armchair (which was nearly afloat now); he looked in ridiculous places: the silverware drawer, a Tupperware bowl. He waded with his arms down, feeling below the surface, dragging his fingers along the floor. The only sounds were of his lower body splashing along and the smaller percussions of waves he'd made lapping against the walls.

He found her on his third pass through the family room. She was in her bassinet, atop the highest shelf of his wife's plant stand, against the foggy window, her eyes wide, a blanket over her shoulders. Her yellow wool cap on her head. Her blanket was dry. "Grace," he said, lifting her out, "who put you up there?"

Emotion flitted across her face, her lips tightening, her forehead wrinkling. Just as quickly, her expression eased. "It's okay," he said. "We'll get you out of here." He held her against his chest, waded through the hall, and dragged open the front door.

Water sighed in from the yard. The street had become a clotted, makeshift river. The sugar maple on the Sachses' lawn was lying immersed across the street. Plastic bags, snagged in the branches, vibrated in the passage of water and sent up a high, unearthly buzzing, a sound like insects swarming. No lights were on. Two cats he had never seen before paced a low branch of the front yard oak. Dozens of possessions were adrift: a lawn chair, a pair of plastic trash cans, a Styrofoam cooler — all slathered with mud, all parading slowly down the street.

He waded down the steps of the front walk. Soon the water was to his belt and he held Grace high against his shoulder with both arms and fought the current. Her breath was small in his ear. His own breath stood out in front of them in short-lived clouds of vapor.

His clothes were drenched and he had begun to shiver. The force of water — slow, but heavy with sediment and sticks and whole clumps of turf — pushed resolutely at his thighs and he felt it trying to raise his feet and carry them away. A hundred yards up the street, behind the Stevensons' place, a small blue light winked among the trees. He glanced back at the entrance to his own house, dark, already far away.

"Hang on, Grace," he said. She did not cry. From the location of the telephone poles standing in the dimness he could discern where the sidewalk was and made for it.

He clawed his way up the street, hanging with one arm on to lampposts and the trunks of trees and pulling himself forward as if up the rungs of an enormous ladder. He would reach the blue light and save them. He would wake, safe and dry, in his bed.

The flood hissed and murmured, a sound like blood rising in his ears. The taste of it was in his teeth: clay and something else, like rust. Several times he thought he might slip and had to stop, propped against a mailbox, spitting water, clutching the baby. His glasses fogged. His legs and feet were numb. The flood sucked at his boots.

The light behind the Stevensons' wavered and blinked and rematerialized as it passed behind obstacles. A boat. The water was not as deep up here. "Help!" he called. "Help us." Grace was quiet: a small weight against his wet shirt. Far away, as if from a distant shore, sirens keened.

A few steps later, he stumbled. Water surged to his shoulders. The river pushed at him the way wind pushes at a sail and all his life, even in dreams, he would remember the sensation: the feeling of being overwhelmed by water. In a second he was borne away. He held Grace as high as he could and clamped her little thighs between his palms, his thumbs in the small of her back. He kicked; he pointed his toes and tried to find bottom. The upper halves of houses glided past. For a moment he thought they would be carried all the way down the street, past their house, past the cul-de-sac, and into the river. Then his head struck a telephone pole; he spun; the current washed them under.

The evening had gone to that last blue before darkness. He tried to hold Grace above his chest, her little hips in his hands; his own head stayed under.

His shoulders struck submerged sticks, a dozen unseen obstacles. The undercurrent sucked one of his boots off. A few hundred feet down the block they passed into an eddy, full of froth and twigs, and he threw his legs around a mailbox — the last mailbox on the street. Here the flood coursed through wooded lots at the terminus of the street and merged with the swollen, unrecognizable Chagrin River. There, somehow, he managed to stagger to his feet, still holding Grace. A spasm tore through his diaphragm and he began to cough.

The bobbing, shifting point of light that had been by the Stevensons' was miraculously closer. "Help us!" he gasped. "Over here!"

The mailbox swiveled against his weight. The light drew nearer. It was a rowboat. A man leaned over the bow waving a flashlight. He could hear voices. The mailbox groaned against his weight. "Please," Winkler tried to say. "Please."

The boat approached. The light was in his face. Hands had ahold of his belt and were hauling him over the gunwale.

"Is she dead?" he heard someone ask. "Is she breathing?"

Winkler gulped air. His glasses were lost but he could see that Grace's mouth hung open. Her hair was wet, her yellow cap gone. Her cheeks had lost their color. He could not seem to relax his arms — they did not seem like his arms at all. "Sir," someone said. "Let her loose, sir."

He felt a scream boiling up in his throat. Someone called for him to let go, let go, let go.

This was a dream. This had not happened.

5

Memory gallops, then checks up and veers unexpectedly; to memory, the order of occurrence is arbitrary. Winkler was still on an airplane, hurtling north, but he was also pushing farther back, sinking deeper into the overlaps, to the years before he even had a daughter, before he had even dreamed of the woman who would become his wife.

This was 1975. He was thirty-two years old, in Anchorage, Alaska. He had an apartment over a garage in Midtown, a 1970 Chrysler Newport, few friends, no family left. If there was anything to notice about him, it was his eyeglasses: thick, Coke-bottle lenses in plastic frames. Behind them his eyes appeared unsubstantial and slightly warped, as if he peered not through a half centimeter of curved glass but through ice, two frozen pools, his eyeballs floating just beneath.

It was March again, early breakup, the sun not completely risen but a warmth in the air, blowing east, and with it the improbable smell of new leaves, as if spring was already happening to the west — in the Aleutian volcanoes or all the way across the strait in Siberia — the first compressed buds showing on whatever kinds of trees they had there, and bears blinking as they stumbled from their hibernal dens, whole festivals starting, nighttime songs and burgeoning romances and homages to the equinox and the first seeds being sown — Russian spring blowing across the Bering Sea and over the mountains and tumbling into Anchorage.

Winkler dressed in one of his two brown corduroy suits and walked to the small brick National Weather Service office on Seventh Avenue where he worked as an analyst's assistant. He spent the morning compiling snowpack forecasts at his little veneered desk. Every few minutes a slab of snow would slide off the roof and plunge into the hedge outside his window with a muffled whump.

At noon he walked to the Snow Goose Market and ordered a salami and mustard on wheat and waited in a checkout lane to pay for it.

Fifteen feet away a woman in tortoise-shell glasses and a tan polyester suit stopped in front of a revolving rack of magazines. Two boxes of cereal and a half gallon of milk stood primly in her basket. The light — angling through the front windows — fell across her waist and lit her shins below her skirt. He could see tiny particles of dust drifting in the air between her ankles, each fleck tumbling individually in and out of sunlight, and there was something intensely familiar in their arrangement.

A cash register clanged. An automatic fan in the ceiling clicked on with a sigh. Suddenly he knew what would happen — he had dreamed it four or five nights before. The woman would drop a magazine; he would step over, pick it up, and give it back.

The cashier handed a pair of teenagers their change and looked expectantly at Winkler. But he could not take his eyes from the woman browsing magazines. She spun the rack a quarter turn, her thumb and forefinger fell hesitantly upon an issue (*Good Housekeeping*, March 1975, Valerie Harper on the cover, beaming and tan in a green tank top), and she picked it up. The cover slipped; the magazine fell.

His feet made for her as if of their own volition. He bent; she stooped. The tops of their heads nearly touched. He lifted the magazine, swiped dust off the cover, and handed it over.

They straightened simultaneously. He realized his hand was shaking. His eyes did not meet hers but left their attention somewhere above her throat. "You dropped this," he said. She didn't take it. At the register a housewife had taken his place in line. A bagboy snapped open a bag and lowered a carton of eggs into it.

"Miss?"

She inhaled. Behind her lips were trim rows of shiny teeth, slightly off-axis. She closed her eyes and held them shut a moment before opening them, as if waiting out a spell of vertigo.

"Did you want this?"

"How — ?"

"Your magazine?"

"I have to go," she said abruptly. She set down her shopping basket and made for the exit, almost jogging, holding her coat around her, hurrying through the door into the parking lot. For a few seconds he could see her two legs scissoring up the street; then she was obscured by a banner taped over the window, and gone.

He stood holding the magazine for a long time. The sounds of the store gradually returned. He picked up her basket, set his sandwich in it, and paid for it all — the milk, the cereal, the *Good Housekeeping*.

Later, after midnight, he lay in his bed and could not sleep. Elements of her (three freckles on her left cheek, the groove between the knobs of her collarbone, a strand of hair tucked behind her ear) scrolled past his eyes. On the floor beside him the magazine lay open: an ad for dog biscuits, a recipe for blueberry upside-down cake.

He got up, tore open one of the cereal boxes — both were Kellogg's Apple Jacks — and ate handfuls of the little pale rings at his kitchen window, watching the streetlights shudder in the wind.

A month passed. Rather than fade from his memory, the woman grew sharper, more insistent: two rows of teeth, dust floating between her ankles. At work he saw her face on the undersides of his eyelids, in a numerical model of groundwater data from Shemya Air Force Base. Almost every noon he found himself at the Snow Goose, scanning checkout lanes, lingering hopefully in the cereal aisle.

He went through the first box of Apple Jacks in a week. The second box he ate more slowly, rationing himself a palmful a day, as if that box were the last in existence, as if when he looked into the bottom and found only sugary dust, he'd have consumed not only his memory of her, but any chance of seeing her again.

He brought the *Good Housekeeping* to work and paged through it: twenty-three recipes for potatoes; coupons for Pillsbury Nut Bread; a profile of quintuplets. Were there clues to her here? When no one was looking he set Valerie Harper's cover photo under a coworker's Swift 2400 and examined her clavicle in the viewfinder. She consisted of melees of dots — yellows and magentas, ringed with blue — her breasts made of big, motionless halos.

Winkler, who in his thirty-two years had hardly left the Anchorage Bowl, who still caught himself some clear days staring wistfully at the Alaska Range to the north, the brilliant white massifs, and the white spaces farther back, the way they floated on the horizon less like real mountains than the ghosts of them, now found his eyes drawn into the dream kitchens of advertisements: copper pots, shelf paper, folded napkins. Was her kitchen like one of these? Did she, too, use Brillo Supreme steel wool pads for her heavy-duty cleaning needs?

He found her in June, at the same

market. This time she wore a plaid skirt and tall boots. She stepped briskly through the aisles, looking different, more determined. A shaft of anxiety whirled in his chest. She bought a small bottle of grape juice and an apple, counting exact change out of a tiny purse with brass clasps. She was in and out in under two minutes.

He followed.

She walked quickly, making long strides, her gaze on the sidewalk ahead of her. Winkler had to half jog to keep up. The day was warm and damp and her hair, tied at the back of her neck, seemed to float along behind her head. At D Street she waited to cross and Winkler came up behind her, suddenly too close — if he leaned forward six inches, the top of her head would have been in his face. He stared at her calves disappearing into her boots and inhaled. What did she smell like? Clipped grass? The sleeve of a wool sweater? The mouth of the little brown bag that held her apple and juice crinkled in her fist.

The light changed. She started off the curb. He followed her six blocks up Fifth Avenue, where she turned right and went into a branch of First Federal Savings and Loan. He paused outside, trying to calm his heart. A pair of gulls sailed past, calling to each other. Through the stenciling on the window, past a pair of desks (with bankers at them, penciling things onto big desk calendars), he watched her pull open a walnut half-door and slip behind the teller counter. There were customers waiting. She set down her little bag, slid aside a sign, and waved the first one forward.

He hardly slept. A full moon, high over the city, dragged the tide up Knik Arm, then let it out again. He read from Watson, from Pauling, the familiar words disassembling in front of his eyes. He stood by the window with a legal pad and wrote: *Inside me a trillion cells are humming, proteins stalking the strands of my DNA, winding and unwinding, making and remaking . . .*

He crossed it out. He wrote: *Do we choose who we love?*

If only his first dream had carried him past what he already knew, past the magazine falling to the floor. He shut his eyes and tried to summon an image of her, tried to keep her there as he drifted toward sleep.

By nine a.m. he was on the same sidewalk watching her through the same window. In his knapsack he had what remained of the second box of Apple Jacks and the *Good Housekeeping.* She was standing at her teller's station, looking down. He wiped his palms on his trousers and went in.

There was no one in the queue, but her station had a sign up: PLEASE SEE THE NEXT TELLER. She was counting ten-dollar bills with the thin, pink hands he already thought of as familiar. A nameplate resting on the marble counter read, SANDY SHEELER.

"Excuse me."

She held up a finger and continued counting without looking up.

"I can help you down here," another teller offered.

"It's okay," Sandy said. She reached the end of her stack, made a notation on the corner of an envelope, and looked up. "Hello."

The lenses of her glasses reflected a light in the ceiling for a second and flooded the lenses of his own glasses with light. Panic started in his throat. She was a stranger, entirely unfamiliar; who was he to have guessed at her dissatisfactions, to have incorporated her into his dreams? He stammered: "I met you in the supermarket? A few months ago? We didn't actually meet, but . . ."

Her gaze swam. He reached into his knapsack and withdrew the cereal and the magazine. A teller to Sandy's right glanced over the partition.

"I thought maybe," he said, "you wanted these? You left so quickly."

"Oh." She did not touch the cereal or the *Good Housekeeping* but did not take her eyes from them. He could not tell but thought she leaned forward a fraction. He lifted the box of cereal and shook it. "I ate some."

She gave him a confused smile. "Keep it."

Her eyes tracked from the magazine to him and back. A critical moment was passing now, he knew it: he could feel the floor falling away beneath his feet. "Would you ever want to go to a movie? Anything like that?"

Now her gaze veered past Winkler and over his shoulder, out into the bank. She shook her head. Winkler felt a small weight drop into his stomach. Already he began to back away. "Oh. I see. Well. I'm sorry."

She took the box of Apple Jacks and shook it and set it on the shelf beneath the counter. She whispered, "My husband," and looked at Winkler for the first time, really looked at him, and Winkler felt her gaze go all the way through the back of his head.

He heard himself say: "You don't wear a ring."

"No." She touched her ring finger. Her nails were clipped short. "It's getting repaired."

He sensed he was out of time; the whole scene was slipping away, liquefying and sliding toward a drain. "Of course," he mumbled. "I work at the Weather Service. I'm David. You could reach me there. In case you decide differently." And then he was turning, his empty knapsack bunched in his fist, the bright glass of the bank's facade reeling in front of him.

Two months: rain on the windows, a pile of unopened meteorology texts on the table in his apartment that struck him for the first time in his life as trivial. He cooked noodles, wore one of the same two brown corduroy suits, checked the barometer three times a day and charted his readings halfheartedly on graph paper smuggled home from work.

Mostly he remembered her ankles, and the particles of dust drifting between them, illuminated in a slash of sunlight. The three freckles on her cheek formed an isosceles triangle. He had been so certain; he had *dreamed* her. But who knew where assurance and belief came from? Somewhere across town she was standing at a sink or walking into a closet, his name stowed somewhere in the pleated neurons of her brain, echoing up one dendrite in a billion: David, David.

The days slid by, one after another: warm, cold, rainy, sunny. He felt, all the time, as if he had lost something vital: his wallet, his keys, a fundamental memory he couldn't quite summon. The horizon looked the same as ever: the same grimy oil trucks groaned through the streets; the tide exposed the same mudflats twice a day. In the endless gray Weather Service teletypes, he saw the same thing every time: desire.

Hadn't there been a longing in her face, locked behind that bank-teller smile — a yearning in her, visible just for a second, as she dragged her eyes up? Hadn't she seemed about to cry at the supermarket?

The *Good Housekeeping* lay open on his kitchen counter, bulging with riddles: *Do you know the secret of looking younger? How much style for your money do cotton separates*

39

offer? How many blonde colors found in nature are in Naturally Blonde Hair Treatment?

He walked the streets; he watched the sky.

6

She called in September. A secretary patched her through. "He has a hockey game," Sandy said, nearly whispering. "There's a matinee at four-fifteen."

Winkler swallowed. "Okay. Yes. Four-fifteen."

She appeared in the lobby at four-thirty and hurried past him to the concessions counter where she bought a box of chocolate-covered raisins. Then, without looking at him, she entered the theater and sat in the dimness with the light from the screen flickering over her face. He took the seat beside her. She ate her raisins one after another, hardly stopping to breathe; she smelled, he thought, like mint, like chewing gum. All through the film he stole glances: her cheek, her elbow, stray hairs atop her head illuminated in the wavering light.

Afterward she watched the credits drift up the screen as if the film still played behind them, as if there would be more to the story. Her eyelids blinked rapidly. The house lights came up. She said, "You're a weatherman."

"Sort of. I'm a hydrologist."

"The ocean?"

"Groundwater, mostly. And the atmosphere. My main interest lies in snow, in the formation and physics of snow crystals. But you can't really get paid to study that. I type memos, recheck forecasts. I'm basically a secretary."

"I like snow," Sandy said. Moviegoers were filing for the exits and her attention flitted over them. He fumbled for something to say.

"You're a bank teller?"

She did not look at him. "That day in the market . . . It was like I knew you were going to be there. When I dropped the magazine, I knew you'd come over. It felt like I had already done it, already lived through it once before." She glanced at him quickly, just for a moment, then gathered her coat, smoothed out the front of her skirt, and peered over her shoulder to where an usher was already sweeping the aisle. "You think that's crazy."

"No," he said.

Her upper lip trembled. She did not look at him. "I'll call next Wednesday." Then she was moving down the row of seats, her coat tight around her shoulders.

Why did she call him? Why did she come back to the theater, Wednesday after Wednesday? To slip the constraints of her life? Perhaps. But even then Winkler guessed it was because she had felt something that noon in the Snow Goose Market — had felt time settle over itself, imbricate and fix into place, the vertigo of future aligning with the present.

They saw *Jaws*, and *Benji*, talking around the edges. Each week Sandy bought a box of chocolate-covered raisins and ate them with the same zeal, the indigo light of the screen flaring in the lenses of her glasses.

"Sandy," he'd whisper in the middle of a film, his heart climbing his throat. "How are you?"

"Is that the uncle?" she'd whisper back, eyes on the screen. "I thought he was dead."

"How is work? What have you been up to?"

She'd shrug, chew a raisin. Her fingers were thin and pink: magnificent.

Afterward she'd stand, take a breath, and pull her coat around her. "I hate this part," she said once, peeking toward the exits.

"When the lights come on after a movie. It's like waking up." She smiled. "Now you have to go back to the living."

He'd remain in his seat for a few minutes after she'd left, feeling the emptiness of the big theater around him, the drone of the film rewinding up in the projection room, the hollow thunk of an usher's dustpan as he swept the aisles. Above Winkler the little bulbs screwed into the ceiling in the shape of the Big Dipper burned on and on.

She was born in Anchorage, two years before him. She wore lipstick that smelled like soap. She got cold easily. Her socks were always too thin for the weather. During the earthquake of '64 a Cadillac pitched through the front window of the bank, and she had been, she confessed, *thrilled* by it, by everything: the sudden smell of petroleum, the enormous car-swallowing graben that had yawned open in the middle of Fourth Avenue. She whispered: "We didn't have to go back to work for a week."

The husband (goalie for his hockey team) was branch manager. They got married after her senior year at West High School. He had a fondness for garlic salt that, she said, "destroyed his breath," so

44

that she could hardly look at him after he ate it, could hardly stand to be in the same room.

For the past nine years they had lived in a beige ranch house with brown shingles and a yellow garage door. A pair of lop-sided pumpkins lolled on the front porch like severed heads. Winkler knew this because he looked up the address in the phone book and began driving past in the evenings.

The husband didn't like movies, was happy to dry the dishes, loved — more than anything, Sandy said — to play miniature golf. Even his name, Winkler thought, was cheerless: Herman. Herman Sheeler. Their phone number, although Winkler had never called it, was 542-7433. The last four digits spelled the first four letters of their last name, something Herman had, according to Sandy, announced at a Friday staff meeting as the most remarkable thing that had happened to him in a decade.

"In a *decade*," she said, staring off at the soaring credits.

Winkler — behind his big eyeglasses, his solitary existence — had never felt this way, never been in love, never flirted with or thought about a married woman. But he couldn't let it go. It was not a conscious decision; he did not think: We were meant to be, or: Something has predetermined that our paths cross, or even: I choose to think of her several times a minute, her neck, her arms, her elbows. The shampoo smell of her hair. Her chest against the fabric of a thin sweater. His feet simply brought him by the bank every day, or the Newport pulled him past her house at night. He ate Apple Jacks. He threw away his tin of garlic salt.

Through the bank window he peered at the bankers behind their desks: one in a blue suit with a birthmark on his neck; another in a V-neck sweater with gray in his hair and a ring of keys clipped to his belt loop. Could the V-neck be him? Wasn't he twice her age? The birthmarked man was looking up at Winkler and chewing his pen; Winkler ducked behind a pillar.

In December, after they had watched *Three Days of the Condor* for the second time, she asked him to take her to his apartment. All she said about Herman was: "He's going out after the game." She seemed nervous, pushing her cuticles against the edges of her teeth, but she was perpetually nervous, and this, Winkler figured, was part of it — Anchorage was not a huge city and they could, after all, be seen at any time. They could be found out.

The streets were dark and cold. He led her quickly through the alternating pools of streetlight and shadow. Hardly anyone was out. The tailpipes of cars at stop signs smoked madly. Winkler did not know whether to take her hand or not. He felt he could see Anchorage that night with agonizing clarity: slush frozen into sidewalk seams, ice glazing telephone wires, two men hunched over menus behind a steamy diner window.

She looked at his apartment with interest: the block-and-board shelves, the old, banging radiator, the cramped kitchen that smelled of leaking gas.

She picked up a graduated cylinder and held it to the light. "The meniscus," he explained, and pointed to the curve in the surface of the water inside. "The molecules at the edges are climbing the glass." She set it down, picked up a typed page lying on a shelf: *I measured spatial resolution data of atmospheric precipitable water and vapor pressure deficit at two separate meteorological stations . . .*

"What is this? You wrote this?"

"It's part of my dissertation. That nobody read."

47

"On snowflakes?"

"Yes. Ice crystals." He ventured further. "Take a snow crystal. The classic six-pointed star? How it looks so rigid, frozen in place? Well, in reality, on an extremely tiny level, smaller than a couple of nano-meters, as it freezes it vibrates like crazy, all the billion billion molecules that make it up shaking invisibly, practically burning up."

Sandy reached behind her ear and coiled a strand of hair around her finger.

He pushed on: "My idea was that tiny instabilities in those vibrations give snow-flakes their individual shapes. On the out-side the crystal looks stable, but on the inside, it's like an earthquake all the time." He set the sheet back on the shelf. "I'm boring you."

"No," she said.

They sat on his sofa with their hips touching; they drank instant hot chocolate from mismatched mugs. She gave herself to him solemnly but without ceremony, undressing and climbing onto his twin bed. He didn't put on the radio, didn't draw the shades. They set their eyeglasses beside each other on the floor — he had no nightstands. She pulled the covers over their heads.

★ ★ ★

It was love. He could study the colors and creases in her palm for fifteen minutes, imagining he could see the blood traveling through her capillaries. "What are you looking at?" she'd ask, squirming, smiling. "I'm not so interesting."

But she was. He watched her sort through a box of chocolate-covered raisins, selecting one, then rejecting it by some indiscernible criteria; he watched her button her parka, slip her hand inside her collar to scratch a shoulder. He excavated a boot print she'd left on the snowy step outside his apartment and preserved it in his freezer.

To be in love was to be dazed twenty times a morning: by the latticework of frost on his windshield; by a feather loosed from his pillow; by a soft, pink rim of light over the hills. He slept three or four hours a night. Some days he felt as if he were about to peel back the surface of the Earth — the trees standing frozen on the hills, the churning face of the inlet — and finally witness what lay beneath, the structure under there, the fundamental grid.

Tuesdays quivered and vibrated, the second hand slogging around the dial. Wednesdays were the axis around which

49

the rest of the week spun. Thursdays were deserts, ghost towns. By the weekends, the bits of herself that she had left behind in his apartment took on near-holy significance: a hair, coiled on the rim of the sink; the crumbs of four saltines scattered across the bottom of a plate. Her saliva — her proteins and enzymes and bacteria — still probably all over those crumbs; her skin cells on the pillows, all over the floor, pooling as dust in the corners. What was it Watson had taught him, and Einstein, and Pasteur? The things we see are only masks for the things we can't see.

He flattened his hair with a quivering hand; he walked into the bank lobby shaking like a thief; he produced a store-bought daisy from his knapsack and set it on the counter in front of her.

They made love with the window open, cold air pouring over their bodies. "What do you think movie stars do for Christmas?" she'd ask, the hem of the sheet at her chin. "I bet they eat veal. Or sixty-pound turkeys. I bet they hire chefs to cook for them." Out the window a jet traversed the sky, landing lights glowing, her eyes tracking it.

Sometimes she felt like a warm river,

sometimes a blade of hot metal. Sometimes she took one of his papers from a shelf and propped herself on pillows and paged through it. "One-dimensional snow-pack algorithms," she'd read, solemnly, as if mouthing the words of a spell. "C_d equals degree-day melt coefficient."

"Leave a sock," he'd whisper. "Leave your bra. Something to get me through the week." She'd stare up at the ceiling, thinking her own thoughts, and soon it would be time to leave: she'd sheathe herself in her clothes once more, pull back her hair, lace up her boots.

When she was gone he'd bend over the mattress and try to smell her in the bedding. His brain projected her onto his eyelids relentlessly: the arrangement of freckles on her forehead; the articulateness of her fingers; the slope of her shoulders. The way underwear fit her body, nestling over her hips, slipping between her legs.

Every Saturday she worked the drive-up teller window. *I love you, Sandy*, he'd write on a deposit slip and drop it into the pneumatic chute outside the bank. *Not now*, she'd respond, and send the canister flying back.

But I do, he'd write, in larger print. *Right now I LOVE YOU.*

51

He watched her crumple his note, compose a new one, seal the carrier, drop it into the intake. He brought it into his car, unscrewed it on his lap. She'd written: *How much?*

How much, how much, how much? A drop of water contains 10^{20} molecules, each one agitated and twitchy, linking and separating with its neighbors, then linking up again, swapping partners millions of times a second. All water in any body is desperate to find more, to adhere to more of itself, to cling to the hand that holds it; to find clouds, or oceans; to scream from the throat of a teakettle.

"I want to be a police officer," she'd whisper. "I want to drive one of those sedans all day and say code words into my CB. Or a doctor! I could go to medical school in California and become a doctor for kids. I wouldn't need to do big, spectacular rescues or anything, just small things, maybe test blood for diseases or viruses or something, but do it really well, be the one doctor all the parents would trust. 'Little Alice's blood must go to Dr. Sandy,' they'd say." She giggled; she made circles with a strand of hair. In the theater Winkler had to sit on his hands to keep them from touching her. "Or no," she'd say, "no, I want to be a bush pilot. I could get one of those passbook accounts of Herman's and finally save enough to buy a used plane, a good two-seater. I'd get lessons. I'd look into the engine and know every part, the valves and switches and whatever, and be able to say, 'This plane has flown a lot but she sure is a good one.' "

Her eyelids fluttered, then steadied. Across town her husband was crouched in the net, watching a puck slide across the blue line.

"Or," she said, "a *sculptor*. That's it. I could be a metal sculptor. I could make those big, strange-looking iron things they put in front of office buildings to rust. The ones the birds stand on and everybody looks at and says, 'What do you think that's supposed to be?' "

"You could," he said.

"I could."

Every night now — it was January and dark by 4 p.m. — he pulled on his big parka and drew the hood tight and drove past her house. He'd start at the end of the block, then troll back up, the hedges coming up on his left, the curb-parked cars with their hoods ajar to allow extension cords into the frost plugs, the Newport slowing until he'd come to a stop alongside their driveway.

By nine-thirty each night, her lights began to go off: first in the windows at the far right, then the room next to it, then the lamp behind the curtains to the left, at ten o'clock sharp. He'd imagine her passage through the dark rooms, following her with his eyes, down the hall, past the bathroom, into what must have been the bedroom, where she'd climb into bed with *him*. At last only the tall backyard light would glow, white tinged with blue, all the parked cars drawing energy from the houses around them, the plugs clicking on and off, and above the neighborhood the air would grow so cold it seemed to glitter and flex — as if it were solidifying — and he'd get the feeling that someone could reach down and shatter the whole scene.

Only with great effort could he get his foot to move to the accelerator. He'd drive to the end of the block, turn up the heater, roll alone through the frozen darkness across town.

"It's not that he's awful or anything," Sandy whispered once, in the middle of

Logan's Run. "I mean, he's nice. He's good. He loves me. I can do pretty much whatever I want. It's just sometimes I look into the kitchen cupboards, or at his suits in the closet, and think: This is it?"

Winkler blinked. It was the most she'd said during a movie.

"I feel like I've been turned inside out is all. Like I've got huge manacles on my arms. Look" — she grabbed her forearm and raised it — "I can hardly lift them they're so heavy. But other times I get to feeling so light it's as if I'll float to the ceiling and get trapped up there like a balloon."

The darkness of the movie theater was all around them. On-screen a robot showed off some people frozen in ice. In the ceiling the little bulbs that were supposed to be stars burned in their little niches.

Sandy whispered: "I get happy sometimes for the younger gals at work, when they find love, after all that stumbling around, when they've found their guy and get to talking about weddings during break, then babies, and I can see them outside smoking and staring out at the traffic, and I know they're probably not a hundred percent happy. Not all-the-way happy.

55

Maybe seventy percent happy. But they're living it. They're not giving up.

"I've just been feeling everything too much. I don't know. Can you feel things too much, David?"

"Yes."

"I shouldn't tell you any of this. I shouldn't tell you anything."

The film had entered a chase sequence and the varying colors of a burning city strobed across Sandy's eyeglasses. She closed her eyes.

"Thing is," she whispered, "Herman doesn't have any sperm. We got him tested a few years ago. He has none. Or basically none; no good ones. When they called, they gave the results to me. I never told him. I told him they said he was fine. I tore up their letter and brought the little scraps to work and hid them at the bottom of a trash can in the ladies' bathroom."

On-screen Logan careened down a crowded street. Suits in the closet, Winkler thought. The guy with the birthmark?

In his memory he could traverse months in a second. He imagined Herman crouched like a crab on the ice, guarding the net, slapping his glove against his big leg pads, his teammates swirling around the rink. He imagined Sandy leaning over him, the tips of her hair dragging over his face. He stood outside their house on Marilyn Street and above the city, streamers of auroras — reds and purples and greens — glided like souls into the firmament.

Now a soft hail — lump graupels — flew from the clouds. He opened all his windows, turned off the furnace, and let it blow in, angling through the frames, the tiny balls rolling and eddying on the carpet.

Near the middle of March she lay beside him in the darkness with a single candle burning on his sill. Out beyond the window a trash collector tossed the frozen contents of a trash can into the maw of his truck and Winkler and Sandy listened to it clatter and compress and the fading rumble as the truck receded down the street. It was around five and all through the city, people were ending their workdays, mail carriers delivering their last envelopes, accountants paying one more invoice, bankers sealing their vaults. Tumblers finding their grooves.

"You ever just want to go?" she whispered. "Go, go, go?"

Winkler nodded. Without her glasses,

that close to his face, her eyes looked trapped, closer to how they had looked in the supermarket, standing at a revolving rack of magazines but trembling inside; her whole body, its trillions of cells, quivering invisibly, threatening to shake apart. He had dreamed her. Hadn't she dreamed him, too?

"I should tell you something," he said. "About that day we met in the market."

She rolled onto her back. In five minutes, maybe six, she would leave, and he told himself he would pay attention to every passing second, the pulse in her forearm, the pressure of her knee against his thigh. The thousand pores in the side of her nose. In the frail light he could see her boots on the frayed rug, her clothes folded neatly beside. He would tell her. Now he would tell her. I dreamed you, he'd say. Sometimes I have these dreams.

"I'm pregnant," she said.

The flame of the candle on the sill twisted and righted.

"David? Did you hear me?"

She was looking at him now.

"Pregnant," he said, but at first it was only a word.

7

He parked the Newport in a drive-up lane and tugged a deposit slip from the slot.

Can you get away?

No.

Only for an hour?

He could just make her out through the drive-up window, wearing a big-collared sweater, her head down, her hand writing. The pneumatic tube clattered and howled.

This is not the time, David. Please. Wednesday.

Between them was fifteen or so feet of frozen space, bounded by his window and hers, but it was as if the windows had liquefied, or else the air had, and his vision skewed and rippled and it was all he could do to put the Newport into gear and ease forward to let the next car in.

He couldn't work, couldn't sleep, couldn't leave her alone. He went by the house every night, patrolling Marilyn Street, up and back, up and back, until one midnight a neighbor came out with a snow shovel and flagged him down and asked if he was missing something.

In Sandy's backyard the one blue street lamp shivered. The Chrysler started away slowly, with reluctance, as if it, too, couldn't bear to leave her.

Each time the office phone rang, adrenaline streamed into his blood. "Winkler," the supervisor said, waving a sheaf of teletype forecasts. "These are atrocious. There are probably fifty typos in today's series alone." He looked him up and down. "Are you sick or something?"

Yes! he wanted to cry. Yes! So sick! He walked to First Federal at lunch but she wasn't at her station. The teller in the station to the right studied him with her head cocked as if assessing the validity of his concern and finally said Sandy was home with the flu and could she help him instead?

The banker with the birthmark was on the phone. The gray-haired one was talking with a man and a woman, leaning forward in his chair. "No," Winkler said. On the way out he scanned the nameplates on the desks but even with his glasses on couldn't make out a name, a title, any of it.

She came to the door wearing flannel pajamas printed all over with polar bears on toboggans. Something about her standing in her doorway barefoot started a buzzing all through his chest.

"What are you doing here?"

"They said you were sick."

"How did you know where I live?"

He looked across the street to where the other houses were shuttered against the cold. Heat escaping from the hall blurred the air.

"Sandy —"

"You walked?"

"Are you okay?"

She stayed in the doorway, squinting out. He realized she was not going to invite him in. "I threw up," she said. "But I feel fine."

"You look pale."

"Yes. Well. So do you. Breathe, David. Take a breath."

Her feet were turning white in the cold. He wanted to fall to his knees and take them in his hands. "How is this going to work, Sandy? What are we going to do?"

"I don't know. What are we supposed to do?"

"We could go somewhere. Anywhere. We could go to California, like you said. We could go to Mexico. You could become whatever you wanted."

Her eyes followed an Oldsmobile as it passed slowly down the street, snow squeaking beneath its tires. "Not now, David." She shook her head. "Not in front of my house."

March ended. Community hockey ended. She consented to meet him for coffee. In the café her head periodically swiveled on her shoulders, checking back through the window as if she had ducked a pursuer. He brushed snow off her coat: stellar dendrites. Storybook snow.

"You haven't been at the bank."

She shrugged. A line of meltwater sped down one lens of her glasses. The waitress brought coffee and they sat over the mugs and Sandy didn't speak.

He said: "I grew up over there, across the street. From the roof, when it was very clear, you could see half the peaks of the Alaska Range. You could pick out individual glaciers on McKinley. Sometimes I'd go up there just to look at it, all that untouched snow. All that light."

She glanced again toward the window and he could not tell if she was listening. It struck him as strange that she could look pretty much how she always looked, her waist could still slip neatly into her jeans, the blood vessels in her cheeks could still dilate and fill with color, yet inside her something they'd made had implanted into the wall of her uterus, maybe the size of a grape by now, or a thumb, dividing its cells like mad, siphoning from her whatever it needed.

"What I really love is snow," he said. "To look at it. I used to go up there with my mother and collect snow and we'd study it with magnifying glasses." Still she did not look up. Snow pressed at the shop window. "I've never been with anyone, you know. I don't even have any friends, not really."

"I know, David."

"I've hardly even left Anchorage."

She nodded and braced both hands around her cup.

"I applied for jobs last week," he said. "All over the country."

She spoke to her coffee. "What if I hadn't been in that grocery store? What if I had decided to go two hours earlier? Or two minutes?"

"We can leave, Sandy."

"David." Her boots squeaked beneath the table. "I'm thirty-four years old. I've been married for fifteen and a half years."

Bells slung over the door handle jangled and two men came in and stamped snow from their shoes. Winkler's eyeballs were starting to throb. Fifteen and a half years was incontestable, a continent he'd never visit, a staircase he'd never climb. "The supermarket," he was saying. "We met in the supermarket."

She stopped showing up at the bank. She did not pick up the phone at her house. He'd dial her number all day and in the evenings Herman Sheeler would answer with an enthused, half-shouted "Hello?" and Winkler, across town, cringing in his apartment, would gently hang up.

He trolled Marilyn Street. Wind rolled in from the inlet, cold and salty.

Rain, and more rain. All day the ground snow melted and all night it froze. Winter broke, and solidified, and broke again. Out in the hills, moose were stirring, and foxes, and bears. Fiddleheads were nudging up. Birds coursed in from their southern fields. Winkler lay in his little bed after midnight and burned.

At a welding supply store he compiled a starter kit: a Clarke arc welder; a wire brush; tin snips; a chipping hammer; welder's gloves, apron, and helmet; spools of steel, aluminum, and copper wire;

64

brazing alloys in little tubes; electrodes; soldering lugs. The clerk piled it all into a leftover television box and at noon on a Tuesday, Winkler drove to Sandy's house, parked in the driveway, took the box in his arms, went up the front walk, and banged the knocker.

He knocked three times, four times. He waited. Maybe Herman had put her on a plane for Phoenix or Vancouver with instructions never to come back again. Maybe she was across town right then getting an abortion. Winkler trembled. He knelt on the porch and pushed open the mail slot. "Sandy!" he called, and waited. "I love you, Sandy! I love you!"

He got in the Newport, drove south, circled the city lakes: Connors and DeLong, Sand, Jewel, and Campbell. Forty minutes later he pulled down Marilyn past her house and the box was gone from the front porch.

Baltimore, Honolulu, and Salt Lake said no, but Cleveland said yes, handed down an offer: staff meteorologist for a television network, a salary, benefits, a stipend to pay for moving.

He drove to Sandy's and pulled into the driveway and sat a minute trying to calm his heart. It was Saturday. Herman answered the door. He was the gray-haired one: the one with the key ring permanently clipped to his belt loop. Gray-haired at thirty-five. "Hello," Herman said, as if he were answering the phone. Over his shoulder Winkler could just see into the hall, maple paneling, a gold-framed watercolor of a trout at the end. "Can I help you?"

Winkler adjusted his glasses. It was clear in a half second: Herman had no clue. Winkler said, "I'm looking for Sandy Sheeler? The metal artist?"

Herman blinked and frowned and said, "My wife?" He turned and called, "Sandy!" back into the house.

She came into the hall wiping her hands on a towel. Her face blanched.

"He's looking for a metal artist?" Herman asked. "With your name?"

Winkler spoke only to Sandy. "I was hoping to get my car worked on. Whatever you like. Make it" — he gestured to his Chrysler and they all looked at it — "more exciting."

Herman clasped his hands behind his head. There were acne scars on his jaw. "I'm not sure you've got the right house."

Winkler retreated a step. His hands were shaking badly so he stowed them behind his back. He did not know if he would be able to say any more and was overwhelmed with relief when Sandy stepped forward.

"Okay," she said, nodding. She snapped the towel and folded it and draped it over her shoulder. "Pull it into the garage. I can do whatever I want?"

"As long as it drives."

Herman peered over Sandy's head then back at her. "What are you talking about? What's going on here?"

Winkler's hands quivered behind his back. "The keys are inside. I can come back in, say, a week?"

"Sure," she said, still looking at the Newport. "One week."

One week. He went to Marilyn Street only once: creeping on foot through the slushy yard and peering through the garage window toward midnight. Through cobwebs he could just make out the silhouette of his car, hunkered there amid boxes in the shadows. None of it looked any different.

What had he hoped to see? Elaborate sculptures welded to the roof? Wings and propellers? A shower of sparks flaring in the rectangular lens of her welding mask? He dreamed Sandy asleep in her bed, the

67

little embryo awake inside her, turning and twisting, a hundred tiny messages falling around it like snow, like confetti. He dreamed a welding arc flickering in the midnight, a bright orange seam of solder, tin and lead transformed to light and heat. He woke; he said her name to the ceiling. It was as if he could feel her across town, her tidal gravity, the blood in him tilting toward her.

In his road atlas Ohio was shaped like a shovel blade, a leaf, a ragged valentine. The black dot of Cleveland in the northeast corner like a cigarette burn. Hadn't he dreamed her in the supermarket? Hadn't he foreseen all of this?

Six days after he'd visited their house, she telephoned him, whispering down the wire, "Come late. Go to the garage."

"Sandy," he said, but she was already gone.

He closed his savings account — four thousand dollars and change — and stuffed whatever else he could carry — books, clothes, his barometer — into a railroad duffel he'd inherited from his grandfather. A taxi dropped him at the end of the block.

He eased the panels of the garage door

68

up their tracks. She was already in the passenger's seat. A suitcase, decorated with red plaid on both sides, waited in the backseat. Beside it was the television box stuffed with welding supplies: the torch still in its packaging, the boxes of studs unopened. He set his duffel in the trunk.

"He's asleep," she said when Winkler opened the driver's door. He dropped the transmission into neutral and rolled the car to the end of the driveway and halfway down Marilyn Street before climbing in and starting it. The sound of the engine was huge and loud.

They left the garage door open. "The heater," was all she said. In ten minutes they were past the airport and on the Seward Highway, already beyond the city lights. Sandy slumped against her door. Out the windshield the stars were so many and so white they looked like chips of ice, hammered through the fabric of the sky.

8

The convergences of a life: Winkler on an airplane, fifty-nine years old, St. Vincent receding behind him; Winkler waist-deep in a flood, his chin at the gunwale of a rowboat, men prying his drowned daughter from his arms; and Winkler again at thirty-three, speeding toward Cleveland with someone else's wife — this, perhaps, is how lives are measured, a series of abandonments that we hope beyond reason will eventually be reconciled.

Vast tracts of country reflected off that big hood: the Coast Mountains, Hazelton's lava beds, Alberta's steel-blue granaries. Every hour he was seeing new things, wiping his glasses clean: Saskatoon, Winnipeg. An awe at the size of the continent swelled in Winkler's chest — here was the water in his cells, moving at last, cycling between states. He could not resist pointing out nearly everything they passed: a jackknifed truck, a sagging billboard barn, a tractor bucking like a lifeboat in the ruts of a field.

Sandy hardly said anything. Her entire countenance was pale and several times they had to stop so she could go to the bathroom. At meals she ordered dry cereal or nothing.

Three days out, he summoned the nerve to ask: "Did you leave him a note?" They were in Minnesota, or maybe Illinois. A roadkilled doe, dragged to the shoulder, flashed past in the headlights — a gory snapshot — and was gone.

He waited. Maybe she was asleep.

"I told him," she eventually said. "I said I was pregnant, that it wasn't his child, and that I was leaving. He thought I was joking. He said, 'Are you feeling okay, Sandy?' "

Winkler kept his hands on the wheel. The center stripe whisked beneath them; the headlights pushed their cone of light forward.

Eventually: northeast Ohio, a grid of brick and steel nestled against Lake Erie. Smelter fires burned on mill stacks. Huge Slavic-looking policemen stalked the sidewalks in crisp uniforms. A wind hurled particles of sleet through the streets.

They stayed in an eastside motel, looked at real estate: University Heights, Orange,

Solon. Sandy tiptoed through rooms, trailed her fingers over countertops, interested in nothing. In a ravine they found a subdivision called Shadow Hill, the Chagrin River sliding along at the end of a cul-de-sac, a feeder creek beside the road in a landscaped trench. Above the street on both sides the walls of the ravine rose up like the berms of a ditch.

The house was built on a form and each of the neighbors' was identical. Two floors, two bedrooms upstairs, an unfinished basement. A pair of mournful saplings in tubs flanked the front steps. A brass knocker shaped like a goose was bolted to the door.

"Your own little paradise," the Realtor said, sweeping an arm to take in the hillsides, the trees, the wide stripe of clouds churning above.

"Paradise," Sandy said, her voice far-off. "We'll take it," Winkler said.

His job was straightforward enough: he pored through Weather Service data, studied the station's radar output, and compiled forecasts. Some days they sent him into gales to stand in front of a camera: he clung to an inverted umbrella shouting from beneath his rain hood; he sat three hours in a spotter's shack on top of Municipal Stadium predicting game-time weather.

Sandy stayed indoors. They had hardly any furniture, the dining room empty, nothing in the kitchen but a card table encircled by stools. He bought a TV and they propped it on two milk crates and she'd lie in front of it for hours, watching whatever came on, her forehead wrinkled as if puzzling through it. In the basement her box of welding supplies waited untouched. Every few days she threw up into the kitchen sink.

At four in the morning she'd wake hungry, and he'd tramp downstairs and feel his way through the kitchen in the dark to get her a bowl of Apple Jacks, measure a half cup of whole milk into it. She'd eat with her head propped against the pillows, her whole body lean and warm. "Tell me no one can find us here, David," she'd whisper. "Tell me that right now, nobody in the world knows where we are."

He watched her chew; he watched her swallow. In nearly every way they were still strangers, trying to learn each other.

"You sleepwalk," she told him once, her head off the pillow.

"I do not."

"You do. Last night I found you in the

kitchen standing at the window. I said, 'David, what are you doing?' but you didn't say anything. Then you came back in here, put on socks, took them off, and climbed back into bed."

But it was Sandy, Winkler thought, who woke and disappeared from the bed several times a night, walking the house or descending into the basement, and although she told Winkler it was pregnancy keeping her up, he guessed it was Herman. She didn't want to answer the phone or doorbell; she never got the mail. At dusk her eyes went to the windows. As if from the growing shadows, at any moment, Herman might clamber onto the porch, aflame with retribution.

"My Crock-Pot," she'd say, staring into a cupboard. "I left my Crock-Pot."

"We'll get you a new Crock-Pot, Sandy."

She looked at him but did not answer.

Eventually she regained color and energy. She scrubbed the sinks; she cleaned out the basement. One evening he came home and found new dishes in the cupboards.

"Where did you get these?"

"Higbee's."

"Higbee's? That's twenty miles from here."

"I hitched."

He stared at her. She shrugged. That night she served him lasagna, the first meal she'd cooked since they'd moved.

"This is delicious," he said.

"Marry me," she said.

He said yes. Of course. Tremors of happiness rose through his chest. He kept his imagination fixed on the future: the child, the thousand small rewards and punishments he imagined fatherhood would bring. There were the customary preparations: painting the upstairs room, shopping for a crib. The questions were obvious: "Are you going to divorce Herman? Won't you be technically married to two men?" But she was washing dishes, or staring at the TV, and he was afraid to ask.

In the basement she began welding, cannibalizing sheets of metal from the house itself: the furnace cover, the front of a kitchen cabinet. Weekends he drove her to salvage yards and garage sales to claim anything metal: the hood of a Ford Fairlane; forty feet of copper pipe; a brass captain's wheel. At night he'd hear her banging around down there, the clangor of the aluminum hammer, the hiss and pop of the welding torch, a smell of singed metal rising; it was like living on top of a foundry. And at night she'd slide into bed, sweating and wide-eyed, her whole body hot, her coveralls hanging on the closet door. She'd splay her legs on top of the comforter. "The TV says the blood volume of a pregnant woman increases fifty percent," she said. "Same body, fifty percent more blood."

"Are you being careful?" he'd whisper. "Do you know what you're doing?"

She'd nod; he'd feel the heat pour off her.

A six-foot-six Indian magistrate married them; a half dozen Channel 3 employees sidearmed rice at them on their way out. For a honeymoon — Sandy insisted they have one — she filled the empty dining room with houseplants she'd bought at a moving sale: ficus, philodendron, a dozen hanging ferns. He took four days off and they went to sleep each night on a blanket in the center of the floor, surrounded by plants. "We're in the jungle," she whispered. "We're on a raft on the Amazon." When they had sex, she wept. Each morning he brought her eggs, scrambled and chopped, and a bowl of Apple Jacks with a half cup of milk. Inside her now the fetus had eyes, four chambers to its heart, neuroelectric pulses riding the arc of its spine.

By July, Sandy was spending five or six hours at a time downstairs in her workshop. She had settled on a project, she said, a "Paradise Tree," something he sneaked downstairs one morning to glimpse: a single, nine-foot pole, partially rusted, with the beginnings of shapes fused onto it: sections of coat hangers and unfurled springs for branches; flattened lamp finials and metal scrap for leaves.

For Winkler each hour was another hour between Cleveland and Anchorage, between who they were becoming and who they had been. That summer was the first truly hot weather he had ever experienced; he hiked the riverbank, watching fishermen, inhaling the aroma of warm soil, feeling the humidity wrap his body like a net. A pair of mallards paddled shyly through an eddy. A plastic bag came rafting down.

Ohio, he decided, bore less of the everyday vulnerabilities: there wasn't as sharp an edge to the air, or the threat of winter always hovering beyond the horizon; there were no tattered prospectors or pipeliners mumbling into their beards in the grocery stores. Life here was sane, predictable, explicable. The backyards had fences; the neighborhood had covenants. Each night, with the burgeoning, hot shape of Sandy sweating beside him, he found himself entering a mild and dreamless sleep. If he dreamed of things to come, he did not remember them when he woke. There were days when he could almost pretend that he had never even had such dreams, that his nights had always been like anyone else's, that there wasn't anything more Sandy could know about him.

Each morning, leaving to drive to Channel 3, he'd stop at the door and glance above the roof at the slope of the ravine. The light seemed to bring a stabbing clarity: the edges of clouds, the illumined leaves, early shadows playing beneath the trees — Ohio teemed with small miracles. Standing there some mornings he imagined he could glimpse the architecture of the entire planet, like an enormous grid underlying everything, perfectly obvious all along — the code of the universe, a matrix of light.

I have never, he thought, seen things so clearly.

A robin hopped through the blades, hunting worms. The woods beside the river rang with singing insects. Tears gathered at the backs of Winkler's eyes.

Soon Sandy would descend to the basement, the child inside her waking from its own fetal dreams, the bones in its ears hardening, its hooded eyes peering into the flaring darkness.

9

Winkler remembered his mother as a supremely pale woman: hands like they had been dipped in milk, hair a creamy silver. Even her eyes were almost pure white, the irises pale, the sclera devoid of visible capillaries, as though the color had been rinsed out of them, or else her blood ran clear.

She had lived her first thirteen years in Finland before coming to the New World with a grandfather who promptly died of pneumonia. She finned salmon on a floating fish processor, then waitressed for Lido's Café, then washed sheets at the Engineering Commission Hospital; she worked her way through nursing school, joined the Women's League, married the milkman. In 1941 they moved into a bankrupt furrier's storehouse converted to apartments, a small fourth-floor flat blessed with a trio of huge parlor windows that overlooked the pharmacy across the street, the rail yard, and Ship Creek beyond. All during the Second World War P-36 Hawks descended across those windows left to right and disappeared behind Government Hill to land at the airfield at Elmendorf. And every summer thereafter those windows buzzed with the comfortable drone of passing two- and four-seaters, hunters and prospectors, gliding in and out of the bush. Men bent on gold, oil, wilderness. She would live in that apartment the rest of her life.

The rooms existed in his memory as clearly now as they always had: the big-beamed ceilings, the smells of fur still lingering in the corners, as though invisible foxes and marmots moved silently inside the walls. His bedroom was a broom closet with a door that opened inward — he had to fold back his mattress each morning to get out. The smell in there, he decided one night, was of caribou, and he imagined their ghosts snuffling in the sitting room, nosing through the pantry.

His mother loved the building: its drafts and big-paned windows; the way the floors, no matter how much you scrubbed, smelled permanently of tannins. She walked barefoot over the cold boards, and dragged open the curtains, and showed David how if they scratched their names into the panes with a pin, winter frost would freeze around the letters. On the roof she'd gather palmfuls of snow and press them into her mouth and make pronouncements on their quality: sweet or pure, grainy or velvety. "Back home," she'd say, "there is a snow my grandfather called *santa lunta*. It came one night a year, always around Christmas. He'd pack it into little tin funnels and pour fruit juice on it and we'd eat it for dessert. Like ice cream. Only better."

His mother the Ice Queen. The only thing he still had of hers was a book: *Snow Crystals*, by W. A. Bentley. Inside were thousands of carefully prepared micrographs of snowflakes, each image reproduced in a two-inch square, the crystals white against a field of black, arrayed in a grid, four-by-three, twelve per page. Bound in cloth, it was a 1931 first edition her grandfather had bought at a rummage sale. She would page through it carefully, almost devotedly, occasionally calling David over to ask him his favorites. She'd hold his finger and trace the outlines of whatever shapes lay hidden within: six hippos' heads, six dragons' eyes, six tiny sea horses in profile.

Eight-year-old Winkler would wrap a board in black felt and climb to the roof to catch snowflakes as they floated down. He studied them with a Cracker Jack plastic hand-magnifier. Only rarely was he able to capture an individual crystal, undamaged in its journey from the clouds, and he'd sit with a pencil and a damp notebook, trying to sketch it before it melted: the corollas, the interstices, the kaleidoscopic blades. When he'd accumulated twenty or so drawings, he'd take the damp pages downstairs, staple them together, and present the book to his mother with grave ceremony.

"It's beautiful, David," she'd say. "I will treasure it." She'd set the little booklet on top of Bentley's *Snow Crystals*, on the shelf beneath the coffee table.

In grade school he read about irrigation, ice fields, clouds. He could still remember a poster on the wall of his fourth-grade classroom: THE WATER CYCLE — oceanic clouds creeping over a town, dropping rain on steeples and rooftops, rainwater pooling in a river, the river charging through a dam's spillway, easing back into the ocean, a smiling sun evaporating seawater into tufts of cartoon vapor, the vapor condensing into clouds.

By high school he was beginning to understand that the study of water and its distribution phenomena yielded again and again to sets of reassuring patterns — Hadley cells, cycling air in the troposphere, dark bands of nimbostratus. To consider water on any scale was to confront a boundless repetition of small events. There were the tiny wonders: raindrops, snow crystals, grains of frost aligned on a blade of grass; and there were the wonders so immense it seemed impossible to get his mind around them: global wind, oceanic currents, storms that broke like waves over whole mountain ranges. Rapt, seventeen years old, he mail-ordered posters of seas, lakes, calving glaciers. He caught raindrops in pans of flour to study their shape; he charted the sizes of captured snow crystals on a handmade grid.

His first week in college he met with a counselor and made earth sciences his major. A chemistry unit on the hydrologic cycle that had other students yawning seemed to him a miracle of simplicity: condensation, precipitation, infiltration, runoff, evapotranspiration — water moved around and through us at every moment; it leached from our cells; it hung invisibly in front of our eyes. Theoretically, water was inexhaustible, endless, infinitely recycled. The ice in his mother's freezer was millions of years old. The Egyptian Sphinx was carved from the compressed skeletons of sea animals.

But in graduate school the opportunities to study water, particularly snow, were limited. Professors wanted to teach hydraulics; students wanted curricula with engineering applications. And when he was allowed to study snow it was often in the most mundane ways: stream flow forecasts, precipitation assessments; snow as resource, snow as a reservoir of meltwater.

Winkler was not popular at school. Parties blazed in A-frames set back in the spruce, and couples strolled arm in arm along the boggy paths, and leaves fell, and snow, and rain, and he went on in a state of more or less permanent solitude. He carted around stacks of books; he examined drops of Lake Spenard under a microscope. Water was a sanctuary — not only hot showers or condensation on his window or the sight of Knik Arm on a fall day, but reading about it, collecting it in an eyedropper, freezing it, sublimating it. Two hydrogen atoms bonded to one oxygen — always — at a 104.5 degree angle. The distances between atoms was — always — .095718 of a nanometer. Every thirty-one hundred years a volume of water equivalent to all the oceans passed through the atmosphere. These were facts, bounded by inviolable laws: water was elastic and adhesive, it held its temperature longer than air, it was perpetually in motion.

But he sensed, even then, that any real understanding would continue to exist beyond the range of his capacities. The more he studied water, the more he examined snow, the more mystified he became. Ice could be unpredictable and baffling. Unforeseen variables could set the entire hydrological cycle reeling: an unsuspected front, riding an unexpected event (a deep ocean current, a shearing microburst), could transform a clear, blue noon into an afternoon deluge. A predicted blizzard — snowplows rumbling on highway shoulders, workers in roadside salt huts braced over their shovels — did not arrive. Rain threw itself at the windows while the radio burbled out a forecast for sunshine. Scientists had engineered elaborate models, radar, radio beacons — now satellites coasted above the atmosphere, peering in — and still it was nearly impossible to gauge the size and shape of a raindrop. No one knew exactly why an ice crystal bothered with such elaborate geometry; no one knew why liquid water was able to carry so much heat; no calculation was able to account qualitatively for the surface tension on top of a simple puddle.

Water was a wild, capricious substance: nothing solid, nothing permanent, nothing as it appeared.

10

When Winkler was nine he dreamed a man he had never seen before would be cut in half by a bus three blocks from where he lived. In the dream he watched — paralyzed — as a hatbox flew from the man's arms and landed on its corner, dented. The lid fell; a gray fedora spilled out. He woke with his mother's hands on his shoulders. In front of him the apartment door was ajar and he was sitting on the doormat with his school shoes pulled halfway onto his feet.

"You were screaming," she whispered. "I was shaking you." She soaked a washcloth in the bathroom and pressed it to the back of his neck. "I watched you do it. You went to the door and opened it and tried to pull on your shoes. Then you screamed." Her hands trembled. She led him to his bed and brought him tea thick with honey. "Drink it all. Do you want the lights?"

He shook his head.

She moved past him in the darkness. He heard the faucet rumble and cough and heard her put more water in the kettle, and heard her push the door shut and set the chain. After a while she settled into his father's chair and he went to her and climbed into her lap. She closed her arms around his shoulders and they sat there until the windows brightened and the sun lit the clouds, then the building across the alley, and at last the rail yard and Ship Creek below.

She kept him home from school, brought him to work, where he stuck labels on files for forty cents an hour. Two days later it was Saturday and they were heading home from Kimball's with boxes of groceries in their arms when the air became abruptly familiar: a smell like boiled crab drifted from the restaurant beside them; the low winter light struck the bricks of Kennedy Hardware across the street in a way that was unmistakable. He had been here; these moments had played themselves out before.

Ice, glazing the road, sent back wedges and sheets of glare. The whole scene trembled, then fused with radiance. A woman exited a storefront with two little girls in tow; a green and white cab chunked over a pothole; three Aleuts in rubber bibs walking past burst into laughter. Every small, concurrent event had slowed down and assumed an excruciating clarity: through his glasses he could see each blue polka dot on one of the little girls' wool hats; he watched the shadow of the passing taxi slide black and precise over the ice. His mother turned. "Come along, David." Her words condensed in the air. Her eyelids blinked once, twice. His shoes felt as if they had been frozen to the sidewalk. A teenager in a green muffler tugged a wooden toboggan past them, whistling. Did no one see? Could the future ambush people so completely?

His eyes roved to the revolving door in Koslosky's across the street. Each pane flashed as it turned and reflected the light. From up the street came the sound of a bus chugging down the block. He dropped his box of groceries and the potatoes inside rolled about and then settled.

His mother was at his ear. "What is it? What do you see?"

"The man. Leaving the store."

She squatted on her heels with her own box of groceries in front of her. "Which one? In the brown suit?"

"Yes."

A man in a brown suit was stepping into the street from the revolving door. In his left arm he carried a hatbox. He had his head up and seemed to be watching a place directly across the road, just to the left of Winkler and his mother.

"What is it? Why are you watching him?"

He said nothing. He heard the tires of the bus hum over the ice.

"What do you see?"

The man stepped from the curb and began to cross the street. He walked carefully so as not to slip. A van passed and left a short-lived cloud of vapor and exhaust in the man's path but he did not slow. His skin was pale at his throat and his hair looked thick and glossy and lacquered. His lips were almost orange. The sound of the bus came whistling down from the man's right.

"Oh my God," his mother said, and added something else in Finnish. Already she was lunging forward, too late, her hands waving in front of her as if she might wipe the whole scene away. The bus entered the boy's field of vision, bearing down, but the man in the brown suit kept walking forward. How could he not see? The sun flashed a square of light from the toe of his shoe. The hatbox swung forward on his arm. The bus's horn sounded once;

there was the wrenching, metal-on-metal shriek of brakes, the whisper of space being compressed. The bus lurched on its frame and began its skid. All too quickly the man was struck. The hatbox flew, making an arc through the air, catching a star of sun at its apex, then falling to the street, landing on a corner, and denting the box. A fedora spilled out, gray with a black band, and wobbled in the road. The bus slid to a stop — nearly sideways now — thirty feet farther on. His mother had knelt and taken up the dying torso of the man in her arms. The fists at the ends of the man's arms closed and unclosed automatically. A first thread of blood had appeared beneath one of his nostrils, and finally a lock released somewhere in the boy's chest and he began to scream.

In the deepest part of that midnight there was no sound but a water pipe ticking somewhere in the walls. His mother stood with him by the big parlor windows. She had changed her clothes but there was still a spot of the man's blood on her wrist, perfectly round and toothed at the circumference, a tiny brown saw blade. Winkler found himself incapable of taking his eyes from it. In his mind, over and over, the hatbox sailed through the air, caught a star of sunlight, and came down uncaught. The man had been George DelPrete, a salmon merchant from Juneau. For years the boy would keep a clipping of the obituary in his pencil box.

"How did you know?" she asked.

Winkler began to cry and raised his hands to cover the tears.

"No, no," she said. She reached for him and stroked his hair. His eyeglasses were hard against her side. Her eyes were on the window. The space above the city appeared to stretch. The moon stepped lower. Any moment, it seemed, something could tear the sky and whatever was on the other side would push through.

Once, a year before, her son had told her, as they sat on the rooftop watching the sun settle behind Susitna, that the tumbler of iced tea she held in her hand would slip through her fingers and fall to the street. Not three minutes later, the glass fell, each chip of ice spinning and sending back light before disappearing, the tea falling in a spray, the tumbler exploding on the sidewalk. Her hands shook; she had hurried downstairs to fetch a broom.

Even though it was beyond the range of

her understanding, she had the evidence before her, and intuition filled in the gaps. Two weeks after George DelPrete was killed, she sat beside David at the big dining table as he ate graham crackers. She watched him until he was done. Then she took his empty plate to the sink and said, "You dreamed it, didn't you? That night. When you got up and opened the door with your shoes half on?"

The color rose in his cheeks as if he were choking. She came to him and knelt beside him and pried his hands from the arms of the chair and embraced him. "It's okay," she said. "It's okay."

From then on she slept out in the main room, on the sofa outside David's bedroom door. She had always slept lightly, and David's father did not complain. She slept there for the rest of her life. Even then it was clear David could not talk about it, was too afraid. Only rarely would she bring it up: "Do you have the dreams often?" or "Did you sleep through the night?" Once she said, "I wonder if the things could change. Between the time you dream them and the time they happen," but by then, after George DelPrete, the dreams had ceased coming, as they often did, retreating somewhere else for years, until another event of sufficient significance neared, and the patterns of circumstance dragged them to the surface again.

11

Dust shifting and floating above the bed, ten thousand infinitesimal threads, red and blue, like floating atoms. Brush it off your shelves, sweep it off your baseboards. Sandy dragged sheets of tin across the basement floor. Winkler cleaned the house, fought back disorder in all its forms, the untuned engine, the unraked lawn. All the chaos of the world hovering just outside their backyard fence, creeping through the knotholes; the Chagrin River flashing by back there, behind the trees. Wipe your feet, wash your clothes, pay your bills. Watch the sky; watch the news. Make your forecasts. His life might have continued like this.

In October of 1976, Sandy was in the last, engorged weeks. Winkler coaxed her into walking with him through a park above the river. A generous wind showed itself in the trees. Leaves flew around them: orange, green, yellow, forty shades of red, the sun lighting the networks of veins in each one; they looked like small paper lanterns sailing on the breeze.

Sandy was asking about the anchor of the morning show who always had two cigarettes burning beneath the desk, and why she couldn't see any smoke on TV. She walked with her hands propped beneath her distended abdomen. Winkler gazed up periodically at the twin rows of clouds, *altocumulus undulatus*, sliding slowly east. As they crested a hill, although this was a place he had never been, he began to recognize things in quick succession: the enameled mesh of a steel trash can, broken polygons of light drifting across the trunks, a man in a blue windbreaker climbing the path ahead of them. There was a smell like burning paper in the wind and the shadow of a bird shifted and wheeled a few yards in front of them, as — he realized — he knew it would.

"Sandy," he said. He grabbed her hand. "That man. Watch that man." He pointed toward the man in the windbreaker. The man walked with a bounce in his step. All around him leaves spiraled to earth.

"He wants to catch leaves. He'll try to catch leaves."

A moment later the man turned and jumped to seize a leaf, which sailed past his outstretched hand. Another fell, and

97

another, and soon the man was grasping around him and stepping from the path with his hands out in front of him. He lunged for one and caught it and held it a moment in front of his eyes, a bright yellow maple leaf, big as a hand. He raised it as if hoisting a trophy for cheering on-lookers, then turned and started up the hill again.

Sandy stood motionless and quiet. The wind threw her hair back and forth across her face. Her cheeks flushed.

"Who is he?"

"I don't know. I saw him in a dream. Two nights ago, I think."

"You saw him in a dream?" She turned to look at him and the skin across her throat tightened — she looked suddenly, he thought, like Herman, standing in the doorway to his house, looking him over.

"I didn't even remember it until just now, when I saw him again."

"What do you mean? Why do you say you saw him *again?*"

He blinked behind his eyeglasses. He took a breath. "Sometimes I dream things and then, later, they happen in real life. Like with you, in the grocery store."

"Huh," she said.

"I tried to tell you. Before."

She shook her head. He exhaled. He thought he might say more, but something in her face had closed off, and the opportunity passed.

She went on, walking ahead of him now. Again she laced her hands at her belt, but this time it struck him as a protective gesture, a mother hemming in her cub. He reached for her elbow. "Take me home, please," she said.

Dad will soak his new pipe in the sink; Mom will come home with a patient's blood smeared across her uniform; the grocer will hand down two pretzel sticks from the jar on top of his counter and wink. A man, strolling through a park, will try to catch leaves.

Who would believe it? Who would want to think time was anything but unremitting progression, the infinite and indissoluble continuum, a first grader's time line, one thing leading to the next to the next to the next? Winkler was afraid, yes, always afraid, terminally afraid, but it was also something in Sandy herself, an unwillingness to allow anything more to upset the realm of her understanding. Her life in Cleveland was tenuous enough. He never brought it up to her again except to ask:

"You ever get déjà vu? Like something that happens has happened before, in your memory or in a dream?" "Not really," she had said, and looked over his shoulder, toward the television.

But he'd dreamed her. He'd dreamed her sitting on top of him with her eyes closed and her hands thrown back and tears on her cheeks. He'd dreamed the revolving rack of magazines, the dusty light of the Snow Goose Market, the barely visible vibrations of her trillion cells. And hadn't she dreamed him, too? Hadn't she said as much?

It was a thorn, a fissure, a howitzer in the living room, something they taught themselves not to see, something it was easier to pretend did not exist. They did not speak on the drive home. Sandy hurried downstairs and soon afterward he could hear her torch fire up, the high, flickering hiss, and the smell of acetylene rose through the registers. From the kitchen window he watched leaves curl into fists and drop, the landscape revealing itself, deeper and deeper into the woods, all the way back to the river. He checked the barometer he'd nailed to the family room wall: the pressure was rising.

12

The daughter came on November 4, 1976. She was beautiful, slick, and dark red: tiny lips, tiny toes, splotches of orange on her cheeks, delicate crinkles in her palms as if her hands were bags her metacarpals had yet to grow into. A flower of black hair on her scalp. Tiny exit bruises dotted her forehead.

They named her Grace. Grace Creek, Alaska, was a place Sandy had been only once, for a few hours with her father, on pipeline business. "The farthest north I've ever been," she told Winkler, and when she described it — the dome of the sky all white, and the ground white, too, so that you felt you were standing in a place devoid of all perspective, like standing in a dream — it made him think of the view of the Alaska Range from the roof of the apartment where he'd grown up, that white folded into white, so brilliant you'd get a headache if you looked too long. "Grace," he'd said. "Okay."

He could not look at his daughter without feeling his heart turn over. The redness of her lips, the extravagant detail of her eyelashes. The fields of blood vessels on her scalp. The smell of her neck. They would be equals, friends, confidants. After dinner some evening they would lean over their plates and she'd tell him jokes. They'd talk through her loves and fears. Her dreams.

And Sandy in the hospital bed: flushed, deflated, four drops of blood on the sheet by her hip. She held the child, whispered to her; he fell in love over and over again.

In the following weeks Sandy seemed more comfortable, her body regaining its shape, her eyes quicker and more alive. She spent only an hour at a time in the basement; she found time to make meals and wash diapers. A first snow fell and she stood holding the infant at the window watching snow sift lightly through the illuminated cones of streetlights. Joining them, he felt his heart lift with the thought of it: family.

The neighbors brought rattles and packets of formula and nippled bottles. It pleased him when they said that Grace was Daddy's girl, that she was pretty, that she had his eyes. He felt like holding her up to the sky and shouting, "Here is something perfect! Here is a miracle!" Sucking on her bottle, her legs and toes flexing against his chest, she raised a tiny, perfect hand to his chin: pink around the fingernails, an impossible intricacy to each knuckle.

Sandy would bring her into the basement and set her in a bassinet and work on her huge metal tree, and the baby would be silent, eyelids slowly falling, amid flaring blue light, the sounds of metal cracking and spitting.

Winkler, sleepless, sat in a Channel 3 staff meeting and scribbled on the agenda: *I can watch my daughter for an hour.*

He began sleepwalking again. Perhaps he had never stopped. He woke to find his feet in wet socks, mud tracked over the carpet. His coat was not hanging where he'd left it; a dresser drawer was upended, his T-shirts scattered over the floor. In nightmares he was encased in ice; he balanced precariously on the lip of Chagrin Falls, river water hurtling past his knees. After midnight he'd wake choking beneath the comforter and hear Grace crying; he'd go to her, lift her from her crib, take her downstairs, and wander with her among the dark shapes of furniture, the striped shadows of the blinds, the submarine comfort of unlit rooms.

Weeks passed. His dreams went, again and again, to Grace. He dreamed her fist would close around his thumb; he dreamed she would balance herself against the edge of the coffee table and take her first, tottering steps. There was no way for him to know if these were merely dreams — the firing of three billion neurons, the neural pyrotechnics of REM sleep — or if they were more than dreams, apparitions of what would be.

He brought his mother's old copy of Bentley's *Snow Crystals* to his cubicle at Channel 3 and sat with it in his lap. Ten thousand snow crystals, white on black. Ten thousand variations of a single, inexorable pattern: hexagonal planes, each extension at sixty degrees. Out the weather room window the wind beat Lake Erie into whitecaps.

The irises of Grace's eyes abandoned their near-black for a thoughtful gray. A more developed face began to emerge from behind her baby fat; Sandy's cheeks, Sandy's pale, thin nostrils. But she had Winkler's eyes; the shape of them distinctly familiar, like almonds turned down at the corners, absurdly large in her small, round head.

104

Christmas, New Year's, the snows of January and February, and then it was March. Sandy's Paradise Tree in the basement was growing, the highest branches appearing on it, capped with gilded angels clipped from the tops of trophies; a copper sun soldered to the top, each ray ribboned and sharp. He could hear her working late into the night, hammering and soldering, talking to their daughter.

The earth froze; the sky hovered blue and flawless above the city. Banners of vapor fluttered above storm drains and vents on the roofs of buildings; the Chagrin waterfall hung frozen from its ledge, bulbous and brown, shellacked with icicles.

He had the dream: rain on the roof, water three feet deep in the street. The downstairs was flooded; Grace cried from the plant stand. He collected her, carried her outside, and they were caught in the flood. He held her to his chest; he went under; someone called for him to let go, let go, let go.

13

After midnight he hovered over Grace in the orange glow of her night-light and watched her blanket rise and fall. Lately she slept a subterranean, vacant sleep, as if some invisible huntsman came to put her consciousness in a sack and hold it until morning.

Five months old now, she could hold her head at midline and focus her eyes on him. And she smiled — a raw, toothless smile, a hockey player's grin — any time he raised her to the ceiling or swung her through his legs.

Three days had passed since he first dreamed her death and each subsequent night the exact same dream had returned. He stood at her window and gazed down at the Newport in the driveway. He could take her. It wouldn't matter where. They could find a hotel, wait it out. Up and down Shadow Hill Lane the faces of the neighbors' houses were dark and blank.

After a few minutes he went instead to the backyard, where the remnants of summer's tomato plants lay gray and withered in the mud. The evening rain had let up and the sky above the ravine had split apart and in the gaps burned stars. Scraps of dirty, twice-frozen snow hid in the corners of the yard. A wind came through the trees and sent droplets flying through the air. One landed in the hairs on the back of his wrist and he studied it: a magnificent, tiny dome, a rhombus of sky reflected on its cap. Suddenly he forgot how to stand — his knees gave way and there was a slow, helpless sinking. He knelt awkwardly in the yard. The house loomed in front of him, dark and angular. Beneath the thin layer of mud he could feel massed shafts of ice, slender as needles. He remembered the way his mother's plants had absorbed the water she'd poured into them, the liquid slowly disappearing, a kind of flight. He thought: So this is how it will be. Not a sudden collapse of all function but instead a gradual betrayal.

How much easier it would have been if he and Sandy could have fought: a skirmish in the night, some harsh words, some measure of the truth actually spoken aloud. Maybe even — was it too much to hope? — a final belief: "I believe you," she would say. "It's impossible, but I believe you. We have to leave."

But he would be given nothing so dramatic. Everything invisible stayed invisible; everything unsaid remained unsaid. The following week progressed like any other: Sandy tended Grace, made dinners, soldered more and more objects onto her Paradise Tree. He had not even told her about the dream.

He tried every kind of sleep evasion: caffeine pills, push-ups, cold showers. He'd sit at the kitchen table over a mug of coffee and wish Sandy good night and watch the backyard darken and stars crawl over the lip of the ravine, the Milky Way rotating out there on its concentric wheels. He'd play solitaire. He'd eat tablet after tablet of Excedrin. He'd climb Shadow Hill and stand beneath the naked trees listening to dogs bark and houses settle in the night.

But he could not keep it up. Eventually he'd sleep — in bed next to Sandy, or sometimes in the Newport against the steering wheel, or at the kitchen table, chin propped on a palm — and he'd dream, and what he saw was always minute variations of the same original nightmare: Grace cold and drowned against his chest, hands prying her out of his arms. Let go, let go. The future waited for him to keep his appointment. The creek crawled through its ditch beside the lane and emptied into the river.

Yesterday he had brought home real estate flyers for houses across town; he begged Sandy to take a trip to Florida, or North Carolina, two weeks, three weeks, whatever she wanted. "We can't afford that," she'd say, or, "Why are you acting so strangely?" Here was the worst curse: he managed to force the dream from his conscious mind often enough that when it returned to him (opening the pantry door, say, recalling the sweep of floodwater), the experience of it became fresh and bleeding once more. At moments he found himself wondering how he'd gotten himself into this life: a wife? a child?

Did time move forward, through people, or did people move through it, like clouds across the sky?

For months after George DelPrete had been killed by the bus, Winkler couldn't sleep for more than a couple hours at a time. He'd wander the apartment in the dark, try to locate that smell of caribou he used to love, try to imagine big reindeer sniffing at the kitchen wastebasket, standing quietly in the shadows of his parents' bedroom. As often as not he'd find his mother at a window, watching the night, and she never seemed surprised or upset to find him out of bed at such a late hour — she'd extend an arm and bring him to her side, the pair of them at the glass, the city sleeping below. She'd pull him closer, as if to say, "I believe you, David; you're not alone," though she rarely said anything at all, just kept an arm around him, both of them watching the slow blinking of lights on far-off antennas, the all-night trains shunting into the railyard.

Now, kneeling in the frozen mud behind his house, he saw it again: a hatbox flying through the air, coming down dented on one corner. He hauled himself up from the garden and went on creaking legs back inside and checked the barometer. Falling. He studied the roiling, silvered sky through the window but felt no presence there, no sympathetic gaze.

At unpredictable moments he began mistaking people for Herman Sheeler. Herman was urinating in the Channel 3 restroom; he was salting the walk in front of a pizza restaurant; he was pulling open Winkler's mailbox and shoving a phone book inside. Each time Winkler had to calm his heart, wait for Herman's face to fade, a stranger's to reestablish itself.

What must it have been like for Herman to walk out into that garage for the first time, to open a closet and see all the clothes and shoes Sandy had left behind? Sandy's underwear in the dryer. Their wedding silver. Their West High yearbooks. Their fifteen and a half anniversaries.

At work Winkler spilled coffee through the cooling vent of a six-hundred-dollar television monitor. He stubbed his toe; he zipped his shirttail in his fly and didn't notice until the head meteorologist pointed it out to half the office.

Sandy bounced Grace on her thigh and watched him eat dinner. "You've started sleepwalking again," she said. "You went into the baby's room. Last night I was feeding her and you came in and started going through her drawers. You took out her clothes and unfolded them and piled them on top of the dresser."

"I did not."

"You did. I said your name but you didn't wake."

"Then what happened?"

"I don't know. You went downstairs."

A sudden front. Warm air pressing over the lake. Storms riding down from Canada.

He handed his forecast to the morning anchor: rain.

From the Channel 3 parking lot he watched black-hulled cumulonimbus blow in like windborne battleships. Across the freeway, lake ice banged and splintered. Dread rose in his larynx. On the way home he parked in a neighborhood in University Heights with the windows down and waited.

Any minute now. The wind lifting leaves from the gutters, a first dozen drops sinking through the branches. The sky curdled. Trees bucked and reared. Rain exploded on the Chrysler's roof.

"You're all wet," Sandy said. She folded a diaper between the baby's legs and pinned it neatly. Rain coursed down the windows and wavered the light.

He rolled up his left sleeve and wrung it in the sink. The water clung, pooled, slid toward the drain. "Sandy. I keep having this dream."

"I can't hear you, David. You're mumbling."

"I said, I keep having this dream."

"A dream?"

From the shadows he could feel Grace's gaze turn on him, dark and strange, not her eyes at all. He shuddered, backed away from the sink.

"What kind of dream?"

"That something will happen. That Grace will be hurt."

Sandy looked up. "Grace? And you think this dream'll come true?"

He nodded.

She looked at him a long time. "It's just a dream, David. A nightmare. You're dripping all over everything."

He went down the hall and stood before the bathroom mirror in his damp suit a long time. Rain hummed on the eaves. "Just a dream," he said. After a while he could hear her pick up the baby, her footsteps fade down the basement stairs.

Midnight or later. He woke up in the driveway. Mud gleamed on the tires of the Chrysler. One red leaf was stuck to the bottom of his shoe. Rainwater murmured in the gutters. Sandy was quaking in front of him. "What are you doing out here? Have you lost your mind? Were you driving the *car?*"

She was reaching for him — he was holding Grace, he realized, and she was crying. Sandy took her (collecting her neatly, expertly, always so much better at holding the child than he was) and hurried back inside. Through the open door he could see her undressing the baby, wrapping her in a blanket. The cries were screams now, long wails that even out in the driveway seemed improbably loud. He stood a moment longer, feeling sleep melt from him. His shirt was warm where he'd been holding the child. The car ticked behind him in the driveway and the driver's door stood open. *Had* he been driving? How long had she been crying like that? It seemed like it had been awhile: when he concentrated, he could remember her bawling, as if the residue of it still hung in the air.

Before he went in he watched the rain sift past the floodlight mounted beneath the eave: sheets of drops like a procession of wraiths, shifting, tumbling.

Sandy was running water in the bath. Her chest heaved, still out of breath. Grace lay on the carpet beside her, sucking her fingers. "It's going to flood," he said.

"What were you doing, David? My God, what were you doing?"

"The ground is frozen. It can't absorb this water. We can go wherever you like. Florida, Thailand — wherever. Just until this weather is gone. Or longer if you want.

114

Forever if you want."

Water surged and bubbled in the tub. "At first it was kind of charming, you know," she said. "Sleepwalking. And you did it so rarely. But now, David. I mean, come on. You're doing it every *night!* You had Grace out there!"

She unwrapped the baby and set her in the bath. "There," she said. "It's okay." She swirled the water with an index finger.

"Sandy." He reached for her but she pulled away.

"You've barely slept in, what, five days, David? Get some rest. I'll sleep in the baby's room. And Monday you're going to Dr. O'Brien's."

The rain kept up all night. Sandy whispered into the phone downstairs. He did not sleep. The sound of the water on the shingles sounded to him like insects chewing away at the roof. Twice before dawn he wrapped himself in his poncho and went out to the Chrysler and held his keys at the ignition but could not bring himself to start the car. Water ran down the lenses of his glasses. Inside the Chrysler it was damp and cold.

The next day was Sunday and still the rain had not let up. Over an otherwise silent breakfast he begged her twice more to leave. Her eyes glassed over; her lips went thin. There was no water in the streets, nothing on TV about flooding, not even on his own network. None of the neighbors were going anywhere.

"Our house is lowest," he said. "Closest to the river."

Sandy only shook her head. "I made an appointment for you. At Dr. O'Brien's. To-morrow. One p.m." To appease him she carried food up from the pantry and arranged it on top of the dresser: three boxes of Apple Jacks, a tub of oatmeal, bread and jam. Grace began to cry around noon and would not let up. He couldn't bear it and had to go stand in the bathroom, pretending to relieve himself.

Sandy called from the top of the basement stairs, her welding mask braced on her head. "You better go see the doctor, mister! You better go tomorrow! You tell him about sleepwalking. Tell him you think you can see the future."

He took Grace's yellow hat and hid it. Not ten minutes later Sandy was calling him: "Have you seen her yellow woolie?"

"No."

"But you just had it. I saw you with it."

He withdrew it from the toolbox in the

closet and handed it back.

One o'clock the next day he did not go to Dr. O'Brien's. The dream floated just beneath his consciousness, huge and eager. He had not slept in fifty hours except for two catnaps in the file room at the network office and in all that time the rain had not ceased. By 3 p.m. the river had surpassed its embankments in several valleys and sent thin sheets of water speeding through neighborhoods. At intersections, firemen waved away traffic or ferried sandbags through the mud. Telephone poles along the road shoulders stood rootless, their bases submerged. The river climbed over a bridge on Miles Road and carried it off.

Winkler clambered out of the car on the way home from work and watched the water lick at the banks. A camera crew from a rival network pulled up and splashed out of their van. "Are you getting this?" the producer shouted at the camera operator. "Are you getting it?"

A policeman waved them back. The concrete at the edges where the bridge had been was left clean and dark as if cauterized. A child's red plastic snow sled came floating down.

At home, water was coming through the

foundation. Sandy had removed many of her things from the basement already, her soldering kit, a crate of salvaged metal, sheets of paper with the ink running off in long purple tendrils. But her tree — huge now, as broad at the base as the hood of the Newport — would never fit up the stairs. Winkler doubted three men could lift it. Sandy splashed beside him, pulling her fingers through her hair.

He waded beside the washer and dryer with a five-gallon bucket and brought it up to the porch and upended it over the lawn. Then he descended again. Grace wailed. After a half hour of bailing, he could see how futile it was — water was seeping into the basement in a thousand places. The water he carried out probably rifled through the topsoil, met ice, and flowed right back through the foundation. His feet had gone numb in their boots. The drizzle would turn to sleet later in the night.

"We'll get a hotel room," he said, carrying a box of copper piping upstairs. "Across town."

"You didn't go to the doctor's." Her hands were shaking lightly. "I called."

"Sandy. The house is flooding."

"We'll be okay." But Sandy looked haggard, her face drawn, her shirttails soaked.

She held Grace as if marauders might at any moment storm the kitchen and pry her away. "Channel five says it'll end tonight. None of the neighbors are leaving."

"They will."

"We'll get a room in the morning. If it hasn't stopped raining."

Rain was assaulting the roof. They could hear it pouring over the shingles and through the downspouts. "Sandy. Please."

She looked toward the basement door. "My tree."

But she relented. They sat in the car, the three of them, wipers ratcheting back and forth. Moisture fogged the windows. It felt immediately better to him, to be together in the car, hemmed in by the dark, the doors and windows of the Chrysler fogged, the smell of wet clothes close around them. Lightning, or a downed power line, flashed somewhere. Overlapping tides of rain washed over the windshield. The dashboard sent forth its frail orange glow.

They took a motel room on Eaton Road, six miles away.

"Will you be okay tomorrow? If I take the car to work?"

"I guess. We can eat in the diner."

He looked at her, still clutching Grace. "I'm sorry about your tree, Sandy."

"Let's just get through this."

Around midnight the rain turned to hail and the motel roof sang underneath it, a sound like thousands of buckets of pebbles being emptied onto plastic. Maybe she believed him now. Maybe they would get through this and be stronger; maybe she would ask him someday to tell her everything. The blanket was heavy on his chest. The muscles in his eyes were giving over to sleep.

He woke to sudden pain and brought his fingers to his lip. He was in the parking lot of the motel. The neon sign above him sputtered in the rain. The car was running and the driver's door hung open — Grace lay asleep on the front seat. Sandy had hit him across the mouth. "Are you crazy?" she shouted. She rushed to Grace and collected her in her arms. Sandy's hair was getting damp and she was standing in her bra and pajama bottoms, barefoot on the gravel. The rain washed down over them. "What the hell are you doing with her out here?" She backed away, bracing Grace's head against her shoulder. He looked up and watched the onslaught of rain, half a million drops riding down.

Sandy was already across the lot. "What's

happening to you, David? Why are you doing this?"

He could not answer — he did not know. Sleep was slowly washing from him. Had he been dreaming?

He followed her to the door. She closed it most of the way and spoke through the gap. "Don't come in, not tonight. Don't come near us." The door shut — a red number seven painted above the peephole — and he heard the bolt slide home.

Winkler stood in the rain a long time before splashing back to the car. His jaw clattered. He could feel his lip swelling against his teeth. He was wearing his suit but his shirt had been buttoned improperly and his tie was tucked into his trouser pocket. Everything — his clothes, his hair, the seats and mats of the Newport — was wet. His hands shook in front of his eyes.

There was no traffic. From the River Road Bridge he realized he could no longer make out where the river originally ran — it had become a lake sliding through trees. A police car ahead of him rolled haltingly through a deep pool. For a moment he wondered if the sun had burned out and the entire planet was listing off into space.

He locked himself in the weather room

at Channel 3, hung his suit over two chairs, and sat in his wet underwear watching the rain-spattered window and the slurred lights of the city. In the morning he taped three outdoor spots in a poncho emblazoned with the network logo. Throughout the watershed, streams were collecting and merging. Even when the rain let up, he told the camera, it would be at least another fifteen hours before the river reached floodpoint. Churches and gyms were filling; neighborhoods lining drainage creeks were evacuating. The mayor had petitioned the governor; the governor was mobilizing the National Guard.

He called the motel, room 7. No answer. It wasn't until early evening that he could get back there. The manager had to let him in.

They were gone. Not in the shower, not in the bed. Sandy's sweater hung in the closet; a stack of diapers waited by the television. There was no note. There was a familiarity to the room that he felt outside of; it was as if, already, he was trespassing, as if the red plaid suitcase on the floor and the green toothbrush on the sink belonged not to Sandy but to some stranger whose possessions he had no right to.

He checked the diner, but they weren't

there; he dialed the house, but no one picked up. He had a half hour until his evening spot — he was supposed to be on the Main Street Bridge interviewing volunteer sandbag fillers.

Were they eating somewhere? Walking? The only theory that made any sense was Sandy's Paradise Tree — Sandy was at the house, trying to save it. She had hitched a ride somehow, and had brought Grace with her, and was trying to save her sculpture.

He backed out of the room. Out in the street the daylight was failing. The clouds were matted tightly. He pointed the Chrysler toward the house. When he reached the base of Shadow Hill he could not believe how much water had collected there. The parking lot of the middle school had become a foaming brown lake. Spirals of debris eddied against the gymnasium wall.

It was impossible to drive farther. He parked on a small knoll and climbed through wet, naked trees, hurrying along the ridge above the neighborhood. Soon he was near the top of Shadow Hill, a couple hundred feet above the lane. Below him the rooftops of neighbors' houses looked like the peaked roofs of so many houseboats. Three separate creeks funneled in at the head of the street and poured through the center of the neighborhood; the front yards and the half of the lane closest to the Chagrin had become a river of mud.

The sound of all that water was pervasive: gurgling, spitting, swallowing, pouring down the hillside and down the trunks of the trees — it sounded as if the atmosphere had liquefied. He counted rooftops: the Stevensons, the Harts, the Corddrys, that Italian family who had barbecues every Saturday. The Sachses' lawn was entirely underwater, just the candy-striped apex of their daughter's swing set showing. In the backyard of his own house the heads of fence posts were the only things visible, wooden buoys marking a shore.

Rain ran down his neck; his soles were heavy with mud. A lesson, half remembered, rose in his memory: Water craves, water is hungry — look at what it does to the stems of roses left in a vase too long. Who had said that? A professor? His mother?

Shades of mist ascended from the hillside. A helicopter shuttled past, passing in and out of low clouds, winking a small light. Already there was an odor in the air like mildew, like wet carpet, as if the houses were great moldy tea bags that had begun to steep.

As he gazed through the rain, at the flooded neighborhood, the tall and stately maple in the Sachses' front yard fell. It leaned grandly, then gave out with a singular groan, a thousand rootlets tearing and snapping, the trunk splashing down, the high branches reaching across the street, a series of percussive waves going out. The current pushed; the tree turned a bit, and held steady.

The smell, the collapsed maple, the sound of water rising and muttering — it was hopelessly recognizable. He wavered a long moment, studying the wet shingles on the roof of his house, feeling every minute of his life funnel into an instant. Here was a line from one of his hydrology texts: *convergence, confluence, conflux;* a point at which two or more streams combine, and a new stream forms by their combining.

And if Grace was in there? If he waded into the house, looked upstairs, downstairs, found her finally on the top shelf of Sandy's plant stand? If he gathered her in his arms and tried to carry her out, up the street? Her yellow woolie, her bassinet, the cereal boxes on the dresser — everything was in place.

He took a few steps forward, then turned, and walked back over the hill, the way he had come. Down through the mud and leaves. He fell once, twice, lurching back to his feet. He did not run but tried to keep his pace steady, resolved. The soles of his shoes slid in the wet leaves. He staggered to the Chrysler, started it, and turned south on Music Street, Shadow Hill at his back.

He taped his spot in borrowed waders on the Main Street Bridge above Chagrin Falls. Rain was running down his glasses and he could see only the light mounted on top of the camera, a white smear on a field of gray. Behind him men in slickers shoveled sand into burlap sacks. The falls roared.

At the end of the segment he faced the camera and said he hoped the river would crest that night. He said he hoped the rain would not turn to ice. He said we would all have to keep our fingers crossed, and watch the sky, and pray.

14

By 10 p.m. he was crossing the Springfield line into Pennsylvania. He rented a motel room in Erie and burst through the door and switched on the television. There were two and a half minutes of footage: a car floating in the library parking lot; an uprooted tree rolling over the falls; a gymnasium lined with cots. Lampposts sparked and drowned in the night; there was the customary video of stop signs submerged to the letters. But no mention of fatalities, injuries, drownings. The anchor signed off, and a movie came on — soldiers storming a hillside, shouting to one another. He turned to the window. A breeze came in, damp, stinking of diesel. He dialed the house — no ringing, just static. He dialed the motel on Eaton Road and asked for room 7 but the phone rang on and on and no one answered. He let it ring until he could not hold his eyelids open.

Exhaustion trundled over him. In a dream he piloted the Chrysler back down Music toward Shadow Hill, descending into the valley. The car stalled a few hundred feet past the middle school, swamped. He waded out into the cold, muddy water. It was soon at his waist; the light was failing. He half waded, half swam the inundated street. Bloated magazines hung in branches; dolls rode the current facedown. Whole clumps of sod turned in eddies. He entered the house, climbed the stairs, roved the rooms. Grace was crying; it was dusk. He lived through the dream again: finding her on the plant stand, lifting her out of the bassinet, wading with her into the street. He slipped. They went under. She drowned.

He had fallen asleep in his still-damp suit and woke to a chill deep inside him, as though he had been sleeping underwater. Beside the window two cords, caught in the updraft from the heater, knocked against the blinds. He bent over the sink and rinsed his face.

It was 5 a.m. Again he dialed: no one in room 7; no connection at the house. Already he had reached a state where he expected the phone to ring on and on, for no one to be there. At Channel 3 the station attendant said she knew of no fatalities. "When are you coming in?" she asked. He hung up.

Everything seemed intractable. What were his choices? To return home and possibly be the instrument of his daughter's death? How many times would she have to drown? The future had become a swarming horizon, an advancing wall just down the road, raging forward, black and insatiable, swallowing houses and fields as it came.

He left the room key on top of the television, went to the Chrysler, and guided it not toward home, but east. He kept his hands firmly on the wheel and at dawn did not turn back. I have run away before, he thought. It is merely a matter of keeping your foot on the accelerator and not letting it off. The clouds had pulled back and there were only the occasional trucks rumbling in the night, last fall's leaves blowing across the interstate.

All that day he drove, stopping only for gas and to buy chocolate bars, which he ate mindlessly, dropping the wrappers to the floor between his legs. Scranton? Philadelphia? New York? He settled on the latter, as much for its size as anything, its supposed impassiveness, its positioning at the terminus of the freeway. At dusk he brought the Chrysler up through the northern miles of New Jersey and soon was navigating beneath the Hudson in the Lincoln Tunnel, where exhaust-caked girders groaned past in the blackness above him, and when he emerged he was in Manhattan. He was drained and his vision was lapsing badly behind his glasses and what he saw appeared as little more than a hubbub of steel and mirrors, as if he were entering some vast and awful funhouse that would soon seal him into a dead end and pinch off the exits.

He parked the Chrysler in an alley and left it. On the street, big band music played from a portable stereo and the people on the sidewalks appeared to step in concert with the song — a nun with a blue backpack, an Indian man in a tracksuit carrying flowers, a woman ducking into the backseat of a cab — all of them seeming to fulfill some greater orchestration, stepping up, stepping down, swinging their arms, blinking their eyes, oblivious, hurrying to their ends.

15

Above a tavern he found a cheap room with a bricked-over window and a hot plate and an orchestra of crickets performing beneath the cot. He lay on his back and watched the cracks in the ceiling as if they might hand down a sentence that did not come. The light, from a dusty and naked bulb, was constant, day or night; he couldn't find a switch or reach the fixture to unscrew it. Every few hours he descended the iron staircase to the bar in his rumpled suit to order coffee and scan the newspapers like some deranged businessman. He dialed home from the pay phone in the back but service must still have been interrupted by the flood — a buzz rose in the line, each time, electrons piling up against a resistor, and the signal clicked off. At the motel on Eaton the clerk said that he could not reach anyone in room 7, that the room had not been paid for, that no one had yet checked out.

Directory Assistance got him the number of Tim Stevenson, the neighbor six houses up. Tim answered on the second ring. "We haven't seen anyone. Your place is a mess. The whole street is a mess. There's crap everywhere; all the septics are backed up."

"A mess?"

"Where are you?"

"Have you seen my wife?"

"Haven't seen anyone. Where are you staying?"

"And my daughter?"

"No one. Are you okay? Hey, which insurance were you on?"

Winkler washed his face and armpits in the bathroom sink; graffiti had been etched into the mirror: CHUCK WANTS SUE BUT CAN'T HAVE HER. CANDY IS EASY. On the national news the Ohio flooding warranted seventeen seconds, the rushing falls, the half-drowned street signs, a clip of two firemen in a skiff coaxing a Doberman off a garage roof. An anchor came back on; stock indices rolled across the screen.

A telegram:

Sandy —
I know you must think what I've done is unforgivable. Maybe it is. But I had to go. In case. I think I would have harmed

Grace. I'll be back as soon as it is safe.

The first bank wouldn't let him transfer funds; the second allowed him a one-day maximum withdrawal of seven hundred dollars. From a corner stand he bought a sheaf of newspapers and read that the flood had receded. The thawing soil was choking it down, funneling the water into its aquifers. Only two deaths, the paper reported, old men unwilling to leave their homes.

He dialed from a dozen different payphones but no operator could get a call through. Had he gone far enough? Would time take care of itself? Somewhere was there a tally of souls that had marked his daughter's and would seize it regardless of agent?

What if Sandy had drowned in the basement and doomed them both in the process? But wouldn't their deaths have been reported? Not if they hadn't been found. Not if he was the one who should have been reporting them.

A greater fear: What if by leaving he had somehow tampered with the order of things, removed a thread and left the fabric snagged and incomplete?

Or worse — maybe worse than anything:

What if years of studying water had manifested themselves into a dream that was nothing more than a nightmare, something to wake from and shake off, a manifested fear, merely an instance of what *could* be? What if he had left his daughter in that house to die?

It didn't matter. What mattered was that his daughter might still be breathing somewhere, smiling, sleeping, grasping Sandy's ear, gurgling some unintelligible communication.

He wandered the thronged sidewalks and peered up at the sky: spring in New York, the first trees unfolding their leaves, a depthless, pristine blue poised between buildings. Tulips rising from beds on Park Avenue, a woman laughing in an open window — these things seemed impossible, unreal.

During three and a half days, he did not sleep more than twenty minutes at a time. Finally his body gave out on the floor in front of the bed. He managed to haul a chair in front of the door, and sleep took him, and when he woke he had slept twelve hours. What he could remember of his dream was that Sandy had stormed the hall toward his room, the arm that did not hold Grace swinging violently as if to clear demons from her path, her hair standing uncombed and snarled above her head. She was beautiful in her fury; she kicked a hole in his door with the toe of her boot. In the dream he was lying on the cot and she stood over him and unleashed a thousand curses. He raised his hands over his face: spittle flew from between her lips. Grace had begun to scream. He sat up.

"Not in front of the baby," he said, and in his dream was overcome with happiness — his daughter was saved, the flood had passed, they could begin again. But Sandy was shaking Grace; he rose and gathered her from her mother's arms, wrapped her in a blanket and was leaving the room, moving down the hall, Sandy's voice behind him cracking at its peaks, as if her voice somehow had become the arc of her welding torch, sizzling and snapping, and the child still screaming in his arms, reaching the top of the iron stairs — he would get them all out of there, they would find the Chrysler and drive home, or all the way back to Anchorage if Sandy wanted — and he tripped. Horror plunged through him. The blanket unraveled; Grace hovered, out of his arms, for an instant, her forehead wrinkling. Sandy screamed. He tried to close his eyelids but in the dream they were wide open, as if propped by invisible toothpicks. Grace dropped spinning down the flight of stairs and landed with a muffled crack, an egg breaking inside a towel.

What was sleep? What was sentience? He studied his reflection and realized he was not sure if *this* was a dream — would he wake at any moment and find himself somewhere else? Was he sleepwalking even now? That night in a state near desperation he crouched in his doorway with his hands wrapped around a quart of coffee. He had stacked the frame of the bed and chair against the door.

Each time a cupboard closed somewhere in the building, or a siren started, or footsteps emerged from the stairwell, an impulse shivered through him: *Run. Run farther.* It was only a matter of time until he would wake and Sandy would be at the door and he would kill his daughter.

In the morning he roved the city. He rented two more hotel rooms and each time the dream was the same with the setting altered. In the second dream he was sleeping on a sidewalk grate with steam rising around him. Beside him slept another man, wrapped in an orange plastic raincoat. Down the sidewalk came the echoing footsteps of his wife, each heel clapping the pavement, and she was shaking him awake, shouting, he was taking the child from her arms, dropping her, killing her.

The terror of sleeping was no better than the terror of waking. His hands seemed pale, strange devices — not his own. He had already spent five hundred and eleven dollars of his and Sandy's money. Any moment now the future — that black, swarming wall — would arrive.

He was at the cage on the first floor of a hostel. A muffled pounding echoed from the ceiling. The clerk had a dozen tattoos beneath his cardigan. "Booked. You've got to check in by three p.m."

"I'll pay double."

"No beds."

"I'll take anything. A closet."

"We're full. You need a hearing aid?"

He stood awhile in front of the desk and then went out. It had gone cold that evening, a last paroxysm of winter, and wind rasped through the buildings. Subways shook the sidewalk as they passed beneath. He drew his suit jacket around him. Above the city nimbus clouds raced to sea. It began to snow: small, wet crystals that seemed to groan as they dropped through the air.

He was downtown in an all-night gyro place, bent over the table, beginning to nod off on his forearms. It was the sight of dust on a vase of fake irises, and then a smell when someone entered, cold air rushing through the door, a smell like oiled metal, like slush, and he knew he was entering the dream. He left the restaurant. A half block away, a figure in an orange plastic raincoat knelt over a grate. Sleep clawed at Winkler, clutched his eyelids; how easy it would be to lie there, up the block in that rising steam, to doze, to let the future catch up with the present.

Instead he ran. He ducked through alleys and tried not to pay attention to the turns he made. His legs ached and his feet chafed in his shoes. After a dozen or so blocks he was passing the faded green awnings of a shore market, and had reached the edge of the island. Out on the pier a crane was loading a freighter and snow floated beneath its floodlights in slow coils. He stopped, breathing hard, knees trembling, a pain in his lower legs as if his shins had begun to splinter.

He had not seen Sandy for nine nights.

A security guard with a clipboard led him aboard and showed him the captain. The ship was the *Agnita* — a Panamanian-registered British merchant freighter bound for Venezuela. For two hundred and thirteen dollars, all the cash he had left, the captain allowed him passage.

"Caracas?" the captain asked.

"Anywhere," Winkler said.

Snow flew among the telegraph wires and down through the varied masts and antennas in the port and disappeared wherever it touched the harbor. He climbed to the foredeck and watched the city, its thousand muted corridors. A police launch motored past, its spotlight illuminating a taper of falling snow. Small, granular flakes collected on the shoulders and sleeves of his jacket. He raised his cuff to his eyes: Triangular forms with truncated corners? Hexagonal plates? He looked away, feeling sick.

After an hour or so the loading crane swiveled away and a tug brought the *Agnita* out from the pilings and into the harbor. From the stern he watched as the ship slid through the Narrows. The engines rumbled to life; a great boil went up behind the ship. The tug turned and faded, and the lights of Manhattan reflected off the rimpled water like the lights of ten cities. The outer harbor waited black and huge off the bow. The freighter sounded two blasts; somewhere a buoy clanged. They steamed past Coney Island and Breezy Point and soon he could see only the lights of fires along the Jersey shore and finally those, too, waned.

Ice glazed the rails. He clambered down to the bunkroom. The ship fell into a steady buck and sway as the long swells of open water took hold of her.

Book Two

1

Frost, like a miniature white forest, backlit by sun, fringed the bottom of the window. Dendrites, crystal aggregates, plumes of ice — an infinite variety. Strange to think that a few million water molecules frozen now on the fuselage of a 757, hurtling toward Miami, could feasibly be the same molecules that seeped through gaps in the foundation of his house, molecules Sandy might have sopped with a towel and wrung into the yard, to evaporate, become clouds, precipitate, and sink to earth once more.

What is time? he wrote in his pad. *Must time occur in sequence — beginning to middle to end — or is this only one way to perceive it? Maybe time can spill and freeze and retreat; maybe time is like water, endlessly cycling through its states.*

A flight attendant came by and asked him to pull the shade. The movie was starting. The woman in the middle seat tore headphones out of a plastic bag and clamped them over her ears. Winkler removed his eyeglasses and wiped the lenses.

Before Darwin, before Paracelsus, before Ptolemy even, for as long as memory had existed, humans carried it in a corner of their hearts: We live in the beds of ancient oceans. We carried it in our terrors of drowning, our stories about ancestors delivered from floods: *In the beginning God separated the vapors to form the sky above and the oceans below.* The end of the world would be watery as well: a resolving storm; a cleansing tide; glaciers grinding over everything.

Overlap, succession, simultaneity — how Noah must have sweated, hammering together his raft, the first raindrops striking the neighbors' roofs.

The sound of the engine mounted on the wing outside his window made a constant, lulling wash. The sky, pale blue, seemingly infinite, eased past.

A quarter of a century before, the *Agnita* traversed the rough gray of the Atlantic, moving in the opposite direction. Six hours out, the sun pushed over the edge of the sea. He climbed to the deck and watched the last gulls sail over the cargo booms.

The steely green of the Blake Ridge, the floating weed of the Gulf Stream. Never had he seen so much sky, so much water. Near the Bahamas a gale drove ranges of hissing swells against the hull and he clung to the life rail, yellow-faced, sick, the ship rolling beneath him. Scraps of memories surfaced: Sandy stepping into the cold from First Federal, drawing the ruff of her big hood around her face; the way Grace had begun to look up when he entered a room; Herman Sheeler bent over his desk, penciling an appointment onto his calendar: *Hockey, Wednesday, 4 p.m.*

Sandy, he assumed, would by now be careening toward ultimatum. He imagined her first night back in the house, propping cushions to dry on the porch, draping curtains over the backyard fence. How much sediment and sludge would have to be pumped out of her basement workshop?

She'd phone the police and Channel 3; she'd make a list of necessary repairs; she'd stand in the doorway looking out at the space in front of the hedges where the Newport should have been. Maybe she'd board off the basement door and leave her Paradise Tree underwater, an Atlantis in the basement.

The telegram would be delivered; maybe she would shred it, or stare at it, or shake her head, or nod. At some point she'd have to answer difficult, uncomfortable questions: from the neighbors, from an insurance representative. *Where* is he? By now, perhaps, she would have stuffed Winkler's clothes into boxes and taped them shut.

Or she was making funeral plans. Or the house was destroyed and she and Grace were halfway to Columbus, or California, or Alaska. Or she was dead, lodged underwater, snared in the branches of a tree beside Grace, mother and daughter, their hair fanning like ink in the current.

All the cruelties of conjecture. Was he simply too weak? Too afraid? Had he *wanted* to flee? Maybe she had fled, too. Maybe she was glad Winkler had gone: no more tossing in the bed at night, no more sleepwalking, no more waking to find her husband empty-eyed over his sock drawer. Maybe she and Herman had been corresponding all along, while Winkler was at work, while Winkler was asleep. Maybe, maybe, maybe.

To even think of Grace set a voltage tingling through his skull. Even then, twelve nights since he had last seen his daughter, the continent receding steadily behind him, a small part of him understood that he might not be able to return. After a measure of time — a month, six months, maybe, or a year — Sandy would recover and seal herself off and then she would be finished with him, finished completely, living again in the present, clerking in a savings and loan, making her sculptures. He would be relegated to a past best left fastened and buried, a Paradise Tree in the basement, a body at the bottom of a lake. Grace — if she had lived — would ask about him and Sandy would say he was a deadbeat, nobody.

He slogged through the hours. At night stars spread across the sky in unfathomable multitudes and pulled through the dark, dropping one by one beneath the sea as new ones emerged on the opposite horizon.

The crew was mostly Brazilian; the mate was British. The only other paying passengers were a threesome of Malaysian pepper merchants who whispered furtively to one another in the forecastle like conspirators plotting a hijack. He avoided everyone — what if someone should try to start a conversation? *What do you do? Where are you going?* Neither was a question he could answer. At meals he chose between the galley's daily offerings: grilled cheese, boiled sausage, or a shapeless pudding that shuddered grotesquely with the ship's vibrations. Sleep, if it came at all, arrived weakly, and he entered it as if it were a shallow ditch. When he woke he felt more exhausted than ever. Around him men snored in their bunks. Water roared through the ship's plumbing.

The vast blue fields of the Sargasso Sea. The Windward Passage. The Antilles. The Caribbean. Birds began to appear: first a pair of frigate birds riding over the bow; then jaegers; finally a squadron of gulls riding over the foredeck. Land came into sight on the seventh day: a trio of islands floating in vapor thirty miles to the east.

The *Agnita* docked at a half dozen ports. At each, customs officials swarmed her holds and went away with bribes: cases of single-malt, a lawnmower, a New York Yankees jersey. She took on grain in Santo Domingo and sugar in Ponce; she disgorged mattresses in St. Croix, a bulldozer in Montserrat, three hundred porcelain toilets in Antigua.

One noon, as the ship was piloted out of open water and toward harbor once more, he climbed to the deck and stood at the rail. A steep island, with the broad green shoulders of a volcano at its northern end, approached. The sea was unusually calm, and the swell driven in front of the bow held a wavering image: the tall gray hull, punctuated only by the starboard hawse-pipe; then the row of scuppers, and the thin spars of the rail; lastly Winkler's own small and insubstantial shape, hanging on.

It was the cargo port in Kingstown, St. Vincent. Maybe two thousand miles from Ohio, but it might as well have been a million. Far enough.

He disembarked in the lee of three containers of tractor parts and took refuge near the wharf in a ruined hotel, the roof partially caved in, a half dozen warblers preening on the window frame. Within an hour the *Agnita* sounded twice and pulled out. He watched it all the way to the horizon, the hull fading first, then the white superstructure, finally the tops of the stacks disappearing beyond the curvature of the sea.

2

St. Vincent's hillsides were a foreboding emerald, patched with cloud shadow and the paler green of cane fields. From his window he could see a row of tin warehouses, an arrowroot-processing plant, a dirt field with netless soccer goals at either end. Knots of pastel-colored houses clung to the mountainsides. A syrupy, melancholy smell that Winkler associated with old meat permeated the air. Frigate birds hovered in drafts high over the port.

That first night he hiked a nine-hole golf course left to ruin behind the hotel, six-foot stalks of peculiar, spiky plants nodding in the fairways; ivy creeping over the tee boxes; a family of gypsies in semipermanent encampment on what had been the third green. Few lights burned except fires along the beaches, the mast lights of yachts, and a dozen or so flashlights conveyed by unseen commuters, shuttling between leaves like misplaced stars.

The palms stirred. Tiny sounds took on

distorted importance: a pebble rattled under his shoe; something rustled in the scrub. Frogs shrieked from the branches. He wondered if he had not fled New York but the present as well.

A sign for a public telephone was bolted to the wall of the post office. He took up position with his back against the entry gate and fell in and out of nightmares. In the morning a woman dressed neck to ankle in denim nudged him awake with her toe. A crucifix swung from her neck: a cross as big as her hand with an emaciated Jesus welded to it.

"I need to make a phone call," he said. "Can you speak English?"

She nodded slowly, as if considering her answer. Her cheekbones were high and severe; her hair was straight and black. Spanish, maybe? Argentinean?

"I have to call America."

"This is America."

"The United States."

"Twenty E.C."

"E.C. What's E.C.?"

She laughed. "Money. Dollars."

"Can I call collect?"

"Will they accept?" She laughed again, unlocked the gate, and ushered him inside the post office. He wrote the number on a slip of paper; she went behind the desk, spoke into the receiver a moment, and passed it to him. In the line he could hear miles of wires buzzing and snapping, a noise like a thousand switches being thrown. There was a sound like a bolt sliding home, then, miraculously, ringing.

It astonished him that a sequence of wires, or maybe satellite relays, might actually run from that island all the way to Shadow Hill, Ohio — how was that possible? But he was not so far away, not yet. He could imagine the phone on the kitchen wall with ruinous clarity: fingerprints on the receiver, the plastic catching a rhombus of light from the window, the bell's mechanical jingle. What time would it be there? Would the ringing wake Grace? Would the house still be damp, would he have been fired, would an insurance check have arrived?

He was fairly certain he had been gone eighteen days. He imagined Sandy plodding to the phone in her pajamas. She was flipping on lights, clearing her throat, lifting the receiver from its cradle — she would speak to him now.

The line buzzed on and on: a simulation of ringing he wasn't used to. His tongue was like a pouch of dust in his mouth. It

152

rang thirty times, thirty-one, thirty-two. He wondered if the house was submerged underwater, at the bottom of some new lake, the phone still clinging dumbly to the wall, the cord brought horizontal and fluttering in the current, minnows nosing in and out of the cupboards.

"Not home," the operator said. It was not a question. The post office woman looked at him expectantly.

"A few more rings."

The wall of the post office was white and hot in the sun. The silos of a sugarcane mill, painfully bright, reared above the town. At a kiosk he bartered his suit jacket with a man whose patois was so thick and fast Winkler could not understand any of it. Winkler ended up with a salt cod, a pineapple, and two jam jars filled with what he thought might be Coca-Cola but turned out to be rum.

A pair of women strolling past, carrying baskets, nodded shyly at him. He followed them awhile, down an unpaved street, then turned and descended through thorny groves to a beach. Small green waves sighed in from the reef. He heard what he thought were occasional voices in the trees behind him but even in full sunlight it was dark back there and he could not be sure. From high on the hills came the bells of goats moving slowly about.

That sweet, carrion smell crept under the breeze. The cod was oily and stirred in his gut. He raised the first rum jar and stared at it a long time. Tiny gray clumps of sediment floated through the cylinder.

He had been drunk only once before, at a chemistry department party in college when, in a fit of introversion, he quarantined himself on top of a dryer in the hostess's laundry room and gulped down four consecutive glasses of punch. The room had begun to spin, slowly and relentlessly, and he had let himself out through the garage and thrown up into a snowbank.

Dim clouds of mosquitoes floated at the edges of the trees. He sipped rum all that morning and afternoon and rose from the sand only to wade into the sea and relieve himself. By evening strange waking dreams possessed him: a dark-haired girl hauled a sack through woods; a rowboat capsized beneath him; the woman from the post office prayed over a halved avocado, her crucifix swinging through the light. He dreamed freezing lakes and Grace's little body trapped beneath ice and the heart of an animal hot and pumping in his fist.

Finally he dreamed of blackness, a deep and suffocating absence of light, and pressure like deep water on his temples. He woke with sand on his lips and tongue. The sun was nearly over the shoulder of the island — the sky seemed identical to the previous morning's. The same cane mill stood brilliant and white in the glare.

Another day. Beside him a tiny snail worked its way around the rim of an empty rum jar. His dream — the asphyxiating blackness — was slow in dwindling. Dark spots skidded across his field of vision. He rose and picked his way through the grove behind the beach.

In an alley behind a series of hovels he pulled lemons from a burl-ridden tree and ate them like apples. An old woman tottered out, shouting, shaking a mop at him. He went on.

In the days to come he telephoned the house on Shadow Hill Lane a dozen times — each time the call went unanswered; each time he begged the operator to wait a few more rings. He wondered again if the freighter had carried him to a new location in time, a future or past that did not coincide with Ohio's. Here it was a day like any other: a hot, dazzling sky, blackbirds screeching at him from the trees, boats sliding lazily in and out of harbor. There what day was it? Maybe it was years later — maybe, somehow, it was still March, maybe he was still asleep in his bed, upstairs, beside Sandy, Grace sleeping her steadfast sleep down the hall, the first raindrops fattening in the clouds.

But it was April 1977. Back home the yard was coming to life, the flood receding into memory. Were they burying Grace? Maybe the funeral had already happened and now there were only memorial-fund canisters beside checkout registers, a grave, and leftover vigil programs neighbors had kept on their kitchen counters too long and now were guiltily folding into the trash. Grace Pauline Winkler: 1976–1977. We hardly knew you.

The American Express office could not reach his wife, they said, to see if she would wire money. A tall, purple-skinned man at the bank said he could not access Winkler's checking or savings without a current passport. "Technically, sir," he stage-whispered, winking, "I make a call and you get locked up at Immigration."

He pawned his belt; he pawned the laces from his shoes. He ate stale croissants salvaged from bakery seconds, a dozen discarded oranges with white flesh. When he couldn't bear his thirst he took sips from the second jar of rum: sweet, thick, painful.

In a moment of courage he asked the post office woman to dial Kay Bergesen, Channel 3's "News at Noon" producer. Kay accepted the charges. "David? Are you there?"

"Kay, have you heard anything?"

"Hello? I can't hear you, David."

"Kay?"

"You sound like you're in Africa or something. Look, you have to get in here. Cadwell is pissed. I think he might have fired you already —"

"Have you heard from Sandy?"

"— you just disappeared. We didn't hear squat, what were we supposed to think? You have to call Cadwell right now, David —"

"Sandy," Winkler said, wilting against the post office wall. "And Grace?"

Kay was shouting: "— I'm losing you, David. Call Cadwell! I can't fend —"

Twenty-one days since leaving Ohio. Twenty-two days. He tried the neighbor, Tim Stevenson, but no one answered; he tried Kay again but the connection broke before it could be completed. The post office woman shrugged.

In the afternoons, storms came over the island and he sheltered on the fringe of his small beach under the low-slung palms. Every few hours more blood seemed to drain from his head, as if his heart was no longer up to the task of circulation, as if this place held him in the grips of a more powerful form of gravity. At night tiny jellyfish washed ashore and lay flexing in the sand like strange, translucent lungs. Sand fleas explored his legs. He took to sleeping in long stints and when he woke his same dream of blackness faded slowly as though reluctant to leave. Somewhere out past the reef lightning seethed and spat and he turned over and slept on.

3

He had been in St. Vincent six days when he went to the post office and passed his wristwatch to the woman behind the counter.

"I need to make another call."

"You won't reverse the charges?"

"Not this number."

"Will these people be home?" She started to laugh.

"Goddamn it."

Her smile wilted. She raised a hand to her crucifix. *"Permiso,"* she said. "I am sorry. I should not make fun." She held the watch at arm's length and studied it in a pantomime of interest. She raised the buckle up and down; she squinted at the second hand, which stood motionless over the nine. "What do I do with this?"

"Tell the time. Sell it. They wouldn't take it at the market."

She glanced behind her at the thin man who managed the place but he was paging through a newspaper and paying no attention.

"Is it broken?"

"It works. It got a bit waterlogged. It just needs to dry out."

"I don't want it."

"Please."

She looked over her shoulder again. "Two minutes."

He told her the number for Herman Sheeler's house in Anchorage and she dialed and handed over the receiver. After the first ring he thought he might pass the phone back and tell the woman no one was home but then he heard the handset being lifted on the other side and it was Sandy.

There was a satellite delay in the line. Her two syllables — "Hello?" — repeated, tinny and distant, as if she had spoken through a culvert pipe. Somewhere inside the connection an electronic beep reverberated. His throat caught and for a long moment he thought he might not be able to speak. April in Anchorage, he thought. Wind against the garage door, slush sliding off the roof. The trout print in the paneled hallway.

"Hello?" she said again.

He supported his head against the wall. "It's David."

Silence. He had the sense she had covered the mouthpiece with her palm.

"Sandy? Are you there?"

"Yes."

He said, "You're okay."

"I'm okay?"

"You're all right, I mean. Alive. I'm glad."

The line fizzed; the beep sounded. "Alive?"

"I keep trying the house."

"I'm not there."

"How long have you been gone? Are you back with him?"

She did not reply.

"Sandy? Is Grace there? Is Grace okay?"

"You left. You just got up and left."

"Is Grace with you? Is she all right?"

There was the sound of the receiver clattering onto a counter or maybe the floor. A second later Herman's voice was in his ear. "Don't call here again. Get some help. You need help. Do you understand?" Then a click, and the static fell off.

He stood a moment. The wall was warm and damp against his forehead. The air smelled like wet paint. He had a sudden image of Sandy in the doorway of that house, toboggan-riding polar bears printed on her pajamas, her bare feet whitening in the cold.

"I was disconnected," he managed to say.

The woman's voice was low: "I'll dial again." The line rang, and rang. Finally it picked up and then clicked off.

He listened to the dead space in the line for a moment, then passed the receiver back. "Lord," the woman said. "You sit down for a moment." She clasped the telephone over the big crucifix on her chest. "I'll get some tea."

But he had already turned and was blundering through the doors into the throbbing green light. What was left? His shirt was stiff with sweat and grime; the knees had come out of his trousers. He had a half jar of rum and three Eastern Caribbean dollars in his pocket, enough for nothing: a bag of crackers, maybe, a tin of luncheon meat.

Below the town the ocean gleamed like a huge pewter plate and the sun beat murderously upon it. He stopped in the middle of Bay Street and braced his hands on his knees a long time. The asphalt seemed to tremble, the way an image reflected in water trembles. Inside him a slow vertigo had started. He had the odd sensation that the light in the sky was entering his skin somehow and penetrating the cavities of his body. Any minute now he would not be able to contain it.

He raised a hand to his mouth and retched. A man, passing on a bicycle, gave him a wide berth. Two small boys pointed at him and covered their mouths with the hems of their T-shirts. The faces of the pastel storefronts seemed to leer and pitch. Somewhere in the harbor a ship sounded. He staggered down the thin track south of town. Each cell in my body is disconnecting, he thought. All the neurons have torn loose.

The light was such that he could only keep his eyes open for a few seconds at a time. A bus with PATIENCE AND GOD painted across it, its windows full of sleepy women, churned past and left him dusty. He found the path leading off the road and picked his way through the dense growth. On his little beach he knelt and watched horizontal scraps of clouds inch across the sky. *Cumulus humilis fractus*, he thought. Everything I know is useless.

He crouched in the sand and shivered. Twice in the hours to come he woke to feel another man's hands in his pockets and he reached to grab the wrist but it was gone. The first had robbed him of his remaining money and he wondered hazily what the second had found. In half dreams in which he wasn't sure if he was awake or asleep, he watched regiments of crabs sidle onto the beach, cantering among the tide pools on their needle-tipped feet, pausing, then moving on again.

4

He woke to the smell of meat and the sound of gums smacking. A potbellied man was squatting beside him, eating rice and mutton dedicatedly, hardly pausing to swallow. A bar of yellow light pulled over the back of the island. Among the rocks, tide pools reflected jagged circles of sky. Winkler had not eaten in two days and the wet sounds of the man chewing made him want to gag.

The man said, "Could've robbed you."

Winkler tried to balance his head on his knees but it would not stay. "It's already stolen," he said. His voice cracked and sounded to him like the voice of a stranger. The potbellied man shrugged and ate; the sky accumulated light.

"What day is it?"

"Sunday."

"Sunday what?"

"Sunday Easter. Here." His accent was Spanish. He handed over rice wrapped in a glossy yellow leaf. Winkler raised it to his nose and passed it back.

"Eat it."

Winkler raised it again and closed his eyes and bit off a tiny corner. His mouth was entirely void of saliva. The rice felt like tiny bones between his molars.

"My wife," the man said. "Soma." He paused, waiting perhaps for Winkler to react. His forehead puckered. "She hasn't slept all week. She says Easter is forgetting. No, for" — he snapped his fingers in search of the word — "for giving. For forgiving."

Winkler chewed carefully. His teeth had loosened in their gums and felt as if they could at any moment unmoor altogether. "Eat the leaf too," the man said. Winkler studied it: thick, glossy, something like a broad and yellow rhododendron leaf. He shook his head.

The man took it and folded it carefully into quarters and ate it. "Good for the bowel," he said, and smiled. He wiped his fingers on the backs of his calves and stood. "I am Felix. Felix Antonio Orellana." He seized Winkler's hand and hauled him to his feet. Streaks of light leaked slowly across Winkler's vision.

"I am a chef. I cooked in the Moneda in Santiago, Chile. I cooked once for Cuban presidente Fidel Castro. I made callaloo soup and he called me from the kitchen to tell me it was fabulous. That is the word he used. *Fabuloso.* He said he would like me to send his cooks the recipe." He nodded a moment. "I sent it, of course.

"Come." He led Winkler along the beach and over several embankments clotted with seagrape. Winkler's feet were swollen in his shoes, and his head felt poorly anchored to his neck, as though it might tumble off. Despite his paunch, Felix walked easily and quickly, balancing his torso on agile, chicken-bone legs; several times he had to turn around and wait. They picked their way down to a cove where a barefoot girl, maybe five years old, sat on the bow of a long, wide-hulled canoe, tossing stones into the sea.

Felix said something to the girl that Winkler did not understand and she splashed into the water and stood minding the bowline with one hand on the gunwale.

"Please," Felix said and waved toward the boat. "We take you home." He gestured with his chin toward the sea. "Not far."

The planking was loaded with crates of food and charcoal. Winkler flattened himself across the middle bench and Felix folded himself between crates and took the tiller. The girl coaxed the boat off the sand and waded with it until it drifted free and hauled herself aboard. At the stern hung a rusted outboard and Felix gave it two quick pulls and it coughed and smoked and gasped to life.

The bow rose as the boat accumulated speed. Winkler watched the green slopes of St. Vincent recede behind them. Flying fish soared in front of the bow wake, gliding along for long stretches, then knifing back into the water. Felix produced a flask from somewhere in his shirt and uncapped it with one hand and drank meditatively. He appeared to be making for an island, a black lump on the horizon.

Winkler's vision lapsed occasionally in the dazzle of the early sun and the seething water and the jolting of his eyeglasses against the bridge of his nose. The horizon bounced and heeled. A sour taste rose in his throat and he felt his face blanch. He turned and spat. When he looked up he saw the girl staring at him with bright eyes. "*¿Mareado?*" she shouted. Winkler turned away and swallowed.

The island drew closer; he could make out trees, a cane silo, a few houses dispersed over ridgelines. It looked smaller than St. Vincent and not as steep, three green hills fringed in black, dwarfed by sea and sky.

Just when he felt he could bear the nausea no longer, Felix let off the throttle and backed the motor. "Reef," he announced. Ahead of the bow the island disappeared and reappeared and disappeared again. The backsides of swells frothed and broke ahead of them. Peering over the side Winkler could see the dark shapes of coral passing below. They passed a battered green channel marker, sucking and nodding in the swells. The boat yawed; the propeller came free for a moment and screamed, then cut back in. The girl shouted, "It is daaangerous!" and beamed at Winkler.

Felix seemed nonplussed. He raced the engine, and they were rushing over the coral, surfing almost, and the loaded canoe lilted sickeningly. For a brief moment Winkler found himself staring past the bow at a wall of foaming water. Then they were through and into a lagoon. The boat settled. Combers broke placidly behind them. The girl looked at Winkler, and he nodded to show he was okay and she laughed. "No?" she asked. "No more?"

They landed at a wharf, one rotting jetty leaning into a calm bay and a few scattered pirogues painted in pastels. Beneath the trees on the far side stood a clump of fishermen's cottages. "Everyone is at the harbor," Felix said. "For the regatta."

He cut the motor and the girl leapt onto the seawall and tied up. Without a word they began ferrying their purchases ashore, and soon the three of them set off, carrying boxes and jugs up a dirt track, a meter wide with tall, heavy grass on either side. Occasional white houses stood back from the trail, small and ragged, with corrugated roofs. A few goats trailed them and dark children watched them pass from doorways and called to the girl, who called back. The sun followed them above the treetops. Red dust rose in small clouds around their feet. Winkler carried a box of eggplant and followed behind potbellied Felix and his daughter, both of them toting bigger loads than his.

They stopped eventually in front of a tiny light blue house with a thin crack running through it, corner to corner, as if a gigantic hand had reached through the sky and broken off the top half and then replaced it. Felix set down his crates. "Home," he said.

In front of the door they paused and Felix bent over the girl to say something and she produced a clean white dress from a box and pulled it on over her T-shirt. An assortment of stringy-looking hens flapped across the yard and seethed around their feet. Felix produced his flask once more and emptied it into his mouth. Then he ran a comb through his hair and passed the comb to the girl, who tugged it once through her hair and passed it to Winkler.

Inside, three boys, maybe eight or nine years old, in identical white shirts, played jacks on the dirt floor. Behind them a thin woman in a yellow dress and scarf sat in a chair reading. She was, Winkler saw, the woman from the post office on St. Vincent. She set down her book, stood, and held out the back of her hand. "I am Soma. Happy Easter."

Winkler stood blinking a moment. She laughed. He took her hand. She lined up the children one by one and introduced them and each in turn shook his hand shyly and would not meet his eyes.

Then Soma moved in front of them and made a sort of half curtsy. "I am sorry," she said, "for my joke at the post office. You must forgive me."

Felix cleared the boys out to the yard and unpacked the crates of food. "You," he said, waving a knife at Winkler. "Chop these." He handed Winkler a sack of small yellow onions and Winkler stood at the counter peeling and slicing. Twice he had to lean over the counter, eyes watering, swallowing bile. The little girl, a miniature of her mother, watched him from the other side of the window, her fingers looped through the wire of the screen.

The walls of the house were unpainted. In places hung photos: a city backed by steep, blue mountains; a rolling grassland dotted with tents; a laminated image of the Virgin in a blue cloak with a snake beneath her sandal. In the corners of the central room were stacks of books, most of them in Spanish: *La Iglesia Rebelde*, *Armas de la Libertad*, *Regional Socialism in Latin America*. And on the sills were tiny, clumsily made boats: models of sloops and yawls, longboats, a scow — some with tiny brass halyards, balsa tillers, rigging made from thread.

Felix cooked in a state of near frenzy, banging pans, inhaling steam, occasionally bursting into song. He wiped away sweat with a forearm; he stole drinks from an unlabeled bottle hidden behind the charcoal box. He ordered Winkler to slice the eggplant in long, fine sheets and supervised each slice. "Thin now. Thinner." Felix took them up, like strange, wet slips of paper, and fried them crisp in a skillet and tucked them between sheets of newspaper. He made an elaborate mango chutney. He scalded and plucked small hens, slathered them in pepper, and set them in the charcoal stove. From far away, beyond the trees, came the sounds of fireworks, and the boys returned an hour later flushed and sweaty and Felix lifted the sizzling hens from their pans. "Okay," he said.

They ate at a picnic table at the other end of the room. Felix had covered the slivers of eggplant with chutney and arranged the roasted birds on top. Soma bowed her head and the children bowed with her and she thanked the Lord for the food before them and for the bounty of the island and for preventing one of the boys from failing his mathematics exam the previous week. Then she raised a glass and, holding a hand over her heart, said: "To the health and fortitude of our guest." The children raised cups of milk and knocked them against one another.

They fell to the food. Winkler faced a window and through the screen he watched swifts hunt insects over the yard.

The chickens had gone quiet; a gecko breathed silently on the ceiling. It seemed impossible that he was there, listening to this family eat roasted birds. Felix asked several questions about American cattle raising, sizes and calving rates, and seemed disappointed to learn Winkler knew nothing about it. The boys finished first and sat restlessly over their plates. The girl poked at her meat. Finally Felix wiped his mouth and belched and pushed his plate forward and released presents from under his bench: three small wooden sloops, simple hulls with a dowel glued to their decks as masts and tiny captain's wheels just fore of the stern. The boys clamored and fought over colors and settled in with their respective selections. For the girl he handed down a glass jar with wire mesh stretched over the top and she beamed and reached for him and hung her arms around his neck.

Soma smiled and said, "Nothing for me?"

"For you," Felix said and gestured at the children, "is later." She laughed.

The three boys pretended to crash their sloops into the walls. The girl crawled beneath the table trying to trap a beetle in her jar.

Soma ordered the boys to wash the dishes and they collected buckets from beneath a shelf and went out. He could hear them in the yard sloshing water and clanging plates together.

The light began to fade. Out in the yard the swifts had been replaced by bats. Soma lit an oil lamp and set it at the center of the table, where it hissed and sputtered. Felix leaned back in his seat smiling with a kind of thoughtless beatitude. As though everything was going as planned. As though his small kingdom resounded with harmony.

He lifted the little girl off the floor and onto his lap. She raised her eyes from her jar to Winkler and smiled and blinked rapidly.

"This is Naaliyah," Felix said. "Our daughter." A mosquito landed on the girl's forearm and she watched with astute attention as it pulled blood from her. It swelled, withdrew its proboscis, and disappeared. Naaliyah rubbed her wrist absentmindedly. In her jar a black ant touched at the glass walls with its antennae.

"She is beautiful," Winkler said. He wanted to ask about her, how old she was, if she went to school, but tears were flooding his eyes and he had to get up from the bench and go out into the night.

The room they gave him was the boys', in the back of the house, a sun-faded poster of some Chilean soccer player tacked to the wall, two bunk beds built into the wall with a single crosspiece for a ladder. Stacks of their little clothes were arrayed on a shelf in the corner. The boys lay down wordlessly on the kitchen floor, side by side, their heads on a single pillow. The girl lay on one of the picnic table's benches, beneath the window, still in her white dress, watching Winkler with big, slow-blinking eyes.

Winkler climbed into the lower berth. A scattering of glow-in-the-dark stars shone dully along the underside of the top bunk. The smell was sweet: laundry, and boys' sweat.

Leaves riding the wind like commuters; filaments of air trapped within the arms of a snow crystal; his mother tamping soil into a terra-cotta pot. Dreams creeping like shadows from the edges of the yard. When he'd asked about Grace, Sandy had dropped the phone.

Soma tiptoed in, a book in her hand, reading glasses pushed up over her hair. "David."

He sat up. "I can't . . ." he began, but she held up a palm.

"Felix does his best cooking in the morning. You will stay?"

He shook his head.

"Sshh . . ." She pulled the hem of the sheet to his neck. "For me."

A beetle crashed into the wall and dropped to the floor and sat whirring there as if shaking off the impact. He watched Soma sweep away through the doorway and kiss the girl good night and then disappear behind a curtain into the other room in the house. Soon the place was silent, and he could hear the steady, shallow breathing of the boys as they slept, and the clamor of the insects out in the tamarinds along the path.

He felt himself tilt toward sleep. A memory, unbidden, rose: in the evenings, as a boy, he used to crouch beneath his mother's ironing board as she pressed her uniforms, and the cotton would cascade around him, fragrant and white and warm, and through the folds he'd watch his father in his undershirt smoking his pipe, snapping the newspaper taut as he turned its pages.

5

In the predawn, hens scuttled on the roof of the house and he heard the screen door open and clap shut. When he woke next it was fully light and Felix was singing over the stove. Winkler rose and tucked the sheet back over the little mattress. Had he dreamed? He couldn't remember.

He put on his glasses. Out the window, in the lower quarter of sky, a group of clouds huddled above a hill. "Rain," he said.

The girl, Naaliyah, watched him from the doorway. She came to the window and peered out. "The sun."

He nodded. She said: "No rain."

"It's sunny now," he said, "but see those clouds on the hill? How they are pushed up? Like hats? It means there's a convective — warm air — rising along the hillside. The air up there is unstable. It means there's a chance of rain."

She stood on her tiptoes and hooked her fingers around the sill. "Really?"

He stepped into the kitchen. Felix was wearing a wool watch cap and a teal T-shirt with *Miami Dolphins* silk-screened onto it. He sliced a mango and handed a half to Winkler with a spoon.

Winkler watched him move through the kitchen on his skinny legs. His hair stuck through little moth holes in his cap. He took a drink from his bottle.

"You are not from here," Winkler said.

Felix turned. "No. I was born in Punta Arenas. Soma in Santiago."

"Chile."

"Yes. Chile." He rolled the word in his mouth, as if tasting it. He looked at the girl. "But this is home now, isn't it, Liyah?" She shrugged.

Felix went on: "Soma says everyone on this island is a refugee. Africa, or South America, or Asia. Even the Caribs, this was not their island." He turned back to the eggs.

"And your sons? They are from Santiago?"

"They are not our sons. Not by blood. Yes, from Santiago. Their parents lived there."

Winkler frowned. He dug into the mango. "How much," he asked, "would it cost for a flight to the United States?"

179

"Maybe four or five thousand? Expensive."

"How do I get back to St. Vincent?"

"The boys could take you. When they return. They are at school now. They take their mother to the post office. But you are welcome to stay more. Soma has told you."

"I'd like to repay you for your kindness."

"You owe nothing."

He mulled this over. He owed something. But what position was he in to repay anyone? He did not even know the name of the island he was on.

Felix drank from his bottle. After a while he said, "We are building an inn. I am going to be the chef — perhaps you will work there?"

Felix and Naaliyah led Winkler through the chickens and along another path past more houses, each with an air of happenstance as though it had been placed there by the recession of a massive flood. They climbed a hill and traversed a cleared paddock and then descended into dark thickets toward the western edge of the island. Through breaks in the canopy Winkler glimpsed glittering expanses of sea and the ragged white borders of the reef. Every few minutes Naaliyah glanced over her shoulder at the clouds shifting and piling over the hills.

The inn — or what Winkler assumed would become an inn — was hardly anything: a pile of lumber, a pallet of bricks. One tin shed tucked under a welter of bush. Maybe a quarter mile out frothy breakers collapsed over the reef. Wind-stooped palms fringed the place; the clearing was brown and sandy; a single breadfruit tree at the corner of the property was wreathed by a ring of its own fallen fruit. The beach was crowded with drift logs and mats of morning glory and empty cable spools like huge upended coffee tables.

A half dozen men sent a slow volley of greetings at Felix and then they all waited, a few men smoking as they squatted, the lit ends of their cigarettes glowing and drifting in the dimness. Naaliyah chased ground lizards through the shadows.

Eventually a jeep arrived, pressing its way over a tangled access road. A man in a yellow suit got out and opened the hatch and the men filed forward and took shovels and picks from the back. When Felix reached the rear bumper, the man in the yellow suit stooped and they exchanged a few words. Felix turned and waved Winkler over.

"This is Nanton. It is his inn."

Nanton looked Winkler up and down, then turned and closed the back of the jeep. "What can you do?"

Winkler glanced over at the sullen company dragging tools toward the stacks of lumber and said, "Whatever they can."

Nanton seemed to consider this. "You work on the foundation today. Work two weeks. If you still here after two weeks, maybe I keep you." His teeth were a dull green and his breath was salty, as though he had been drinking seawater. "You work today," he said and his lips eased into a smile. "Maybe you don't come back tomorrow."

Nanton had two men haul what looked like a lifeguard's chair out from the shed into the shallows. He climbed to the top, opened an umbrella, and sat above the crew, watching them and chewing coca leaves.

Winkler took a shovel and followed Felix to the pile of lumber but Nanton called him back. "No." He waved Winkler toward the lagoon. "You work out here." Winkler went to the edge and waited until Nanton beckoned him forward again. "Out. At the flags." Small orange markers had been driven into shallow places in the lagoon. They waved silently with the passage of water. "You dig beneath each one."

"Beneath the flags."

"Correct. Now please. While the tide is still low."

Winkler squinted, then adjusted his glasses and waded out to the first flag. The water reached halfway up his thighs. The flag's thin shaft was anchored by a bag filled with sand. He began hacking at the rock and coral heads below. The shovel skewed out beneath him in the water and it was nearly impossible to get any leverage.

The sun came fully over the island then, brassy and merciless. The other men worked in the shade, on a stretch of rock at the end of the beach. Their shovels chipped and sparked.

Nanton produced a newspaper and slowly turned its pages. There was a sense of laziness and melancholy beneath the trees and most of the men slunk away at noon to nap or drink rum or stare out at the sea. The blade of Winkler's shovel bent; the tide climbed his thighs. It was impossible to keep memories at bay: water seeping into the basement; Sandy glowering in the driveway.

These perhaps were his weakest moments. He had fled, yes, but with reason. Grace's life had been in danger, but surely the danger had passed by now? Yet here he was, surrounded by strangers, hacking away at rocks with a half-ruined shovel. Weren't there other ways home? He could have been begging or sneaking, selling his labor directly for passage, stealing his way to an airplane ticket. He could pilfer a raft and paddle it home. He could swim. Wasn't each passing minute a betrayal?

Was it fear? Was it that if he returned, and she was still alive, he might still inadvertently kill her — her fate waiting all this time for him to fulfill it? Was he simply afraid to face what he had left behind? Had he been hoping, all along, to leave, each moment stretched thin with it, exhausted by the pinioning of obligation against desire: the staying, and the longing to flee? He heard Sandy's voice, echoing down the telephone line: *You left. You just got up and left.* No. He loved her. And he loved Grace, so much that little fissures started in his heart each time he thought of her.

He stared a moment through the water at the base of the flag and wiped his forehead and realized he had made no perceptible progress.

In the early afternoon sheets of diffuse

clouds, dragging scuds, eased off the sea, and it began to rain. Most of the workers retreated beneath the palms, but the girl, Naaliyah, stood in the little clearing, watching Winkler, holding her palms out. Drops spattered the lenses of his glasses; he worked on.

Nanton descended from his perch in the evening and collected the shovels and picks and stowed them again in the back of his jeep. Winkler stood dripping at the fringes of the small excavation and watched Felix speak to Nanton in low tones and finally the jeep drove away.

The rain slowed and the clouds relented. He returned to Felix and Soma's house. The boys washed dinner plates in the yard. Felix dragged a battered tacklebox out of the back room and opened it on the picnic table. Inside were the tiny makings of model boats, little saws and screwdrivers, dowels, tiny brushes, tubes of glue, jars of model paint. He withdrew a small piece of wood and began sanding it carefully. Soma quizzed him about Winkler's day.

Naaliyah tugged Winkler's sleeve. "What else," she asked, "do you know about clouds?"

Every day Nanton sent him out into the

lagoon to hack at submerged rock. "We need half-meter excavations," he said, but did not elaborate. Winkler was the only white man working for Nanton, and Nanton appeared to take a perverse pleasure in the historical irony of it, occasionally descending from his perch and asking Winkler to hold up a shovelful of rock so he could inspect it and smile broadly and spit his coca juice into the water beside them. The skin between Winkler's fingers sloughed off; sores bloomed on his palms.

He let the rhythm of work overwhelm him, chopping with a shovel and pick until the tide was nearly at his chest. Then he would wade dripping ashore and work alongside the other men. He walked back each evening with Felix and Naaliyah, climbing through the forest and the paddock, then dropping down again. He began sleeping on the floor of the kitchen, so the boys could have their bunks back, and when he woke, with the boys and their mother, he would go into the yard and watch the light accrue and listen to the frogs go quiet and roosters crow on the hills. Gazing up at the patchwork of fields, cane plots like clear-cut timber, a sea wind pushing at his neck, it was almost possible to pretend he was eight years old, in a park somewhere with his mother, on a cool, blue Anchorage morning.

A day passed, then another, and another. As long as he did not think of Grace, it was almost easy. Had it been twenty-five days or twenty-seven? A month? The sun came up, the sun went down. Sandy did not appear at the door of Felix and Soma's little blue house fuming with rage. No one appeared. He thought of his year with Sandy in the house on Shadow Hill, how her eyes went to the windows, the silent desperation of everything they never said — gaps and absences in every conversation, the past circumscribing the present, the future hemming in the past. He tried to imagine life as it must have been for Herman, how he must have let each day fall away, going to the bank, tuning out the inevitable gossip, each hour that much more distance between himself and his wife. Maybe he had found a new job. Maybe he had never given up hope.

Winkler's first weeks at the inn passed like that: sun and wind scorched his shoulders; his skin went pink, eventually assumed an even brown. On his palms blisters rose and opened and rose again. Felix told him that Nanton had made his money building tenements in Venezuela and that he planned this inn to fund his retirement.

"Nanton is honorable. He will pay you. He is only testing you now."

"But what are we doing hacking away at rocks? Why does he have me out in the water?"

"Ah." Felix smiled. "It is Nanton's secret."

"A secret."

"Yes. A very special idea." He made a sweeping gesture that took in the whole lagoon. "It will bring guests from all the world."

Out in the inn's lagoon brightly painted fishing boats shuttled back and forth, and onshore strange, long-billed birds cried at the workers from the canopy. Clouds sat down over the distant silhouette of the volcano on St. Vincent to the north. At night the lights of Kingstown glittered across the channel. Felix brought rice or curry or papaya wrapped in leaves for their lunches, and Winkler would sit with him and watch Naaliyah scurry through the sand or beneath the palms, chasing insects, capturing hermit crabs in the cups of her palms. "Papa," she'd whisper, holding up a pair of mating dragonflies. "Look how they're attached."

★ ★ ★

In the course of those evenings he assembled what he could of Felix and Soma's story. Both had worked in the Moneda, which Felix said was like the White House in Washington, only "more Chilean." When the current president was deposed in a coup (he had been shot or perhaps shot himself in a subterranean corridor), his entire staff had fled, including the cooks. There were disappearances. Several of their friends, including Felix's supervisor, were picked up and never heard from again. Soma would not speak about these parts and closed her eyes and played with the chain of her crucifix.

This was, Felix said, international news and he wondered aloud if it was possible that Winkler was the only person alive who had not heard about it.

Felix's eyes were on his hands, where he was using what looked like rusty nail clippers to trim the tiny rigging on a model. His fingers kept missing and the rigging would sag through the little eyelets and he'd have to start again.

Immediately after the coup, Felix and Soma had traveled to Patagonia to hide among his family. When the three boys showed up, sons of the former commerce minister, a friend to them both, Felix and Soma took them in. The mechanics of their departure from Patagonia he would not discuss, nor would he say how they had accomplished this with four children, nor what specifically had catalyzed their flight. They met Nanton in Caracas, who hired Felix and paid for their voyage on a third-rate liner to St. Vincent.

"Will you go back? If it ends? If this current leader gets ousted?"

Soma stopped at the door and turned. "This is our home now. We live here." She swung open the screen and went out into the yard.

Felix did not look up from his boat. Winkler shifted in the heat. Far off they could hear the shouts of the boys where they played stickball in the road.

"And you?" Felix asked. "You are fleeing something also?"

In Winkler's mind came an image of Sandy fluttering her fingers, a habit she had, a gesture, as if she were trying to brush aside all the things that were wrong with their lives. "Yes," he said. Out the window Soma scattered seed corn for her chickens, staring off into the tamarinds.

Late into Winkler's second week, Nanton climbed down from his lifeguard chair, splashed ashore, and called him to the jeep. From the backseat he dug out a roll of blueprints. "You are wondering why I have you in the lagoon, under the sun," he said. His teeth were bright green. "You are thinking I am crazy. You hack apart rocks around a little flag and think I am wasting your time."

Winkler shrugged. "But don't you want to see, really, what you are doing?" Nanton unrolled the plans over the tailgate cautiously, as though they were secret, or illegal, and watched Winkler carefully as he examined them. A lattice of girders, dim blobs of color, blue rectangles representing windows. Winkler shrugged. "I don't get it."

Nanton's face eased into a smile. "A see-through floor. So the guests can look down at all the creatures of the sea."

Winkler turned the page and studied the elevations. Nanton beamed. The reasons for his enthusiasm became plain: a huge glass floor in the lobby where fish might come browsing beneath the shoes of the guests. A big stainless steel kitchen behind that, a dozen guestrooms onshore, a lantern-studded deck for the dining room. There would be footbridges over creeks and low, tasteful light fixtures lining the paths, and underwater spotlights so guests could watch the reef at night.

But for now it was just a dry lot with stacks of cinder blocks and bamboo and roofing piled under tarps.

"If you work like this all the time," Nanton said, gesturing at the shovel in Winkler's hands, "maybe I use you after it is done. Maybe you clean pipes for me." He laughed and showed his green teeth. "My American doctor toilet-scrubber!"

"I won't be here that long," Winkler said.

And anyway the foundation wasn't even halfway finished. He chipped and shoveled out rock; sand slid in to cover his work. Schools of tiny fish wheeled past his legs; the tide crept up and down again. The men studied him but barely spoke to him. When they did, he could hardly understand what they said. At dusk, before heading back to Felix's, he watched their fire at the end of the beach, their shadows reaching across the sand, elongated and warped, their low voices like the voices of the trees.

These were the beginnings of a new existence; Winkler could feel it gestating. One day passed like every other — time would not be a sequence as much as a repeated rhythm: the sunrise, the roosters, the jeep and shovels and rock. No interruptions, no studies, no forecasts. His body was becoming an instrument, a tool — he would wade into the water and lose himself in the cadence of work, and days would be one like every other: clear in the morning, rain in the afternoon, stars burning above branches at night.

Still, of course, memories found gaps: the soft, almost impossibly pink hue of Grace's cheeks; the burned smell of Sandy's hair dryer lingering in the bathroom. The curve of her rib cage against his palms.

Naaliyah watched Winkler from the shadows. The holes beneath the little orange flags deepened. At times, swinging the blade of his pick, he felt he was chiseling his own underwater grave.

6

Fourteen days after he'd begun working for Nanton — over a month now since leaving Ohio — he waited in line at the back of the jeep with the others and was paid: $60 E.C. In the yacht supply at Port Elizabeth he bought pants, a secondhand pair of boots, and a packet of airmail envelopes.

Dear Sandy —

I can remember so many things. I remember skipping rocks across the river, your hand wiping down the kitchen counter, freckles on your cheek. I remember how you hated it if my nose touched your glasses because it smudged the lens, and how you stopped talking and stared whenever we passed a baby.

All I ask is that you tell me if Grace is alive. Just tell me what happened.

I will write you every day. I will work until I have enough money to return and then I will come back. If you'll have me, we could start again. We could always start again.

All day he'd slash away at underwater rocks and at night he'd write letters, leaning over Felix's picnic table in the light of the sputtering oil lamp, scribbling, re-hashing, restarting.

Subsequent letters were even less adequate than the first: disjointed pleas, nearly impossible to compose. He said he was sorry; he hoped someday she would understand. Then he crossed it out. Then re-wrote the same words. At times, just penciling her name onto the front of the envelope was nearly intolerable. But the alternative, which was never to try, to have left for good, was worse. Then he truly would be gone, and he had the sense that a cord like that, once cut, would not grow back. He thought of the feeling he'd had leaving the post office in St. Vincent: a sensation as if his body might dissolve into light — a cracking at the back of his skull, a damp sigh, a thread pulling apart.

Naaliyah peered over his shoulder at the pencil crossing and re-crossing the page. "Are you writing your family?" she would ask. "Are you writing your home?"

Dear Grace —
Sometimes I hope your mother tells you lies. Maybe she tells you I am stationed

overseas: a submarine captain, or a diplomatic spy. Maybe she tells you the man you live with, if you live with him, is your father.

Sometimes I see things and then they happen. It has always been this way — I don't know why. In my more lonely moments I imagine that you, too, might dream things that come to be. If you do, I hope you see better places, and a better life. If you think I'm crazy, that's probably all right. It may help you understand. I love you. I always will.

He addressed the envelopes to Marilyn Street or occasionally — optimistically — the house on Shadow Hill Lane and handed them to Soma in states of near panic. "Mail it," he'd ask, "even if I tell you not to later." One, two, sometimes three a day. Maybe the idea was that he could write so many letters, deliver so many envelopes back to Sandy, eventually he'd have sent all of himself, and could exist more there than he did here.

He imagined Herman shredding each letter and depositing the pieces in his trash can with the pedal-operated lid. In you go, down the lid slams. The Anchorage summer outside the window, failing already.

196

But Winkler kept on, writing at least once a day, using the Kingstown post office as a return address. Sometimes he'd write more than an apologia; he'd describe Felix's elaborate dinners, or his family, little Naaliyah chasing butterflies down the road, cornering a lizard against a rock. *She reminds me of Grace*, he'd write. *Her eyes are always open.*

A steel crew arrived, silent indigo-skinned men who drove trucks onto the beach and unloaded pallets of three-inch-thick Plexiglas. Within an hour they had erected a rudimentary crane and were sinking an auger into one of the holes Winkler had begun. They rolled enormous barrels off a barge, anchored ties in them with concrete, stones, and coral, and sunk them in the lagoon to serve as piles. Within a week an entire framework of steel was poised above a section of the lagoon where the little orange flags had been. A half dozen carpenters boated in and set up camp on the beach and in seven more days framed the entire building. Nanton watched all this unfold from his perch, computing rows of numbers on a legal pad, frowning, erasing, refiguring.

Now Winkler guided a raft loaded with

breeze blocks back and forth across the lagoon. He folded his earnings inside a plastic box; he helped the boys with the dishes; he wrote his letters.

On Sundays he walked the island. Naaliyah would trail him at a distance and eventually he'd call her forward and hoist her onto his shoulders. He'd try to name the few plants he recognized for her: bamboo, Caribbean pine, tree ferns, cecropia. "Clouds like those," he'd show her, "are called *cumulus congestus*. Each one is riding along on a big column of slowly cooling air. Like a big invisible ice-cream cone. That small cloud there probably weighs five hundred thousand pounds."

"Nooo," she'd say. "It's floating — it weighs nothing." Still, she would not look away.

Dripping groves, high fields. Century plants and organ-pipe cacti. The island, viewed from a ridge, was a lumpy, six-mile hill ringed with palms and coral gardens, the sea teething at its reefs. And the skies: in one day the sky could travel from green at dawn to a noontime blue so severe it was almost black to hot silver in the afternoon to roiling burgundy at sunset. Just before night it flowered in yawning, imperial violets. Wedges of mauve, cauldrons of peach — skies more like drugs than colors.

"See that dark line at the horizon? That's called the wind line. It means it's storming out there."

Naaliyah leaned into him and followed the sight line of his arm. "Will it come here? The storm?"

"It might."

They passed a sugar works gone to ruin: an abandoned waterwheel, a rusted tread-mill, relics of slavery. He thought: Our shadows are our histories. We drag them everywhere. Naaliyah stood outside looking up, waiting for rain. He thought of the small weight of her in his arms, her thin and bristling hips, and a blade of guilt turned inside him.

At poorly lit tavern tables with a bottle shining in front of him, Nanton penciled elaborate landscape drawings onto sheets of butcher paper. "Here," he'd jab with a coca-stained finger, "flowers. And here royal palms. I want a row of them by the creek."

He had good ideas, Winkler could see, a feeling for how things could look.

"Is good?" Nanton asked, frowning. "There will be enough water?"

"Yes. It will be nice."

Dear Sandy —

It feels good to work with my hands. At the end of a day I'm truly tired. I understand now my father's pleasure in his work. He used to park his truck at the end of the block and slog upstairs and sigh when he got through the door. He looked forward to dozing in his chair, his pipe beside him at the end of a day.

Felix, the friend I've told you about, makes little model boats, still using his hands at the end of a long day. He is not very good at it — his masts are always lopsided, his rigging is always falling off — but he seems happy, working on small things in the lantern light with a bottle beside him.

I'm sleeping better here, having dreams I cannot remember. Are you okay? Do you think of me?

Naaliyah would wade out and hang from the girders that would soon brace the glass floor, or she'd climb through the shell of the dumbwaiter where pupating caterpillars had already wrapped themselves to the walls and pale wasps shuttled between shafts of light, her small hands grasping after them. She and Felix and Winkler would walk home from the work site at dusk, the girl on her father's shoulders and the husks of palms blowing and skeltering over the path and the ocean crashing out behind them against the reef.

"What do moths do in the rain, Mr. Winkler? Do their wings get wet?"

"I'm not sure, Naaliyah."

"I bet they crawl up under big leaves," she'd say. "I bet they sit under there and peek out at the rain. Happy as rabbits."

She'd come to him, her pockets full of lichens and seeds and shells. "Look," she'd exclaim, and spread her hoard over the ground and take it up one item at a time. "I found this on the side of the cistern, and this in the muck below the standpipe. . . ." Once she brought Winkler a piece of blue sea glass and he began to ask her if it might be a sapphire or some rare gem but she shook her head. "No, Mr. Winkler, it's glass from a bottle that got smoothed by the sea."

The facts and truths of the world around them. Tiny snails appeared in her hands. She'd tug his sleeve: "Mr. Winkler, do ants sleep?" Once he woke and saw her at the kitchen window, holding his glasses over her eyes with both hands and blinking out at the night.

I have questions, Sandy, of course I do.

Whole days pass and all I feel sure of are questions. What if I'd been able to save that man — Mr. DelPrete — in front of the bus? What if I'd been able to carry Grace safely up the street? What if knowing had been enough? If I'd been able to hold her a bit more cautiously?

The funny thing is, people don't want to hear about the future. They go to palm readers and fortune-tellers but in the end they only want to hear that they're doing well, that everything is going to be fine. They want to hear that their kids will take over their world. No one wants to hear that the future is already determined. Death's success rate has been 100% so far, yet we still choose to call it a mystery.

He was reminded of how he'd felt at his mother's funeral: neighbors glancing around the pews to see who else had come, a girl he'd never seen before smiling in the vestibule, whispering something to a friend about how she was going to take her coat back to Koslosky's because it was too small. The dead are gone and so their power over the living is only temporary. You lose sleep, you lose your appetite, but eventually you fall asleep and eventually you eat — you may hate yourself for it, but the body's demands are incontrovertible. He had always felt guilty about that, that he went on living, eating tomato sandwiches, going to Iditarod Days with his father, making snowballs, when his mother could not.

All he had to do was close his eyes. He could see the two saplings flanking the front door, the roof of the house as it looked that last hour, viewed from atop Shadow Hill, a thousand wet shingles beneath which Grace may or may not have been. He could watch, over and over, the Sachses' big maple lose its hold and come groaning out of their lawn, roots tearing, the trunk splashing down, a hundred branches bouncing and clattering and finally going still.

Any of the freighters plying the horizon — any of the airplanes descending into St. Vincent — could hold a letter in its compartments, bound for him. When Soma returned from St. Vincent, still making the crossing each day, so the boys could go to a better school, she'd lift her shoulders slightly, hold her palms up: nothing. He'd be left shut out, her hands an empty mailbox, the rest of the afternoon paler somehow. But each morning the thought would resurface: some letter sorter in Kingstown might be funneling an envelope in his direction, laying it neat and flat in a cubbyhole for Soma, for *him*. The sun clambered over the horizon, the well of hope refilled. Somewhere Sandy might be sealing an envelope with his name on it, touching her tongue to the back of a stamp.

The bank in Cleveland reported that all his accounts had been closed. The American consulate in Kingstown would work on reissuing his passport. He phoned a shipping agent in Grenada, a freight company in Port Elizabeth, the American Airlines office in Kingstown. The best he could find was $1,100 to Los Angeles. Twenty-nine hundred E.C. He would keep working.

7

A dream: Naaliyah was grown, maybe twenty-five years old. She lowered a cinder block from the stern of a boat. An anchor chain, looped through the block, paid out through her hands. The chain picked up speed, rifling into the water as the block sank; a bight of chain caught her ankle, jerked her off her feet, and dragged her over the transom. Water closed over her head. Winkler watched all this from a beach, a hundred yards away. Fog swept over the boat. She did not surface. He sprinted into the lagoon and swam toward her, but the boat seemed to recede; water poured into his lungs. The boat was too far away. His chest overflowed.

He woke panting over the girl where she slept on the bench of the picnic table. He was shirtless and barefoot in his torn work pants. The three boys cowered in the doorway to their room. The remnants of the stove fire cast the kitchen in a dim red light. Naaliyah's ankle was in Winkler's fist and he realized he was holding her leg at his chin as though he might take a bite. Her eyes were serious and trusting. She flexed her foot and he could feel the muscles in her calf contract. Although it was dark and he did not have his glasses, Winkler could see the sheen of the picture of the Virgin above the bench; his eyes were level with hers.

Felix threw back the curtain to his bedroom. Winkler set down Naaliyah's leg. "Go back to sleep," Felix told the boys. He hefted the girl like a house cat in his arms and brought her across to the bedroom and pulled the curtain shut. When he re-emerged Winkler could hear Soma speaking softly to Naaliyah and he realized that she, or perhaps one of the boys, had almost certainly shouted. Felix went out into the yard and motioned for Winkler to follow.

The sky was drawn back and the Milky Way made a soft avenue overhead. A single star fell. Felix bent and collected stones from the path and began pitching them one by one into the high grass.

"I sleepwalk," Winkler started to say. "I —"

Felix held up a hand. Without his watch cap on, his hair stood up from his head in all directions. He tossed another stone. "You find somewhere else to stay. To-morrow. Someone will take you in."

"I'll leave now."

"No. In the morning."

But he left that night, collecting his air-mail envelopes and pencils and his plastic box of savings, carrying them out the gate, over the hill, and down to the construction site, where the frame of the inn stood dark and empty with the wind passing through the shells of the rooms. He dragged a tarp under the palms and lay the rest of the night on the sand with the waves reaching for his feet and the sheeting snapping in the breeze and the most desolate kind of lonesomeness in his heart.

8

Sandy —

It must be nearly autumn in Anchorage by now. Are leaves falling? Are you even reading this there? It's hard to believe seasons go on when one is in a place like this, where every day is so much like the one before. I miss cool weather. I miss rain. Here we have rains but they are nothing like rain at home. Here the rain never seems to last more than twenty minutes. The clouds haul back and unleash these enormous droplets, then quickly dissipate. And then the heat builds back up. The surface of the sea gets so bright you cannot look at it.

Out on the water, right now, I can see virga — fallstreaks — where rain leaves clouds but evaporates before it reaches the ground. It looks like hair blowing out there. It is hard not to think about Grace every few minutes. I miss her. I miss you. I am truly sorry I left.

One day:

Sandy — Please write back. Send a photo. So I know she's alive. Write just one word.

And another, in his ungainly cursive, across the first line of the page:

Is she alive?

9

They still sat beside each other at lunch, and Felix might hand over a packet of rice, or boiled eggs wrapped in cheesecloth, but when they worked Felix always seemed to find a spot away from him, in what would be the kitchen, or out on the porch, or by the band saw helping the framers halve bamboo for siding. Six-year-old Naaliyah did not come with her father to the site anymore. Weeks passed and Winkler did not see her. When he finally mustered the nerve to ask, her father said they'd enrolled her in the island school.

Sometimes, in the evenings, Winkler would walk the dusty road past the small blue house and watch the hens scratch at a corner of the yard. Maybe he'd hear, through the screen door, one of the boys shout, or the stove door clang shut, but that was as close as he and the family came. He wrote his letters, still using the Kingstown post office as a return address. He cooked beans in a salvaged pot; he kept to himself. In the darkness from his spot on the beach he listened to lambs bleating from their paddocks high on the hills. A steady rain fell on the sea and small waves lapped at the framework of the inn and there were no lights save the washed-out gloss of the moon on the water and leaves, and no sounds but the lambs and wind moving the trees and drops slipping into the understory, and the two-note frogs, and the sea, always the sea.

Like most people in Anchorage, his father had shut out night. He drew curtains, dead-bolted the door, switched on lamps. In the depths of winter, by mid-February, Winkler could see the strain in his father's face, would see him study a travel ad in the newspaper with almost preternatural longing: a surf girl smiling beneath a thatch umbrella, her skin drenched with sunlight.

But his mother had welcomed it. "Please, Howard," she would say to Winkler's father, "do we need all these lights on?" The hospital, she said, was bright enough. Her eyeballs hurt. In late September, after the days had broken and night made its long, cool entrance, she would take Winkler to the roof to watch. Lights came on up and down the rail yards, and above them a chevron of geese would laze along, and far off the mountains would go blue and hazy, seeming to gather a thinness as day fell, as though they were fading off into another dimension. The smell of his mother's container garden, frosted once already, on its way to death, would rise. Stars emerged, one by one, and soon enough by the hundreds — the sky would be studded with lights.

"There's plenty of light in winter," she'd tell David. "More than enough. Your father isn't paying attention."

The roof of that building seemed as real to him now as it did then: scraps of snow in the shadows, fumaroles of smoke rising from the tar-specked chimneys, his mother's tomato plants sagging against their stakes in the southwest corner. On rare nights — the Perseids, the Orionids, the Leonids — they'd sit on blankets and watch meteorites sizzle through the thermosphere. "Count them, David. See if you can get every single one." He marked them in a little notebook and in later days his father would find the untitled pages littered about, covered with dashes, and wonder what the boy had been tallying.

Once Winkler asked his mother if the

constellations would be left with holes in them but she said no, that shooting stars were merely flecks of iron burning in the air, no bigger than thumbtacks, and that the stars above him were huge and ancient and would never leave nor change their positions and in the following nights he saw that it was so.

Sandy —

I'm sleepwalking again. I woke up in the ocean last night. I was up to my waist, standing there. I'd dragged my sleeping tarp in behind me, and I must have taken my shirt too, because I can't find it anywhere. The tarp was covered with snails and after I got back to shore I had to pull them all off. You were right — I should have gone to Dr. O'Brien's, a sleep lab, somebody.

Every night I hope to dream of Grace. If I could just dream her once, in your arms, in her crib, then I might believe she's still alive. But I never do. Lately I dream mostly of darkness. What am I doing here? Am I following a path already laid out for me, or am I making it myself?

Am I scaring you? I don't mean to. There were so many things we should have talked more about.

It was nearly impossible to write the Marilyn Street address on an envelope, to walk to the village to mail it: he imagined Herman in the hall, shuffling through bills, stopping when he saw another envelope, another postmark, more of Winkler's handwriting. He'd burn it; he'd shred it and bury the pieces in the backyard.

Would he let her sleep in the bedroom? Would she want to? Would he even have her back? Would Grace be across the hall, out in a taxi, screaming her lungs out in some foster home? Here was something he could imagine: Sandy reentering First Federal Savings and Loan, the looks from the other tellers, the whispering down the line. Herman watching her from his big desk. She would keep her face up.

He could be in Kingstown in an hour. He could be in Ohio in one revolution of the sun. Eight hundred more dollars.

To close his eyes and be on the hillside above their house, the big wet trees blowing and murmuring. To cross the lawn and peer through the glass door into the kitchen: the high chair, the card table ringed by mismatched stools. A light would come on. Sandy would bring Grace downstairs — to see their shadows rise along the stairway wall would be enough.

Memory, dreams, water. Through an unfinished hall of the inn a paper bag dragged about in the wind.

10

They completed the inn in March 1978. He had been gone almost a year. The inn was not, Winkler thought, as glamorous as Nanton had hoped. It had twelve guest rooms, a bar at the end of the dining deck, a huge dry molasses vat that was to become the swimming pool. The grounds were still scrubby, the beach still overgrown, and littered with sea logs and nylon ropes, and every Wednesday, when they burned garbage at the dump, the wind carried smoke through the rooms, and with it the reek of smoldering plastic.

At night, though, it did possess a certain enchantment; with the lanterns of the restaurant aglow, and a few lamps switched on inside the lobby, the inn stood on its pylons half-submerged in the lagoon like the top floor of a skyscraper in a flooded metropolis: wall sconces visible through the windows, a yellow radiance hanging in the tide.

Inside, square-meter sheets of Plexiglas

windowed the reef and indeed fish did swim and skirt in lazy loops beneath, and the tide sucked and pushed great flexing air bubbles along the bottom of the floor like foamy, hypnotic jellyfish. Wrasses, jacks, ladyfishes, once — Nanton insisted — a spotted eagle ray as wide across as a dining room table, flapping along down there. Winkler would see Nanton and Naaliyah down on their hands and knees looking into the floor and pointing out wonders to each other as if an engrossing film played ceaselessly on the sea floor.

There were dinghies for guests to shuttle between their yachts and the beach; there was a paved shuffleboard court beside the driveway. Big wooden loungers studded the lawn and nautical maps framed the walls of the lobby. A rope bridge hung between the shore and restaurant. Music piped through outdoor speakers. Sea fans and wooden parrots stood on bedside tables. Felix began ordering food for the kitchen and Nanton took up post behind the front desk.

Guests came, boating in or taking the water taxi from St. Vincent. They would hang about a few nights, marveling at the weather and the glass floor, and be replaced by others. As an exchange for staying on to tend the grounds and maintain the glass flooring, Nanton allowed Winkler to move off the beach into the old boat shed at the corner of the property, a tin structure with one glassless window, a dirt floor, and a door that consisted of the entire western wall, swinging upward in a rusted aluminum track. Inside Nanton helped arrange a cot, chair, and basin. "This is fine," Winkler insisted. "I won't be here long."

Each night, before he lay on the humped, musty mattress, he barricaded himself in by wedging a two-by-four between the door and a guide wheel.

He went about his work diligently enough, staining lawn furniture, distributing seeds and laying flagstones, planting whatever decorative ferns and flowers he could harvest from the hills. Nights he walked the dark, rustling thickets, returned to his shed for a few fitful hours of dreams, and was up before dawn, pushing barrows of dirt, raking clumps of beached weed off the sand.

He did not buy clothes or spend money on rum. In his plastic box he had accumulated somewhere around two thousand E.C. He calculated his wages in the sand. Maybe by June. Home by June. He allowed himself images of a reconciliation: the goose-shaped knocker in his hand, Sandy pulling back the door. Behind her leg a shy little girl — Grace — smiling up. "Dad?" It was a kind of hope. But his dreams spoke to none of that: when he slept he dreamt of darkness, or of people he did not recognize, or of water closing slowly, almost gratefully, over his head.

A May evening. Soma called him out of a flower bed near the back steps of the kitchen. The crucifix on her chest heaved. "I came as quickly as I could. Something arrived for you last night." From inside the screen door she produced a cardboard box. One end was partially crushed. On top his name was printed in lowercase. It was Sandy's handwriting — he knew this without thought — her big looping D's, circles floating above the I's. The lettering was dark, and definite, as if she had pressed so hard she had nearly driven the tip of the marker through the cardboard. His breath stopped somewhere in his throat. He took the box from Soma and shook it.

A thudding inside. Cheap brown packing tape. An Anchorage postmark.

"Is it from home? Is it what you've

been waiting for?"

He could not take his eyes from his name. He managed to say yes.

Soma let out a sigh. "Oh, I am glad. I'm happy for you, David. I have prayed for you." Already he was turning away. "Take it," she said. "Of course."

He crossed the yard to the boat shed and raised the door and lowered it behind him. It was nearly dark inside, and he dragged the chair to the window and sat in his damp shirt trembling and looking at his name on top of the box.

Twelve months. Out in the yard a few guests on the deck laughed and fell quiet. A wasp buzzed against the window. He had to remind himself to breathe. After several minutes he withdrew a pair of pruners from his rear pocket and brought the blade across the seam of the box.

Inside was a thick bundle of letters. His letters: the ones he had sent to Anchorage and what looked like most of the ones he had sent to Cleveland as well. Many, the first ones, had been opened, but some — maybe a hundred — had not. Not a single letter had been opened since January. She had bound them between two rubber bands, so that the packet was pinched at the ends and bulged in the middle.

Clamped beneath one of the elastics sat a folded square of paper, its creases sharp. That was all.

His rib cage thudded. The air in the shed tasted faintly of burning garbage, smoke from the dump. He unfolded the note: *Don't come back. Don't write. Don't even think of it. You are dead.*

She did not even sign it. Outside the last light was failing and the clouds freighted a tenuous red and the long shadows of frigate birds glided across the lawn and over the roof of the shed and continued out over the sea. After maybe ten minutes the bundle of letters fell from his lap. He held the note and the gloom stretched over him. Soon it was fully dark. Frogs started screaming in the trees. A window banged at the inn.

What might have been an hour passed. Then another. In the lobby tourists held their inconsequential conversations and asserted their hierarchies and praised the qualities of the states in which they lived and feigned yawns and retired to their rooms. Nanton closed his book, switched off his lamp. A mile inland Felix bent over a sleeping Naaliyah and set a kiss in the center of her forehead.

It was after midnight when Winkler rose

and hauled open the door and made his way in the darkness to the beach. The inn stood rigid and immobile in the water, all the lamps extinguished. One of the dinghies was turned hull-up on the sand with its oars under the thwarts. He flipped it, and dragged it into the water.

Big combers were breaking far out on the reef, but in the lagoon they came low and small and the boat rose and fell lightly on the water. He clambered in. Little waves slapped the bow. It was the same handwriting she used for any note. *We need milk. The sliding glass door is broken.* Or: *How much?* The stars sent wavering lines of silver onto the water. The inn was dark and still. The few yachts in the anchorage bobbed and turned against their moorings. The Earth at that latitude rotated at a thousand miles an hour, sailed around the sun at eighteen miles per second, spun with the entire solar system around the two billion stars of the Milky Way at something like 135 miles per second, and yet, he thought, it went so silently, whispering on its axis, roaring soundlessly through the vast, prehistoric jug of space.

Don't come back. Don't even think of it. He unshipped the oars and rowed out.

It took twenty minutes to reach the edge

of the reef. The breakers howled as they pummeled the seaward side. The oars dripped and the little boat wobbled in the foam. A trio of gulls squabbled in mid-flight and veered past his head, heading in-land.

In alcoves he saw large blue blotches, maybe jellies. An iridescent crab cantered sideways through the shadows, big and hurrying. If anything made noise he could not hear it; the waves disallowed any other sounds — a rising and falling, violent and ceaseless, the abiding element.

The spring after his mother had died, he tried to restart her garden, stepping through the slush on the roof with leftover seeds and pressing them into the potted soil. But for some reason the seedlings, if they appeared at all, came up weak and pale, as if they could tell who planted them, as if grief overwhelmed their roots. Maybe he watered them too much.

Why him, why now? What use are memories when memories can do little more than fade? The air in the box had smelled of nothing, cardboard, old paper.

In the lagoon whirlpools left by his oar blades pulsed with phosphorescence. The dinghy listed uncomfortably. Behind him another comber reared and detonated across the coral. Grace was dead. She had to be. How few days are left in the lives of anyone. How few hours.

He reset the oars and stroked toward the reef, across overlapping sheets of foam. It took only three or four strokes — the hull ground over rocks, he pried it free, and then he was into the waves. The first came bowling low over the bulwarks, throwing water past his feet. The next lifted all the way over the bow, and broke over his back. He marveled at the size and strength of them. They were nothing a person on shore or the deck of a freighter could appreciate — you had to be in among them. He fought to keep the oars tracked but it felt as if the blades were caught in cement and they slipped on the tholepins.

His arms were not up to the task anyway. Foamy water rolled through the bottom. In a matter of seconds the boat began to turn. The oar shafts sang under the stress. A third wave exploded against the hull. He could see — for one moment, as the boat plunged into a trough — the ledge of the reef as it fell away beneath him, illuminated by starlight, plummeting into blue darkness. Then the little boat stood up on its stern, and went over.

The oars fell away. He thought: Take me.

The dinghy landed upside down with him beneath it. He was dragged across the coral.

An undertow hauled him out and down. The next waves were passing over his head, and he was driven two fathoms deep, the reef shelf looming in bubbles in front of him, and still the tow swept him back, past a slope of sand studded with delicate, waving ferns, past a swarm of tiny phosphorescent shrimp, grazing against the current. They vanished, too, receding as quickly as if a window shade had been pulled, and he was hauled into deep water. The pressure of the sea filled his ears: fierce, grumbling, a thousand tiny cracklings. His eyeglasses were taken from his face. The surface — a roiled sheet of quicksilver — seemed a mile away.

The ocean was so warm it was almost hot, and the feel of the rip and the darkness against him was not unlike the feel of a damp, insistent wind. Urgency traveled through his chest, but despite it a kind of seduction fell over him. How easy it would be to open his mouth and pull water into his lungs.

Above him swells sucked and pulled. Pain squeezed the tips of his jawbone. His ribs began to throb; his epiglottis swung shut over his larynx like a trapdoor.

A body drifting in the sea. A corridor into the light. Suddenly he had all the time in the world to consider things. To the propeller of a passing yacht, to a bird, to the sky, he would be dead, a floating object, little more than a log, a thousand organisms trying his orifices, the world without him precisely as it had always been, or nearly so: waves turning over on the rocks, sun flaring in the eastern sky. Blood would sink in his corpse, gravitating toward the sea floor, purpling his face, his tongue. Plankton would venture into the tunnels of his ears.

For a hydrologist these things were not hard to imagine; they were even acceptable: he would dissolve into the great blue cauldron; his skin into the gastric sacs of sea life; his bones into shells and exoskeletons; his muscles into energy, rifling through a claw, a fin.

Water around him, water inside him. Two hydrogens, one oxygen; after all, it was the ultimate solvent. Who had he been? A failed father, a runaway husband. A son. A packet of unopened letters. He was dead; he was dead.

Across his eyes passed the fleeting blues and greens of dreams. The stars he had been watching were now like the flood-lights of some slow undersea vehicle, toiling the murky bottom. There was time for one fleeting vision: Grace and Sandy at a kitchen table. Sandy passed an orange cereal box and Grace took it with a careful hand. Sandy poured milk into their bowls. A television flickered over their shoulders. That was all he could see, really: a houseplant in the corner, a painting he didn't recognize above it. Behind them a glass door reflected light from a naked bulb. They were talking but he could not hear what they were saying. Grace was two years old, perhaps. She raised a spoon to her lips.

Saltwater poured into his mouth. He would have given his life a hundred times over to continue peering in at them. Little Grace had curls bunched up against the back of her head. Her pajama top was too small, tight across her belly. She chewed a mouthful of cereal.

But the sea bore him up. His head was at a trough in the swells; he surfaced. A switch threw in his lungs somewhere and he was gasping.

All night he grappled with a luminous doom. The rip had carried him nearly a quarter mile out. A smashed thwart, still nailed to one of the dinghy's bilge panels, drifted past and he clung to it. Every few moments a star rose over the islands and another disappeared on the opposite side, under the horizon. Was the galaxy turning or was it the Earth?

By morning he had drifted closer and the sea had calmed to a fluid, rolling glass. The island rose and fell on the horizon. Birds traveled the lagoon. Even without his glasses he could identify Mount Pleasant, and the thick cane smoke pluming from the sugar mill. He kicked toward it until his lungs and heart throbbed, then rested, clinging to his float, occasionally letting his face down. In a few hours he was riding a wave through a channel in the coral, his knee striking something hard and sharp at the reef crest, and he was washed onto the packed, ridged sand of the intertidal flat, coughing, paddling forward. When he reached the shallows his legs would not bear him up. He crawled out of the wave-break and fell onto the beach. The piece of the dinghy floated up beside him.

The sand was searing hot against his cheek. The pain in his knee was enough to make him faint. A deep, elegant blue rose up along the fringes of his vision.

11

Two dive operators motored his body the mile north to the inn. Nanton helped carry him up from the beach. A doctor dining at the restaurant stitched his knee; a hotel guest donated a plastic vial of painkillers. Soma fetched pillows, gauze, and water; Felix brought beef tea. Even the boys helped, fulfilling Winkler's obligations around the inn.

But it was Naaliyah's vigil. She slept on the floor beside him; she waved mosquitoes away from his face; she poured water into his mouth at regular intervals. His eyelids quivered; sweat shone on his forehead; he slept on.

During four days and nights he woke only twice. A thousand splinters of narrative passed in front of his eyes: surface formations in the sand of a shoal; snow blowing through trees; the viscera of an animal steaming in his hands. Were these memories or dreams? He watched a boy sprint down a row of planted saplings; he saw air bubbles cycle through a fish tank. A mantis perched on his thumb, methodically cleaning her face with her forearms.

Eventually he woke. A smell like phosphorus and sulfur, as if a match had been struck, hung in the air. Droplets from the trees plunked onto the shed's roof. Naaliyah was asleep on the floor, rolled in a sheet. Beside her, beneath the window, waited the box of his returned letters.

He stood and lifted her onto the bed. Then he went out. A half-moon hung over the horizon, its reflection a tapering trail across the water. The lawn was wet beneath his feet and water murmured in unseen streamlets toward the beach.

No lamps in the inn, no sailboats in the lagoon; the lights of St. Vincent six miles away veiled by rain; drops trilling in the understory and the popping and bubbling of saturated ground — for a moment he wondered if a tidal wave had broken over the Grenadines and hauled everyone away. *Don't come back,* she had written. *You are dead.* Maybe he was. Maybe he was dead and this island was a purgatory from which he could only watch the souls of the more deserving go shuttling past to their various Edens. What is death, after all, but a cessation of involvement with the world, a departure from those you love, and those who love you?

Grace had died in the flood. Standing beside the inn that evening he was certain of it. His flight had been in vain. There would be no going back.

He returned to the shed, collected the box of letters and a matchbook from the sill, and brought them out to the beach. In a hollow near the tide line, he tore up every sheet of paper and set the shreds afire.

The sea churned under the moonlight. Smoke rose into the palms. A breeze caught a burning scrap of paper and sent it flying over the lagoon, glowing at its fringes, then going black and disappearing as it touched the water.

He marveled at the indifference of the world, the way it kept on, despite everything.

Book Three

Book Three

1

Winkler would not leave the Grenadine Islands for twenty-five years. A quarter of a century, a third of a lifetime. The years passed as clouds do, ephemeral and vaporous, condensing, sliding along awhile, then dispersing like ghosts. He mended leaks and planted trees and scrubbed coral deposits from the underside of the lobby's glass floor with a system of magnets. He mowed the lawns, planted young trees, culled dead ones. He washed beach towels. He fixed toilets.

His knee healed beneath a net of scars. An optometrist on St. Vincent ground him a new pair of eyeglasses. He spent $1,100 of the $2,100 E.C. in his plastic box to replace Nanton's lost dinghy. No one, not Nanton, or Felix, or any of the islanders who knew him, asked what he had been doing that night, why he had tried to take a ten-foot rowboat over the reef. Perhaps the reasons were obvious enough.

He bought a shortwave radio, balanced a

series of nerite shells on the windowsill, fashioned a hot plate from a propane tank and an old burner element. Every day he wore a pair of canvas trousers and a T-shirt; his skin browned further; his hair gradually went white. Insomnia slowly carved hollows around his eyes, so that the sockets looked permanently bruised, and the eyes themselves were gradually failing — objects at a distance quivered among halos; small flecks of color began traveling the periphery of his vision. Without glasses he could no longer read a sign thirty feet away.

But these were physical things, remote from him: no more real than if they were the actions and hours of another person. His thoughts skirted Sandy and especially Grace as if they were fatal chasms into which he might tumble. Out of habit his eyes noticed clouds, signs of cycling weather, rainbows flowing into the Atlantic, and wreaths of moisture around the moon, but the information did not interest him as it once did. It was as if banishment from his nascent family included a banishment from his curiosity as well. Somewhere icebergs were calving off glaciers. Somewhere it was snowing.

St. Vincent won its independence in

1979 and islanders shot Roman candles from rooftops but to Winkler it was just the end of October, Nanton nailing pinwheels to palm trees, Felix drinking an extra fifth of rum. The war in the Falklands was a rumor, a breath, an English couple on vacation sharing coffee.

Gnats whined at his ear. Clouds scaled the mountainsides. Twice in those years Soufrière belched steam and tephra a mile into the sky, and the Caribs on St. Vincent's northern slopes scurried across the channel to wait it out and some never went back.

Maybe six months after he had nearly drowned, Soma stood in his doorway with a basket of eggs. "For you," she said.

"Thank you."

She went to the window and stood fingering the shells aligned on his sill. "It was that box? From the post office?"

He nodded.

"I'm sorry I brought it. I wish I had burned it."

"I needed to know."

"You are okay now?"

He shrugged.

"You can come by the house, you know," she said. "You are welcome with us."

He nodded and rubbed his chin. Her

fingers worked the shells, flipping them, rotating them.

"You would like to meet girls?" Felix asked. This was December, or January. Nineteen eighty-one. Or '82. The kitchen closed for the night, and he appeared in Winkler's doorway wiping his hands on an apron. "Go to a . . . what is the word? Rendezvous?"

"Date?"

"Yes, dates. Dates are very fun. I know girls on St. Vincent. And others from church. Even one of the maids, maybe? They might like to go to dates." He winked.

Winkler sat on his bed. "*On* dates."

"Yes. Go *on* dates."

"I don't much feel like it."

"You'd be okay. They'd like you."

"It's all right, Felix."

"Huh," said Felix, and took off his watch cap and turned it inside out and pulled it on again. "It is because of your family?"

"I don't know. I suppose. Something like that."

"You were asleep. When you held Naaliyah's ankle? In our house?"

Winkler said nothing.

"It is okay," Felix said. A shutter at the

inn banged in the wind. Someone at the restaurant bar burst into laughter.

"Well," Felix finally said. "In Patagonia we say: God needs His priests and His *ermitaños* all the same."

"His what?"

"His *ermitaños*. His hermits. Like hermit crabs? Carrying around those shells?"

Later Winkler would wonder: A hermit? Is that what I have become? He thought of Felix, marooned in his own way: the cracked blue house filling with model boats; the way he worked as if he were building little arks that might deliver him across the sea, back to Chile.

When he dreamed it was the now familiar blacknesses, or standard human phobias: he was signed up for a geology course he never attended; he had inexplicably turned in blank pages for his dissertation. He did not dream of Ohio, or Alaska, or Sandy, or Grace. It was as if he had trapped them underwater, beneath a Plexiglas floor, and though he may have stood over them all this time, just a few feet away, he could not look down to see. Eventually they would stop struggling. Eventually they would go away.

Life still contained pleasures: leftovers

from Felix's kitchen, which a waiter would periodically leave steaming on Winkler's doorstep — pumpkin soup, whelks steamed with garlic, scungilli or snapper, lobster roasted with nutmeg and lime, prawns, ratatouille, roasted christophene, a warm slice of banana bread slathered with butter. There was the reassuring hum of rain on the roof, and the wind in the plants he tended — hibiscus and anthuriums, arrow ginger, oleander, the big symmetrical fans of a traveler's palm — and there were the thousand colors of sky and ocean, and the clouds that trundled over the island in ceaseless ranks: infinite variations of cumulus, sprawling sheets of stratus, a smear of cirrus troweled against a ceiling of air. In that place the sky was a vast magician's bowl where miracles brewed up hourly.

And there was Naaliyah. Weeks would pass without his seeing her, but then there she'd be, tapping at his window on a Sunday morning. Each time, seeing her, his heart lifted. She brought him leaves silvered with rain; she broke open urchins on rocks, hunted eels in the shallows, dragged him into the lagoon to rescue a wounded octopus. He helped her build a butterfly net from old T-shirts and wire; he explained to her what he knew about waves, how they revealed the topography of an ocean's floor, how they told the stories of offshore storms. And he watched her grow up. Her body elongated; she started wearing lipstick, and complaining about the restrictions of her mother. Soon she was laughing on the steps of the general store, sipping beer from the cans of older boys; she had school, friends, interests he did not know about. Her tapping at the shutters came less and less frequently.

The boys had dropped out of school one by one and moved to Kingstown to take jobs. They would return for holidays in clean shirts, wearing gold-rimmed sunglasses and speaking in quiet, polite voices, carrying gifts for Soma and Felix: a radio, a Coleman lantern, packets of batteries. By the time she was in secondary school, Naaliyah spent most of her waking hours on St. Vincent. Only once in a rare while would Winkler see her, walking the ferry road in her St. Mary's uniform (white blouse, navy skirt, high socks), her hair knotted and bunched about her head like a helmet, her blouse dirty, a pile of books clasped against her breasts. "Hi, David," she would call, and he would stand as straight as he could and smile and con-

241

tinue past as if on critical errands.

She had, Felix told him, removed the posters of soccer players from her brothers' room and replaced them with photos torn from Chilean magazines: a shanty town, the Torres del Paine, a man in a gas mask carrying a rifle. "She blames her mother for leaving," Felix said. "She thinks we left too easy. But she does not understand. How there were soldiers, how we were afraid to answer the telephone. How Soma's friends were taken."

Naaliyah turned fourteen; she turned fifteen. They sat and watched a hundred birds, small brown sparrows Winkler did not know the names of, land on the roof of the inn and rest along the gutter with their wings half-folded, panting for a minute, before taking off again, one brief reprieve along a three-thousand-mile migration.

Trolling his shortwave at night, Winkler sometimes came across a frequency where a Spanish-speaking girl read seemingly random numbers into a transmitter: 24. 92. 31. 4. 229. *Tres, ocho, dieciseis.* Her enunciation was painstaking, as though each numeral were a vital, fragile thing. Whenever he found her, tracking along the dial, he would sit and listen until she signed off. Often this could last as long as two hours. Indeed, after a while, he found himself seeking her out, searching the dial for that voice, those mysterious numbers.

Nanton told him, in his cryptic way, that the broadcasts were codes for spies to pick up when they were in hostile territory. Each sequence corresponded to some message from back home: *Your mother has gout. Your son had his first communion.*

Winkler would take the radio to the end of the beach and lie in the blue shadows beneath the palms and rove the frequencies. It was not difficult to hope that somewhere there was a channel on which his own daughter was transmitting numbers — a code he might eventually break. 56. 71. 490. *I have an aquarium, Daddy. I'm trying out for the swim team. I like pizza but not pepperoni.*

Past midnight: a tapping on the shutter. Naaliyah. She was breathing hard; the front of her T-shirt rose and fell. She seemed darker somehow, a brooder, a dreamer. Her hair slashed into a ragged bob. Wind shouldered through the doorway. She squirmed as if anxious to leave.

"Are you okay?"

"I'm running away."

The knobs of her collarbone stood out above the collar of her shirt. He thought of his Sunday walks with her, years ago, her hands in his hair, the way her pelvis felt against the back of his neck.

He made tea. They stood side by side in the open door, cradling their mugs and watching stars through the shifting crowns of the palms. She chewed a fingernail. Shadows milled around them. "Where will you go?"

"What's it like in America?"

"Well. I don't know. It's huge. There are a thousand different places."

"What's your home like? Where you were born?"

"Alaska? Not as cold as everybody thinks. It's dark a lot in December and January. But it's not really dark: it's more purple, like twilight all the time. And there are mountains, real mountains, with glaciers. When the wind is from the east, or the north, you can smell them. A smell of trees and stones and snow."

"Maybe I will go there."

"Maybe you should wait until tomorrow."

She didn't laugh. The breeze picked up again and out in the lagoon the yachts swung around and an anchor line moaned.

Naaliyah's voice came out of the dark beside him. "What's snow like?"

Something inside him stirred and he waited for it to settle. "It's full of air. And light, too: each crystal can act as a prism, so when the sun is shining, and the albedo is right, snow glitters, like fires are burning in it."

She nodded, studying him. "You miss it."

He sipped his tea.

"You do. I can tell."

"Maybe."

"I can't even remember where I'm from, and I miss it. My parents left their friends and their histories and everything. To come here." She gestured at the walls of the shed, the island beyond them. From a recess in his memory he heard Sandy's voice: *I look at his suits in the closet and think: This is it?*

"My father misses it," she said. "They left because of my mother."

"They left because people were dying."

Naaliyah shrugged. "That was a long time ago."

"There are worse places to be than here."

Later, watching her pad across the lawn, past the dark, slumbering inn, he wondered if such things were born into people. If perhaps we cannot alter who we are — if the place we come from dictates the place we will end up.

He shut the door, braced it with the two-by-four, and sat on his bed. She was sixteen years old.

Soon afterward Naaliyah moved permanently to St. Vincent. He saw her on the island only once more, as he paused to knot a shoelace on the road toward town, her face flashing past in the crowded flatbed of a truck. She raised an arm at him; she might have smiled. Then she was gone. The foliage seethed in her wake, and stilled, and the pursuing dust hung awhile in the air, collecting on his shirt as it sifted down.

Felix only shook his head and Winkler did not have the heart to ask Soma about it. Naaliyah had failed out of school, he heard, stopped going to classes. One night Felix showed him her knapsack of abandoned schoolbooks. In the margins of her notebook were drawings of shells or a husk of a nymph fastened to the underside of a leaf. But nothing else — she didn't seem to take any notes. Crushed at the bottom of the bag was a geometry exam: she'd written only her name, then made idle sketches beneath each problem. An anemone standing beneath a question about scalene triangles; a cricket crouched beneath the Pythagorean theorem.

Whole months passed. The only contact he had with her parents was if he worked near the kitchen and could hear Felix barking orders to his dishwashers. Soma began sleeping in an apartment above the St. Vincent post office during weeknights. Sunday nights she'd eat leftovers on the inn's back steps with a plate balanced on her thighs, chewing thoughtfully and staring off into the dark spaces between the trees. She joked less; her attention strayed when he spoke to her. Hen feathers clung to the hems of her skirts.

Felix, too, wore a certain distance in his eyes. Winkler would see him gazing into the space above the grill, or at the tiny planking of one of his models, as if something invisible floated there, and Winkler knew he was back in Chile, weighing the things he had now against the things he had been forced to give up.

Each Christmas he walked with the two of them to St. Paul's, a round, thatch-roofed church built on stilts halfway up a hill. He'd sit behind them in a back-row

pew and watch the half dozen or so coun-
trywomen in the choir — each a different
shade of brown — croon and flash gold
teeth. Fat yellow flowers in baskets would
line the altar and moths would crowd the
candle flames and a smell of sweat would
rise as the priest delivered his homilies in a
cautious voice — perhaps afraid that if he
preached too loudly, the church might tear
off its stilts and go cartwheeling down the
hillside — and the whole building would
sway while the congregation nodded as if
the father had located truths they'd fumbled for all their lives.

Afterward, leaving the church, with the
lights of St. Vincent trembling across the
sea in front of them, Soma would reach for
Felix's hand, and they would walk together, the frogs howling, big night clouds
passing across the stars, Winkler trailing
his friends, down the steep, crumbling
road, to the small blue house, to eat. Sometimes the boys would come, wearing
shark's-tooth necklaces and drinking beer
after dinner, speaking in their mixed ac-
cents of investment schemes or trade laws
or the Truth and Reconciliation Committee in Santiago, how it was progressing,
how families might be paid reparations.
But Naaliyah never came.

And each time, leaving in the darkness, walking the dewy footpath over the paddocks and down to the inn, Winkler would have the sensation that he moved neither forward nor backward in time, but merely endured variations of the same day over and over. Maybe *he* was the one trapped underwater, under a Plexiglas floor, while the world moved on, men and women checking in and out of rooms, lugging overstuffed suitcases, the soles of their shoes passing lightly above him.

2

Thirteen. Seventy-two. Forty-nine. The voice of the girl on the radio aged, deepened, but her articulation — even through a roar of static — was as careful as ever. Maybe it was Naaliyah, leaning into a microphone half a world away. *I am in Irkutsk, now, crossing into Siberia. I am in Lima; I am in Toronto. Tell everyone I love them.*

There were rumors, of course: Naaliyah had fled with a French charter captain and was somewhere in the Arctic Ocean; Naaliyah had a string of boyfriends all the way to Cuba; Naaliyah was living in Barbados, working as a waitress. He imagined her in Chile, in Puerto Montt, wrapped in a dark coat, crossing some weathered square and staring up at the stark spires of a church.

The seasons traded places. Guests glided in on rented catamarans and ate at the restaurant and raved about the stars or the soup or the clarity of the sea. Felix went from table to table with his hands clasped behind his back and explained the night's menu and Nanton stood behind the front desk turning pages of his newspaper and Winkler went from lantern to lantern at the end of the night extinguishing little flames.

Once a week a cruise ship steamed past, maybe a mile out, stuffed to the portholes with creamy light, and in the lulls between waves Winkler could hear music drift across the lagoon. The entire island was changing. Vacation houses sprouted on hillsides; local boys deemed themselves sailfish hunters and swaggered along the quays hawking charters. The cane mill closed; forests were cleared to make room for a copra plantation, an airstrip, even a golf course. Bed-and-breakfast bungalows popped up, boasting wicker chairs and elaborate latticework and complimentary American newspapers.

The inn itself began to slump, as though it had simmered too long in a covered pot. Sea stars climbed walls and crept into gaps in the mortar like disembodied hands trying to undo the place. Toilet flappers failed; showerheads rusted; potato bugs built empires of tunnels beneath the linoleum. The Plexiglas flooring had buckled slightly, so that the armchairs did not sit flush anymore and tipped from side to side whenever a guest sat.

Worse, Nanton's little rectangle of reef was dying. Shaded from sunlight, pressured by discharge, the coral slowly died, elkhorns collapsing into rubble, and algae moved in, coating the abandoned fingers and struts with a waving black fuzz. Fish still roved beneath the lobby but they were mostly chubs now, greedy, trained to wait below the railing for the shadows of crumb-dispersing tourists.

In storms cocktail glasses fell from lobby tables; kitchen pots swung and clanked. Occasionally a groundswell rose high enough to slip beneath the porch doors and push a sheet of water through. Nanton would scream and curse and climb on his stool clutching his guest book, and Winkler would slide the armchairs aside and push the water back with a rubber squeegee.

Some days, pulling on his rubber boots and wading into the lagoon, prying anemones or urchins off the glass bottom with a paint scraper, he felt like a damkeeper, attempting to keep an overwhelming quantity of water at bay, managing a truce that was doomed to eventually fail.

Mice chewed tunnels through the thinning thatch of the inn's roof and seedlings sprouted in the eaves and the tide swirled against the lucent floor of the lobby and the world — somewhere, out there — fought its wars and constructed its cease-fires while Winkler managed what remained of his life as microscopically as possible, head down, unwilling — or afraid, perhaps — to look up. The same Spanish girl read her same numbers into her same microphone, and an antenna somewhere flung them into the ionosphere in huge electromagnetic waves, across the ocean, through the walls of the shed, penetrating his shirt and skin and bones and cells and nuclei and smaller still — radio signals in his dreams, in his soul.

He endured Nanton's indignities: wearing the same flower-print shirt every day, renting teeth-ravaged snorkels and leaky masks to guests, pushing the perpetually full bin of dirty towels from beach to laundry, and pushing the clean towels back again. Perhaps, he'd think, staring at the sky above his shed — a brightening green bowl of light — *this* is a dream. Any moment I'll wake and be thirty-three years old, in Ohio, in bed, in the middle of the night. The warm shape of Sandy will breathe beside me; I'll hear Grace mumbling in the nursery. I'll pull back the blanket; I'll go to her.

Or he could wake in his childhood bed inside the coat closet and smell the ghosts of all the animals who gave up their coats there, the foxes and minks and caribou; he'd pull open the door and hear trains shunting through the snowy rail yard, his mother stepping through the apartment, pouring a glass of water, chewing a piece of toast at the window before work.

There was that chance. But each time he woke, there was the dusty, cramped interior of the shed. The springs of his cot creaked beneath him; a pain throbbed two-thirds of the way up his spine. A smell like rust, like failure; the cool emptiness of his bed; the sound of the sea sighing into the reef and a fly writhing in a corner-spun web: he was forty-eight, he was fifty; he was alone.

Once — 1993, or '94 — he was walking the road to the pier, north of the inn, when he stopped outside Felix and Soma's house. It was a Tuesday, and Soma was on St. Vincent, working at the post office, and Felix, Winkler knew, was at the inn, working through lunch orders.

The gate was closed with its loop of wire,

and before he could think too much about what he was doing, he unfastened it and entered the yard. The hens came running, heads bobbing, scratching up dust with their dinosaur legs. He waded through them to the screen door.

"Hello?" he called. But no one was home. He knew no one was home. He ran his hand over the crack in the wall, its edges a rawer white against the blue paint.

Inside it was dark and cool. Most things were as he remembered them, as they had seemingly always been: the ungainly boats sitting on everything, painted in their Popsicle colors; Soma's books in the corners; the light blue picnic table with its laminate hanging from the underside in long, deciduous strips. On the counter sat a flat of two dozen eggs waiting to be wiped clean.

But there were changes, too, or maybe it was being in the house like this, uninvited, the kitchen devoid of noise and activity. It felt emptier, less hopeful. Not so much haunted as abandoned, as if even its ghosts were away, at work on more pressing concerns.

Felix had since installed a sink and several chipped plates sat in the bottom, one with a mostly eaten tortilla on it, a soggy quarter-moon. Outside, in one of the neighboring yards, a dog began to bark.

The stove smelled like caramelized onions. The charcoal box was tidy and full. In the corner room that had been the boys' and then Naaliyah's still hung the poster of Chile's Torres del Paine, faded so the sky had gone white and all the granite pink. A menagerie of stuffed cartoon rabbits sat mute on the shelf; a fistful of dried herbs stuck out of a pebble-filled wine bottle. On the underside of the top bunk the constellations of glow-in-the-dark stars still clung, pale and stiff, the adhesive failing.

Once, he remembered, for a whole summer, Naaliyah had wanted to learn to walk on her hands. She wore a purple one-piece bathing suit every day, frayed at the straps and hems, and she'd bend and spring onto her hands and ask Winkler to hold her calves in his fists and she'd walk on her palms through the sand, her suit slipping off her buttocks, legs straight. They'd shuffle a few dozen yards until her arms gave out. "How many did I make that time?" she'd ask, breathless, shaking out her arms.

"Fifteen, I think."

"Fifteen," she'd say, savoring it. "Okay. Let's try for twenty."

Outside someone passed along the path carrying a radio and Winkler froze beneath the archway of the bedroom. Soma's clothesline creaked in the breeze. The music was a long time in fading.

They still slept behind a curtain. Their bed was unmade, its sheet kicked to the foot. A row of dresses hung from a dowel in the closet; rumpled cook's tunics were piled in one corner. And a little TV, with a complicated aerial rigged on top, and a battery-powered clock radio, and a glass of stale-looking water, bubbles arrayed along the bottom.

He lifted one of Soma's blouses from the floor to his nose and inhaled and held it there for a minute or so. Then he set it down carefully and retreated, walking quickly, past the picnic table and the wary eyes of the laminated Virgin, easing the screen door shut behind him so it would not clap, and hurried out through the yard.

3

Before dawn, December 1999. Some first guests were moving about — he could hear doors groaning and water traveling through pipes. He stood at the entrance to his shed and listened to the clamor of the birds. Venus shone a distant white above the shoulder of the hills to the south. The black of the sky blanched into a pale green, and three tiny clouds appeared — *cumulus humilis* — carrying a wilting pink in their undersides, drifting west.

He picked his way down the coral stone path to the beach. Bats, on their final hunts, swung overhead like black motes. Soon there was a horizon, ironed flat as if by the load of the sky, and a sailboat toiling across it. He let himself into the kitchen, crossed the inn, over the glass floor, and climbed to the porch. There he drew open each of the louvered doors, and swept sand from the boards, and watched it sift and disappear into the water below.

The sun was fully up when he returned

to his shed and found a blue folder leaning against the door. Inside was what appeared to be a lab report, or a draft of one. On the cover was a photograph of a shrimp, one of its claws lumpy and oversized. The hand-written title read "Social Structures of Sponge-Dwelling Snapping Shrimps." And beneath that, a name: Naaliyah Orellana. Across the title page someone — Naaliyah herself? — had scribbled: *What do you think?*

He brought the report into his shed and set it on the table and read it cover to cover.

It was Naaliyah's work, he could tell right away. There were exclamation points after nearly every sentence: *The shrimps feed on their host sponges almost exclusively, but never so much that they endanger the sponge — think of that! Symbiosis is every-where! Did evolution select the shrimps with the most gastronomic restraint?*

Apparently she had harvested exposed sponges from a variety of reefs and peered into their tunnels in search of tiny shrimp, no bigger than a grain of rice. She'd main-tained a controlled environment some-where — for two years, evidently — and according to her research, certain species of these crustaceans lived in eusocial groupings, like termites or bees, in service of a single reproducing queen.

It was an ambitious and marvelous and amateur effort all at once. She blamed discharge from cruise ships for population declines but never demonstrated that such pollution was in the water. And the report had no structure: no abstract, no introduction, no citations.

By candlelight he flipped through it again. There were astonishing observations: *After feeding the dominant brooding female, a juvenile male will sometimes invert and lie on his back, flexing his telson. Like a submissive dog! I have seen the female climb on top of him and repeatedly tap his thorax delicately with her major cheliped. Is she asserting her dominance? Maybe she is teasing him!*

In the past years he had kept up with science less and less, almost solely now out of coincidence — fog shoaled over the sea in the morning, the condensation of water vapor on plumbing pipes, the high mark of a spring tide on the lobby's eastern wall. If a yachtie left an issue of *Nature* in the lobby, or if he overheard charter captains discussing fish stocks, he could not seem to muster the energy to be interested beyond a vague and stifled curiosity. As if he had a faraway brother who cared for such things. But now here was Naaliyah, writing like an adult, like a scientist, a piece of her delivered to his doorstep. Did Felix know? Did Soma?

He sat over her pages well into the evening, making notes in the margins with a pencil.

February came and went and he did not see her. He gathered what he could from Soma as she cleaned a henhouse, hacking apart waste caked onto the plywood floor: Naaliyah had completed secondary school on Barbados; she had found work with the Caribbean Institute of Oceanography, scrubbing aquariums, maintaining research boats. She'd crept into classes, read instructors' texts. One of them had eventually allowed her to use a launch, in the mornings, to record her own observations. Now, after four years of this, she had moved to their satellite school on St. Vincent, where she was completing a degree.

Soma had seen her only once, glimpsing her from the post office package dock, as Naaliyah hurried up Back Street with a garden hose coiled over one shoulder. She looked older, Soma said. Different. But when pressed she could not explain what, exactly, had changed.

Vestiges of the dream he'd had, twenty-three years earlier, tugged at Winkler's consciousness: Naaliyah's ankle, a loop of chain.

"All this time so close," Soma said.

The acrid, nitrous smell of waste saturated the air. Winkler blinked a few times.

In the hot shade Soma looked smaller than ever. "An angry daughter," she said, dragging the blade of her shovel across the plywood, "is like an angry hen. The more you chase, the harder it is to catch her. You wait, and be patient, and hope that eventually she comes to you."

He rubbed his eyes. Shadows of that old dream — an empty skiff, a taut anchor line — dragged through the bottom of his stomach. He watched the dust hanging inside the henhouse, three divergent sunbeams slanting through it, tiny coronets rotating in the light.

Was she in danger? If she was, wouldn't the dream come back? He dreamed and woke and remembered hardly anything: the green paint on his high school locker, a wire and chrome hubcap he'd caught rain in as a child.

That dry season was very dry. No rain

for thirty days, then forty. The wind carried dust devils out to sea, where they whirled and elongated like miniature red tornadoes and finally spun themselves out. His flowers wilted in their beds. "Damn," Nanton would mutter, peering into the cement reservoir set behind the inn, stretching on his tiptoes, his curse echoing back. But the tourists still came, raving about the lack of cloud cover, and took their showers, and swam in the molasses-vat-turned-pool, and ran their faucets, and Winkler cringed to hear it: more water disappearing through pipes, flushing into the sea.

The shrimps live in twisting networks of canals within their host sponges — hundreds of crooked, scrambled tunnels, yet they always seem to know where they're going. Duffy et al. argue that it is the sponge itself who pumps water through those tunnels, providing the shrimps with their steady supply of oxygen. As payback they defend the sponge from other colonizers. And they give their lives! They are little soldiers! They are lions!

In March he saw her. She was rounding the cape in a small motorized launch with navy blue markings, her hand flat above her eyes to block the sun. He was on the beach raking spent sparklers and plastic cups from a volleyball party the night before and leaned on his rake and raised a hand. She did not see him or else pretended not to. Stacked in the bow in front of her were what looked like traps made of rusted chicken wire. She sat in the stern with one hand on the tiller. A yellow T-shirt ruffled against her chest. Although she was far away and his eyesight was poor, he could see that her mother was right — she was older: something in the way she held her frame, in the confidence with which she piloted the boat. He remembered the feeling of her small weight on his shoulders, shifting as she ducked to avoid an overhanging branch.

How many times had she passed without his noticing? He lowered his hand and watched the boat as it passed the lagoon along the last line of coral and finally disappeared, just her wake coming in toward shore, and the whine of the motor fading into silence.

4

Twenty-four years before, he and Sandy had been driving from Anchorage to Cleveland in the Chrysler. They were in Manitoba, maybe, or northern Minnesota. It was early morning and the Newport climbed a low rise, pushing east toward a darkness broken only by a thread of white. On a grassy slope beside the freeway, eight small deer, like little impalas, stood chewing. All of them faced westward, staring into the receding gloom. Their shadows — long and hazy in front of them — shrunk slowly back along the hillside.

"Sandy," he said, and nudged her where she was slumped against the door. "Sandy, look." But she had not even bothered to raise her head, asleep or feigning sleep, and soon the deer were behind a hill and out of sight. I should stop the car, Winkler remembered thinking. I should double back and force her out and we should climb that hill and watch those deer. But he hardly slowed. The box of welding supplies rattled softly in the backseat; the hood of the Newport cut the wind. He had the strange thought that what he had seen were not deer but the ghosts of them, that if Sandy had looked she would have seen only a hillside, an empty swath of grass.

Were they already seeing things so differently, only two days away from Anchorage? It was hard not to think, back then, of Herman Sheeler calling detectives, hiring private investigators.

Later that day Winkler saw more deer, all of them dead, their bodies broken open on highway shoulders and the dark miscellaneous stains they left on the asphalt. Sandy held her bladder in silence beside him.

Easter Monday. Dusk. He stood on the beach watching the sun recede in a soundless panoply of color, the rays separating and refracting a thousand times in the fields of dust blowing over the sea.

Before he saw her, he could hear the hum of the outboard. Then the launch came into view, crossing the lagoon from the south this time, the same rusty traps stacked in the bow, a wake rolling from the stern. As she passed she turned the boat and killed the motor and coasted onto the

266

beach. She climbed out and dropped a cinder block anchor onto the sand and came up barefoot and stood beside Winkler watching the smear of color on the horizon. She wore a one-piece bathing suit printed with magnolia flowers and a pair of jeans sawed off just below the pockets. Her fingers were cut and scarred in places; her face was broad and smooth and brown and older. But still so young, still the face of the little girl who had taken his eyeglasses and held them over her eyes.

"What?" she said, smiling.

He could not look away. She laughed and hugged him. He felt her breasts press into his chest, and the lean strength of her arms around his back. He wondered how long it had been since he was last embraced.

He blushed. She tilted her head toward the kitchen. "Is he . . . ?"

"Serving dinner."

"Did you get it? My thesis?"

He nodded.

"It's only a draft. I've collected more data since that one."

From the deck of the restaurant they could hear silverware clinking. A waiter navigated between tables with a tray on his shoulder. Winkler didn't know what to say, how to begin. She was a grown woman. The sun burgeoned as it neared the horizon. "Take a walk with me," she said. They crossed the grounds and went out onto the road in the failing light. A hundred yards farther down, a trail switchbacked to the summit of Mount Pleasant, a path they had taken many times when Naaliyah was a girl.

It was a short, steep hike. They didn't speak. By the end of it Winkler was struggling to catch his breath. From the tight, stumpy clearing at the summit they could see lights in the towns along the necklace of islands to the south, illuminated like small piles of glitter on a black platter. The wind had finally come up and it was blowing hot down from the north and pushing dust through the sky, and the last light of the now vanished sun made a blue stripe at the horizon. Above it the troposphere hung rose-colored in all that haze as if a great fire burned just beyond it. Lights strung along the market and condominiums on the hillsides and along the riggings of boats in the harbor farther off shirred and quaked in the wind and the microwave tower erected beside them on the summit moaned. Small flowers of fireworks bloomed over the neighborhoods to the west.

Yesterday the priest at St. Paul's had told his congregation in his quiet voice that the risen Lord was wandering among the people now, showing them the wounds in his palms. Afterward, during the Nicene Creed, the choir rose to such a pitch that Winkler worried that this Easter, finally, the church was going to tear off its stilts and go careening down the hillside.

Naaliyah smelled faintly of shellfish. She worked her hands in her pockets. "I need a favor," she said. From her shorts she produced a half dozen envelopes, folded in half, addressed and stamped. "I need letters."

"Letters?"

"I'm applying to school. To get a doctorate."

He took the envelopes and held them close to his eyeglasses. They were addressed to schools in the United States: Texas A&M, UMass Boston, Portland State University. Even the University of Alaska at Anchorage. "Graduate school," she said. "Like you. Like you did. I'll need funding, of course, but my advisor thinks I have a shot."

"Naaliyah . . ." The light was failing. A single rocket arced above the harbor and guttered and faded. What did he know about getting her into a graduate program? What clout would he have now? He'd never had any to begin with.

"Will you do it? I don't need it until the end of the month."

The crowns of the trees below them billowed and shone. A chain of firecrackers erupted somewhere. Naaliyah was saying something about how hard she had worked, how she wanted her thesis to break ground.

"What about the instructors at the institute?"

"I've asked them, too. But I thought one from you . . ."

Winkler leaned against the cement base of the microwave tower. "I'll try," he said.

"Thank you." They stood a bit longer watching the small, ephemeral flourishes of fireworks below them, and the ganglions of smoke they left behind. He thought he should say something about her parents, how her father stood sometimes on the beach and gazed over the six miles of sea at St. Vincent. How every Monday morning her mother walked the footpath to the interisland ferry alone, the big tangled trees looming above her.

"Your thesis," he said. "I'm not sure I'm

qualified, but I made some notes and —"

Naaliyah reached over and held his hand. "They'll take me, won't they, David? Some school will let me in?" Out in the harbor the fireworks pitched toward the finale, dozens of green and carmine blossoms that left ribbons of fading gold sparks as they drifted back. "Yes," he said. "Of course." He felt as if she might float off into the sky and burn, as if he were what kept her from it.

That night he had the dream again. Even as it began, he felt himself entering a scene at once familiar and intolerable. He was hurrying down a path, crashing through thorns. Off to his left, out at sea, Naaliyah was lowering a cinder block from the stern of a small boat. Every detail was concentrated and intensified: mica shining in the sand, a thousand reflections of sky on the water, each oscillation of her launch. A chain, rifling into the water, caught her ankle and jerked her off her feet. She clung to the transom. The boat tipped. She went under. He was maybe a hundred yards away. He sprinted into the lagoon and swam for all he was worth, but she was too far. The chain hung taut from the stern; the launch turned slowly against it. She did not surface. He stroked forward but the boat seemed to recede. He woke with water in his lungs.

5

A trend recurred over and over: Winkler was on an airplane, returning home after twenty-five years; Winkler was on an island, dreaming of the future. George DelPrete stepped in front of a bus; his hatbox flew through the air. Grace suffocated in his arms. Now — again — Naaliyah drowned before his eyes. All these deaths, ordained perhaps by chance, or choice, or the complexities of some unfathomably large pattern — was there a difference? Would he be forced to relive the same events over and over? Would he always be compelled along variations of the same trajectories?

Studying ice crystals as a graduate student, he eventually found the basic design (equilateral, equiangled hexagons) so icily repeated, so unerringly conforming, that he couldn't help but shudder: Beneath the splendor — the filigreed blossoms, the microscopic stars — was a ghastly inevitability; crystals could not escape their embedded blueprints any more than humans could. Everything hewed to a rigidity of pattern, the certainty of death.

He was supposed to fix a failing toilet in room 6; instead he ran the mile and a half to town in the still-dark and paid a fisherman $60 E.C. to ferry him to Kingstown. His heart thrummed in his ears. Scraps of the dream resurfaced: an empty launch, a chain hanging motionless. The hull of the boat smacked the waves.

At the post office he cut to the front of the line. Soma frowned. "Did you run here?"

"Where does Naaliyah live?"

"Somewhere near the market. Get your breath, David."

"Please. Do you know the address?"

"No."

"Can't you look it up? You've never looked it up?"

It was a concrete building, eight apartments, a flat roof, a strip of front lawn gone to clay. Across the street a butcher cut steaks behind a grease-smeared window. Winkler sprinted the stairs, rapped the knocker. "Naaliyah!" he called. "Naaliyah!"

After a minute a shirtless man with dreadlocks swung back the door. Behind him music played softly in a dark room,

sheets tacked over the windows, a weath-
ered-looking couch littered with Heineken
bottles, a glass coffee table with a wedge
chipped off the corner. "What's this?"

"Where is Naaliyah?"

"Work." He gestured toward the stairwell, the street beyond. "You having a
heart attack?"

"Where is that? Where is work?"

"At the institute. By the quay. Here now,
man," he scratched his hip with the back of
his thumb, "what you up to? You the old
guy she talks about?"

But Winkler was already down the stairs.
He was halfway across the street when the
sheet over the apartment window pulled
back and the shirtless man leaned out.
"Hey," he called. "Liyah is fine! You got to
relax!"

The institute was a series of boats along
a jetty and a low trailer lined with sinks.
Two men outside the trailer carefully lowered large pieces of coral into a roiling
aquarium. Winkler huffed her name. They
pointed to the sea. "Collecting. Won't be
back for a while."

"Does she have a radio?"

The men rolled their eyes and laughed.
"You here to make a donation? We'll take
some radios."

275

He jogged to the end of the pier. Barnacles. The white shapes of rocks twenty feet down. A few needlefish flitted past, dim and silver. The sea swung slowly up and back down, leaden and inscrutable. What cove was she in now? Would she be lowering anchor? His heart shook. Wisps of an older nightmare resurfaced: water at windowsills, his legs wrapped around a mailbox post.

His hamstrings ached and it felt like bones had collapsed in his feet. All this running — and for what? His memory summoned an image of her, maybe twelve years old, tapping at his shutters before dawn. She was breathing hard; the front of her T-shirt rose and fell. Grass clippings clung to her bare feet and she stood before him with a kind of electricity in her body: her fingers quivered; her teeth gleamed. He had struck a match and set it to a candle and swung open the door.

She slipped over the transom; links of chain tightened around her ankle. Bubbles rose like flexing jewels to the surface.

She did not return until nearly dark, easing the launch against the tire casings hung beside the pier, and hauled herself up the ladder. She stopped when she saw him.

"You look terrible."

He took her hand. He practically knelt on the planks. Maybe she was a ghost. "You have to stop collecting, Naaliyah. You can't go out anymore."

"What are you talking about?"

"Isn't your research completed?"

"Is it ever completed? I didn't do that work just for my thesis, you know. Just to get into a school."

"Can't you research in the lab from now on? Don't you have enough specimens?"

"What is this? Did my father put you up to this?"

"No. No." He dragged a palm over his forehead. "Please. Don't go on the water anymore. We need to get you to dry land." He followed her to the door of the institute and paused outside, unsure, his fingers on her elbow.

"David," she said, "you're the one we should be worried about. You should go home." In her hand a net bag full of coral pieces dripped. "Please."

He waited in front of her apartment, leaning against the butcher's front window. She went up and came down an hour or so later with the dreadlocked man. He tailed them to a café, watching from a distance.

He saw her smile over a plate of rice; the boyfriend leaned over and kissed her neck. Heat built around Winkler. His eyes stung. An emaciated hound emerged from a lot beside the restaurant and barked him into the shadows.

He walked to the post office, which was closed and still bore the rotting gate where he had spent his first night in that town more than two decades before. Nanton would be furious by now, hammering at the door of Winkler's shed. The beach chairs would need to be folded and stacked; umbrellas taken down; lanterns around the dining deck extinguished. Towels folded. Lawns watered. Walkways swept.

At the wharf two cables hanging from a crane swung heavily against a purple sky. All around him the small lights of houses burned behind their shutters.

He passed the night in a motel meant for tourists that smelled of cigarettes and bleach. Before dawn he was again outside her window.

After an hour or so she left the apartment and hurried up the street. He followed at a distance. A rum-and-cake vendor unbolted his kiosk and propped the awning. Three women on bicycles pedaled past. Naaliyah waved and they waved back. The sun broke the line of Grand Bonum above town and striped the street with light and shadow. He followed her another block and then called her name and she turned to face him as though both were players in some gunfighters' burlesque.

"David?"

"Don't go out. Don't go out today."

Her shoulders heaved and she passed a hand over her temples. "Why are you doing this? You of all people are trying to stop me?"

A woman towing a child's wagon full of melons passed and nodded at Naaliyah, and Naaliyah nodded back. Winkler approached. "I can't let you out on the water."

She stared at him. "But what does that mean? Why can't I? What are you talking about?"

"Please."

"If I don't go I won't be paid. You have to give me a reason."

Winkler closed his eyes and inhaled. He was a yard away, within reach. "For me."

"David." She turned as if to go. He lunged and caught her T-shirt at the shoulder but she spun away and his hand slipped to her neck and she staggered for a moment. On the sidewalk a man in a white shirt with a short tie stopped and frowned. Naaliyah pushed forward with her legs and Winkler lost his balance and fell.

She stood a few feet away. "Christ!" she said, examining her collar. "What's wrong with you?"

Winkler scrambled on the asphalt for his glasses. "You can't —" he said.

"No. No way." And she was walking away.

He gathered himself and followed her to the institute but she was nowhere. Her launch bobbed beside the jetty; the little trailer stood dark and empty. Was she watching him from somewhere? Had she taken another boat?

He clambered down the ladder, stood in her wobbling skiff, seized three black tubes leading to the outboard powerhead — a thirty-five-horsepower Evinrude — and pulled as hard as he could. Two of them gave; one squirted liquid onto his hand. Gasoline, mixed with oil. A multihued bloom of petroleum spread across the surface of the water. He climbed back up to the pier and wiped his hands on his trousers. A light flipped on inside the institute. He turned, nodded to a man who stepped out of the trailer, and went on toward town.

★ ★ ★

Nanton stalked the lobby, throwing his hands periodically toward the ceiling. "You think I cannot hire another gardener? In a minute? You think you are so skilled you cannot be replaced?" Winkler bore it, his gaze on the floor and the waving gray shapes of algae on the rubbled coral below. A tiny trumpet fish nosed along beneath the glass, turned its eye up at Winkler, then darted away.

At the yacht supply, he bought swimming fins and a large pair of chain cutters. Soma was at the shed door when he returned. He went inside and set his purchases on the table and began stuffing clothes into a two-ply garbage bag.

"What is this? You're leaving?"

He grunted. He unclipped socks from his clothesline.

"I have not seen you behave like this in a long time. Not since the first year you arrived." She pushed open his shutters and light poured in. "I don't know everything that happened, David. I know you used to write letters. I know you left somebody at home, who you used to telephone. And I know that the box I brought upset you terribly."

Insects shrieked in the mounds of cut

grass beside the shed. A wind came up and stirred dust on the floor. "Naaliyah's a woman," Soma said. "An adult. She can make her own decisions." She pulled one of Winkler's shirts out of the bag and snapped it and folded it on the bed.

"Naaliyah will drown," Winkler said.

Soma studied him. "What do you mean?"

"I know that she will drown. Soon."

"You *know* it? I don't understand. She swims like an eel."

"I need you to tell her to stop going out in her launch. We need to keep her from the water."

"You think she will listen to me?"

"Please, Soma."

"You *know* she will drown?"

He looked at the floor between his feet for a long time. The sensation of an invisible hand crimped itself around his windpipe. "I dreamed it, Soma. I dreamed she would fall off the back of her boat and get tangled in the anchor."

"You dreamed it."

"Yes."

Soma smoothed the edges of the shirt she had folded and put her hands on her hips. "You dreamed this about my daughter."

"You don't believe me. It's all right."

"I believe that you dreamed it. But how do you know the dream will come true?"

"I don't. Not exactly."

She went to the doorway and stood gazing out. "I just want everyone to be okay. Why do we let things that have already happened torture us?"

Winkler braced his hands on the sill of his window. He felt like rocking the wall back and forth until it collapsed and brought the shed down on top of them. "But this hasn't happened yet."

"Those, too. The things that have happened, and the things that could happen."

A half hour later he was on the ferry to St. Vincent. He toted his sack of clothes through the streets and rented an unfurnished room above the butchery across from Naaliyah's apartment. The odor of old meat rose through the linoleum. Ants patrolled the walls. In the bathroom a lustrous green moss had grown over the toilet tank. He bought a dented aluminum chair for $20 E.C. and plugged his hot plate into the extension cord the butcher had run up through the window.

The harder he tailed her, the harder she worked to conceal herself. It might have been comical if it had not been so awful: Naaliyah ducking behind fences, Winkler half jogging after her, a block away. Cat and mouse. But who was the mouse? Winkler chasing Naaliyah, the future chasing Winkler.

Her outboard had been repaired; she began collecting specimens in the early hours, in the evenings. He felt the arrival of his dream grinding like a bus toward him. I have become a stalker, he thought. An obsessed savant, slouching in the shadows outside her apartment, slumping past baskets of oranges at the market.

In the aluminum chair, facing her window, he tried writing the recommendation letter. *Dear Admissions Committee,* he'd try. *Naaliyah Orellana is remarkable.*

Dear Admissions Committee, You will not believe how extraordinary Naaliyah Orellana is.
Dear Admissions Committee. Naaliyah Orellana is. Naaliyah Orellana is. Naaliyah Orellana is.

Naaliyah sat across from an overweight white man, perhaps the same age as Winkler. They sipped ice water on a restaurant balcony, waiting for their dinners

284

beneath a faded umbrella emblazoned with red and green roosters. Behind them huge purple batiks shifted uneasily in a breeze. The overweight man gestured at Naaliyah with his fork; she smiled.

"I only need one minute," Winkler told the hostess. He had to interlock his fingers so his hands would not shake. "They are friends of mine."

When Naaliyah saw him, her face paled. "David," she said. "Hello. This is Dr. Meyer. He is my advisor at the institute." The big man shifted his napkin, half stood, and held out a hand.

"Mr., ah —"

"Dr. Winkler," Naaliyah said.

"Ah," Meyer said. "The mysterious other recommender."

Winkler did not take the man's hand. "Naaliyah," he said. He crouched so his eyes were level with hers. "We have to talk."

"Is this the best time for that?"

Meyer sipped his ice water. Naaliyah held her hands very carefully in her lap. "Are you all right, David?"

"I had a dream," Winkler whispered. Meyer was looking over Naaliyah's head. "I don't think you should go out in the boat."

A group of children, passing below in the street, began to sing "Happy Birthday." Naaliyah managed a small, forced smile. "You've said this before, David."

The hostess was standing behind Winkler. "Everything okay?"

"Yes," said Naaliyah.

"No," said Winkler.

The hostess leaned over. "Come now, mister. Let's leave them to eat, yes?"

"Please," Winkler said. He was being led out. "Please, Naaliyah."

"A pleasure, Dr. Winkler," Meyer called after him.

He tailed her home; he tailed her to work the next day. From the shadows of the institute, swallowing hard, he watched her start her Evinrude.

But still she did not drown. Still she came back, motoring beside the jetty, apparently whole, apparently breathing. He watched her unload her net bags and empty them into aquariums. He felt like sneaking up behind her and poking her in the side, to see if she was real.

Monday — seven days after he had his dream — there was a knock on the door of the apartment. Soma stood on the iron staircase squinting in. She wore gold bangles through her ears and her crucifix over her sternum and a discolored lace-hemmed dress that stopped at her knees. "The butcher told me you were here," she said, and stepped through the door and surveyed the gritty tiles, the chair by the window. Over her shoulder hung a bag of books. Winkler returned to his chair and sat down.

"She's inside," he said. "I'm nearly positive. If she slipped out this morning, I didn't see it."

"When was the last time you slept?"

"Last night. I think. Did you talk to her?"

She went around in front of him and squatted on her heels. "David, can you look at me? Can you listen? You're afraid for her, that is all. And rightly so. It is dangerous for anyone to be alone on the water. But you can't watch over her every moment. You must learn to let go. Believe me, it's not easy. But you must let whatever will happen, happen."

"No," Winkler said, shaking his head, looking past her. "You don't get it." Pale rectangles of light fell through the panes and divided their bodies into parallelograms.

Soma put her hands on his shoulders.

"You had a daughter, no?"

He felt a voltage rising behind his eyes. "Grace."

"What was she like?"

He looked away. He shut his eyes. Over time his images of the baby, like photographs handled too often, had worn down and creased, lost their definition. No longer could he recall her face precisely, or her fingers, or the smooth, new skin on the bottoms of her feet. What was the shape of her cheekbones? Of her mouth? All he could remember was Sandy's copy of *Good Housekeeping*, Joyce Brothers and Tupperware, how to trim sugar from your family's diet, a promise to reveal Valerie Harper's real-life loves.

"She had my eyes," he said. Electricity sizzled behind his forehead.

Still squatting, Soma brought her body toward his, a disjointed embrace. "Okay, David. It is okay. I will talk to Naaliyah. It will be okay."

A snowflake, a honeycomb, a spider's web stretched across the doorframe. He found a dead katydid in the corner of the apartment and turned it in his hands, the small, polished thorax, ten thousand tiny hexagons in its diaphanous wings. Sixes and sixes and sixes. Were there solutions here, clues to what he was missing?

Roiling skies, burning skies, skies bleached silver with heat. Emaciated dogs dozing in doorways. The levels in the town reservoirs shrank as though drains had been unplugged beneath them. Irrigation canals ran at half their normal levels, then less. Even the banana plantations, the big, hardy trees on the flanks of Mount St. Andrew, seemed to lilt and acquiesce in the heat. In the evenings a hot wind would start up from the west and heave red dust over the island: dust on the sills and louvers, dust in his rice, dust in his throat. The entire island seemed dimmer somehow, as if its hills were crumpling back into themselves.

Insomnia, a pending calamity: Hadn't he been through all this before? He thought of graduate school, growing ice on a supercooled copper pipe. Each dendritic arm of a snow crystal always corresponded precisely to the others, as if, as they formed, each knew what the other five arms were up to. Was this so different from the shape of his own life, the way his personal history seemed to repeat itself: George DelPrete, Sandy, Grace, now Naaliyah? Who next? Himself? He was trapped in the lattice of an ice crystal, more molecules precipitating around him every second; soon he would be at the center, locked in a hexagonal prison; one of them, a quarter billion of them.

Soma came through the door, her dress soaked with sweat, the skin beneath her eyes swollen. She sat on his aluminum chair and blew her nose into a yellow handkerchief. "She wouldn't even open the door. She said I was trying to keep her from the only thing she loved."

Her cheeks drew inward; her fingers trembled. She opened a book on her lap and turned pages without reading. A few moments passed, just the two of them in the apartment, a truck passing in the street. Then he took her head in his arms, smelling the back of her neck, a smell like salt, and hens, and soap. The book fell from her lap and neither moved to pick it up. They sat like that, her head in his arms, watching the window go dark.

From then on, Soma joined him every evening after her shift and together they stared across the sandy, unpaved road at the sheets in Naaliyah's windows. They managed to keep watch in a kind of unspoken rotation, Soma blinking in the chair, Winkler retreating to lie on the folded blanket in the corner every dozen or so hours to close his eyes and feel the heat and hear the bananaquits sing from the rooftops behind them.

"You have been fired," Soma told him. "Nanton put your things in a cardboard box. He says he'll burn them."

"Let him," Winkler said.

"He's just talking. I think he misses you."

"I bet Felix misses you."

"Let him. He has his rum."

In the afternoons, with Soma at work and dark stratocumulus banking up overhead, the light in the trees would go so flat he could see no more than a few feet into them, and an immense stillness would accumulate, and he'd get a gagging feeling, as if the oxygen had been choked out of the air. In those moments everything felt as if it were waiting: himself, Soma, Naaliyah's concrete building across the way, the vendors fanning themselves in their stalls, the masts wobbling out in the harbor. A hot, sickly smell would rise from the tiles, and the cathedral bell would clang, and he'd get a slow, certain sense of the impermanence of his life, the vastness of the universe and his own insignificance in it. Eventually he would run out of hours; eventually Naaliyah would slip away and die.

He crept through town to the pier to sabotage her launch a second time. He snipped a foam-covered hose running out from the Evinrude and yanked out what he thought might be plugs. He cut the anchor chain and heaved the cinder block overboard — the water closed over it with a clap.

Thunderclouds dragged black tendrils of evaporating rain through the sky. Lightning rang back and forth over the horizon and pelicans labored up from warehouse roofs on their huge, prehistoric wings and skimmed the telephone wires.

6

To the Selection Committee —

Here are some of the things Naaliyah Orellana showed me, one afternoon, when she was ten. A hermit crab trying out new shells; a large underwater shape (sea turtle? ray? monk seal?) swimming lazy circles between two groupings of coral; boobies raiding each other's eggs; tropic birds (red- and white-footed, with a long white feather trailing behind them); a shining winged beetle like a drop of mercury on a fence post; a militia of tiny ants invading a bag of cereal; black crabs dashing sideways into burrows; a white urchin the size of her thumbnail; two long-necked anemones in a tide pool engaged in slow-motion wrestling; an emaciated feral cat trotting up the path behind us, then carefully stepping back into the vegetation; clown fish, triggerfish, iridescent and turquoise fish; yellow and white angelfish; brackish pools squirming with tadpoles; goats and ewes and one white horse snapping at flies in the corner of his paddock; a tortoise upside down in the road that hissed and groaned at us as we righted him; a beautiful crest-headed bird like an oversized blue cardinal; a half dozen cattle egrets high-stepping behind a lawnmower; a tiny chick in a hole on the ground, its back to us, looking around in the dark; a snail the size of a tennis ball making its way toward the kitchen trash, its eyes waving on stalks. "Look in one spot for a minute," Naaliyah told me. It was a game she'd play. "Choose grass or sky or beach or water — and something will cross it." And these are just the things I can remember.

To live in the tropics is to always be reminded (I find a hornet in my rice, a minnow in my shaving water) of the impossibility of ownership. The street in front of me belongs more to whatever is tunneling up those hundred or so little mounds of red dirt than to any of us. The beams of this apartment belong to houseflies; the window corners to spiders; the ceiling to house geckos and roaches. We are all just tenants here. Even the one thing we believe is ours — the time we're given on earth — does that belong to us?

"An amazing book," Naaliyah once told me, "could be written about mites." To *know her is to realize the thousand forms of inquiry. The least things enrapture her: she used to lie on her stomach and watch a tiny square of reef through a plate of glass for hours. Her shortest excursion into the world is a field trip. For me it is a reminder of the poverty of my own vision.*

Naaliyah possesses all the things that keep us from giving up: exuberance, curiosity, hope. She is a gift to the world. I pray you will find it in you to grant her the opportunity for more study.

It had taken him a dozen drafts. Soma was asleep and he laid it in her lap to make copies and mail in the morning. "I hope they will accept it handwritten," he said aloud, into the shadows. It was the first letter he'd been able to finish in twenty years.

7

Now, in the last hours, he noticed patterns everywhere: a template in the glistening trail left by a slug in the bottom of the sink; another in the veins of a leaf, blown across the sill; yet another in the arrangement of condensation droplets on the toilet tank. He stared at them for minutes, convinced there were answers locked there, correlations, a code he couldn't quite break.

Soma came in the door late — she had missed yesterday altogether. Did she even believe him about his dream? In a borrowed fry pan she cooked a dozen eggs over a foam of butter and they sat watching the dark windows across the way and passing the pan back and forth, eating with their fingers. As if across the street an engrossing film played. But there was only the wind against the sheets in Naaliyah's windows and the isometric reflections of the street lamps.

"You can't keep her from what she wants, David. Even if it means letting her reach a destiny you fear. You have to leave that up to God. If you push at her, she'll just push back harder."

He closed his eyes; he thought he could hear, although he did not have his radio on, the girl on the shortwave whispering outside the window: 13, 91, 7 . . .

Soma laid a sheet across him, pulled it up to his neck. He shook himself awake. But he could not fight it; his eyelids fell. There was a noise, grains of sand grinding beneath a chair leg. Did dreams, he wondered, when they arrived, make a sound? The smallest kind, like the noise of an embryo being conceived, or a snowflake touching down? The shadows in the corners of the room pooled toward the center, and at some point the floor of the apartment had become the floor of Nanton's lobby, a window into some greater darkness, the seams giving way, a black, eager liquid rushing the gaps.

In a nightmare Naaliyah dragged chains onto a beach and shook still-living fish from her hair. "These things happen," she said, "not because you foresee them but because you foretell them. The telling makes it so." She grabbed his shirt and pushed him down. Then Naaliyah was turning into Sandy, and Sandy into

Herman, and the beach was a rainy driveway beneath his back, and Herman had hockey pads strapped to his legs, and skates on his feet. He kicked Winkler; he braced the blade of a skate over Winkler's throat. Numbers dropped from the clouds like leaden kites, huge and spinning.

Winkler moaned in his chair. Soma crept down the iron stairs, made her way to the waterfront, caught the last ferry home. Naaliyah's boyfriend, Chici, came across the road in the final darkness before dawn and set a plate of chicken, wrapped in plastic, by the stairs to Winkler's apartment.

8

In the end he did not need chain cutters or snorkeling fins. She exited her building in the predawn on Sunday morning and he hurried down the iron staircase, as usual, to follow her. A fog clung to the buildings and the street lamps hummed. They were the only two people about. He had the sense she knew he was there, a hundred yards behind. She moved up Halifax Street, walking quickly, the cuffs of her sweatshirt pulled over her hands, the shops dark, the kiosks padlocked, the second-story windows shuttered as if a hurricane had been forecasted, or some worse scene not even buildings could bear to watch.

At the pier she descended the ladder into her launch, unlocked the Evinrude, topped off the tank, and motored out, heading north, keeping the shoreline to her right. He began to run, glimpsing her through the fog and gaps between houses. She gained on him, of course, disappearing around one point, then another. But he ran on, leaving the road when it ended, and crashing through scrub. The hillside shanties petered out; soon there was only a thin trail, and the jumbled prop roots of screw pines, and the sound of her engine, far ahead of him.

Brush lashed his legs. Spiderwebs wrapped and clung to his face. Twice he stopped and walked, clutching a stitch beneath his ribs.

Maybe a mile from town, she killed the motor in a sapphire-blue cove, probably a hundred meters from shore. The trail climbed and he glimpsed her from a low knoll and then kept on. By the time he caught up she had been there a couple of minutes and was already drifting, leaning over the stern, peering into the water. He stood huffing on a rocky beach, beneath a stand of palms. The muscles in his legs felt unraveled and overstretched; the sound in his ears was of blood.

Naaliyah reached beneath a thwart and produced what looked to Winkler like a diving mask. She strapped it over her head. The air was alive with salt and wind; a pair of fat, golden gulls glided past him and landed placidly in the water.

Then everything was familiar: an imprecision to the shadows, a smell in the fog like decomposing leaves, the sound of palms rasping behind him. Her back was to him; the launch wobbled beneath her movement. The dream broke over him like a wave.

He took off his glasses and set them in the sand. He thought: Here it is again. Naaliyah stooped over something in the stern. Then, impossibly, since he had sunk it five nights prior, she was raising what looked like a cinder block. Before she had dropped it over the transom he was pulling off his shoes and socks, charging forward.

Sharp rocks; a spread of corrugated sand in the shallows; clear, warm water breaking at his thighs; a last glimpse of Naaliyah clinging to the stern. He dove. His arms swept forward, one then the other, and a thought emerged: I should have practiced. She was too far away. His legs kicked, his arms rotated. Almost immediately he was exhausted. The muscles in his neck and upper arms stiffened and threatened to lock.

He forced his shoulders to roll forward. The pain built to a point where he felt his arms melt into a kind of mist and he became, for a moment, limbless, a stone sinking toward the bottom. By now she would be trapped a fathom down and working against the bight of chain around her ankle. The empty skiff would make slow pivots around its stern.

The water was almost impossibly clear. Even without his glasses he could see the sea floor recede slowly away from him, pastel poufs of coral and blizzards of tiny fish and one lone grouper hunkered among the shadows, slowly fanning its pectoral fins.

He breathed, marked his bearing, and forced himself to keep on. The sea buzzed and cracked in his ears, matching the sound of his blood. One arm. Then the other. He found himself thinking of water, how it is never still, how even in our bodies water never relents: ceaselessly vibrating, each electron in each molecule in each cell orbiting, spinning, nine independent vectors of position and force, a rapture of movement.

His arms became dowels in a vat of honey; his heart inflated until it pressed against the backs of his ribs.

Then, quite suddenly, she appeared ahead of him in the water, a few streaks of sunlight angling past her. She looked as he knew she would, hanging upside down and bent at the waist, scrabbling at the chain, which had looped twice around her ankle and pulled taut, extending in a thin vertical column toward the sea floor. Bubbles rose from her mouth and hair. The chain quivered sluggishly.

His heart pushed through gaps in his chest. The noise in his ears built to a crescendo. Her body slackened, unfolded; her arms swung beneath her. He dove and tried to raise the chain but the cinder block was heavy on the bottom and the chain was fast to her ankle.

He ascended, breathed, and dove again. This time he went below her and hauled on the chain until he had a few seconds of slack as the cinder block rose, and with a final spasm of energy, he loosened the coil enough to free her ankle. She floated up. He watched her head break the surface and grasped the chain a half second longer, little stars bursting across his vision, blazes of light swaying and shifting on the roof of the water.

He surfaced. Her eyes were open but not blinking and her breath would not start. "No," he heard himself saying. "No no. No no no," denying not only this moment but every preceding one, all the houses and bridges of time, his thrashing heart, his exploding lungs: George DelPrete, Sandy, Grace — he would deny himself, deny structure, dissolve into the ocean, spin in a tiny, dissociated cloud somewhere in the depths.

A moment passed: silence, just water lapping at their necks and the boat turning calmly against its anchor. A sheet of gold mist lay quivering all around them. Water ran down her face and into the corners of her mouth. A feeling like waking from a dream came over him; the dream melting away, a sharper, more coherent reality dawning. Sandy's voice reverberated in his memory: "I hate this part. When the lights come on after a movie."

He fit his hands beneath her rib cage and squeezed. The tide was coming up. With each breath the bottom of the sea, maybe a dozen feet below, sank imperceptibly away. The raging of his heart subsided. Passing swells, low and warm, pushed past them and moved on. Strands of Naaliyah's hair floated into his mouth. "Wake up," he said, and embraced her as firmly as he could. "Wake up."

Mucus leaked from her nostrils. He turned her, and with his arms locked around her waist, pressed his lips against hers and blew into her mouth. He inhaled, readjusted his grip, breathed into her again. Her body accepted the air; he could feel her lungs swell against it, her body float a fraction higher in the water.

He thought of Felix and Soma, just now waking. Was this the conclusion of his dream after all? Two refugee parents, lying on their sad, crumpled mattress, while their daughter drowned six miles away?

How easy it is to let water take you. Warm and smooth — it is like surrendering to the bluest sleep. Don't all of us, at our ends, whether we die in a desert or a quiet white room, drown in some way?

He inhaled once more; he breathed into her. Her eyelids fluttered. She coughed and spewed mist. He compressed her midsection and she inhaled a ragged breath. "Thank you," he said. "Oh thank you." At the horizon stratocumulus clouds gathered in silent, big-shouldered stacks.

9

Thunder, a sound like furniture being dragged across the sky. He hauled himself up from his sheet on the floor, put on his glasses, and went to the window. Lightning ran on in the twilight, flaring mostly in the clouds, but a few fingers dropped now and then to touch the hillsides above town. The power to the street lamps had been knocked out and in the blue, vaporous light he could just see the tossing crowns of palms and the rearing black arcs of utility wires. Lightning strobed close by and Naaliyah's building stood small and bright for a moment, its windows and decaying facade, before it was sucked back into shadow.

Wind threw sand and leaves and plastic bags down the street. He unlatched the window and let the first raindrops blow over the sill. In his imagination he could hear trees on the hills stretching to catch the water, roots perking, trunks leaning, leaves reaching out. Up the street a shutter pushed open and someone cranked in her clothesline. A few people — little more than shadows — stepped from doorways and held up their palms, gaping at the sky. After a minute or two the tile around his feet was wet, and he drew the shutters.

In the hospital the whole family had showed up, Felix and Soma and the three boys, and the doctor said Naaliyah was fine, no lung or chest complications, just sore ribs, just shock. She was discharged that night. Nobody asked him how he had been there. Felix shook his hand. Soma hugged him a long time. His clothes left wet marks on her dress.

Now the wind stilled and the rain came harder and he retreated inside and listened to it thrum on the roof and let sleep come over him.

The following afternoon Soma walked with him down Back Street and together they stood at the quay beside a vast produce warehouse watching the rumbling queue of farmers' trucks and the athletic pivots of loaders as they passed crates of bananas down a human chain. Behind them, in the market, a nutmeg merchant collapsed his umbrella and shook its water into the runnels.

"What now?" Soma said.

He glanced at her face, the wide, planarian-shaped nose, the light brown cheeks, the skin freckled lightly over her cheekbones. Nanton had cleaned out the shed at the inn and was now storing the riding mower there. The new grounds-keeper, Felix said, was a teenager from Kingstown who brought friends in there to smoke marijuana.

"I've been thinking about work," Winkler said. Out in the harbor a few un-rigged sailboats bobbed at their moorings, and halyards chimed against their metal masts, a sound like church bells. "Not for Nanton, but here on St. Vincent."

Soma turned to him and let her arm rest on his shoulder. He pivoted slightly, and was embraced, the warm column of her body, the thin cotton of her dress, the sweet, living smell of her neck.

For a desk he unhinged the bathroom door and laid it across two waxy boxes used for shipping beef. The first days it was a notebook and pencil, but soon it was out in the streets, on the switchbacked paths above the town, even as far north as the slopes of Soufrière. He started with de-scriptions of water, or sketches; he'd crouch over a rivulet running from the forest into the sea: the braided channels, driving miniature landslides of sand before them — the way the surface of the water flashed and stretched in the wind, the way it poured on, seemingly endless.

In the afternoons he walked to Kingstown's only library, an antique two-story gingerbread with books stacked on every available piece of furniture and trade winds stirring everything on the second floor so that, after particularly strong gusts, the place fluttered wildly with papers.

There were so many things he had not known: researchers with remote-controlled submersibles had found sea life two miles deep, beside volcanic vents called black smokers — and not just microbes, either, but meter-long worms, clams as big as hubcaps. There were new phenomena, thousands of them: global climate change, reservoir pollution, rising sea levels. Physicists theorized that a trillion subatomic particles called neutrinos passed through a person's body every second — through a body, its bones, the nuclei of its cells, and out again, into the ground, into the core of the earth, out the other side, and back on into space. There were older notions, too: FitzRoy, captain of Darwin's *Beagle*, pored through fossil beds of mollusks determined to find evidence for Noah's global flood. An Englishman named Conway argued that sparrows left farm ponds in autumn not for warmer climates, but for the moon.

Were they so wrong? Who was to say their guesses were any less applicable than the theories of scientists who strapped radio collars onto geese? They were all aspirations toward the same unknowable truths.

Gates were creaking open inside him — paths, long sealed off, revealed themselves once more. He would write a book. He would write a treatise on water, a natural history of it: it would be new and popular and fascinating; it would be the *Double Helix* of water. He would start small, with the attraction between hydrogen and oxygen atoms. This would in turn illuminate everything else, glaciers and ocean and clouds — what had he been doing for so long at Nanton's inn?

He filled one notebook, started another. Every day he could feel whole segments of himself waking. The sight of the sea just after dawn was enough to make him stand and watch for an hour. Boobies chased one another across the reef line; light touched the tops of the swells; shadows shrunk in the troughs. He lay on his back in a buzzing, abandoned cane field and watched cumulus bloom, growing across seventy miles of sky, a movement so slow you could hardly observe it, a gargantuan puffing, a heart-pulling tumescence. He ate dinner at Soma and Felix's; he shared a cigarette with Naaliyah's dreadlocked boyfriend. He saw Naaliyah herself only occasionally, running up the stairs to her apartment, or running down, toting a sheaf of papers, a bag of groceries, but to see her brought a quickening to his pulse, and he found he could not keep himself from smiling.

In the evenings he'd sit in the alley with the butcher, a small, very black-skinned man with shiny forearms and improbably delicate hands. He smoked and rebladed his saws and told Winkler stories about the 1902 eruption of Soufrière that killed 1,600 islanders, or how his grandfather would kill pigs with a ball-peen hammer. "One whack," he said. "Back of the neck. Over and over. All day, every Friday." He pronounced "Friday" like "Frey-dee."

Winkler would wake at midnight with his mind active, revving high, and scribble sentences into his notebook: *Do starfish grow old?* Or: *Water, impossibly, is in the sun — a wreath of steam, unfathomably hot, floats around the corona.*

In June, Naaliyah appeared on the iron stairwell outside his door. She was wearing a rubber raincoat and her legs were like tan sticks between the hem and the tops of her boots. Mist rolled on the landing behind her. She smiled. "Got an hour?"

She led him to the institute and they stood a moment on the pier looking down at the launches bobbing and clattering lightly in the dark. She chose a larger boat, stacked as usual with wire traps in the bow. A winch stood on scaffolding over the stern. The anchor, he noticed, was brand-new, an aluminum trefoil with symmetrical flukes, set into the bow.

Wordlessly, she lowered the motor and steered them clear of the last pilings. He could not help the fear from starting: something would capsize them and she would be trapped again in the chain and drowned. But he had dreamed nothing and the day felt new and unportentous. All around them the sea glided past black and glassy. Moisture in the air condensed on his forehead and hands.

She found a gap in the coral benches that headed the harbor and maneuvered north. They passed beaches Winkler knew,

the island sliding past dark and silent beneath the noise of the motor, to a place he
had never seen, where the shoreline was
rocky and beachless, crenellated cliffs beneath an unbroken forest. The water here
was pocked with buoys. She eased the
throttle and let them drift.

"Eels," she said, as she clambered to the
stern and reached for a green buoy with a
long gaff. "For one of the professors." She
caught the buoy line in the gaff hook,
pulled the launch closer, and snapped an
eyelet at the end of the line through a
carabiner on the winch. The unclipped
buoy she tossed into the bow. Then she
threw a switch, the drum turned, and the
line began to coil. "He's studying some
photochemical in them. He thinks it might
help in human neurology. Something like
that."

Winkler felt his way to the stern to
watch. The cable tightened; a deep boil
rose. A dark cloud, flecked with silver,
bloomed in the surface water. Tiny white
crabs clung to the line, hauled up from the
depths, blind, hanging on. As the crabs
reached the surface, each slipped off in
turn and floated back down in slow spirals.
Haze drifted over the water. The launch
rose and fell. The sound of the winch

groaned out into the fog, on and on.

Eventually a trap came into view, abruptly visible from the deep green, rising past the descending flurry of crabs, and it broke the surface and Naaliyah switched off the winch, swung the trap over the stern, and emptied it onto the deck. A few fish and a dozen eels writhed around her boots. She rebaited the trap with sardines, clipped it to a new buoy, and swung it overboard.

Winkler retreated into the bow and listened to the eels, like sleeves of muscle, slap the boards. The fog washed down, thick and otherworldly, a trillion minute beads. The great unbroken swaths of trees on the flanks of the volcano seemed impossibly still. Birds — jaegers, maybe — wheeled in slow, primitive circles.

Naaliyah stood with her hands on the stern, looking east. The sun was flaring suddenly in a rift of cloud. Around her boots the eels flopped and writhed. "How many times does a person get to see this?" she asked. "Maybe twenty? Ten?" She leaned over the bulwark and filled a bucket with seawater and set it at her feet and looked out at the swells. "And yet it all seems infinite."

Winkler shook his head. "Not to me."

She flipped the fish overboard, then gathered the slick eels with both hands and stowed them in the bucket, where they popped and seethed. He watched her arms as she worked, thin and brown; he could see the lean strength in them. When she had emptied three traps, she peered into the plastic bucket and said, as if addressing the eels, "I got a letter. Yesterday. From the University of Alaska in Anchorage."

A swell passed under them and he clutched a cleat in the gunwale.

She looked at him. "Don't you want to know what it said?"

"If you want to tell me."

"They accepted me. With a tuition waiver."

He shook his head. Another swell came in beneath them. "Congratulations."

"Thank you." She leaned over and braced her hands on the rim of the bucket. "Thank you for everything."

10

Nanton let them use the inn. Felix was in rare form, sprinting through the kitchen with a ladle in one hand and a pair of tongs in the other, grilling snapper, stewing plantains, producing plates of ginger cookies, bowls of chutneys and pigeon peas, banana bread, steamed whelks.

Maybe forty people came. Naaliyah's boyfriend, Chici, plucked an electric bass in the corner and sang island songs with a girlish voice. The three boys were there, drinking coladas and smiling behind their sunglasses, two of them with dark, handsome girlfriends. Tourists gathered at corner tables, tapping their feet. Even Nanton came out for a while, sitting nervously and sipping ginger ale through a straw, nodding at whoever nodded at him, periodically brushing something invisible from his suit.

Naaliyah smiled and touched the arms of guests, the priest from St. Paul's, girlhood friends and their husbands. Winkler sat for dinner beside Dr. Meyer, who proved to be a cordial and soft-spoken man.

"Naaliyah tells me you are a hydrologist."

"I was," Winkler said. "Years ago."

"You don't work anymore?"

"I've been doing some reading. But I have not worked seriously in a long time."

Meyer nodded. He took a bite carefully with his plastic fork and wiped his mouth.

Winkler ventured further. "I was thinking about writing. Maybe a book, something for a wider audience."

"It's never so late you can't start again."

"I suppose not," Winkler said.

Later, after dessert and toasts, he walked the beach and watched the reflections of table lights play across the lagoon. Chici was still singing softly and his voice carried over the water. Someone was dancing on the deck — Soma, perhaps, her thin arms swaying back and forth like ropes.

Three days later he stood in the street in front of the butcher's to say good-bye to Naaliyah. The boys were there, and Felix in his cook's whites, and Soma. Chici had borrowed a truck and stood leaning against its fender, smoking a cigarette and periodically tapping its ashes against the edge of his sandal. The sky was huge and blue. Naaliyah wore a pair of canvas shorts, a tank top. Her hands worked over a trio of suitcases a hundred times.

Felix beamed as he produced a giant box sheathed in newspaper and ribbon. "What is this?" Soma asked. Felix winked.

Naaliyah removed the frangipani tucked under the bow and folded back the newspaper and opened the box. "Oh!" she said. She hauled out the contents: a puffy blue parka. The brothers laughed.

She pulled the coat over her bare arms and spun in it a few times. Chici pitched her bags into the flatbed. "Thank you, Papa," she said. Her mother looked away.

Winkler offered his present: a glass bottle, filled with seawater and stoppered. "So you don't forget what it's like at home," he said. She thanked him, tucked the bottle into a bag. Finally she made her way down the line, hugging her brothers, her mother. She finished with Winkler. "Come see me," she said.

He held on, the smell of her hair in his nose.

"I'll write. I'll miss you," she called. "I'll miss you all!" Then she was stepping into the cab, still wearing her oversized blue parka, and Chici was easing the truck out, up the black road, and they watched it get smaller and turn onto Bay Street, and she was gone.

11

In the evenings he sat with the butcher and unburdened himself. Furtive meetings with Sandy, leaving Alaska, the birth of Grace. Describing Anchorage or Cleveland brought those places back: the look of the Chagrin River rumbling brown and heavy beneath a bridge; the awful lurch of an Anchorage city bus on ice. All during the days, at unexpected moments, images — Sandy folding a sweater, or his father wheeling a dolly of milk crates — would seep in front of his eyes, as if by cracking the door on recollection, he was unable to shut it again, and now memories that had been staved off for years were shoving their way out.

And indeed in the fringes of sleep he was often back in his old life — a school bus turning into the middle school parking lot; yellow leaves hung up in a chain-link fence; Sandy's face beneath the high, blue light of the Fourth Avenue Theater. For long, tentative moments, just after waking, it would be as though he'd never left, and he often wondered if, in some divergent world, he hadn't — if he lived in Ohio still, staking tomato plants in the backyard, the Newport rusting in the driveway, the river slipping innocently past the end of the street.

He filled a third notebook with sketches and disjointed findings cribbed from books.

Our entire bodies, flooded with water, are governed by electricity. Bring any two molecules close enough together and they will repel each other. We cannot ever touch each other, not really. We repel at a distance. Actual touch — real contact — is not possible. A fistfight, one person lifting another, even sexual intercourse — what you feel is only electrical repulsion, maybe a few thousand molecules sloughing off your skin. Even our own bodies are not cohesive. Photons pass through our eyeballs, through the webbing of our fingers.

He began to dream of snow: ice glazing a parking meter; slush in the treads of Sandy's boots. There was the feeling of turning up blinds and seeing the whiteness of everything — snow on fence posts, snow limning branches — a banquet of light. He thought of his mother, and the way the mountains looked from the rooftop of his childhood: shimmering, insubstantial as ghosts.

He sat in the alley with only the light of the butcher's cigarette and the pale, reflected glow from the street lamps on the far wall. "You know why I left the States? You really want to know?" The butcher grunted. His hands smelled of bleach.

"I dreamed I was going to inadvertently kill my own daughter trying to save her from a flood."

The butcher nodded. "And did you?"

"No. But I may have left her to die. I may have left her to drown in our house."

"But you were not there when she drowned. You did not see her drowned."

"No. I fled. I came here."

Something rustled in the pile of boxes beside their chairs, then fell silent. The butcher carefully stretched his back. "You still don't see it?"

"See what?"

He shook his head. "This woman. Across the street. What did you dream when you dreamed her in the water?"

"I dreamed she would drown."

"But did she?"

"No."

The butcher inhaled and the tip of his cigarette flared and in the sudden light his features were antic and strange. "Maybe this is because you changed it. You altered it. Maybe you changed the dream with your daughter, as you did with the girl across the street. Now do you see?" He flicked away his cigarette and it fizzled in a puddle.

"But my wife sent a letter."

"And said your daughter is dead?"

"No. Well. No, she did not say that."

Suddenly Winkler was standing, backing against the wall.

"So you see it then," the butcher said. He passed a hand over his thin scrub of hair. "You see."

But Winkler was already clanging up the stairs, in the hot, frog-loud night.

Hope was a sunrise, a friend in an alley, a whisper in an empty corridor. All night he stayed awake, pacing, making notes, going to the window. It felt as if a last lock had ruptured: the hinges were giving way; light was rushing in.

In his fingers he could feel Grace's forearm, bonelessly soft. He smelled her: the smell of a crushed maple leaf; he remembered that Sandy could vacuum beneath the crib and still Grace would not wake. And the crib itself — enameled metal, the feeling of the screws in his fingers as he'd assembled it . . . If she had lived, if she had lived. The phrase vibrated dangerously in his brain. If she had lived, she could right now stroll down Market Street and he would not know it. That very day he had passed a half dozen possibilities: a newlywed strolling the beach, another paddling a rented kayak slowly across the harbor. A blonde with plump, sunburned calves examining lemons at the market; a freckled redhead turning magazine pages on a hotel balcony. Was one of them Grace? Was it so impossible? A woman now, a wife, a tourist who swam the breaststroke in a resort pool, or held hands with an overloud car salesman, or ordered carrot sticks from Felix's kitchen?

The rich, sudden smell of Sandy's hair — the smell of metal in it, tin or lead — used to stay on his fingers all day. The way she rubbed her feet together even as she slept; the way she would pull hairs from her hairbrush and drop them onto the floor of the bathroom instead of into the trash — it was as if all these memories had been hibernating in him, not dead but merely dormant, weathering it out, and now they stumbled out of their thousand dens.

The butcher had said: "Now do you see?" He scrambled for a notebook.

I have not seen snow since 1977. But now, in my mind, I see it perfectly: Flurries swirling through the beam of a street lamp. Like tiny dried flowers. Like a million insects. Like angels descending.

12

David —

*You were right about this city. It is gray
and bleak, but also beautiful in many
ways. I especially love the lakes. The other
day I brought my lunch to Lake Hood and
watched the float planes land and take off
— over a hundred in a single afternoon.*

*I'm studying insects now. Their similari-
ties to shrimps are astounding. The work is
not as hard as I expected, and I'm doing
better (I think) than most of the others.
Next winter there is an opportunity to
study cold weather insects in the north. I
hope to go, but Professor Houseman says it
will be difficult and very cold, too cold for
someone from such a warm place. What
does he know? I trust you are well. Hi to
everyone.*

He went to sea one last time in a rowboat.
He lay across the thwarts and felt the water
raise the boat and set it back down, and
stared at the sky a long time.

The day he left for college his father had waited on the landing, a string of smoke rising from a cigarette in his fingers. What had they said to each other? Maybe a good-bye, maybe nothing. Winkler had set down his cardboard box of books and grasped his father's hand. After his mother had died, he and his father lived together like timid roommates, almost strangers, never touching, speaking softly over meals about nothing important. Each evening his father sat in his chair and smoked and read the *Anchorage Daily News* cover to cover. This was how he had finished out his days: brokenhearted; smoke suspended around him like grief; settling into the rituals of newspaper stories — lost hunters, plane crashes, basketball scores — wheeling dollies of milk into the backs of stores.

He turned the boat and rowed back. The sun was over Soufrière and the sea was drenched with light. He paused a minute and feathered the oars and let them drip.

The passport had taken two months. After that it went quickly. He booked a ticket, returned his library books, told the butcher he'd be moving out. He visited Nanton, and they stood on the porch sipping tea, saying nothing much, and when his mug was empty Nanton nodded and went back inside to tend to a guest.

Fifty-nine years old and what had he accumulated? Two dozen pieces of staghorn coral, each smaller than the next. His nerite shells from the windowsill of the shed. A pair of avocado seedlings in ceramic pots. A couple towels, a couple sets of clothes. In Kingstown he went to a tailor and ordered a two-button suit, gray with high-notched lapels. He bought two white shirts and a nylon duffel bag. At the bank he withdrew his savings and exchanged the currency, $6,047 U.S., his life's savings.

The night before he was to leave, a uniformed driver knocked on his door and said a car was waiting. In the street the butcher stood smiling. "On me," he said. The driver took Winkler to the ferry, which brought him the six miles across the channel. At the inn Nanton led him across the rope bridge to the restaurant. "Your friend," he said. "He wanted to do this."

A table was set with linen and a single votive. Felix brought out chicken and slips of eggplant fried crisp. "One of Soma's birds," he said. He stood beside Winkler, sipping a short glass of rum. Afterward they led him to a room where he lay down for the night on a king-sized poster bed with mosquito netting and a ceiling fan.

In the morning he shaved in the porcelain sink mounted on the bathroom wall — a sink he himself had installed twenty-three years before. He dressed in his new suit, distributed his money into his shoes and each of his pockets. Then he made the bed, collected his duffel, and went through the lobby, across the glass floor. From the porch he peered out at the lagoon and grounds one more time. Tacit good-byes: the reef, the shed, the breadfruit tree.

He walked to Soma and Felix's, climbing through the sheep paddock and stepping carefully over the fence so as not to catch his pants on the wire. At the top he paused and peered back down into the cove where the lobby of the inn stood on its stanchions in the early light. It looked like an architectural model down there, idealized and small, nestled into the cove, something close to how Nanton had probably always wanted it to look. Then he descended the grassy field to the blue house with its crack running through the center and the tiny boats crowding the sills. Soma was in the doorway. She folded her arms around him.

"You can come back."

He nodded. They separated; she fished a

handkerchief from a back pocket and blew into it.

Behind her shoulder Felix smiled. "Ready?"

"Before you go," Soma said, "I have something." She set a wristwatch into his hand — his watch.

He turned it over in his hands. "You saved this?"

"You still owe me for a phone call."

Winkler smiled. "We can take you across," Felix said. Soma stood beside him with her arms crossed over her chest.

"I'd rather take the ferry."

"We'll take you."

"No," Winkler said. "Thank you."

They stood a moment longer, in the kitchen, Soma with her big crucifix lying atop her blouse and Felix with his hands folded over his belly, the smells of that kitchen and the eggs stacked on the counters and the old picnic table and the hens outside and the tradewinds muscling through the window screens all suddenly and plainly obvious to Winkler — all this family's thousand kindnesses, their own expulsion still not finished, their haunting, perhaps, more permanent than his own.

Before he left, Felix gave him a pair of meat pies, wrapped in newspaper. His last image was of the pair of them standing at the gate, a dozen or so hens like shadows scratching in the dust around their feet.

The ferry ride across the channel was like a film running in reverse. From the stern he watched the jetty recede, and the small pastel shapes of the fishermen's pirogues, and the ferry churned and shifted slightly and thirty or so scuba tanks stacked along the stern rang against one another as the diesel pushed through the gap in the reef, past the big combers to the east, past the two lonesome channel markers, their bottom halves crusted white.

Book Four

1

Flight attendants collected cups and newspapers; passengers levered their seats forward. From the window he watched the city of Miami assemble itself: antennas and rooftops gliding into view, two trucks like toys curling through a freeway exit, a green band of smog hovering over the shoreline. A crowded marina scrolled past, each boat's windshield in turn reflecting the sun.

From the wing came the whine of flaps threading down. The runway whisked beneath them; the wheels touched, a slight jolting, and their bodies tilted forward as the airplane decelerated.

Beside him the woman clapped her novel shut and tucked it into the leather bag between her feet. Without turning to him, she said, "When you got on, you saw the bin wasn't latched. That's all."

The jet taxied into its gate. Passengers stood, yawned, hauled bags out from overhead compartments. "I —" he began.

"You could have at least relatched it.

Now Dirk's martini glasses are all ruined."

He pretended to busy himself with magazines in the seat pocket in front of him. The woman and Dirk pushed into the aisle. The frost on the window, Winkler saw, had softened to water. He had meant to watch it change.

In the terminal he waited for his connection and scanned commuters as they rushed past, families, businessmen. There was a certain transparency to them, tides of human beings washing back and forth, and to what end? An enormous woman settled into the seat next to him, pulled a cinnamon roll from a wax paper bag, and put half of it in her mouth.

Our bodies are water, too, he wrote in his pad. *Our skin and eyeballs. Even the parts we think will last: fingernails, bones, hair. All of us. It's no wonder doctors keep it in intravenous bags, at the ready. We are dust only after all our water evaporates.*

On the flight to Cleveland he sat by the window and grappled with a slow and unyielding nausea. States slipped beneath: Georgia, North Carolina, West Virginia, low hills broken by the geometric quilting of fields. The sky darkened toward violet. Platoons of cumuli ascended past the window, each shot through with light.

★ ★ ★

An airport hotel in Cleveland. A hot shower, condensation on the mirror. He lay on the coverlet watching steam roll out of the bathroom and dissipate into the room.

Every few minutes a jet landed or took off, quaking the window glass. Soon a thin, almost granular light seeped through the curtain. If he had slept at all he was not aware of it. He dressed in his suit and went to the lobby and paged through a newspaper (the president denying rumors of war; Asian smog clouds threatening millions; home sales up, prices down), heading for the classifieds.

Only one of the lobby payphones accepted coins. A local call cost 30 cents. He dialed a number and an hour later a boy and his father were in the parking lot walking Winkler around their Datsun. "Most of the miles are highway," the father said. "Got a nice sporty clutch. Good brakes. Just rust-proofed it."

Winkler tried to remember what was expected of him. He nudged a tire with the toe of his shoe; he checked the odometer — 110,000 miles.

"Fine," he said, and ran a finger over the hood. "I'll take it." Eight hundred dollars.

He pulled the bills from his pocket and folded them into the boy's palm and the father signed over the title and all three of them shook hands and the car was Winkler's.

He checked out of the hotel, took his packet of nerite shells from his duffel, and aligned them in front of the speedometer largest to smallest. A memory of his old Newport rose: the smell of vinyl, the feel of the starter grinding against the cold. That expanse of hood stretched out in front of him, reflecting sky.

It was August 2002. He didn't have a driver's license, didn't have insurance. With a magnifying glass he studied a road map left in the glovebox. A convulsion of freeways. He eased the key into the ignition, cranked it, and the car gasped to life.

2

The boy had outfitted the dashboard with a low-end Hifonics digital receiver with push-button volume controls that Winkler could not figure out how to turn down. Electric guitar screamed out of speakers in the door panels. He stabbed buttons randomly as he drove but managed only to stop the tuner halfway between stations. Static deluged the car, punctuated by bursts of distant-sounding jazz. He rolled down the windows.

The roadsides had changed — a strip mall at an intersection; new developments labeled Meadowlark Ridge or Woodchuck Hollow — but the roads themselves were the same: the same iron bridge over Silver Creek, the same low and comfortable hill on Fortier Avenue, even the same weeds along the shoulder: Queen Anne's lace and thistle bucking in the wake of a passing car.

At a convenience store he bought three wilted roses wrapped in cellophane and drove with them in his lap. Despite the howl of static, his heart was oddly steady; the Datsun griped through its gears.

East Washington, Bell Road, Music Street. The middle school — still a middle school! — marquee read: CONGRATULATIONS BOMBERETTE DANCE TEAM! In front of the entrance a giant poplar he didn't remember stood sentinel. The parking lot was empty, save a trio of school buses parked at the back. He turned in and switched off the car and the speakers mercifully stopped their hissing.

He had spent one August in Ohio, a month of thunder: distant clouds in the far corner of the sky muttering most mornings; by afternoon whole colonies of storms illuminated in the radar's sweeping radius, like spots of blood saturating a disc of gauze. By evenings, he remembered, the air would get so heavy with moisture he imagined he could feel each bloated molecule as it toppled into his lungs.

Memories heaved up: a ball of hail melting in his palm; sheets of rain overwhelming the windshield; a calendar darkening and turning in the whirlpool of the basement stairwell. The goose-shaped knocker. A smell of acetylene rising through kitchen floorboards. This place was the Ohio he had left, but it wasn't, too:

the hurtling traffic, a buzzing electrical tower where he was certain a tract of forest had been twenty-five years before.

He got out of the Datsun and exhaled. This was just a day. Just a late-summer morning, a few stratus clouds skimming over fields. To a passing car he would be nothing more than a man out for a walk. Who knew — maybe he had a family here; maybe — in some fundamental way — he *belonged*. He took the roses, locked the Datsun, and started up Shadow Hill Lane. A warm wind eased past.

Here was the subdivision, all the houses still standing: the Stevensons', the Harts', the Corddrys'. On the Corddrys' mailbox stood a new, hand-lettered sign: THE TWEEDYS. In the driveway that had been the Sachses', a bald man in painter's coveralls took a bucket from the back of a van and carried it inside. There was no sign of the fallen sugar maple, just a young crabapple besieged by tent caterpillars.

He peeked inside the Harts' mailbox, where a yellow strip of tape read *Mr. Bill Calhoun.* The same was true of the Stevensons: moved away, replaced by another name, updated lives.

New houses had been built at the end of the cul-de-sac — smarter-looking houses, with skylights and outdoor central-air units and art deco numerals. An image of the road awash in floodwater flashed in front of his eyes, flotsam and detritus, swirling brown water, his legs locked around a mailbox post.

Still, he could not suppress tendrils of hope: Sandy coming to the door, photos of Grace hanging in the hall, an eventual reconciliation. Had he wanted so much from life? An interesting job, a view of sky. A car to wash in the driveway. Sandy plucking weeds from a flower bed; his daughter pedaling a bike cautiously to the curb. A straightforward, anonymous existence. The odds were astronomical, he knew, but his brain floated the idea forth — they could be here — and he was reluctant to dispel it.

He scanned the houses but could not discern a trace of flood damage. Warps in the frames? Stains on the foundations? He saw nothing. It was as if the entire place had been rebuilt, the old houses hauled away, memories erased. Grass, trees, birds — even the smell of barbecue somewhere — every sound and sight bore a quiet, summertime complacency: no mysteries here, no secrets.

But everywhere corpses were rising from

graves, shambling toward him: the odor of wet, mown grass, of weeds, of the river — each was a key to a memory: the card table in the kitchen, leaves in the backyard, a slap across the face.

Four houses, three houses, two. The cellophane around the roses crackled in his fist. "She won't be here," he said. "Neither of them will be here." Still, spiders of sweat crawled his ribs.

Nine-five-one-five Shadow Hill Lane. The saplings flanking the front walk were now rangy, gangling adults. The walk and driveway were the same, the hedges unruly and full. The same eaves. The same front steps. A new garage huddled at the end of the driveway, clumsily built. In one of the downstairs windows a chain of paper dolls, taped to the glass, held hands.

He could see Sandy taking Grace inside, lowering her into the bath. Clumps of snow dashed against the kitchen window. In our memories the stories of our lives defy chronology, resist transcription: past ambushes present, and future hurries into history.

The brass knocker had been replaced by a doorbell. An orange bulb behind the button flickered. It was strange to think that something added to this house after he had last been there had already become old in the interim.

A piece of slate suspended above the bell was engraved THE LEES. He wiped his palms on his pants and rang the bell. The door was maroon now, and the paint was flaking off. I'll repaint it for them, he thought. I could do that today. Think of the things he could do: edge the beds, weed the lawn, pry moss from the sidewalk cracks — he'd cook them dinner; he'd defrost their freezer. Whomever Mr. Lee was, a guar- dian, Sandy's husband, he wouldn't mind; he'd shake Winkler's hand, invite him into the backyard — by the end of the night they'd embrace like brothers.

There was a shuffling inside and a Korean woman came to the door holding a puppy. She squinted through the screen. "Yes?"

"Oh," Winkler said. Over her shoulder, in the hall, the closet door had the same plastic knobs on it. "You live here? This is your home?"

"Of course." She raised her eyebrows. "Are you all right, sir?"

"And no one named Sandy lives here?"

"No. Is this — ?"

He thrust the flowers at her. "These are for you."

She pushed the screen open a foot and took them and let the door close again. The dog sniffed the cellophane. She turned the bouquet to see if there might be a card.

"It's a nice house," Winkler said.

She looked up expectantly. "Are these from you?"

He shrugged, tried a half wave as he backed off the stoop. The heel of his shoe caught, and he staggered backward onto the walk.

"Sir?" she called.

"I'm okay," he said. She closed the door, and he heard it latch. Blinds in the front windows louvered shut, one after another.

He gathered himself, trembling lightly, and continued to the end of the street, past the end of the cul-de-sac, through a backyard, to the edge of the river. The water was sluggish and low. The caps of a few stones showed above the surface, pale with dried mud. On the far bank, the trees had been thinned and he could see the decks and backyard swing sets of another neighborhood. He listened: a low murmur, a thousand tiny splashes. Somewhere above that, the sound of traffic. That was it. A meek, brown river purling along.

3

Buildings looked smaller, sidewalks more crowded, traffic more hurried, parking meters more expensive. He was unused to seeing shoulder belts in cars, locks on doors, screens on windows, blankets on beds. The smell of the falls, the grapevine of the gazebo, the revolutions of the barber pole — they all seemed smaller, less compelling than he remembered. Other changes were more obvious: the Chagrin Department Store was now The Gap. Goodtown Printers was Starbucks. All the clichés held fast. You can't go home again. It seems like only yesterday.

By noon he was in the Chagrin Falls Library, scrolling unsuccessfully through microfiche of 1977 *Plain Dealer*s. A volunteer pointed him toward a desk where a ponytailed man sat rapt before a computer monitor. "He can help you," she said. "Gene knows the archives as well as anybody."

Gene sat in a wheelchair, a chubby torso balanced over disconcertingly still legs. He held up a finger, typed something on his keyboard, then looked up and clasped his hands over his gut.

"I'm trying to find somebody," Winkler said. "Two people. My daughter. Her name is Grace. Grace Winkler. And my wife, Sandy. They lived here a long time ago. They might be in Alaska now."

Gene pulled down the corners of his bottom lip and inhaled. "I can do addresses in national White Pages and *ReferenceUSA*. Real estate records, maybe. That's about it. You want more, you'll need a private investigator. It can get spendy. Are they hiding?"

"Hiding? I don't know."

"You have social security numbers?"

"Not by heart." A black spot was slowly opening across his field of vision. He leaned on Gene's desk. "I have money," he said. He set a hundred-dollar bill on the keyboard. Then another. Gene looked at the bills a moment, then slipped them inside a fold in his wheelchair. "Okay," he said. "Sandy with a *Y?*"

Winkler dragged a chair from a nearby table and sat down. He had seen desktop computers only in the back of the island church and inside the Shell station, but this machine was larger and sleeker and its hum more quiet and powerful. Gene piloted it with unnerving speed, unleashing a stroboscope of websites; leads, dead ends, more leads. Winkler couldn't make out much, a logo for Switchboard.com, another for something called U.S. Search. Gene breathed slowly through his nose; occasionally his fingers burst into an avalanche of keystrokes.

"Nothing here," he said, "not in Cleveland . . . I can try by age. . . . She married?"

"Married?"

"The girl. Grace. Is she married?"

"I don't know."

Gene turned from the screen a moment to look at Winkler, then looked back. "It's okay, Pops. Go get some water. It'll be all right."

Winkler sat beside him for over three hours. Gene tried everything he said was "in the book" and some things that weren't — marriage certificate databases, real estate transactions, quasi-legal pay-search systems, IRS audit lists. "If they're married, man, or changed their names," Gene said, "we're pretty much screwed." But he tried — his fingers rattled keys; he elicited two more hundred-dollar bills from Winkler. He searched Ohio, Alaska, credit reports, criminal records, a directory for nationals currently living out of the country, an FBI search engine not meant for librarians.

At first there were too many, several hundred at least, daunting numbers, a world populated with Grace and Sandy Winklers. But they were able to rule out some because of age, some because of nationality, a few because of race.

"Anchorage?" asked Winkler. "None in Anchorage?"

"None in Alaska. No Grace Winklers. There's an Eric and Amy Winkler."

"What about Sheelers?"

A burst of keystrokes. The computer searched. "None in Anchorage. There's a Carmen Sheeler in Point Barrow. I don't see a single Grace Sheeler under sixty years old in the whole country."

Winkler pinched his temples and tried to hang on.

"The cops could do better," Gene said. "They've got access to fingerprints, of course, and to CCSC, which I can't touch."

Screens succeeded one another across the monitor. It was well into the afternoon before Gene paused. He did not look at Winkler. "Should I do obituaries?"

"I don't know."

"You know they're not," Gene asked, and cleared his throat, "or you hope they're not?"

Heat, and a rising acidity. He studied one of the wheels on Gene's chair, the treads worn shiny, a wad of chewing gum anchoring a loose spoke. "Hope," he said. In his mind's eye he could see Nanton leaning on his elbow at the desk of his hotel, waiting for guests. A few gray chubs circling in the water beneath the glass floor. He could see the butcher seated on his crate in his bloody apron, smoking a cigarette. Gene shifted in his wheelchair and a smell rose from the seat: musty, overused. "I'll just take a look," he said.

Winkler tried to remember the feeling of Grace in his arms, the weight and warmth of her, but all he could think of was his mother's plants, how in the spring after she had died, he had gone up to the roof and tried to restart her garden but overwatered the seedlings. How months later he had to drag her pots and planters, heavy with soil, down to the street and upend them into a Dumpster.

After a few minutes Gene fumbled for his mouse and blanked the screen. He pivoted his chair back from the desk and turned to Winkler. "Tell you what, come back in an hour."

"I could search on another machine."

"It's okay. I'll get it done. And look, Pops. Make sure you remember one thing. The world is a big, big place. Huge. It may be crisscrossed with fiber optics and spy satellites, but there are still plenty of pockets to hide in. Plenty. I can get you a list of maybe half your Sandys and Graces. I can find the taxpaying ones."

"Half?"

"Maybe more. Maybe all of them. Maybe I'll find every damn one of them."

Winkler nodded.

"All right," said Gene. "You sweet on these girls, then?"

"Something like that."

"They really your family?"

"Yes."

"You going to write them? All the ones I find?"

"I'll go see them. I wouldn't know what to put in a letter."

"Well." Gene turned back to the screen. "See you in an hour."

He walked to Dink's and chewed fish sticks at a veneered table and scanned customers for familiar faces but found none.

Traffic slid past and a police officer drove an electric cart up and down the street ticketing cars. Out the window clouds gradually sealed off the sky. Near the edge of his view, beyond the wall of the candy store, hung a rippling parcel of air, heavy with mist. Just below it, out of sight, the river slipped under Main and over the falls.

When he returned to the library Gene was gone. He had left a manila envelope, which Winkler brought to a carrel. Inside were five folded sheets of paper and the four hundred-dollar bills, all returned. No note.

The first two pages consisted of a list of five Sandy Winklers and eight Sandy Sheelers. He scanned the addresses: Texas, Illinois, two in Massachusetts. No Alaska. The second two pages listed Grace Winklers, nine Graces sprinkled throughout the states. A Grace Winkler in Nebraska, another in Jersey, another in Boise, Idaho.

He could not take his eyes from the name, repeated nine times in black letters, above an address and a phone number. Grace Winkler, 1122 Alturas, Boise, Idaho. Grace Winkler, 382 East Merry, Walton, Nebraska. These names corresponded to real, living women, women with phone numbers and hairdos and histories. He

352

pictured a daughter in some event — graduation or a field hockey game — scanning the crowd, wondering if her father was there, cheering her on. Was it any better if she had lived? To have abdicated all that responsibility?

The last sheet of paper was a photocopy of an obituary notice from the *Anchorage Daily News*, dated June 30, 2000. Even before he reached the end of the first sentence, the air went out of him.

Anchorage resident Sandy Winkler, 59, died May 19, 2000, at Providence Alaska Medical Center due to complications from ovarian cancer. A service of remembrance will be held at 4 p.m., Thursday, at Evergreen Memorial Chapel, 737 E Street. Burial is Friday, at the Heavenly Gates Perpetual Care Necropolis at Mile 14 of the Glenn Highway.

Ms. Winkler was born Aug. 25, 1941, at Providence Hospital in Anchorage. She was a graduate of West High School and worked at First Federal Savings and Loan, Northrim Bank and Alaska Bank of the North.

She enjoyed movies and served as secretary for the Northern Lights Film

Society. She also enjoyed sculpture, pets, and cruise ships. During summers she volunteered at the Downtown Saturday Market.

Her family writes: "Sandy had a big heart. She was kind and compassionate to friends and strangers alike. We will always remember her quick wit, smile, and dedication to her job."

Memorials may be sent to the charity of the donor's choice.

There was a grainy pixilated photo. Beneath his magnifying glass it looked more like a distorted mash of dots than a face. But he could see her inside the pattern: the high cheeks, the off-axis smile. It was Sandy. She wore a pair of tortoiseshell eyeglasses, updated for style. Her eyes were trained on something to the left of the camera. She looked thin and bemused, a prettier, more tragic version of the woman he had known.

She enjoyed sculpture. Pets and cruise ships. She had kept his name. He lowered his head to the desk. All I have to do is wake up, he thought. If I concentrate I will wake up.

Her family writes. Was it Herman? Why was there no "survived by"?

Someone had carved graffiti into the writing surface: *TM loves SG*. He did not see how he could sit there one more second but he couldn't get up either, so he waited and listened to the blood moving through him and ran his fingers over the letters as though they contained some colossal and imperative meaning he couldn't quite crack.

After a while — he would have been unable to say how long — a closing announcement burbled through loudspeakers above the shelves. The lights dimmed. A woman touched him on the shoulder. "Time to go."

He tucked the four hundred dollars and the lists of Sandy Sheelers and Sandy Winklers inside the envelope and handed it to her. "Give this to Gene," he said.

In the parking lot he sat in the Datsun with the list of Grace Winklers in his lap. Beyond him was the town of Chagrin Falls, the neatly painted storefronts, Yours Truly and Fireside Books, the candy-striped Popcorn Shop. Through the drone of traffic, the clanging of a Dumpster somewhere, through the shifting leaves and a lawnmower growling behind the library, even beneath the sound of his own, faltering breath, he could hear it: the rumbling, the long plunge, the churning of the falls.

After a long time he turned the key; static roared from the speakers.

4

She liked cruise ships? Did they mean she liked looking at them? He tried to imagine Sandy finishing out her days in an Anchorage savings and loan, wearing her bank teller smile, cashing people's social security checks. A ranch house, a weedy lawn, a snowblower, an infertile ex-husband, a closet full of cheap shoes. Pain gathered behind his eyes. I hope they gave her cereal, he thought. I hope they brought her Apple Jacks.

From a motel room near Mansfield he managed to get an operator to give him the telephone number for the Evergreen Memorial Chapel in Anchorage. A woman answered; he asked to speak with anyone who might know something about a memorial service for Sandy Winkler in May of 2000. Twice the receptionist asked his name. She put the phone down. He waited. Hold music started.

The lamp beside the telephone buzzed softly and his fingers left tracks in the dust on its shade. She kept him on hold a long time. When she came back on, she said: "Looks like Reverend Jody Stover did that one. He's since moved to Houston. About two years ago."

"I see," Winkler said. "Houston?"

What had he hoped for? Every answer handed to him the moment his plane touched down? An envelope in a safe deposit box, a note taped to the door of 9515 Shadow Hill Lane? He could not face any of it, not yet: the idea that Herman might have shared so much of her life, that Herman might have had the final say. He almost drove back to the library, asked Gene to find Herman.

But it seemed too awful to contemplate, too impossible: Herman the goaltender, Herman the banker, Herman the victor. These things were not about winning or losing, Winkler knew, but clearly Herman had won. Sandy was dead. Herman, ultimately, had been her husband.

At dawn he sat in the motel's diner over a plate of hash browns with the roster of Grace Winklers beside his plate. Sandy had returned to Anchorage after the flood and it seemed likely now that she'd never left again. She'd sent the box of returned letters from there; she'd worked for North-

358

rim Bank there. She'd died there.

But there were no Grace Winklers in Anchorage. And no Grace Sheelers anywhere. Winkler forced himself to consider it — he had been a scientist, after all, he could think analytically. Grace lived in Anchorage under another name, or she, too, was dead, or she had moved away. If the latter, she could be on his list, one of the nine. And this possibility was the one his mind fixed on. She had grieved her mother, left home, started anew. On a three-dollar U.S. map he dotted the locations: Jackson, Tennessee; Middletown, New Jersey; San Diego, California, six others. Then he linked them. The route made a sort of broad, warped loop; a femur shape, a stretched and broken heart: Ohio to New Jersey, south to Virginia, down to Tennessee, across to Nebraska, then Texas, New Mexico, California, Idaho.

New Jersey first: 5622 Skyridge Avenue, Middletown.

He tore Sandy's photo out of the obituary and anchored it in a groove in the dashboard. She stared off to her left, in the slightly cross-eyed way she'd always had, as if she were gazing out the car window at something perplexing. At a gas station he paid an attendant five dollars to permanently sever the power to the car stereo.

Those first miles — despite everything — were miles of hope. Coffee, a straightforward silence in the Datsun's cabin, a list of nine potential daughters — the odds didn't seem so insurmountable. The country was not such a big place. Already he was nearing Pennsylvania. Green faded into green faded into blue.

Along those miles, and the miles to come, he crossed and recrossed a thousand reinventions of his daughter: Grace as housewife, apron lashed to her hips, biscuit dough drying on her fingers. Maybe a tiny granddaughter, polite, madly pleased, some pureed squash smeared across her cheeks, pushing back from the table. Grandfather, she would say, and curtsy, and giggle. Grandfather: like a father who had succeeded so well and so long he'd been promoted.

Grace as schoolgirl, ponytailed and prim, plaid skirt, high socks. Grace as ski racer, Grace as landscape painter, cartoonist, lounge singer, lover, surgeon, dental hygienist, head chef, senator, activist, cereal box designer. Grace as vice president of marketing research. Grace: five letters, a state of clemency, a beating heart.

He thought of Herman Sheeler composing Sandy's obituary, alone at a kitchen table; he heard Gene say, "The world is a big, big place." What of the nagging probability that Grace was gone, not on the earth but in it?

He would not allow himself such thoughts. Gene was chairbound and spent his days goggling at a computer monitor and did not know so much. There were plenty of places to look — nine, at least — and the road ran out like a blank scroll in front of him.

By afternoon his eyes were tiring: sedans floated and swam in the distance and were suddenly on him. Trucks roared past in the left lane, invisible until they were nearly past, spinning his heart in his chest.

Around dusk he left the interstate. Tidy green farms gave way to wild, independent-looking ones, buckling one-story farmhouses, cattle dragging their flanks against fence wire. Every few miles a low-slung convenience store touted lotto tickets and budget beer. Teenagers, scowling on the trunks of muscle cars, watched him pass.

The only motels were cinder block bunkers bathed in neon: the House-Key

Hotel, Jarett's Pay N' Sleep. His mind shaped itself around a notion of 5622 Skyridge Avenue: a guest room with a vase of dried sunflowers on the dresser, a quilt folded over the footboard. Maybe the smell of breakfast, and gulls outside the window, to wake him.

The road reopened into a highway that eventually dumped him onto the Garden State Parkway. The sheer volume of automobiles astounded. He kept as far right as he could. Echelons of tollbooths loomed every eleven miles. Twice he missed the coin basket and had to clamber out the driver's door and scrabble in the gravel for errant dimes.

An all-night photomat attendant off exit 114 gave him directions. It was after 11 p.m. His gut was empty and his back ached and his eyes felt full of sand. He would just take a look, then leave, go to a hotel, rest till morning.

Skyridge was a poorly lit, aging street: brown lawns, asbestos shingles, oversized hedges camped in front of windows. A stoplight flashed yellow; a raccoon sauntered across the road and disappeared into a storm drain.

Five-six-two-two blazed with light. Colorful plastic toys were spilled across the lawn; a sprinkler clicked back and forth. The house itself was single-story, dun-colored. Vines clambered up the siding; two of the three porch pillars had been kicked in, lending the facade a ruinous sag. But if she owned it, he decided, he would compliment her awning, the health of the plants.

Clearly someone was still awake. Every lightbulb in the house was turned on. And where was the nearest motel? He put on his suit jacket, buttoned his collar. Through a window he could see a couch, swathed in clear plastic. A cheap lamp over a side table. A lopsided fan turning. No books on the shelves — didn't she read? He tucked in his shirt and smoothed down the front of his jacket and brought his fist against the door.

Hardly a second later a shirtless boy opened it. His skin was black against his white underpants, and he stood turning the knob back and forth in his small hand.

Winkler cleared his throat. "Miss Winkler? Grace? Is she here?"

The boy looked over his shoulder at a closed door, then turned back.

"Could you tell her a visitor is here? A man with her same name? Tell her I'm sorry about the hour."

But the boy stood dumbly. Perhaps he was mute? Winkler called a "Hello?" into the room. "Grace? Miss Winkler?" He heard a toilet flush and a man turned out from some hallway and opened the closed door and the sound of voices and laughter rose from behind it. The man started down some stairs and the door shut behind him.

"Do you mind?" Winkler asked. The boy stepped aside and gave a sort of bow. Winkler crossed the room. A basement: shadows, a blue light. He could hear voices, but when he called hello down the stairwell, the noise ceased. "Miss Winkler?" The stairs were steep and the railing had been torn out. "Miss Winkler?"

She sat behind a bottle of bourbon on a card table. Even from the bottom of the stairs, twenty feet away, he could see she was not Grace, not his Grace — this woman had a broad face, flat nose, and big, black eyes that swiveled neatly in the domes of her sockets. Four heavyset African women lounged with her around the table. On shadowed lawn furniture about the circumference of the basement sat others, women and some men, a thin one sitting on the washing machine tapping his heels against the metal. All watched him and Grace shuffled a deck of cards without looking at it. She was thin and well-dressed and taken out of these surroundings might have been a marketing rep or copyright lawyer.

On the table beside her sat a homemade machine the size of a microwave with wires and tubes sticking off it. One of the women sitting nearby was clipped to it and, upon seeing Winkler, she slowly unclipped each wire and set them on the table and leaned back.

Winkler explained. "I'm looking for my daughter. I thought you might be her. But . . ."

Grace cut and recut the cards. "You don't know where your daughter is?"

"I've only begun to look." He pocketed his hands. "I haven't seen her in a long time."

"I see," she said. Did she? He could hardly even make out the other faces in the room. Were they sizing him up for the quality of his suit? Were they detaining him so neighbors could ransack his car?

In the room a quiet tension stretched out. There were small footsteps on the stairs behind him and the half-naked boy slipped past Winkler's leg and went to

Grace Winkler and stood beside her, a hand on her skirt, his eyes just clearing the tabletop.

"I should go," Winkler said.

"Stay a bit," Grace said.

"I don't mean to intrude." Was she angry? Smiling? It seemed as though she was smiling. The boy watched him. "You have guests."

"Not at all," she said. "No one minds. Jed here," she patted the boy's head, "was just using his future machine to tell Mrs. Beadle's fortune. Weren't you, Jed?" But the boy only looked at Winkler and did not nod or acknowledge him.

"I should be going," Winkler said.

"Stay," Grace Winkler said. "Someone give Mr. Winkler something to drink." The man on the washing machine stood and with one long arm extended to Winkler a forty-ounce bottle.

"Homebrew," he said, and smiled.

"There we are," said Grace.

Winkler nodded his thanks, uncapped the bottle, and took a drink. The liquid was warm and thick and, he thought, full of sediment. Grit accumulated in his teeth. Conversation resumed. The boy watched him with large white eyes.

"Jed built this future machine," Grace

said, "all on his lonesome. Isn't it something?"

The women around the table whistled. "Lookit here," said Mrs. Beadle, and pointed to an array of dials and switches drawn on the front of the box. "And here," another woman said. She ran her finger over a cluster of blue fibers — more wires, perhaps — that emerged from the box's top and ran out onto the table. "This is where the machine gets its power. Ain't that right, Jed?"

Again the boy did not respond. The beer in Winkler's bottle tasted like hot mulch. Already he could feel his lips numbing. After a while the boy turned to his mother and put his mouth against her ear and whispered.

"Jed here wants to know if you'd like to have your fortune told."

Winkler glanced about. "I really must get going. I've got to get a motel, early start tomorrow."

"Nonsense. You can sleep here. On the sofa. A man with my husband's name can stay with us one night."

"Well . . . ," said Winkler.

"Well, nonsense. Come over here. It won't hurt a bit."

Mrs. Beadle groaned up from her chair

and Winkler took her place. Again the boy whispered into Grace's hair. She laughed. "Jed says the future machine will need ten dollars before he can make it work."

"Ten dollars?"

The people in the room chuckled and the boy watched Winkler. Winkler handed over a bill. The boy folded it twice and poked it through a slot in his contraption.

Winkler could see the machine more clearly now — it looked like the body of an old television with all sorts of basement odds and ends crammed inside. The junction box from a ceiling fan, a simple two-wired motor, a copper pipe elbow. No part of it seemed integral to any other, as if Jed could upend it and dump out its parts with a single shake. But the boy was springing into action. He clipped alligator clips with wires trailing off the tails all over Winkler: to his tie, his cuff, one to the tip of his pinkie, another to his left earlobe. Winkler winced — it felt as if the clip had bitten into his skin and he was bleeding. The boy's hands whispered over him. Winkler reached for his ear.

"Don't take it off, Mr. Winkler," Mrs. Beadle said. "Won't take but a minute."

The boy's hands scuttled over the old television, aligning wires, pulling switches.

Then he lidded his eyes and paddled his arms back and forth. He took the long tress of fibers jutting through the top of the box and stroked and pulled them apart and spat in his hands and rubbed the saliva in.

Winkler lifted his bottle and took a long drink. Amazingly, the bottle was nearly empty. He felt a tingling all through his spine. Were they running a current through him? He thought of the photo of Sandy, up in the car, waiting for him.

"What does it say?" The boy opened his eyes and peered into his side of the box. Winkler tried to see Grace: her hair chopped at the neck, her wide black eyes, an unadorned string around her throat. Not his daughter at all.

"Jed says the future machine was able to see much. He says the future machine ranged across the blanket of time and gathered much information."

The boy glanced at the machine, bent over, and said more into his mother's ear. "Jed says to ask you, Mr. Winkler, if you are sure you want to know what the future machine says."

Winkler shifted in his seat and felt the room make a slow, fluid spin underneath him. He felt suddenly ridiculous and vain in his new suit: he would never find his daughter like this, drinking in some hot basement, enduring parlor tricks. "I'm not paying more," he said, "if that's what you mean."

The others in the room laughed. Grace held up a hand. "Jed says that to know what will come is sometimes the same as making it so."

Winkler swallowed. The boy whispered again. "Jed says you will have a long journey. He says the future machine tells only what it sees and not everything."

Winkler breathed a bit and smiled but Grace did not smile back. "Does it say where my daughter is?"

The boy rubbed his hands over the machine and the room seemed to collectively inhale and Winkler raised his empty bottle to his lips. Grace leaned over to listen and finally said: "The future machine says there are many Grace Winklers and all of them are the real Grace Winkler, so in that way your journey will never be done. He says you will see fire and you will die. The future machine says that to enter a world of shadows is to leave this world for another."

Winkler blinked. The boy came forward and began removing his alligator clips. "That's it?"

"That's it."

5

Someone left the kitchen faucet on and he woke to the sound of running water. On the carpet around the entrance to the basement stood a bevy of empty bottles. Winkler peeled himself from the plastic sofa and stumbled to the sink and shut it off. The house was empty and silent now save the lone dark child still in his underpants who crouched at the door eating animal crackers from a giant plastic tub. Winkler found his glasses on the sofa back and wiped them and put them on. The sky out the windows was gray and overcast. A pale fog slinked along the lawn.

"Hey," Winkler said. "Jed. What time is it?"

The boy did not turn or even flinch. There was an aching at the far back of Winkler's head and a general soreness in his limbs and he gathered his coat and in his rumpled suit unlatched the screen door and went down the steps to his car, which sat as he had left it, unmolested. Before he pulled away, he brought the Datsun beside the mailbox, pulled down the door, and set a hundred-dollar bill inside.

A motel north of D.C. He draped his coat on the table beside a broken television and took a sheet of stationery from the bedside drawer.

Dear Soma —
Supposedly there are over 13,000 Mc-Donald's restaurants in the United States. I drove here on an eight-lane freeway and passed five of them. I miss you and Felix. I miss the whole island. I even miss Nanton. There are comforts in knowing the boundaries of the place you live. Everyone here seems to behave like things are endless.
Once, before she was my wife, Sandy bought a sleeve of chocolate chip cookies and we ate them on a bench overlooking the ocean. I remember she was talking about something, but I couldn't listen. I was watching her lips move as she spoke, the curve of her jawbone. I wanted to grab her and hold her and feed her cookies. I didn't, though. I only watched her, the light on her face, a few stray hairs that had fallen over her ear.
You ever read your horoscope, go see a

fortune-teller? Do you think there's any-thing to people's desire to know what's coming? I always thought they just wanted to hear something nice, that their week will be a happy one, that they might meet somebody who will love them.

The Grace Winkler in Petersburg, Virginia, lived in a russet-colored condominium with a pair of overexcited Saint Bernards. She spoke to him through her screen door with one hand covering the mouthpiece of a cordless telephone. The Saint Bernards slavered at the screen and dripped big ropes of drool onto her bare feet. She listened to Winkler, then shook her head. "I grew up in Raleigh. I work for my dad's software company."

She called, "Good luck," after him, and pushed her huge dogs back from the door with her knees.

From a cavernous superstore outside Winston-Salem he mailed her two twenty-pound bags of premium dog food that cost more to ship than they did to buy. Families clambered in and out of cars in the parking lot. A close, damp sky hovered over them. Mothers, daughters, fathers — stocking their wagons like postmillennial pioneers: bricks of Miller Lite, foil pillows of Goldfish crackers, crates of Campbell's Beef & Noodle. Something caught in his throat and he began to cry.

One squirrel harrying another across the parking lot, an itch halfway up his arm — even in the midst of grief the mind grapples with a hundred impressions: a pain below the heart; an odor on the breeze. He thought of Sandy measuring milk for her cereal; he thought of her smile behind the bank counter, and the dark mouths of her boots standing on his bedroom floor. He thought of cancer devouring her ovaries; of bacteria, and beetles, and the grubs that had by now chewed their tunnels through her body, carrying her off, piece by piece.

The third Grace Winkler lived in Dyersburg, Tennessee, with a soft-spoken grandfather who asked Winkler to sit in a porch hammock while they waited for Grace to return from the night shift at a doughnut bakery. Lightning bugs rose through the spaces between branches. Winkler wondered: Would my daughter live here? He lay motionless in the netting, listening to the old man's dictums: Grace's father had been a master with drywall, her mother (the grandfather's daughter), the best nine-pin bowler in four counties. There were trophies to prove it. This Grace, when she returned, was at least two hundred pounds and looked precisely like a younger and more female version of her grandfather. She fed Winkler and the grandfather fried chicken thighs at three in the morning, a pair of candles burning on the table, tribes of bullfrogs rising to successive crescendos outside the windows. Afterward Grace and the grandfather fell asleep in her California king and left Winkler sweating in the grandfather's twin beneath a pile of afghans. He waited until he could hear the old man snoring, set a hundred-dollar bill on the nightstand, and slipped down the porch, through the humid starlight.

It took a day and a half of driving to cross Missouri and a corner of Kansas into Nebraska. The open ends of cornfield rows ticked past like turnstiles. Six Graces left and he could feel his hope wilting. The country was huge and trafficked and hot. Everything moved more quickly than he imagined it would: music, travel, images projected on screens. Only his search seemed slower, longer, already interminable.

By Lincoln the Datsun was spitting black smoke and listing badly to the right.

Parked, it left pools of oil on the pavement and he had to begin carting a two-gallon jug of Valvoline in the hatchback and draining it into the black and smoking filler neck whenever he stopped for gasoline.

A hollowness settled into him. A feeling like the corridors of his body were cobwebbed and vacant. He lay on a hotel mattress with the air conditioner on high and the TV forecasting temperatures in Hanoi, Istanbul, Jakarta.

There was the Grace Winkler of Walton, Nebraska, now Grace Lanfear, a subdued woman who said probably five words to Winkler and served him the greatest macaroni and cheese he'd ever eaten. She lived in a two-bedroom ranch house with train tracks running through the backyard and a kitchen that reeked of bird droppings. He met Geoff Lanfear, a gangling and excitable husband who spouted all evening about education technologies: "What do you think the classroom is going to look like in 2020, Dr. Winkler? Take a guess!" He showed Winkler his birds: a cockatoo, an African gray parrot, twenty cockatiels in a cage the size of Geoff's minivan. During dessert a freight train stampeded through the backyard, rattling the pictures on the walls and the plates on the table. The family chewed on as if their eardrums had been plucked from their heads. The birds sent up a death racket from the garage.

What Winkler took from there was the macaroni and cheese, in a Tupperware bowl, tasting of Parmesan and bay leaves, a triad of flavors, first the bread crumbs, then the bay, finally the cheese and butter. He ate it for breakfast the next morning on the side of the road, using his fingers for a spoon.

In Austin, Texas, he tripped on the front stairs of Grace Winkler's townhouse and put his teeth partway through his tongue. She was a large Englishwoman who shoved kitchen towels at him and told him to spit the blood in her sink. "My God!" she kept saying. "Holy crap!" She taught at the University of Texas and drove a Datsun identical to Winkler's. No kids. A father back in Manchester. She had antique-looking photos of menorahs on her walls and a giant brass clock, twice as tall as him, shaped like a sun. Who knew?

Dear Soma —

Today a stranger at a truck stop sold me two dozen cans of soup and an "emergency kit." He had maybe a thousand American flag buttons pinned to his jacket. "You've got to keep this stuff in your trunk," he said. "You never know what will happen." And I was so persuaded, so convinced that he was on to something original, what he said about the not knowing. I practically stuffed money into his pockets.

At nights I page through my notebooks and wonder what to do with all these drawings, all this stuff I've gathered about water. Most of it makes very little sense. I have written here that two hundred years ago Urbano d'Aviso theorized that steam consisted of bubbles of water filled with fire, ascending through the air. What do I do with that?

More than once, I admit, I've imagined a ridiculous triumphant publication with lots of people and newspaper articles. My daughter smiling in the front row, flash-bulbs, all that. Ridiculous. I haven't even taken any notes in a week. The whole thing feels like a pool of water that I'm trying to hold in my hands.

Did you know students in U.S. schools now take notes not on paper but on computers? Half the drivers that pass me are talking on cellular phones.

When I sleep now I pray I'll dream of Grace but my dreams are crazy: the bath-

room is stuffed with ice; angels wearing sneakers chase me through the halls of my college dormitory. All I really remember when I wake is that they were bad dreams, and kept me from sleeping.

I've visited five Graces now. Maybe it is stupid to continue; maybe I ought to go to Anchorage and find Naaliyah, see if anyone there can tell me what happened. Perhaps Herman, my wife's first husband. But it seems easier — and better — to do it this way, to try to find her on my own. My best to Felix.

A hundred anonymous dollars in a stamped envelope for Grace in Walton; another hundred for Grace in Austin.

Motel rooms blended in his memory, a mash of polyester bedspreads, air conditioners, soap wrapped in paper. Mirrors were the worst, always big and garishly lit, always revealing an image of himself he cringed to see: a gaunt, white-haired stranger in rumpled underwear, twin ladders of ribs up his sides, a face pinched by glare, permanent hollows beneath his eyes. He learned to draw curtains, use bathrooms in the dark.

In Socorro, New Mexico, a bank sign

read 109 degrees Fahrenheit. The gravel between the Datsun and the front door was so hot he could hear it sizzle. This Grace was a twenty-year-old beauty in a floor-length nightgown who hovered behind the screen giving him laconic answers (" 'Course I know my daddy") until her father appeared in the hallway. "Out," he said, and clapped his hands as if Winkler were a dog that needed frightening. He was a mousy man striped with tattoos and his arms looked capable of nasty, redundant violence.

Winkler veered back the way he came, his shells rattling and sliding across the dash. The car shuddered and limped; the father's words rolled in the passages of his ears like pebbles: *Your. Daughter. Ain't. Here.*

West of there he turned onto I-10 and tried to lose himself in a current of westbound trucks. The whole of the country was off to his right, shining up into the sky. Electric wires slung past in shallow parabolas from tower to tower. Mirages loomed in the distance like lagoons into which the Datsun could plunge. Sandy, immured in her yellowing photograph, watched it all pass.

As he came out of a truck stop bathroom

east of Tucson, he paused in front of a payphone. Rust-colored foothills burgeoned the horizon and heat blurs rose in the distances. The bug-spattered Datsun looked horrific, like some primitive beast driven through the apocalypse and deposited next to the gas pumps to die. The thought of climbing back into the driver's seat made him want to retch.

He pulled Gene's list from his pocket. Three Graces left. Numbers seven and eight lived in Southern California: Los Angeles and La Jolla, still a day away.

The girl at the register traded his ten-dollar bill for a handful of quarters. He pushed into the only phone booth and sat holding the receiver a moment, dial tone failing in his ear. It was 9 p.m. in California. He thought of Sandy holding Grace on her hip, reaching with her left arm to retrieve something from a cupboard. What did the future machine say? There are many Grace Winklers, all of them the real Grace Winkler, so in that way your journey will never be done.

He rifled quarters into the slot. At the first number a man answered. "Not here. At her mom's for dinner. Yeah, her mom. What's this about?" Winkler hung up.

The other decided he was trying to sell

her a new windshield. "I told you to take me off your list," she said. "My windshield isn't even cracked."

"No," Winkler said. He gave his explanation, asked if she had family in Alaska, if she was born in Ohio or knew the name of her father. When he finished, there was a pause.

"Luke?" she said. "It's you, isn't it? Goddamn you, Luke. Nice try. My dad died of cancer five months ago. Real freaking smooth." She swore, and hung up.

6

He sent deer jerky to the Graces in California, a hemp doll in a tiny poncho to the one in New Mexico. All daughters, none of them his. He felt as if he were trapped in some variation of the original dream: a house filling with water, a search through empty rooms.

From a motel in Glendale, Arizona, on the first of September, he dialed the number for the last Grace Winkler, the one in Boise, Idaho, and pressed the handset to his ear. It rang unanswered. It was noon before he could summon the will to stand, fold his clothes into his duffel bag, and slog out to the Datsun once more.

Dear Soma —

In over two weeks I have spoken to eight Grace Winklers and have nothing from any of them, no clues, no answers, just a sore on the underside of my tongue and pain in my lower back. It was stupid to think she'd even use my surname. What could it mean to her? She could be Grace Sheeler; she could be Grace Anything. I should probably go straight to Anchorage, finish this. But I'm afraid there will be nothing — no one — there. Not even Herman. It is strange and awful to feel so alone, to feel like your whole tribe is dead, even your enemies.

My little car is starting to fail me. I have spent more than two thousand dollars already.

All day the Datsun coughed and spat oil. He talked it forward. The highway fringed the faint arc of an ancient lakeshore where fossilized shells lay like small bones in the sand, and by evening he was descending onto a plain thronged with legions of cacti. They went first pink and then purple and finally crimson in the dusk, their shadows lengthening, the sun dragging its light over the edge of the firmament. Little desert bats appeared over the road, swooping through the headlight beams, their ancient and jawboned faces flashing once in the glare and then gone. Winkler pushed on, racing the fuel gauge to empty, stopping only to refill the oil reservoir or scrape husks of bugs from the windshield. Soon the cacti were behind him, or invisible in the dark, and all that remained were gray and corrugated mountains at the horizons and the immense darkening cistern of sky, trimmed at the edges with orange.

The Datsun limped into Utah around midnight, only intermittent highway lights left now casting dim pools that the car and its pilot passed beneath, gliding from one to the next, towed, seemingly, by their own pale wedge of light. Beneath the highway a canyon opened, and a river appeared, sleek and implacable, before vanishing again.

He spent the last hours of darkness in a rest stop between two purring car carriers. All night he half woke to the sounds of truckers swinging open the door of the outhouse and relieving themselves. An echoing trickle; a noise like small, individual lives passing away. In a dream he watched a winged ghost disappear through columns of falling snow. Each time he drew close, the ghost faded deeper down the trail. Finally it dissolved for good, just the faint blush of its wings receding, and Winkler stopped running to gaze up at ranks of descending snow, snow all the way to the limits of the earth. He woke sweating.

The next day he passed through the sun-afflicted towns of southern Utah and the flanks of the Datsun went red with dust and great red walls of that same dust hung over the road incandescent as if lit from within. The little car wound over canyons and followed the course of a river far below lined with the greens of river oaks and cottonwoods.

It was late into his sixteenth day when he reached Idaho along the wind-tortured flats near Holbrook. The sky was purple a long time and finally black. Along the shoulders dim shapes of sagebrush were bundled low against the ground, and at both horizons low walls of mountains stood black and featureless. He felt as if he were entering a trap and would soon be hemmed in. Around midnight he could make out the lights of Boise reflected off a space in the sky and soon after saw the lights themselves, twinkling and burning on the range like a small blue galaxy.

"Almost there," he told Sandy. She merely looked out the window. He braced his hands on the wheel. Already the truth was becoming plain: this place would be no happy ending, no slate wiped clean, no port in the storm. He was arriving at the end of the line, no markers above him, no prospects, no tenth Grace on his list. Sandy was dead and his daughter had likely drowned twenty-five years before, and here he was in Boise, Idaho, after nearly sixty years of living and what did he have to show for it?

7

One-one-two-two Alturas Street was a small slate-colored bungalow with three or four heat-stroked rhododendrons withering in the front bed. He kept his attention on the porch. No one went in or out.

It was the third of September, plenty of broth left in summer's cauldron, and by 10 a.m. the temperature shoved past ninety. Winkler opened his collar and rocked in his seat. Every hour or so a pedestrian ambled by, one of them a sweating mailman who limped to Grace's door and pushed a pile of magazines through the slot.

Cars slugged past. A magpie landed on the Datsun's hood and rested a moment, panting. Winkler took his shells from the dashboard one by one and worked them between his fingers. He ate a convenience store sandwich; he drank a liter of water. In the afternoon a police car rolled past and slowed but did not stop.

Around six a lady in a little white pickup pulled in behind him. She closed her door, polished a smudge from the window with her sleeve. As she walked past, she studied him with a measure of suspicion before trying a wave. He waved back.

Grace, he assumed, was at her office. She likely held a very important job, a scientist, or a surgical intern. She would come home soon and if he was very lucky, she'd invite him inside and give him a glass of ice water.

The white-truck lady disappeared, swallowed by a neighboring house. The sun crept lower. Winkler knotted his tie in the rearview mirror and sat in his damp shirt watching shadows enter the trees. The heat — unbelievably — seemed only to increase.

What were the chances? Ten thousand to one? A million to one? The light concentrated to orange. Red filled the undersides of his eyelids, and drained away, and filled again. Every few minutes he had the sensation of falling out of space and into a dream, then climbing out of the dream and back into the Datsun's misshapen driver's seat once more. At some point, nearing dusk, a Jeep rolled past his window. It parked in front of 1122 Alturas and a young woman in a short-sleeved button-down and slacks bounded out. Winkler's heart stalled; he tried to blink himself into awareness. The woman carried a nylon briefcase and her legs were long and quick and she had a certain exhausted loveliness to her. A short stripe of sweat darkened the middle of the back of her blouse. She took long strides and went straight to the door of 1122 Alturas and let herself in.

"Sandy," he said to the photograph on the dash. "She looks like you." He pushed his glasses up the bridge of his nose. He tried to breathe. He got out of the car.

He was halfway up the walk before he saw she had left her door wide open. Her briefcase lay just inside, a pair of loafers beside it. He glanced up and down the street but there were no neighbors about. The leaves hung still and heavy. It was hardly any cooler outside of the car. "Hello?" he called. "Miss?"

He shuffled forward, climbed the two porch steps, and stopped in the open doorway. Cool air washed out — air-conditioning. His body leaned involuntarily into it. Sweat evaporated from his forehead.

"Grace?" Her mail lay on the tile two feet away, a flyer for a pizza company, a newsmagazine, other envelopes he could not make out. The house looked tidy: little ceramic zebras on the windowsill, a chenille throw on the sofa, a potted ficus in a corner. On an end table behind the sofa were rows of photos in frames.

He rapped on the open door and cleared his throat. "Grace? Grace Winkler? Anybody home?"

Was she in some bedroom farther back? Or on the phone? Her briefcase was beside his foot; he could pick up and smell her shoes simply by bending forward. The photos on the end table were maybe fifteen steps away. Her mail fluttered lightly; the cool air reached his throat.

A slight hesitation, then he let the impulse take him: he walked into the house. There was nothing to hear other than the drone of faraway traffic and the whoosh of her air conditioner as it forced air from a louvered panel in the ceiling.

Five steps, six, seven, eight. He was all the way inside her living room. Soon the front door was a good ten feet behind him. Sweat was drying on his face; his shoes boomed on the floor. Light fell through the western window and lit her curtain. Through an archway he could just glimpse the kitchen: an olive green refrigerator, a rag draped over a faucet arm.

There were two dozen photos on the sofa table. He had to lean close to make them out. One was of a sheepdog, another of a half dozen bridesmaids in purple gowns. There were several of a young man with a woman he was reasonably sure was the woman from the Jeep. The two of them posed on a mountaintop, waved from a canoe, patted the sheepdog. A brother? A boyfriend? In another photo, framed in silver, a family clustered around a Christmas tree. *The Winklers, 12/25/99* was engraved in the frame.

He picked it up. The air conditioner whirred.

The tree in the photograph was a spruce, swathed in strings of popcorn, a plastic angel clipped to the top. A spill of gifts gleamed beneath it. Everyone around the tree was wearing pajamas; the girl from the Jeep in a football jersey and boxer shorts; an elderly grandfather type in union jacks and an undershirt, gazing out from behind impossibly thick eyebrows. There were toddlers, and a mother, too: with white hair in a bob.

He felt the air leave him. This woman could have been her, but she wasn't. The mother was not Sandy — none of them was Sandy. Not even close.

Family — every pattern in a life derived from it. Who you were, how you acted, how you spoke, dressed, fought, worked, died. Here was yet another father, a tired-looking man in an undershirt; here was yet another Grace Winkler. He thought of his mother, carrying a box of groceries into their apartment, how there were hundreds of tiny blue veins visible in her calves.

A toilet flushed behind a door to his right.

The Christmas portrait was still in his hand. She came out of the bathroom buttoning her slacks. When she saw him tendons leapt to attention in her throat.

Run, he thought. *Run.* But she was beautiful, tall, tan — why couldn't she have been his daughter? — and the cool air was washing down from the vent in the ceiling and there was this happy-seeming Winkler family gathered round a tree at Christmas, boys and girls and mothers and fathers, each with gifts bearing his or her name, and one of those girls was named Grace and he had been without her for so long. . . .

She lunged for the ficus tree in the corner, as if she had planned all along, even at its purchase, to employ it as a weapon. She took its trunk in both fists, inverted the entire tree, and came at him. With the heavy clay pot over her shoulder, she managed two steps, shut her eyes, and swung, top to bottom, as if he were a log that needed splitting. At the bottom of the arc the pot slid off the cylinder of roots and smashed down on his right foot, where shoe met shin.

He felt the skin around his eyes stretch. They stood a moment, a tableau of pain: Grace Winkler dropping the unpotted ficus, her hands halfway to her mouth, the sound of impact — like a fist into the back of a sofa — followed by the sounds of the big pot rolling on the floor and the subsequent shower of soil.

He dropped the photo and the glass cracked undramatically — a quiet *tink*. Grace Winkler's shoulders quaked and her upper lip twitched. Her pants were still half-unbuttoned and a small triangle of white underwear showed in the gap. He could feel the tendrils of pain rising through his ankle, as though a fire had started down there, deep in the bone.

"I . . ." he whispered. He smoothed the end of his tie. "It's not what you think."

She shrieked through her fingers: "Are you crazy? Are you totally fucking crazy?"

"Please. My daughter."

She still had her hands over her mouth when he turned and shambled out, nearly tripping over her briefcase. His right foot dragged behind him. He was halfway to the Datsun when she appeared on the porch with a cordless telephone pressed to her ear.

"Come on, come on . . ." she said into the receiver. The street was as empty and hot as ever. The light was the color of blood. A neighbor's sprinkler swung back on its arc.

He fell into the driver's seat. The Datsun — faithful to the last — stuttered to life. He dropped it into reverse and pressed his good foot to the gas and crushed the front fender and right headlight of the white pickup behind him. The Datsun's hatchback dented and the latch sprung. "Oh," said Winkler, and out on the sidewalk the Grace who was not his daughter was crying as she described his car to the police. He wrenched the transmission into drive, the tires screeched and spun, and the car lurched forward.

He ran stop signs, took random turns. The broken hatch flapped and knocked. A birthday party on a front lawn (silver streamers, clusters of Mylar balloons, children skimming across a wet tarp on their bellies) slid serenely past. His right foot felt wet inside his shoe and the pain tunneled deeper. He took a left, a right, sped straight. Where could he go? A motel? Back to the highway? The Datsun — running on one cylinder now — would never make it.

Winkler remembered seeing roads rising into the hills north of the city and he tried to guide the car toward them. The rearview mirror was empty, only road and trees, and a cyclist gliding through a cross street.

Two dead ends, two right turns. Soon the houses ended, and pavement gave way to dirt. The road began to climb sharply and the Datsun grunted over washboarded gravel. A plume of dust rose behind him and hung over the road. The engine moaned.

He coaxed it forward, up a series of switchbacks. He drove with only the parking lights on and in the plunging light could not see more than the broad wash of road in front of him.

Soon bushes scraped the Datsun's underside. The engine bucked. He managed to get it past a last washout to what looked like a trailhead and there the Datsun died, a final groan like a sad and weary beast going to its knees, confused by the world to its end.

He pushed open the door and sat cradling his foot as the last light leached from the sky, a blue hem to the west and the sky dark red and stars coming on.

He pressed his thumbs to the top of his foot and threads of pain, thin as shards of glass, shot up his leg. Broken? It was hard to tell. The skin was not bleeding.

Far below him the apron of city lights shivered in the heat. Behind him were granite hills cloaked in sage. Beyond them: mountains.

He dumped things into the duffel: his three notebooks, two envelopes of money, his extra shirt, the two dozen cans of tomato soup, the emergency kit in its orange pouch. His foot throbbed steadily. He pocketed the nerite shells on the dash, tucked the picture of Sandy into his pocket, and got out of the car. The road had been cut into a hillside and below him it gave way into deepening shadow where clumps of sage faded into darkness. He tested his weight on his foot, pulled the duffel's straps across his shoulders, and started up the trail.

My shoes, he thought. I wish I had better shoes.

8

He passed the night shivering beneath a tangle of bitterbrush. His foot throbbed steadily. Below him the lights of Boise guttered and shook all night as if the wind might extinguish them at any moment. Or else they were about to detach from the valley floor and climb the hills after him.

At dawn he opened the emergency kit. Inside were twenty-four weatherproof matches, two road flares, a plastic canteen, several sleeves of saltines, a bright orange poncho, and a cheap two-blade jackknife. He sliced open a packet of crackers and chewed them slowly. There had to be a town farther north — he did not want to risk going back to Boise.

He shouldered his duffel and descended a few hundred yards and came across a trail heading east. The sun swung over the hills, big and pale.

He limped through a place of burned trees and exposed granite, ascending one ridge, then another. Within an hour he was over a rim and out of sight of the city, descending into a vast, furrowed brushland, hills upon hills, gallery after gallery of sage and bitterroot, all the way to the horizon.

He walked all that day and saw little more than airplanes crossing overhead and large black beetles toiling along the trail beside his feet. The straps of the duffel abraded his shoulders; the pain in his foot flared at unexpected moments. There was not a town farther north, at least not one he could see. A few times he heard the buzz and drone of motorized bikes on trails far below, and once he saw a dust plume, and a flash of reflected sun that might have been a rider's helmet, but since he did not know whether to duck or wave, he merely stood and waited for the sound to fade. The sun seemed to lack the strength of the previous day, and a wind that was not entirely warm came up in the afternoon. He passed the wide, tangled nests of magpies, anthills the size of pitcher's mounds. Fistfuls of sunflowers stood dying and flagging on the hillsides. Clouds blew in from the west.

He decided to retrace his steps but could not — the trails branched almost ceaselessly, descended where they should have climbed, petered out where they should have widened. Over the next three days he would traverse half the northern stretch of the Boise Basin, making a large and ragged arc. He passed logging roads and cattle pastures, a cellular tower, a sun-collapsed shearing shack, a dark and perilous-looking mine entrance, even a graveyard for miners and their children, choked with skeletonweed. Once a pickup truck rumbled far below him across the scrub, flushing quail.

His joints creaked and protested; his ankles rolled in his shoes. He filled his gut and canteen at every stream and tried to drink sparingly as he went on, but water was scarce. The pain in his right foot faded to a steady throb, or perhaps he merely accustomed himself to it, so it was not the pain that diminished but his attention to it. He came to feel that there were figures both ahead and behind him, the one in front standing and departing his resting place seconds before Winkler arrived, the other pressing forward in its pursuit, about to catch up at any moment.

The hills were vast, endless: like an ocean in their immensity and indifference. In the failing light, in the broken faces of boulders slurring and vacillating in the sun, he'd become aware of a patient, invisible menace hiding just outside the range of his vision, something that did not care one way or another if he lived or died.

Even in the dark now he could not see the glow of the city reflecting off the sky and could not have said whether Boise was ahead of or behind him. He reasoned back the panic: perhaps it was better to stay lost a few days. Even if he could get back, then what? Descend into town, stroll past the capitol in his ruined suit? *Well, Officer, I had this dream . . .*

At nights he made fires between slabs of rock. He spent the road flares as fire starters first, then the labels off the soup cans, and on his third night began burning pages from his notebooks.

Wind would buffet and turn the flames and carry them as sparks out into the dark: notes about floods and glaciers, marine limestone in Himalayan peaks, drawings of rivulets, an annotation about FitzRoy captaining Darwin's *Beagle*, studying beds of fossilized oysters, convinced he'd found evidence for the universal deluge. All of it wrinkled and faded into incandescent particles, smoke rising through branches.

His cans of soup would grow black, soup

hissing as it boiled down the sides, and he'd reach for them with his shirt coiled around his hand and set them sizzling in the dust, and — because he was hungry — drink them before they cooled and scorch his tongue. Then he'd roll up in his poncho and watch the fire burn itself out, sparks racing downwind and the embers inside illumined like a miniature castle, complete with balusters and arches and tiny glowing pennants.

Nine Graces and none of them his daughter. He thought of Jed, and the future machine, its dozen clips and wires, none of them plugged into anything. And yet: "To enter a world of shadows is to leave this world for another." Was the boy not exactly right?

In the air on his fourth night hung a smell of struck flint, an odor that started little tremors of fear in the back of Winkler's throat, and all night he found himself glancing uneasily toward the sky, the stars blotting out one by one, a more leaden darkness blowing in.

9

The clouds assembled. These were not mere cumulus but great bossed and flexing cumulonimbus, nearly black in their centers, livid with electrical charges. They crawled slowly toward one another, sealing the gaps, each impossibly tall, all shoulders and necks, seeming to mount from their dark platforms to the limits of the sky. Before them trundled intermittent explosions of thunder.

Winkler shook in his poncho. All night not a single drop fell, but jags of superheated air rained from the sky and charged back up from the ground as though a similar army rode beneath the surface of the earth, firing back. With each stroke the mountains were summoned out of the darkness and sucked back up again and the ozone smelled of iron being forged.

A dry wind came up and pressed the electricity forward and the bottoms of the clouds seemed to glass over, as if liquefying. It sounded to Winkler like the fabric of the sky was tearing over and over again, as if what lay past it, blue and wild beyond his worst imaginings, was now leaking through. Thunder sent rocks skittering from the ridgelines. Tiny charges of static electricity roamed between the hairs on his head.

He zipped his duffel. His poncho billowed and snapped. Hares started from the sage and went wheeling in crazed runs and froze midstride and ran on again. The wind had taken up all manner of things — pinecones and pebbles, even a thrush — and drove them up the floor of the valley below him. He fought his way up a steep ridge and started down the other side. The wind threw grit up the slope and he could hear it striking the lenses of his glasses. Far below he glimpsed what might have been a river. His shoes were fumbling in scree and the slope was steep and he descended in a crab walk with both arms dragging behind him. As he drew closer, he could see broken sheets of water rise and whorling devils of tumbleweed and dust and sleeves of sparks burning out, and rekindling, and turning with the wind. Still no rain fell, just consistent grumbles of thunder and innumerable frayed wires of lightning and small blue fires hanging in the branches of the sage. Already he could smell smoke.

I'm going to die, he thought. I'm going to burn out here and no one will ever find me and no one will even know to look.

He made the bottom of the scree and found the river and lowered his entire face into the water. As if the storm existed only in his eyes. Above him he could feel the reverberating thrill of the air as it electrified, curtains of air fluxing and bending up and down the river's canyon. Water pooled in his stomach — already he could feel his joints easing, his skin stretching.

He bent, and drank, and drank again. Lightning touched a tree not a half mile from him, and it made a profound popping like the sound of water being poured into a deep-fryer. When he finally pulled back from the river, kneeling on the bank, he realized his glasses had been taken from his face.

For what might have been an hour, he fumbled in the shallows but found only gravel. Before dawn the storm was miles to the east and the clouds relented and unveiled a limitless matrix of stars, which appeared only as a huge and terrible ceiling, pocked with light. His duffel bag was to his right. His glasses were nowhere. His clothes were soaked.

Trees became pillars of shadow, the sky a swirling luster, the shapes of his own hands immaterial shadows in front of his face. He crossed the river on an old wire bridge and passed through an empty campground and foundered among rocks. If I keep descending, he thought, I will stay by the river, and if I can follow the river, I will reach a road.

But by daybreak things were hardly better: the forest was a blur, the sky a mess of roiled silver. He made for a dark, cubic structure he thought might be a house but somehow missed it and within a matter of a half hour had climbed two steep ridges and could no longer find the river.

He reached for trees only to lurch into air. At the corners of his vision white spots tumbled like the spalls of meteorites plummeting to earth. By late afternoon he was half-starved and sun-blinded and his vision was nearly useless. He had still not come upon a road. And now he was climbing — should he turn back, and descend again?

All the things he did not see: he walked within thirty feet of a black bear and never knew she was there; Winkler feeling his way along a game trail, the bear raised on her haunches, sniffing for a long moment before settling back down and swinging away into the trees. Two hawks, displaced by the storm, sat on a branch over the trail, preening parasites from their wings and watching him go. And horsemen, harrying sheep far below him, tan ewes like specks circling against a fence, and the faint puffs of dust they kicked up blowing south toward a road, a pickup, a horse trailer. And the next morning: a trio of summer cabins far below him, on the shores of the Deadwood Reservoir, all occupied, all happy enough to feed and water a lost stranger. He saw none of it.

Six mornings out of Boise found him shivering, out of crackers, nearly out of soup, with very little idea where he was. He had unwittingly crossed two broken but traveled roads and now was farther north than he ever would have guessed, with the enormous tracts of the Salmon River Valley ahead of him, and beyond that Marble Creek, and the River of No Return, none of it populated. His feet had blistered in his shoes, and his right ankle had swollen grotesquely: the yellows and purples of contusion had climbed halfway up his shin.

He stumped through the high forests, steadying himself against trunks. The air smelled of pine and sage, sweet and sickly in his nose and at the back of his mouth. Above him giant grasshoppers screamed like panthers in the branches. Occasionally one fell and writhed in his hair or down the back of his collar and he would spasm trying to reach it, his duffel falling from his shoulders, his fingers tearing at his shirt.

This was the darkness he had been dreaming for years. This was the place where events occurred around him heard but unseen, the deep and private blindness his dreams had predicted so many years before. The deep, marine pressure on his brain. The flood of light. At the terminals of circles extremes met: darkness was no different from illumination; an inundation of either was blinding. When he slept now he dreamed of naked, frozen branches: frost growing on windows, snowflakes alighting on sleeves.

The little nerite shells — the three or four he had left — were tiny lumps in the seam of his pocket. His trousers had lost their knees; his socks were little more than anklets, spats of cotton over the insteps of his shoes.

In his farthest moments he sensed, again and again, presences in the shadows: Soma and Felix; Naaliyah and Nanton; Grace and Sandy. He'd be resting on a rock, or in a bed of pine needles, eyes closed, sleep closing in, when he'd hear a rustle in the brush, a pause in the wind. In his ribs, at the tips of his hairs: a slight magnetic draw, the barely perceptible gravitational pull one human body exerts on another.

He'd open his eyes; he'd sit up. There'd be nothing, only the smeary, endless forest, spots dragging across his vision, that pressure in his skull.

He pressed the pad of his finger to a molar and wiggled it back and forth. There was the metallic taste of blood on his tongue. You will see fire and you will die. Your journey will never be done.

"Hello?" he called. "Hello?"

On his ninth night since leaving the Datsun, he reached a land of rocks on a ridgeline cold and smoking in the wind where dwarf trees had grown stunted and hooked and ferns of ice meshed and feathered in clefts between rocks. A cusp of moon floated in the western sky. He tried to start a fire but the wind prevented it. He rummaged in the duffel for a can of soup — his last — and cut it open and drank the thick, salty concentrate cold.

In the night, wrapped in his poncho, the

moon seemed to move closer, filling his whole frame of vision, seeping around the edges of his eyelids, abrading him, his skin and skeleton, until he felt he would become nothing but membrane, a rippling film of soul, until he was lying on the outermost ridge toward heaven, the stars at his feet, the very core of the universe within reach.

The next afternoon he descended maybe a thousand feet into a dense, dusty wood. The muscles in his ankles felt stripped and ragged and the sun was pale but zealous and forced him into the shade. Each time he tried to stand, his eyesight fled in slow, nauseating streaks.

He lay on his back and watched the sky, the only cloud a single, smeary stripe, which after a while he realized was a slowly lengthening contrail at the head of which must have been a jet. An image came to him of the pilots in the cockpit, a panorama of instruments before them, a hundred round glass faces, steady needles and switches, the frozen reaches of atmosphere unrolling in front of them. How strange to be miles below, lying in thorns, while they hurtled through space, a cabin behind them packed with passengers asleep or eating or reading magazines. He raised a hand, squinted, pinched them from the sky.

Not thirty yards from there, through a brace of ferns and across a ditch, came a rising sound, something like an extended sigh. It had crescendoed and faded into silence before Winkler realized a car had passed.

10

He wavered on his legs as a caravan of eighteen-wheelers roared past. On their flatbeds they carried the massive, limb-stripped trunks of trees, ten or so per truck, great streamers of bark trailing behind. The heaving air in their wake smelled thick and sweet, the smell of crushed wood. The last truck threw up its brakelights and began a long, grinding halt that took several hundred yards.

Winkler hurried as well as he could, limping down the shoulder, the ferns at the sides of the road nodding and settling. The door swung open; a hand came across the seat and pulled him in.

"My Lord," the driver said.

Winkler tried to smile but could feel his lips cracking. The truck purred on the shoulder. The driver said, "You been out there awhile?"

Winkler lowered his face into his palms. "Well, I won't ask," the man said. He ratcheted the truck up through the gears.

The road glided past, a blur of gray seemingly way too far beneath them. "You ain't a child-murderer or something?"

Winkler looked up. "No," he heard himself say.

"Where are we headed?"

"Alaska."

The driver laughed. "I can get you to Ninety-five. How's that?"

The roadside blurred; the centerline whisked under the hood. Winkler sagged against the window. Soon placeless dreams were upon him and when he woke it was near dark and the trucker was braking to enter a gas station. "Exit's just past that sign there," he said. "You'll get a ride in no time."

Winkler mumbled his thanks, dragged himself and his duffel bag into the station store, and bumbled through the harlequin light and shelves of candy and crackers and cassettes. He brought a loaf of bread, a bag of tortillas to the counter. The clerk held his twenty-dollar bill to the light.

In the bathroom he sat on the toilet and ate half the bread, feeling his stomach distend and bubble.

When he finished he pulled Sandy's obituary photo from his pocket. It was little more than lint now, a few dots of ink.

He held it in front of his eyes and tried not to weep.

The next driver's name was Brent Royster, a hopped-up, enthusiastic trucker hauling blenders and bread machines to department stores across British Columbia. His face in Winkler's eyes was a wide, pink spread of kindness. He had rigged a turntable on coils in the space between the driver's and passenger's armrests and behind the seats were crates stuffed with records, a thousand at least, all in antistatic sleeves, all jostling and settling softly as the truck rolled on.

"How about Sam Cooke?" Brent offered. He reached behind him and without looking unsleeved a record and notched it on the turntable. The record spun, the needle fell. "Chain Gang" flooded the cabin.

Winkler watched the highway roll past the window, looming green signs and the mile markers flashing past. He tore open a pack of gas station doughnuts and fished them, one after another, into his mouth. "Is this real?" he asked.

"Say what, pardner?" Brent reached to adjust the volume.

"Is this real? What's happening to me?"

Reflectors in the road thwapped beneath the tires, setting a regular, almost re-assuring pace. Thwap, thwap, thwap. *Hooh! Aah!* said Sam Cooke. Brent gave Winkler a curious look.

"Real? It's real as rain, I guess. Real as Jesus."

Around dawn the next morning they stopped at a truckers' diner and bent over steaming mugs of coffee.

"What day is it?"

"September the fifteenth."

"Thursday?"

"Sunday."

Winkler shook his head. He ordered eggs and French toast and a side of fries and three glasses of orange juice. Brent leaned back in his chair. "You can ride with me all the way to Prince Rupert if you like. Then you can get yourself a ferry. You'll be in Alaska by Wednesday."

Winkler blinked. "Wednesday."

"You got friends waiting on you? Or family?"

He thought it over. "Friends."

Brent nodded. The waitress brought the plates. The juice was the best of it: Winkler could taste it in every corner of his mouth. "You're eating like it's the Last Supper," Brent said.

"I'm all right," said Winkler. But ten

minutes later he was in the bathroom.

They were well north of Coeur d'Alene, listening to Van Morrison, when the trucker offered to call Winkler's friends in Alaska.

"No," Winkler said. "Thank you."

"Everyone has someone to call. That's a fact."

"No," he said again, but the trucker had detached his cellular from its cradle. They spent the next ten minutes haggling. Eventually Winkler gave him Naaliyah's name. Brent dialed Information, spelled her name perfectly. When he reached a hall where Naaliyah lived, he handed over the phone. "Here. I've dialed it."

A girl answered. "Naaliyah's not here," she said. "She's up in Nowheresville. On research. What do they call it? Camp Nowhere. Something like that."

"Research," Winkler said. "On insects?"

"Uh-huh. Somewhere way up. In the Yukon."

"Where?"

"I'll look it up." He heard papers shuffle. "Eagle. Eagle City, Alaska."

"Eagle?" Brent said, after Winkler had handed over the phone. "Wow. Girl gets around. Eagle's up by Dawson City. The Yukon."

"How can I get there?"

"There are roads. Might be closer than Anchorage, really. From Haines you can catch a bus into the Yukon. You can probably get all the way to Eagle. Although there isn't much there."

The rest of the journey passed more like dream than reality. Brent drove with his window open and cold, almost hallucinatory air swept ceaselessly through the cabin. Winkler shivered beneath his seat belt. Record after record played; Winkler thought of Naaliyah, of the Caribbean, of fishermen standing in the surf, minding the bowlines of their canoes like the reins of horses.

At the border before Creston, two Mounties had Brent open the big trailer doors so they could see his load, but neither said anything to Winkler beyond investigating his passport, and soon enough they were back on the road. Brent was tireless, it seemed, and Winkler could not keep his eyes open and soon he was asleep, dreaming the country pulling past, the sound of the engine distant and relentless in his ears like the sound of the lagoon at Nanton's inn, and when he woke, a few hours later, he was unsure for a long time if he were still sleeping, if the relentless sweep of trees and valley and stars past the windshield were really an extension of his dream, if from that point onward he would be living in a world of apparitions, and his body would remain asleep on the seat of a long-distance hauler. Another kind of purgatory: a waiting to wake up.

The truck pulled him north, into a land less of Canada and more of sheer imagination, the long freezes, the northern lights, the distance from where and who he had been finally absolute.

Three separate warehouses in Calgary. A truckers' motel near Banff. The up-and-down wastes of western British Columbia: a low and tangled bracken, a smell in the air like mud, and frost; winter on its way. In Prince Rupert, Brent dropped Winkler at the entrance to the ferry where lines of automobiles waited to pile on.

"Here." Brent handed down a pair of shoes from the cab. "They're U.S. nines. Should fit."

"I can't."

"I won't hear otherwise. And when you get home, you get that ankle looked at. Lots of times you think things are healed but they've only healed partway or they've healed wrong and you've got to rehurt 'em to get 'em right."

Winkler took the shoes and stood on the roadside nodding and feeling as if the whole scene was made of paper and could crumple and blow away. "Thank you," he said. Brent Royster turned from putting on another record and gave Winkler a sweet, combustible smile, the smile of a boy, and the truck pulled out and dust pulled in behind it.

In the ferry terminal he bought his ticket and ordered postage and two envelopes at a postal kiosk. *For the broken picture frame,* he wrote on a slip of paper, then crossed it out and wrote: *For your trouble. And for the lady with the white pickup.* He put six hundred dollars in the envelope, sealed it, and addressed it to 1122 Alturas Street in Boise, Idaho.

On the ferry he curled up on gum-splotched carpet between two banks of seats with his ruined duffel under his head and his knees pulled to his chest. The ferry sounded its whistle. The floor heeled gently beneath him. The smell of grilled ham-and-cheese sandwiches drifted through the compartment; two Inuit boys by the windows stared into the screens of their handheld video games with the ardor of believers.

11

He disembarked in Haines and rode motorcoaches through the Yukon Corner: a half dozen isolated towns, most named for animals: Whitehorse, Beaver, Chicken. The highway was gravel, occasionally chipped out of cliff sides, and the bus windows were soon pasted with an oily grime. Mosquitoes traveled the aisle hunting passengers.

The driver indicated highlights as they slid past. Abandoned mining dredges; midnight-sun gardens (like gardens on steroids: inflated cabbages, colossal pumpkins). Vast islands of spruce. A road-killed caribou the size of a dairy cow.

Thirty hours of bouncing in that seat and near the end of it Winkler could feel the minute dissociations between each vertebra. He was the last passenger. A trio of cabins marked the end of the route.

Eagle: population 250. He disembarked on traitorous legs. It was 8:40 p.m. and there was still plenty of light in the sky, shadows reaching across the unpaved street, two boys in a Radio Flyer wagon harnessed to dogs watching the bus turn and start back toward Tok.

He started with them: "Naaliyah Orellana? Dark skin, a scientist?" They picked at paint on the wagon walls. "Hello? Do you speak English?"

They nodded.

"But you don't know her?"

They shook their heads, then mushed the huskies and the wagon started off, creaking up the street.

He could barely read the phone book (thirty or so sheets of paper, clipped together) but there did not seem to be any Naaliyah listed. Out of habit he reached to adjust his glasses but pawed at air.

No one knew her at the Texaco, or the rental cabins, or the propane dealer, or the beadwork shop. He offered the station mechanic a hundred-dollar bill but the man only shook his head: "Can't summon her out of thin air."

The sky was huge and purple and the town was tiny beneath it. Nobody seemed to think his plight was all that urgent. It didn't take long to run out of buildings: a warped box of a bar where a bartender was fast-forwarding a pornographic videotape; the old frame-building custom house; the trading company with its dusty fluorescent lights and neon bags of potato chips shining in plump rows. In his eyes everything was hazy and smeared with light. His ankle ached steadily. Have you seen Naaliyah Orellana? A young woman? Haven't seen her. Anybody? Nobody.

It was September 20 and he'd been in the United States less than seven weeks. The street ended at a series of sad-looking docks where a few houseboats were tied up. Beyond them the vast, khaki current of the Yukon River slid past, a quarter mile across, like some final and insuperable boundary.

"The airstrip," a canoe-rental man told him. "I think I saw a gal like that out there. A couple months ago, maybe? Heading to the university land up there." He waved toward an enormous bluff.

The airfield was less than a mile from town. He trudged the road in half darkness. Off to his right the Yukon rolled on, driving its immeasurable payload of silt northward. He could hardly believe its size: it was a sleek prairie, pocked with boils; it was an avalanche turned on its side.

He felt something uncoiling within him. Brent had warned him — sometimes

things only heal partway, or heal wrong —
but Winkler had been feeling stronger, his
eyes recovering, his pains withdrawing.
Now a cold wind came up, and Winkler
stopped a moment smelling the night. Another town, another empty pocket. Where
would he sleep? All of a sudden his ankle
could not hold him. He teetered, and fell.

The Yukon pushed on and on. Winkler
tried to hold his head up. There was a
sound in the air like women's voices.
"Grace?" he called. "Grace?" He had a vision of her at the bottom of a lagoon, lan-
guid, a grown woman, bound in weeds, her
hair a sea fan nodding in the current. But
the voice came and went, and with it the
vision, and then there was only the incessant glide of the river.

He staggered to his feet and went forward in his tattered suit and borrowed
tennis shoes. The airstrip appeared abandoned, the shells of two Cessna 207s, can-
nibalized for parts, parked beside a barn.

The barn door was not latched. Inside it
was hushed and beamy as a church,
random debris in most of the stalls: tires,
drums, bags of shingles, a row of ruined
ten-speeds, a rusted snowplow. At the back
of the hayloft rose a large, perpendicular
trilancet window, looking over a trembling

island of birch. There was an ancient mattress below the window and he climbed onto it and lay down and listened to the wind against the panes.

A spring, broken somewhere inside the mattress, groaned weakly. What did he have left? A sense of where the moon was coming over the trees, the wispy silhouettes of clouds. And this feeling, permeating every waking minute, that he had made too many wrong decisions, that he should have gone down to the house from the top of Shadow Hill and waded inside to see if his daughter was there. He should even have taken her in his arms and tried grappling her up the flooded street.

But there was a worse feeling: the possibility that it didn't matter what he had done, that outcome was independent of choice, that action or inaction, no decision mattered, and his entire attempt at family was now dead and nobody was left to care whether he gave up or kept on.

He draped his arms over his head and peered up at the clouds. The troposphere, at that latitude, was about seven miles thick: a booming, swirling ocean of air. The clouds blowing through it were nimbostratus — made of ice, improbably blue in the moonlight, a collection of crystals so thin you'd feel nothing, only a chill inside your pores, if you could reach up and pass a hand through one.

Already snow was gathering, flying over the trees.

In his injured foot a dull pain pulsed. The shivering of his body had become something he did not quite understand, something far removed from him, as if the single, lukewarm kernel of his being had been set inside a quivering basket of muscles not its own. Leaves sailed toward the glass. And above them — among them now — the first snowflakes.

The wind assumed its voice: moaning against the window, humming around the roof corners; hissing through drafts. It whispered about darkness, about the coming shadows. *Let go,* it said, *let go.* A solitary snow crystal struck the pane and held there and expired. Then another. And another.

I have already been reduced, he wanted to say. Leave me be.

Who among us, in our lowest hour, can expect to be saved? Have you loved your life? Have you cherished each miraculous breath?

In a dream a rider came to him through

the barn, the horse blowing twin rods of vapor from its nostrils. The rider dismounted and knelt on the boards beside him.

"Can you walk?" A woman's voice. A hood shading her face.

He did not answer; he realized he was incapable. He watched things from a distance. The rider was not a rider at all; she was a woman in a parka, leaning over the mattress. She lifted him by the belt and collar and heaved him into her arms, his head lolling forward. "Is that your bag?" the voice asked.

But she had a horse, didn't she? The two of them were gliding down the hay ladder, floating past empty barn stalls, past the ghosts of horses quarantined there, snuffling and pawing in their beds. He swayed in her arms like a drunk, the skin on his lips sloughing off, his eyes nearly rolling back, spectra blooming across the eyeballs and racing into the corners.

Down the stairs. A first breath of air. She — or was it the horse? — grunted beneath him. The wind swept the crowns of the trees and leaves flew among the snowflakes and the horse raised water as its hooves cleaved the mud.

But there was no horse. He was being

carried to a truck. Snow gusted across the windshield. Heated air whisked through vents in the dashboard. Rescue was not a thing, he knew, that should happen to him. He reached down and felt the horse's flank — skin flexing over a rib. The warmth of it beneath his palm.

"Naaliyah?" he asked. "Did you lift me?"

"Ssshh," she said. "Hush now."

The horse stepped down through the trees. She folded him onto the bench seat of the truck and fastened the seat belt around him. The snow came harder.

Book Five

1

From Eagle, Naaliyah drove him 145 miles south to the medical clinic in Dawson City. He slumped against the doorframe, asleep or deeper: submerged in a kind of torpor. The truck — a three-quarter-ton F-250 diesel four-by-four the university was letting her use for the winter — skidded through the curves.

In the treatment room they plugged an IV into his arm and asked Naaliyah to fill out paperwork she had no way of filling out. Address, insurance information, method of payment — she left it all blank. "I have a credit card," she said. "Please." The nurse swiped it, told her to sit down.

Dehydration, natriuresis, advanced fatigue, giardiasis, a hematoma (but no fracture) in his right foot, fever, corneal burn — the doctor ticked off a lexicon of afflictions. For three consecutive nights Naaliyah slept on the bench seat of the truck. At dawn she'd cross into the trees behind the clinic and watch the insects who had survived the first snow embark on their errands, all of them tentative, floating or crawling uneasily between the melting patches of slush as if conscious that these would be their last days and questioning the purpose of it all.

On the fourth afternoon she walked the hall to his room and stood at his window for a half hour or so: the parking lot beyond the hedge, a row of trucks, then a rising wall of spruce. A broken raft of clouds was driving across the sun and the trees alternately brightened and dimmed, a thousand shades of blue. When she turned back to the bed, his eyes were open.

"What's it like?" he asked.

"What's it like where?"

He swiveled his eyes toward the window.

"Rainy. It rains all the time. But it's beautiful. Back at the camp there's a creek. A laboratory in the cabin. And insects, of course."

He nodded as if this was something he had guessed. She levered the blinds shut. They could hear the quick percussions of a typewriter through the wall.

"They say I won't make it," Naaliyah said. "The other graduate students. The ranger in Eagle. Hell, everyone I meet in Eagle. Even Professor Houseman back in

Anchorage. They say I'll break down and radio for help when the real cold comes."

"They don't know you."

"Maybe they're right anyway."

"I doubt it."

Both of them were quiet. Winkler shifted in his bed. Outside the door, in the hall, a doctor dropped a tray of metal tools, spoons or scalpels, and they listened to her curse and collect them off the floor. A CB in the nurses' station sizzled and went quiet.

"Naaliyah," Winkler said. "Will you take me with you?"

She dressed him in a thrift shop sweatsuit and Brent Royster's sneakers (unlaced to accommodate his swollen feet), helped him sign a voluntary release, and half-carried him to the truck.

She drove fast. Raindrops smacked the windshield and streaked toward its edges. Winkler could still not see very clearly; speed limit signs were smudges of white, the road shoulders long, wet blurs. He had the sense that the endless avenue of spruce was closing off behind them, that they pushed back toward Alaska like an air bubble forced through ice, the exit sealing off behind.

Camp Nowhere was five hours from Dawson, twenty-five miles northeast of Eagle, in a corner of the two and a half million acres of streams and bluffs the government had named the Yukon-Charley Rivers National Preserve. The snow had all but melted and the road was heavy with mud. At a park service station, two sad brown buildings, Naaliyah stopped for a few moments and stood in the drizzle talking with a ranger who touched her shoulder lightly and peered past her into the truck.

Winkler looked away. Out across the river the trees were unbroken, a single gray stain. From the park service cabins she turned east and left the river, ascending a tributary stream along a ragged, switch-backed track. For an hour they saw no one, not the flat, rusted barges on the river behind them, not even contrails of airplanes in the sky above the trees. The truck churned higher; the road became little more than creekbed. Winkler couldn't help the fear starting in his chest. He thought of Idaho, the lightning storm gathering in the air; he thought of the night he had spent in the sea, clinging to a smashed thwart, the hordes of stars crowding above him.

Eventually the track spit them out into a

clearing: an outbuilding, a cabin with one long window and a door, moss growing on the roof, unsplit logs stacked against the outer walls. He blinked through the windshield. "Home?"

Naaliyah nodded. The truck ticked; drizzle sounded lightly against the roof. "Come on," she said.

He breathed, and tried to steady himself. Out of the truck his eyes felt dry and sandy. Even from the clearing, thirty feet away, he could hear her insects inside — a relentless, almost genital thrum.

It was a single twelve-by-eighteen room and three-quarters of it were given to bugs. Along every wall gleamed shelves of insectaries: traditional glass-walled boxes; milk cartons capped with cheesecloth; trees of cotton-plugged test tubes; mulch-filled fishbowls; baby food jars; flowerpots with conical screens braced over them; a half dozen other kinds of containers Winkler with his poor eyes could not make out. Naaliyah was moving among them, prying open lids, murmuring things he could not hear. The smell was of overripe fruit, humid and sticky.

Furniture was arrayed around the space as afterthought: a sawhorse-and-plank table, an army cot draped in mosquito netting, two chairs, a barrel stove, a lantern.

He settled on the cot. His eyeballs throbbed. "You get used to the noise," Naaliyah said. But to Winkler the clamor seemed to rise, waxing, and waxing further still: clacking mandibles, vibrating wings, wet, smacking sounds like something large being chewed.

He tried to nod. "I might close my eyes," he said.

2

He did not get up for two days. Naaliyah moved through the space around him, soaking his foot, tending insects, stacking more and more logs outside the walls. She eased onto a blanket in the corner for a few hours of sleep each night.

It was as if her vigil from the boat shed, decades earlier, had begun anew. In his clearer moments Winkler wondered if, sooner or later, every event recurred, if life consisted of a series of repeated patterns: the scar on his knee; now an injury to his foot. Viewed from above, maybe lives looked like matrices of color, scarves on a loom. He wondered: When I wandered out of that town, heading toward the airstrip, was I planning on coming back? Or was I trying, as I did with Nanton's rowboat, to let the world take me?

A window in a barn; a riptide off a reef. Both eventually gave him back, fishermen hoping for something better. Saved, nursed back again. And to what?

The insects grunted and drummed. She spooned oatmeal into his mouth. "I feel like one of Einstein's astronauts," he said. "The one who travels at light speed and then comes back to Earth and everyone who knew him has aged and died. He has, what, a granddaughter left? But she's so old she doesn't remember him."

Naaliyah frowned. "Don't be ridiculous."

He rolled in the mosquito netting. Her crickets sang without pause, like a throng of deranged egg timers counting him down. And the smell: like old breadfruit, like conch-egg cases stranded in the sun. When he woke it often took an entire minute before he figured out where he was.

He'd try to see Naaliyah clearly: a reflection of light in her hair; a smell on her hands like mashed banana (a paste she fed beetles); a shift in temperature as she crossed the room. It was hard sometimes to believe she was actually there, in the space around him, thousands of miles from the place he had last seen her — as if St. Vincent and its outer islands had been a dream no one could cross over from, a wall erected between two places and times; as if she were still a child, balanced on his shoulders, ducking to avoid an overhanging branch. She could not also — simultaneously — be this grown, competent woman, a young biologist prying larvae from a rotten stick with a jackknife.

But here she was — not a ghost or figment, but *real:* a hand on his ankle, water pouring out of a bucket, a kettle scraping across the stove. She had slipped through a crack somehow, a rift in the fabric, an intersection at the edge of things.

Out the window was a white diesel tank on wheels, rusted around the edges, and a clattering generator in wooden housing. Fifty yards behind that stood a small shed, half the size of the cabin, crammed with unsplit logs. This gloomy assemblage composed the entirety of Camp Nowhere: cabin, shed, generator, and a cracked and mosquito-haunted Porta Potti, all in a boggy clearing encircled by millions of stunted pines. "Is this Canada?" he asked, forehead at the window. "Is it America?"

"It's Alaska," she said, then looked up from her work. "The boundary is east of the river. Out there." She pointed over her shoulder. "We passed it on the way in, don't you remember? They shave it. A thirty-foot-wide swath and they mow it all the way to the Arctic Ocean."

Lice brewing in a mayonnaise jar; arctic wooly bears climbing fishbowl walls; two dozen mosquitoes furring the gap between a cuff and glove. She held a hand lens over their intricate, alien faces; she let them cross her throat, traverse her shirt.

Thirty-one years old, and already Naaliyah was more comfortable with insects than people: they were more chemically predictable, more elegantly designed. Ten billion insects for every square kilometer of land surface — a million ants for every person — *and humans,* she scribbled in the margin of a textbook, *think they dominate Earth.*

Halfway between the cabin and shed hunkered a big trapezoidal desk, warped from rains and frosts, and an office chair with the padding rotted out. It was here Naaliyah worked, in nearly any weather, sitting at that table with a row of specimen bottles in front of her, wearing gloves and a head net against mosquitoes. Up here, she said, things were simpler, the numbers of species smaller, easier to get her mind around.

But she was a romantic still: she could spend a whole morning watching the high-wire act of a garden spider spinning silk; or a pupa chewing at the seams of his chrysalis. At night she'd close her eyes and imagine: over a hundred million billion insects hatching and dying every year — all those bristling, pointed, winged lifetimes: murderers and egg raiders, cooperators and queens. There were the glamorous dragonflies and fearsome widows; slave-holding ants; migrating monarchs; the delicate mantid chewing down her lover; dragonflies making love at thirty miles an hour — all the flagships of entomology.

But lately she had become a fan of the lumpen multitudes: midge larvae and tubal worms, button lice, firebrats, mites no bigger than poppy seeds who weathered nine-month winters as chips of ice tunneled beneath snow. The lesser insects gorged and tumbled their way toward metamorphosis — they were as purely engineered as anything on earth. Not trees or elk or Venus flytraps or humans: none had perfected such singleness of purpose, such diversity of arrangement. A housefly, she told Winkler, made a fighter jet look embarrassingly inept. An ant had the strength of four elephants.

Her desk, Winkler would later decide, was almost like a big insect itself, its warped carapace glinting in the sun, its legs curled as if it might spring away at any moment.

She split wood and heated stews; she took notes, hauled water from the stream, hunted the forest for more specimens: *Upis ceramboides* beneath decaying birch bark; a cluster of hostage *Pogonomyrmex* pupae in the chamber of an ant mound. Her dissertation would attempt a survey of overwintering: both diapause and freeze tolerance — how Alaskan natives and nonnatives reacted to temperature fluctuation: why, where. What triggered the voiding of water each autumn, what triggered the creation of glycerol and antifreeze proteins? How did warming regional temperatures affect reproduction? When winter came, she would let the little woodshed go cold (she had insects in there, too, stacked in terrariums on two metal shelves), while she'd use the generator, heat lamps, and stove to keep her insectaries in the main cabin warm.

In the shed the little animals would face winter as usual: the long freeze, death or diapause; a baseline experiment in the natural course of things. But in the cabin, her insects would be given amnesty: heat, light, food. How they reacted, juxtaposed against the control group, would, she hoped, lay the foundation for her study.

Winkler rose every half dozen hours to

stagger to the Porta Potti and stagger back. After seven days she stood over him with a bag over her shoulder and stirred the truck keys in her pocket.

"Weather's coming," she said. "By the weekend. I'm heading to Fairbanks to get some things. I might be gone a few days."

He sat up. A smell came off him, old and powdery. Inside the mosquito netting, clenching the sides of his forehead, he looked to her like some wasted, malarial sailor.

"I'm okay," he said. "I'm feeling better."

"Fine." They eyed each other through the barrier of the netting. "No," she said. "It's not fine. You can hardly stand up. I'm not a nurse, David. What if you're sick? I've enough to do around here."

He drove the heels of his palms into his eye sockets. For days he had been forcing himself back, again and again, into sleep. "They're dead," he said.

"David . . ."

"My wife and daughter are dead."

"You know this? Without a doubt?"

"Yes. No." He tried to explain: Sandy's obituary, the last address in Boise, how the possibilities had extinguished one by one.

"So you're giving up. From one list. Without even trying Anchorage?"

He shook his head. "No. No."

"Yes. You are. You're giving up."

She roiled her keys in her pocket and looked out across the meadow to the truck. The puffy blue jacket she was wearing, he realized, was the parka Felix had given her when she left the Grenadines. He wondered where Felix was just then, wearing his wool watch cap, his burn-scarred fingers flipping something in a pan, touching the neck of a bottle, the neck of his wife.

"What happened to your notebooks? What about your book?"

He shook his head. "I had to burn them. It suddenly seemed so unlikely to me."

"Don't give up, David. Exhaust the possibilities."

He clutched the edges of the cot and leaned forward. "You ever hope for something so much? So much you can't sleep, so much your skull hurts? But the thing is, you don't even know if the thing you're wishing for is possible? You don't even know if it could ever happen? And it's all out of your control?"

"You mean faith."

"I didn't ask for this. I didn't ask for any of it."

She said nothing for a long time. "I need to take you with me, David. To Fairbanks.

The highway will close soon. Until April."

"I thought I could stay."

She looked away. She shook her head.

"I could help. You're going to stay out here alone?"

"David. It gets cold here. Very cold. All you have to wear is sweatpants, for God's sake."

He didn't move. He tried not to look away. "Where will I go?"

She breathed, and pinched the space between her eyes. She had been preparing for this winter for five months. Were his answers in here? Behind the closed faces of moths and button larvae?

"You'll need snow gear. And more food. We'll need a lot more food."

"I have money."

"And you'll need to get up, feed some of the insects. There are notations on top of the cages. Solutions are in the cabinet. Just change out any plant water. And drop a damp cotton ball in every insectary every morning. Fresh leaves for the caterpillars, if you can find any. The spiders will be all right, I think."

"A damp cotton ball."

"For moisture."

"Okay." He was nodding maniacally. "I can do that."

"I'll be back in a few days." She studied him. "This is a bad idea, isn't it? Tell me this isn't a bad idea."

"This isn't a bad idea."

"Okay," she said. It was nearly a whisper. He watched her cross the meadow to the truck. The sun hung above the tops of the trees, pale and thin. A late cloud of gnats appeared, illuminated in a beam of light, each rising and falling independently like an infinitesimal marionette.

3

Inside his threadbare duffel were three nerite shells, lying spire to spire in a bottom fold. He ran a thumb over their apertures. They were like dreams somehow, in their compactness, their fineness, in the way they seemed complete and incontrovertible.

He rolled in the cot. The crickets shrilled. I'll get out of bed in a minute, he decided.

But he was not up until evening. He eased out of the mosquito netting and managed to cut open a can of tuna and eat its contents with a plastic spoon.

All night Naaliyah's crickets pleaded their same urgent question — *scree-eep? scree-eep?* — but right before dawn they fell abruptly silent, as if they had finally found answers, or else expired from the effort.

Silence. Winkler lay in bed trying to listen but there was nothing to listen to. Blood traveled dully through his ears. He thought: I wish the crickets would start up again. He thought: A person could go mad out here.

He fumbled through a drawer until his fingers closed around Naaliyah's hand lens. With his left eye against the eyepiece, and the focus brought all the way up, he could see whatever was in immediate proximity: creases in his palm, the grain in the wall. He went from cage to cage, peering in.

Caterpillars had forced open a hole in their wire cage; ants streamed out of a test tube and foraged systematically beneath the stove. A dozen pale beetles lay dead on the table, legs cocked at the ceiling. There were earwigs on the cot, spiders beneath the chairs. Several insectaries that may have been recently occupied now appeared completely empty.

He shivered. Was this the normal state of things? Naaliyah's feeding notations were simple enough — sugar solution in eye-droppers, bruised fruit, rolled oats, or wheat bran in dishes. More difficult were the creatures who ate live insects — he was to seize a cricket or moth in forceps and drop it into a neighbor's cage. The moth was the worst: he snared it in a tiny aquarium net and shook it into a jar that contained a praying mantis. With the hand lens he watched the mantid strike, invisibly fast, and her round mouth lap a bead of liquid from the moth's split head; the wings still vibrating, a gray powder smearing the mantid's arms, the moth's arms still clutching her abdomen, like a confused, decapitated lover.

Dozens of awful dramas were climaxing around him every minute: jailbreaks, war parties, ambushes. When he listened closely he could hear them now: chewing, spitting, clacking about. He cringed, felt queasy; he pulled the lens away from his eye and let the world go blurry.

When he finished the main cabin, he went to the shed. There was firewood in every square inch of the place, and stacked around the outside as well. Here, jammed among the logs, the insects seemed calmer, arrayed on their two sets of shelves, numbed perhaps by the cooler air, more assured of their coming ends. The mosquitoes were fewer here, too, as if this was territory they had yet to discover. A draft trickled through gaps in the wood. The air smelled of spruce.

That night he went to sleep not in the main cabin but in the shed, between the shelves, on a narrow bed made from cut boughs and beetle-chewed furs: elk, maybe, or moose. Left here by some previous tenant: scientist, or miner, or trapper. Strange to think that the animals themselves had only been tenants, too, guests inside their coats.

When the cold came, seeping through the gaps like some patient liquid, he tried to imagine it as purifying: a cleansing, an ablution.

In the morning he took a walking stick from the log pile and went into the woods. Spruce, and some willow and what looked like cottonwood. Birch and alder in creases. He wondered if bears were about, and recalled the frontier fables of his childhood, wounded grizzlies swatting hunters, prospectors crashing through creeks, their feet freezing solid. All along, he thought, life has been going on here. For millennia. As it has everywhere. His breath showed in front of him. He wiped the back of his wrist and counted nine dead mosquitoes in his palm.

Along the edge of the meadow was a creek that slashed its way through a few hundred yards of deadfall and muskeg to a small, black pond. The pond, in turn, drained slowly through a jam of bleached trees, down a hill, into a larger waterway: narrow and bouncing, clear to its pebbles. He bent over the riverbank and rinsed his face and arms. The water tasted like copper. He rested his hands against the bottom and felt the pebbles shift beneath his palms, the blood retreat up his wrists.

A half mile farther on he found a break in the trees where he could see the landscape to the west: a series of successive ridges all the way to the horizon: treeless summits and tundra fells — blues fading into whites, little more in his eyes than blemishes of color — the Alaskan interior. No houses, no lights, no antennas, no fire towers. Somewhere beyond it all, five hundred miles away, was Anchorage.

Even without eyeglasses Winkler could see this place had its own kind of light: pale but brilliant, permanently waning, something like the light he had seen reflecting off the Alaska Range from the rooftop of his youth.

He listened to the trees shift and toss, a sound like breathing.

When he returned to the cabin, Naaliyah was unloading things from the truck.

"Next time leave a note," she said. She looked clean, newly washed.

"I was trying to get this foot back into shape."

"Just leave a note." She had more cordwood, bags of rice and sugar, a snowsuit and parka for him. Behind the truck was a tan-colored Skidoo on a trailer, which he helped her unhitch and drag behind the cabin. Through noon they worked together, unloading things and stowing them. She glanced once at the makeshift mattress in the shed, but did not remark on it.

A few hours after dusk he rinsed out his mug and went to the door.

"You're not going to sleep out there."

"I'll be all right."

"You'll freeze."

"There are a bunch of old furs in there."

"It gets cold, David. You don't know how cold."

"I don't mind cold."

"David."

"I'll be fine."

"You'll be in the cabin by midnight."

"We'll see."

She sighed. "At least take these." She held out a small felt sleeve. Inside were a pair of glasses. "I didn't know your prescription, of course. But I knew you were nearsighted. So."

He held them a moment, studying the lenses.

"The doctor said nobody ever came to pick them up."

"Thank you. Very thoughtful."

"Well," she said. "You're welcome." He opened the door and crossed the meadow. He climbed into his makeshift bed and pulled the furs up to his neck. The moon sent its light through chinks in the shed walls. A moth flapped softly against the glass of its cage.

4

The eyeglasses, miraculously, worked. They were wide, aluminum-framed things, heavy on his nose, and the centers of the lenses didn't quite match the centers of his pupils, so that by midday an insistent pain camped out behind his forehead, but he could see. In the dusks and dawns, when the light was mild, everything became momentarily clear: the beauty of spruce, light filtering between the needles. He was even able to read a bit, a few paragraphs of one of Naaliyah's entomology texts (. . . *the subgenual organ, joint chordotonal organs, campaniform sensilla and mechanoreceptors, such as the Johnston's organ in antennae, might be used to detect these vibratory signals* . . .) before his eyes began to feel as if they were being forced in opposite directions, and the headache reasserted itself.

To see again — to discern a tree or face or cloud with an acceptable level of clarity — was the smallest kind of revival, a tiny breakthrough, but enough to start happiness in his heart — the joy of recognizing things, an improvement in his relationship with the world.

Every morning Naaliyah was up before he was, writing at her outdoor table with a battery-powered headlamp strapped around her head net. He watched her press the stinger of a hornet to the pad of her pinkie finger, release the hornet carefully, and take notes with her left hand while the stinger throbbed and ejaculated in her right.

He tried to stay out of her way: he split wood and hauled water, and went for careful strolls beside the river. Each night he drank a cup of tea with her beside the fire, the insects close around them, then said good night and went out to the shed to sleep.

Fridays she took the truck into Eagle for the mail, and to telephone Professor Houseman in Anchorage. She'd grind back up the makeshift road after dusk, and Winkler would tramp to the gap in the trees he had found: her headlights edging up the valley like a pair of sparks, the big opaque acres of the Yukon below sliding on and on. Sometimes, if the wind was blowing, branches or whole trees would blow down across the little gravel track during the hours she was gone, and

Winkler would hear her chainsaw start up — the up-and-down chewing noise of it — as she cut the tree to get the truck through.

The air grew colder. Nightfall arrived sooner and sooner. A more permanent snow line advanced down the contours. And the mosquitoes started expiring — Naaliyah would wipe a thin gray fuzz of them off her table in the mornings.

During the summer, she explained, the university paid men in Eagle to haul firewood to Camp Nowhere, cord after cord of it on trailers. When she swung the maul it fell cleanly through the logs, as if they were already split. When Winkler swung it, it bounced back, nearly into his teeth, or sent slivers flying at his coat. The wood this year was not great, she said, mostly thin stacks of spruce and alder, not much larch (she peered into split logs for sawfly larvae). How did she know all this? Winkler wondered. Where did she learn these things? She was afraid, it seemed, of nothing but the cold, and it was about this that her mind incessantly returned, as if, like her insects, its coming would signal the end of her.

After dark the light of the cabin's lantern mixed with the lights of the heat lamps to produce a carroty, almost garish orange, a glow that escaped not just through the cabin's fogged window, but through chinks in the walls, too, and the piles of wood stacked around them, until in the darkest hours it looked as though the cabin had a tiny sun trapped inside, burning through the night. Winkler would cross the meadow on his way to the outhouse and step through long beams of orange light, his shadow slipping along beside him, antic and huge.

The shed, on the other hand, grew only darker. Already it was quiet, the ants sluggish in their test tubes, the wasps stilled, the whole structure dim and shadowed save Winkler's occasional candle, flickering small and white in the aisle between woodpiles. There was so much wood in there, he thought, they could weather three winters, but Naaliyah did not stop, splitting twice as quickly as he could, working in a T-shirt, her arms pasted with sawdust.

The warblers left. No aircraft traveled the sky.

He closed his eyes and saw Felix and Soma, praying over food at their picnic table; he saw Brent Royster's turntable spinning on and on; he saw Sandy's photo go to lint in his hands. He saw Naaliyah walking away from the inn — not thirty years old, but sixteen — the clean, bare backs of her knees, shadows closing like water over her.

He began to get a sense of how things would change: the insects here in the shed were nearly done, settling into a long sleep or giving themselves up to death — their natural states unfurling, the abominable silence and cold of this uninsulated laboratory, the million distant candles of the stars.

5

In November the freezing began. It started first in hollows and alcoves in high rocks, where structures of frost appeared on the lichen, and whatever soil had gathered there darkened and hardened to the touch, as if the land was contracting, stiffening, like armor plates drawing together on the back of some titanic animal. The mosquitoes vanished altogether, and the birch and alder gave up their leaves all at once, leaching them into the wind as if desperate to be rid of them. Soon the outhouse hole froze over, as did the fringes of the creek, the unfrozen center flowing in a gluey sludge, midstream boulders wearing caps of ice. Each morning they'd find dead insects, bees and flies mostly, arched on the windowsill.

By the middle of that month the sounds of the Yukon freezing — deep, metallic reverberations, as though a Goliath beyond the next hill repeatedly flexed an enormous sheet of tin — sounded everywhere, echoing off hills and seeming to lodge in unseen hollows, only to come spiraling out minutes later, so that the air was filled, always, with the eerie, anchorless sound of water going to ice.

Naaliyah chopped plates of it from small bogs in the woods and turned them over. Beneath were water striders, squirming larvae, macroinvertebrates. "Astounding," she'd tell Winkler, and show him her plunder: a slushy mug livid with tiny swimmers: iceworms; the large-jawed larva of an antlion.

Pockets of life amid all that freezing. It was as if the cold was forcing all of them closer, into tighter and tighter communities, hurrying to find the creases and chinks in the great contracting armor of winter.

After dark, out of reach of the orange, leaking light of the cabin, Winkler would tramp to the edge of the creek and listen: its sound had grown thicker and harsher. It had frozen over now and already successive overflows were lacquering the surface. He could hear ice rolling along the bottom, grinding itself against stones, a sound like dozens of glass tumblers being crushed inside a towel. And above it the sound of the liquid water had deepened, lost some of its animation, the molecules reluctant to give up their bonds. Animals would come down tentative and shy to slurp at the overflows, deer, skunks, chipmunks, even lynxes in the night like big, sleek ghosts (he wouldn't see them but would find their prints frozen in the banks).

Still the snow marched down the mountainsides, mantling summits, filling the high trees. Stones began rising from the ground, thrown up by frost heaves, budding from the earth like strange, monolithic cabbages, and creeping down exposed slopes.

Naaliyah worked harder than ever, almost entirely abandoning her research in favor of gathering wood. She stacked wood everywhere — the shed was filled to the roof, and logs stood around the cabin's perimeter two-deep, and still she was out there, wrestling a big half keg of pinewood onto the block, dropping the maul, cleaving it to its dark, grainy heart.

Sleet, like grains of rice against the windowpane; then the tiny snowballs of graupel, wads of rime skittering across Naaliyah's field desk. Then rain again, and Winkler was disappointed to see it. Winter, he was remembering, was a balky, slow thing — it did not arrive smoothly.

One Sunday, near the back half of the month, he woke to a strange and sad concert, a creaking and yawping that drew him out into the meadow, beneath the impossible spread of stars. The face of the pond had overflowed and the new, upwelling water began to ice over the already frozen surface, and as it froze it ticked, scales of floating ice reaching across, stitching themselves into an unbroken plate, the plate thickening, trillions of water molecules ranging out and lacing. From beneath the new sheet came a sad and eerie moaning, as though the ice had trapped women beneath it.

All month the ice muttered and howled and whistled. The trees echoed back and forth among themselves. Taken collectively, the sound was of deep wounding, of winter inexorably taking the life out of things. That night Winkler stood in the meadow listening as if in a trance — the cold, the answering sounds of grief — until he couldn't bear it. He hurried toward the shed, to bury himself under his furs, to sleep among Naaliyah's thousand slumbering insects.

The night outside, the night within. This was a place where dreams and reality could intersect; where night would be the dominant feature of the landscape.

He could feel snow coming. He could taste it. The mountains were already covered with a half meter.

His right foot had healed as much as it was going to. Probably he would always limp. When he walked it would be as if one foot was permanently a step behind, as if that part of him remained in Boise, Idaho, stepping into a stranger's house, pawing at her photographs. Why couldn't he see the path in front of him? Why couldn't he dream of something to come, some reunion, or at least an answer, some glimpse of who Grace might have been?

There was the Datsun at the bottom of its canyon; the ocean sucking and sucking at Nanton's glass floor; the quiet breathing — in, out, in, out, in, out — of Naaliyah sleeping on her cot. He thought: I should have given Brent Royster all my money. I should have tucked a hundred-dollar bill into every one of his records.

On the twenty-third of November snow finally reached the camp. It battered the cabin window all day. Naaliyah came in and stoked the stove and stood at the glass beside him looking out. "You know," she eventually said, "I see what you meant. How each crystal can be a prism.

How it's full of light."

Winkler did not turn away for several hours. All day — indeed, ever since he'd arrived at Camp Nowhere — a sensitivity had been building within him: the slightest shift in light or air touched the backs of his eyes, reached membranes inside his nose. It was as if, like a human divining rod, he had been attuning to vapor as it gathered in the atmosphere, sensing it — water rising in the xylem of trees, leaching out of stones, even the last unfrozen volumes, gargling deep beneath the forest in tangled, rocky aquifers — all these waters rising through the air, accumulating in the clouds, stretching and binding, condensing and precipitating — falling.

He ate his dinner standing up, forehead at the window.

The flurries didn't stop until well into the night. He tried lying in bed, but his blood was surging, and the pale light of the snow was pouring through the shed walls, touching a place very near the center of him. He pulled on his snowsuit and boots and mittens and went out. Maybe six inches had fallen. His feet passed soundlessly through it — the ice skeleton, one of his professors had called it, that loose scaffolding of new-fallen snow, individual crystals re-forming into lattice; with a vise the professor had compressed a loaf of Wonder Bread into a two-inch cube to demonstrate how much air was trapped within.

Winkler's breath plumed up onto his glasses. The entire valley was enveloped in a huge, illuminated stillness. Above him the clouds had pulled away and the sky burned with stars. The meadow smoldered with light, and the spruce had become illuminated kingdoms, snow sifting from branch to branch. He thought: This has been here every winter all my life.

He tramped along the creek until nearly dawn, his hands and feet stinging with cold, his heart high in his throat. The sky was going a dim olive in the east, and Naaliyah was still asleep in the cot when he returned to the cabin and kicked the ice from his boots. On back shelves, where Naaliyah kept her instruments, he knew, there was a microscope: an inclined Bausch & Lomb Stratalab, probably forty years old, monocular, with a brass arm and revolving nosepiece.

He brought it outside to Naaliyah's desk. He swept snow from the tabletop, switched on the microscope's light source (a battery-powered six-volt bulb beneath the stage) and, trembling, pressed one lens of his eyeglasses to the eyepiece.

It worked. There was a disc of white light, a few specks of debris in it like tiny black commas.

He started with a spruce needle, something big, something easy. He closed the aperture on the light source, turned the focus knob. And there it was: long and green, diamond-shaped, paler on the bottom two planes.

He could not contain himself: he extracted the glass slide, wiped it, and sifted the clumped aggregates of a few snowflakes onto it. Then he slid them onto the stage.

It was like stepping back in time. A thousand frozen bonds, stunted ice structures, even the severed branch of an individual dendrite, all leapt large and backlit to his eye like a memory, like a smell — crushed mint, or his mother's skin lotion. It was as if time was pliable and he was able, for a moment, to become a graduate student once more, standing in the cafeteria freezer, all the succeeding years fallen off him like an old coat. As if the snow had been waiting all this time for him to come back.

It took Winkler the rest of the remaining daylight — only four and a half hours, by then — to locate an individual snow crystal. The snow was already aging, settling in, and he was cold, clumsy with his fingers and breath, and his eyes quickly tired. But he managed to find one, sifting down from a tree — star-shaped, the classic six-branched sectored plate — and spear it with the spruce needle and transfer it, mostly undamaged, onto the glass slide.

When he focused it in the viewfinder, the crystal wavering, then sharpening, he felt the old spark flare: six dendrites jutting off a central hexagonal core, scored with ridges. Adrenaline fired down the length of his body. His breath melted it; he stooped and began searching for another. When Naaliyah finally came out, tramping toward him with a steaming tin can, he was shivering so much he sloshed the tea onto his sleeves.

She persuaded him to go inside. Beneath his furs he saw snow crystals on the undersides of his eyelids. Like birds stirred from a rookery, memories flew into his consciousness: the sound of the fan in the cafeteria freezer, rattling as if ice were caught in its blades; Sandy's frozen bootprint that he'd excavated and preserved in his freezer; the cool, washed-cotton smell of his mother. He saw Sandy's thin form fold itself into a theater seat; he saw his mother take her nurse's uniform from a hanger and spread it across the ironing board, heard her steam iron suck and sigh as she brought it across the fabric.

He thought of Wilson Bentley, whose book of snowflakes his mother used to keep beneath the coffee table, an old farmer peering through the bellows of his camera, and the sound of Bentley's pages turning in her hands.

Thirty-six hours after the first snow, a second arrived, falling like stars, filling the trees. He stood in the clearing and caught flakes in a black plastic tub Naaliyah used to sort ants. When he snared a flake he thought might be an undamaged crystal, he coaxed it onto the glass slide with another of Naaliyah's tools: tiny forceps, intended for a watchmaker.

Hollow bullets, sectored plates, prismatic columns, dozens of elaborate stellar dendrites — soon he was seeing all the patterns of his youth, all melting fast beneath his attention and the heat of the microscope's lamp.

With each shift in temperature or humidity, the crystals' shapes varied slightly, like finely tuned thermometers. He imagined them growing in the clouds, the initial molecules precipitating, the wind blowing them through slight gradations in temperature, each prismatic arm growing — the invisible made visible. He could not, it seemed, grow tired of them — watching light travel their arms, whole spectrums of blues and greens and whites, the edges softening already, wilting toward water.

After dark he went into the cabin and sat with Naaliyah over a bowl of noodles. "You know," she said, "that microscope has a photomicrography kit somewhere in here. I haven't used it, but I'd bet you could get it to work. All you'd need is film."

Winkler stopped chewing. "To take photos?"

"Of course."

He stood. "Can I do that? Do you know how to operate it? Will you order the film? Next time you're in town?"

"Of course." She laughed. "Of course."

She radioed in her request and nine days later brought it back from the post office in Eagle with their laundry and perishables: four-by-five-inch color print Polaroid film in packs of twenty. His hands shook tearing open the package. The pieces were big, and went brittle in the cold, and he creased two of them before he could even load the sheet film holder properly.

These were not the only obstacles. He needed more light — he was afraid to increase the wattage of the tiny bulb in the microscope's base for fear it would melt the crystals even more quickly. He needed steadier hands; he needed better eyesight. He needed more daylight — there was hardly any left. And his breath proved a substantial obstacle: if he breathed in the direction of the crystal, he blew it away, or softened its edges; if he breathed while he tried to hold the camera steady, it shifted and spoiled the image.

In the end what this amounted to was rushing through the snow trying to grasp at seconds. He had to wait for it to snow, then locate a whole crystal among the billions of flying aggregates. Then — if he found one — he had to transfer it undamaged onto a slide, position the slide under the microscope, focus it, ensure the crystal did not touch the lens, screw on the camera, align the film, and speculate a proper length for the exposure.

His first day he made four exposures. His second he made six. None of them came out: each a field of black with a tidy white border.

He was far from discouraged; indeed, Winkler felt he was at the cusp of something, a discovery, a lesson he profoundly needed to learn. Inside him things were unlocking, thawing, or clarifying — something like the sharpening image of a crystal as it came into focus in the eyepiece of the microscope.

Long underwear, two pairs of wool socks, two wool shirts, jeans, a down vest, a balaclava, gloves, and the snowsuit — second, third, fourth skins. Naaliyah had thermometers in several of the shed's insectaries but Winkler decided it would be better if he did not look at them. It sank to perhaps a dozen degrees below zero. The snow that fell was thin and fine as flour.

Cold and darkness became the normal state of things. Marmot tracks written in the snow around the cabin; crows standing in trees; the stovepipe groaning and creaking as the morning fire heated it. Sometimes the sound of the Yukon shifting under its burden of ice — the last water in the valley to freeze — would repeat up and down the valley, a great, internal buckling, as if dwarves were at work, detonating things inside the earth.

In the cabin the insects were as ravenous as ever, some even confused by Naaliyah's artificial lights into singing. But in the shed nearly all of the insects had disappeared. Some of the cages she packed with snow, to insulate them. "They're in there," Naaliyah told him, tapping the side of a Mason jar, her breath fogging, then freezing on the glass. "They're in diapause now."

She spent much of her energy worrying over the generator, paging carefully through its owners' manual, her finger tracing the sentences. Each morning she checked the extension cords, the generator's plugs, put her ear to the alternator casing and listened.

Outside the hills were battered by ice. He remembered how his first hydrology professor had begun a lecture: If water had its way, if geology stopped, the seas would chew up the continents, and rain would wear down the mountains. Water would eventually scour the entire planet into a smooth, definitionless sphere. We'd be left with a single ocean, waist-deep, all over the globe. Then, with nothing left to throw itself at, all the divisions and obstacles eroded — no unworn pebbles, no beaches to crash onto, every water molecule touching another — water would disclose, finally, what was in its molecular heart. Would it stand calm and unruffled? Or would it turn on itself — would it throw itself up into storms?

Winkler turned beneath his blankets and watched stars pass slowly in and out of the gaps in the shed walls: there for a few seconds, shining in the breach, then gone. His dreams were of snow crystals, sifting through trees.

6

For Christmas, Naaliyah thawed a chicken (they stowed uncooked food on the roof inside locked plastic bins) and baked it, and afterward they sat in the cabin watching coals in the stove bank and glow while her insects ate their own meals around them.

"I have something," Naaliyah said, and pulled a box from beneath the cot.

Winkler shook his head. "You didn't."

"It's from my mother."

Inside was a plastic bag of flour mix, and a letter for each of them. The mix had a note in it, a recipe from Felix: they were to beat it with eggs, milk, sugar, and bananas, and bake it. *Happy Christmas, Americans!* Felix had scribbled across the bottom. Winkler and Naaliyah exchanged a smile: they had no bananas or eggs, and only powdered milk. But they stirred it together as well as they could, and set it on top of the stove in a pan. As it cooked it smelled to them like the Caribbean, like Felix, and when it was done they cut the flat, cinnamon-laced loaf in half and ate their portions quietly, with a kind of reverence.

Then they took their respective letters and read them in the firelight. His said:

Dear David —

Sorry to hear your search went so poorly. But have heart. Hope is something that can be very dangerous but without it life would be horribly dry. Impossible, even. Take it from me.

Here things are as usual. Felix is drinking as much as possible, and will sometimes stand on Nanton's glass floor and shout down at the fish. He thinks this is very funny, despite my and Nanton's assurances that it is not.

The boys are all well, running their various shops, and the island is jammed with tourists for the holidays. Knowing you, you haven't been reading the papers so I'll tell you that the Chilean judiciary suspended the charges against Pinochet and dropped the case. All that, and diabetes saves him.

Nonetheless, we are considering a trip back to Chile. Just a visit. Felix is ready, I know — he has been ready for fifteen years. But I'm still not sure. I would like to see Santiago. The parks, the haze on the mountains.

Merry Christmas, David. God bless you.

I hope you will appreciate my gift — I am trying to give you your daughter back, as you once gave me mine.

Soma

Outside Naaliyah's automatic timer clicked, and the generator rumbled to life. The heat lamps flickered, then glowed. Naaliyah had been watching him read his letter and when he folded it closed, she handed him another envelope.

"It's from my mother, too."

Inside was a square of paper with an address:

Herman Sheeler
124 Lilac Way
Anchorage, Alaska 99516

Inside the stove a log collapsed and went to embers with a metallic, hollow sound. Winkler felt his epiglottis open and close over his trachea, as if he were gulping phantom liquid.

"We thought you might want to have the address."

He shook his head.

Naaliyah began to reach toward him, but withdrew her hand. "Are you okay, David?"

Now Winkler could feel anger rising

476

through his chest. He had thought of Herman before, of course: Herman at his big First Federal desk calendar; Herman at hockey practice, crouched in front of a net; Herman at — he could hardly think of it — some event of Grace's, a graduation, a science fair. Herman at Sandy's bedside, Herman at Sandy's funeral. But to see his name printed now in front of him was to somehow make him real again, as real as if Winkler were standing outside Herman's front door, asking if Sandy the metal artist was home.

The address dissociated itself, the letters straying off, becoming cuneiform, meaningless.

Naaliyah watched him with her hands clamped to her knees.

"Soma did this?"

"She wanted to give you something."

"It's not her business." He folded the square of paper and folded it over again.

"We just thought . . ." Naaliyah said, but stopped. The fire was only three feet away and he could have thrown the address in and watched it flare and go to ash. But what would be incinerated?

"Well." She stood and collected the cake pan and began to wash it in the bucket. "Merry Christmas anyway."

7

He set the folded square of paper high on a shelf, between two quart milk cartons stuffed with frozen peat. It was a place he trained himself not to look, a little black hole on a shelf, a location in space too perilous to get close to.

New Year's came and went and he did not allow his mittens or even his eyes to pass over that corner of the shed. Their wood was disappearing quickly — already there was a bit more space in the wood-shed, and most of the logs stacked around the cabin had been given up to heat, and smoke.

Someone had lived in that woodshed before. Lids of tin cans had been nailed over knotholes; strands of twine were stuffed into chinks between the boards. Small enough defenses against winter. But the breaches were too many, and cold air slipped easily through them. Indeed, cold passed through the walls themselves, as if the wood was saturated and could hold no more. Whoever had lived in here before, he decided, had not lasted.

Some mornings he could *smell* the cold, a smell like ammonia, a smell he could feel his bones tighten against. He had to shake his limbs to resurrect the blood in them. Even inside the shed, he breathed through a scarf, and in turn through a balaclava, until the moisture in his breath had frozen the fibers so badly he had to turn, and tramp back to the cabin, to thaw it all out.

Although he had still made no acceptable prints, he worked harder than ever, Naaliyah returning from town each week with package after package of film. After each exposure he turned from the big desk and ran the film into the cabin, dragging the cold in with him, waiting breathlessly to pull out the film leader and separate the positive and negative, only to find his print utterly black, or gray, or a smeary sheen of reflected glare.

But the work suited him, the tediousness of it, the challenge. The way it pushed other thoughts and desires to the edges. The thrill of seeing a magnified crystal, slowly wilting beneath his attention, did not abate. When he woke the day was his, with all its attendant minutes. He and Naaliyah lived simply: they collected the pot of stew from the roof where she'd stowed it and thawed it on the stove. If it wasn't snowing, or hadn't recently, he lost himself in the rhythm of chopping wood or shook snow from tree limbs hoping to dislodge and collect individual snow crystals.

Despite Naaliyah's protests, he continued to sleep in the shed, out of propriety, or obstinacy, perhaps, but also because he had genuinely grown to prefer it. There was something about the cold he liked — it felt purifying, sliding through the dwindling stacks of wood. It was the same thing, he realized, that Naaliyah loved about her insects: the essences of things were clearer with them, the violences and loves of life. Cold demanded a sharper, simpler view of things: in those temperatures death hovered at the margins, offering clarity, providing precision.

But it blurred things, too: the border between dreams and wakefulness, the way it pulled life from fingers and toes, and released them reluctantly, temporarily. The way the wind came, like news from another, more tenuous world, and stirred the trees.

Naaliyah did not mention Christmas again except to ask, each Friday, before she went to town, "Any letters you want to mail?"

In the bitterest parts of January freezing air drained through the woodshed as if it were made of cheesecloth. He rose every hour or so to hurry across the meadow beneath the brilliant, awful sky (the whole arm of the galaxy seeming to drape over the meadow, as if he could reach up and pluck out some blue and frozen sun as he passed beneath it) into the cabin to shove wood into the stove, to try to kick his feet warm.

Naaliyah would be asleep on the cot, and the heat lamps would click off and on, and the stove would groan as its metal stretched. Outside all the water was going to ice and inside steam formed on the windows and frosted over, as though the cabin had become a body itself, jacketed in ice, with the small, insatiable stomach of its stove burning on and on.

Near the end of January it became truly cold. The ranger on the CB told them it was twenty degrees below zero, but to Winkler cold was cold and he was angry that it prevented him from staying outside for more than two or three minutes. The film stuck; the focus knob locked up — work was impossible. It took an hour by the fire to undo what thirty seconds of exposure could do to his fingers. His toes were pebbles, glued together. If he took a cup of boiling water outside and threw it up in the air, it crystallized before it hit the ground.

On most days now the sky was the same color as the trees and the trees were the same color as the snow. Ice fog, they called it. To move through a landscape like this was to find yourself moving through a dream. His own hand loomed before his face, huge and out of proportion. Winkler could see the fear growing in Naaliyah's face, in the scarlet splotches on her throat, in the way she did not get out of bed until the daylight was nearly gone. You could walk in circles out here; you could almost feel yourself entering the old pioneer tales, the survival stories, trappers eating shoe leather, miners frozen into creeks.

Naaliyah had been right to ask: Were they prepared for this? She listened for the generator above the wind as if her life depended on its rumble. Which, in a single, clarifying sense, it did — as did the lives of her insects, all of them attuned to the tenuous orange glow of the heat lamps.

He brought in wood, brought in snow to melt for water. All around them ice touched at the walls of the cabin and the tip of the chimney like a hundred thousand tiny fragments of glass, tinkling softly. At night he tried to sit it out in the shed, the cold coming from everywhere now, like a deep, patient submersion, but he could not make it — it was too cold, too impossible, and he'd have to push himself to his feet and drag his body and the furs across the meadow, back into the cabin. He'd sit by the fire, the cold refusing to leave him, and stare into the coals.

Naaliyah would have her eyes open in the cot, her sleeping bag at her chin, two wool hats on her head, one over the other. The insects were silent.

On the twenty-eighth of January the generator quit. Naaliyah spent almost an hour outside over the wooden housing, examining the points, the fuel filter, and another hour pulling relentlessly on the starter cord, but couldn't get it to turn over. They had plenty of fuel, and their batteries were charged, but the heat lamps would suck them dry in twenty or so hours, and then the CB would go down, and they would have to leave.

They did not talk. Winkler went out to the meadow and stood over her for a moment and watched her shiver and the wind turn the pages of the generator manual. "Let's eat something, Naaliyah," he said. "C'mon. Keep our strength up."

She relented. He put some larch into the stove — the good, hot-burning larch, a piece of two-hundred-year-old tree that had drifted down the river and been trailered up there to save their lives. Naaliyah clambered up on the log pile to retrieve a pot of frozen stew. Together they sat in front of the fire and watched the broth thaw, and the fat begin to rise to the top. When it was ready Naaliyah — who was still shaking awfully — stood to transfer it from the stove to the table, but she was wearing mittens, and lost her grip, and it spilled. A brown, steaming pool spread across the floor, chunks of carrots and beef surfing out at its edges. Within a minute, the broth closest to the walls began to freeze.

Neither said anything. Wind roared across the meadow. The roof sounded as if it was going to tear off. Winkler could hear their food — pounds of it in heavy bins — slide toward the edge. What was left of the stew soon glazed the floorboards and he forced himself to his feet and began to chip it free.

Naaliyah stood in the center of the cabin and put her hands over her eyes.

The wind died around midnight and a thick raft of ice fog settled into the meadow. Winkler went out to the generator and peered into it with a flashlight and touched various parts and screws and cleaned frost off the hour meter with his mittened thumb but could not have told the difference between the alternator and a circuit breaker. After ten or so minutes he went in and stood over Naaliyah where she lay, eyes closed on the cot.

"Can you fix it?"

She turned her head. "No."

"It's totally ruined? A loss?"

She shrugged.

"I think you can fix it. One more try. Give it a half hour. If you still can't do it, then we'll get out of here; we'll go to town and take showers. But I think if maybe you try one more time, you'll get it. I'll keep the fire high. I'll bring you hot tea."

"David," she started, but did not say more. He went to sit by the stove. A half hour passed and he thought she might be sleeping when she got up and pulled on her snowsuit and boots and took the little tackle box full of tools and went out.

All day she worked. He brought her mugs of hot water; he brought her canned soup. Every twenty minutes she came inside to shake the blood back into her hands. Around 3 p.m., with the daylight failing, Winkler heard the generator rumble to life, then die, then start back up again. She came and pushed open the door and looked at him, grease on her face, both mittens black.

Winkler had thawed a package of frozen peas and turned to Naaliyah and winked. "I'll make dinner tonight," he said, and she set her tools down on the table, and after a moment, began to laugh.

8

The generator hung on. Some nights they'd stop whatever they were doing and listen to it as if listening to a beloved tenor. The insects pressed onward, still eating, some even mating, metamorphosing.

Their lives moved deeper and cleaner, as if they were shedding weight. Conversations would lapse for whole hours or even days, and then one of them would pick up the thread again, as though their tongues had frozen midconversation and could only temporarily break free.

"Why not write him, David?"

"What's the use?"

"Why not try?"

He groaned. "She's dead. They're all dead. I'm trying to move on."

"But you can't! You don't want to leave these woods, you don't want to do anything but peer into that microscope. This winter is going to end eventually. And I'm going back to school, back to Anchorage."

He shook his head. The cold was difficult but for some reason the idea that this winter would end was not something he could allow himself to consider. He'd retreat outside to work with his microscope, scanning flakes, maybe — if he was lucky and it was snowing — making a single exposure. In the deep cold the only crystals that fell were columns, or pyramids, devoid of innovation. An hour or two later he was back in, rubbing his hands in front of the stove, feeling the cold slowly — so reluctantly — leave his clothes.

Naaliyah didn't look up from where she was dissecting a mantid. "Don't you at least want to know what happened? Even if they *are* gone?"

He watched the embers in the stove.

"My mother is right," she said.

"No."

"You write him, David. I'll mail it. Just one letter."

"You don't understand. I'm the last person he'd help."

"Try it."

Naaliyah made her Friday trips into town, wrapping herself head to toe in furs, ski goggles over her eyes. Sometimes it seemed like he could hear the chewing, droning engine of the Skidoo all the way to

Eagle, the buzz of it in the high, frozen air, among the glitter suspended there. It would cease for an hour or so, then begin again, growing louder, as she made her way back up the valley. She brought film, vinegar, tomato paste, powdered eggs, five-pound cans of peanut butter, once a bottle of Chianti that froze and cracked on the way back up, so that they had to thaw it in a pot and strain out the glass and drink it hot.

The snow did not accumulate in enormous quantities there — maybe six feet all winter — but it snowed often, nearly every day in February, tiny flakes sifting through the pall of fog, landing in his basin.

On the fifth of February he made his first successful print of a snow crystal, a classic, cold weather hexagonal plate. It was unfocused around the edges, and slightly lopsided, but well centered in the exposure, and a formation very like the shape of a pilot's wheel was braced in- side.

Looking at that tiny hexagon of ice — a crystal now lost to the world — he felt his heart stall; it was like watching an image from one of his dreams appear again in the air and light, right in front of his eyes.

Naaliyah held it to the window. "Lovely."

"It's a start," he said.

Watch the snow fly through the air. Watch the wind come up, and the flakes rise, and swim — each, it seems, travels in a separate direction. The flakes grow bigger; they blow in ghostly waves; they become flowers, raging through the boughs. In the arctic, Winkler had heard, explorers became hypnotized watching snow fall, so entranced they had frozen to death. And what, indeed, he thought, standing at the desk in the outrageous cold, could be more important than watching snow fly into the meadow, and settle on the hills, and gradually conceal the trees?

"Mango," he'd say.

"Passion fruit," she'd say.

"Pizza."

"Oreo cookies."

"Pineapple juice."

"Oh, pineapple juice. How about draft beer? How about curried whelk?"

"Your father's curried whelk. With banana bread."

"With banana bread and fresh butter. And baked grapefruit with honey and cinnamon." On the stove their oats bubbled and murmured as they thickened.

★ ★ ★

February, late afternoon, hours after dark, and Winkler stood over his microscope studying the faint tracery of a snowflake in the wavering light of the microscope lamp (the opaline, almost translucent formation of the snow against the dirtier, more insistent white of the bulb) when Naaliyah appeared at his elbow. "David," she said, and gestured with her chin. "Look up."

A vast curtain flapped in the sky above the trees. It rippled, then became something like a scarf, then a green wedge, a wing, gliding solemnly in front of the Milky Way. He switched off the microscope and they stood in the meadow together, looking up, the vapor of their breath standing out in front of them, and freezing, and settling back onto their cheeks.

Shivering emeralds and blues, trimmed with red. Jades. Violets. An eerie green traveling the meadow, lighting their maze of frozen prints. In the nights to come the auroras appeared around the same time, as if scheduled, and stayed sometimes until after midnight. He'd lie under his blankets and old furs beside the cages of frozen, entombed insects, and the borealis would shuttle and crackle overhead, illuminating the shed through the ever-increasing gaps in the woodpiles, as though a dim and alien craft had landed in the meadow.

He closed his eyes. The light crept through his eyelids. Dreams came over him like tides, like glutinous liquids.

He dreamed of trees freezing, exploding in the night; he dreamed of wolves galloping a ridgeline, and of miniature labyrinths beneath the snow. Maybe, he considered later, they were the dreams of the insects themselves, traveling in the frigid air between them on invisible threads. Maybe they had always been there and he was only now tuning them in, as if he were still on the beach, roaming the frequencies with his shortwave. Their hibernal dreams: ice crystals beneath their exoskeletons, inside their minuscule organs, their blood suspended in filigrees and crowns and diadems. Each dreaming of that day when the thaw would come, when the sun would reach them in their stump or cocoon or tunnel and switch them on like a lamp.

Naaliyah had discovered an odd thing, and had been grappling with it since December. Despite heat, and extended periods of light, even despite the abundant food she placed in their cages, maybe a third of her insects had gone ahead and stowed themselves in their hibernacula anyway. As if they understood that their environments were contrived, artificial. Or as if they understood the changing of the season internally, some chemical turning calendar pages inside them. As if what they were was something inescapable, determined by evolution and independent of circumstance.

Two successful prints. Four. Seven. Ten. He pinned them to the walls of the shed with penny nails, little four-by-five-inch postcards of snow crystals, a hall of fame of departed snowflakes, some prints speckled with white or missing a corner, others blue and curled from the cold. But still, not even a dozen. Bentley had tens of thousands. How had he done it?

Past the middle of February he went out in the early dusk and tramped his way to the gap in the forest, a raven following him as he went, sailing above the trees, as if lonely for company in the silence. He was thinking of his father. Though he had read the newspaper cover to cover each evening, he had never once said: "Hey, David, listen to this," never seemed to know anything at all about current events. Whenever somebody around his father spoke of things going on in the country, his father would say nothing, or worse, look down the street, into the distance, not listening. "Nixon," a neighbor would say. "I said, Howard, what do you think of the vice president?" As if the newspaper were in a different language, or the words were not words at all, or else his father had lost the ability to process them.

The air was so cold that it burned his nostrils. He stood and watched the light seep out of the sky for as long as he could — maybe five minutes — the blue light failing, but another coming up on the hills, as though the snow itself was incandescing. The trees and bare willows below him, out on the floodplains, had become so heavily caked with ice that they'd become other-worldly things, big ice-caked cauliflower heads, and there was no wind, and far below him, like black specks, past the reach of his eyesight, a pair of ravens as big as eagles tore into something dead out on the frozen plains of the Yukon. Out there, beyond it all, in the place where distance merged everything into a swirling, depth-less color like mercury, was Anchorage: where his father had lived his whole life, bringing people milk.

On his way back to the cabin, he stepped in and out of his boot prints, the snow squeaking beneath his weight. He was halfway across the meadow — Naaliyah's cabin light glowing, leaking through the slats in the siding, the chimney blushing smoke, as if the place contained some secret and fortunate enchantment, something worth hiding from the world — when he saw the moose.

She stood at the cabin window, peering in. Her tail flicked back and forth like a milk cow's. Her big eyes blinked. She was almost as big as Naaliyah's F-250.

For a moment he was not afraid, only curious. What must she have thought, staring in there? The heat and moisture escaping through the walls, the smells and sounds of insects — as if summer had been trapped inside a little box and kept in the middle of the woods — it must have stretched her ability to comprehend.

She stood a while longer, huge and quiet. Cold crept up Winkler's arms. Then she turned and contemplated him, entirely unsurprised. A moment later, she trotted off into the trees, light-footed as a fawn, disappearing into the snow.

A slow breeze pushed through the trees and snow unloaded from several boughs.

He thought of those tiny deer he had seen on the roadside years ago, when he and Sandy were speeding toward Ohio — the deer that Sandy had not bothered to look up to see, deer like the ghosts of deer. He wondered if this moose, too, was a ghost, and he knew somehow that when he went in, Naaliyah would not have seen it.

But here were her tracks, right beneath his feet. High on the window glass, far above his head, were two intersecting discs of vapor, quickly fading. He went in and asked Naaliyah for a piece of paper and an envelope.

9

Dear Herman —

My name is David Winkler. I grew up in Anchorage, too. I went to East High School. I met you once in your driveway on Marilyn Street. I was the one who fell in love with Sandy.

Nothing that could fit on this page, or a hundred of these pages, would possibly accommodate all the things I should say to you, all the things you deserve to hear. So please let me say this, although it is barely more adequate than saying nothing: I'm sorry. Sorry for whatever pain we caused you. For whatever pain you might still be in.

I don't know if Sandy's daughter is there with you or ever has been or if she's been dead for twenty-five years. I don't know how much you saw Sandy over the past decades either. But I wanted to say sorry. A lifetime is not really a long time, maybe, but I think I'm finally learning a little bit, coming around, and I hope it is not too late.

Enclosed is a print I made of a snow crystal earlier this month. I hope you will find it strange and beautiful, as I do.

Then:

Dear Herman —
Night makes things simpler, I think. I feel closer to the meanings of things. Here (far more than Anchorage, as I remember) there is no shortage of night. On the solstice we had only three hours and fifty-one minutes of light. The sun didn't even clear the treetops.
But what I never knew was that these are not lightless voids, like we had in the tropics. There, on a moonless night, you can't see your own palm in front of your eyes. The nights here carry their own kind of light, dim purples and navies, the golden stripe of the Milky Way, the snow reflecting and amplifying all of it. You can read newsprint by the light of a quarter moon. Dusk lasts two hours. Sunrise is still happening at noon.
I realize now I knew nothing about snow. It's not white. It's a thousand colors, the colors of the sky or what's beneath the snow, or the pinks of algae living inside it, but none of those colors, really, is white.

How wonderful it is to be my age — our age — learn you were wrong about such a fundamental thing.

What you realize, ultimately, when you have nothing to lose, is that even though the world can be kind to you, and reveal its beauty through the thin cracks in everything, in the end it will either take you or leave you.

Then:

Dear Herman —

Please disregard my last letters if you find them strange. I think you will receive these all at once, because Naaliyah only goes into town on Fridays. Perhaps you'll read this first. If so, maybe tear up the other two.

Naaliyah is the woman I'm with up here. She is an entomologist, and a good one. She spends all her time with her insects, trying to keep them alive in this wicked cold.

We eat noodles and margarine. And tuna. And canned peaches, although they're supposed to be for the bugs. My favorite is curry — Naaliyah can make curry from almost anything. It's a skill from her father, and although (don't tell

499

her this) she is not as good, we beggars cannot be choosers.

If I turn from the fire and set my food outside the cabin door, it steams for only about twenty seconds. It will begin to freeze in forty. Usually the surface of a mug of tea will freeze on the short trip from the cabin where we cook to the shed where I sleep.

But in the cabin, it's warm — even hot. The stove gets cranking and I reach up and find sweat on my forehead.

The enclosed is my best print yet, I think. It has eight arms rather than six because of simultaneous and early growth from two adhering crystals. They locked on to one another high in the clouds, and managed to get all the way down here, into my little black bucket, without breaking. Rare indeed.

Looking at it feels like an unlocking to me, like something inside is finding shape outside. Does that make sense? I hope you are well, Herman. I hope you are beside a heater, with a blanket close at hand.

He'd give the letters to Naaliyah as he had once given letters to her mother, and asked her to mail them for him even if he begged her not to later, and every Friday she came back up the valley with smoked fish or margarine or tea bags but no letters, no answers, holding her hands palms-up exactly as her mother had done twenty-five years before.

Still he worked at photographing crystals, making one or two good prints each snowfall. He was reaching the point now where he could sense snow coming hours before it hit — clouds veiling the sun, casting a pearly light, and the trees throwing their shadows across the meadow. Indeed, he was surpassing that point; he had never known snow so well, or so intimately. A smell would rise, an odor he associated for some reason with flame, and he felt his whole body tune in, as if it were connected to the sky by thousands of invisible wires, as if he himself might precipitate. *Soon it will snow. In fifteen minutes it will begin to snow.* He found he could go so far as to predict the structure of crystals: on warm noons they might get hexagonal plates, or needles; when it got colder, columns like little prisms; colder still, plates again, or equilateral triangles, or stars, or barbells, or scrolls.

In the deep cold the aluminum frames of his eyeglasses would contract and pinch the bridge of his nose, creating a compressed, squeezed feeling, like the cold had his head in a vise. Coupled with the fatigue of working with such small things all day, a simple, clarifying pain emerged behind his temples, and he would have to stand over his microscope, eyes closed, the cold cinching in around him, the blues and reds of blood in his eyelids crawling slowly across his vision.

Before long it was late March, the vernal equinox, pivot between light and dark. Days were lengthening; Naaliyah was dreaming of other seasons. She talked into the CB of pizza, of walking barefoot through sand. "Where I'm from," she'd say, "the sun gets so strong it can melt the paint off boats." Winkler, on the other hand, was almost sad to see the daylight extend; to hear, one afternoon, water dripping from the eaves. Again he thought of Sandy, the way she blinked after a movie had ended, lingering to watch the credits. "Like waking up," she had said.

Indeed they were waking up, he and Naaliyah, and the entirety of Camp Nowhere — reentering life again. Spring: a tapping on the eggshell from the inside.

In winter whole chunks of time calved and fell away, like icebergs from a glacier. It was almost as if time ceased to exist, or asserted itself in a new, previously undiscovered way. In those long, imperceptibly shrinking nights, he might look up and not even realize that the daylight had come and gone, and here it was dusk again — as if the standard method of measuring time — life, death; sunrise, sunset — was only one way, and not necessarily the most relevant one.

But in spring everything resumed: birth, daylight, family.

Dear Herman —

I remember reading this pamphlet by Kepler in graduate school, where he mused about why snowflakes each seemed to have their own individual pattern. He said all things in nature appeared to have a key — invisible to us — inside them that contained the blueprint for their exterior, for what they were. The nucleus inside a cell, the germ inside a seed. This was 350 years before Watson and Crick. Kepler went so far as to call it a soul.

Standing out there in our little meadow, watching crystals come down, I can't help but admire the idea: every snowflake with a soul. It makes as much sense as genetics, as anything — more sense, I think, than the notion that snow crystals don't *have souls.*

You should have seen the ice I used to grow in graduate school — perfect, immaculate little crystals. Little wonders. Out here in the woods crystals break easily, go lopsided under the slightest pressure. But the flakes are magnificent, bigger and more real than they were in the lab, in the way that wild animals make zoo animals seem like shadows.

It is not so much the science of snow for me, anymore. I'd rather just look at it. The light, the way it absorbs sound. The way we feel as if the more that falls, the more we are forgiven.

What were dreams? A ladle dipped, a bucket lowered. The deep, cool water beneath the bright surface; the shadow at the base of every tree. Dreams were the reciprocal of each place you visited when you were awake, each hour you passed through. For every moment in the present there was a mirror in the future, and another in the past. Memory and action, object and shadow, wakefulness and sleep. Put a sun over us and we each have our twin, attached to our feet, dragging about with us in lockstep. Try and outrun it.

He had, ultimately, only one dream left: to know his daughter, to see her hand —

what would have become of Grace's hands? All he could remember was the tiny, intricate detailing of her knuckles, and the way she had slept, as if a huntsman had come to seize her, as if her body had been temporarily vacated.

This was enough, enough to get him up in the morning, enough to break the maul free from where it had frozen against the cabin wall and drive it through a log.

10

On the first Friday in April, Naaliyah returned once more with empty hands. Winkler thought: I am living the same story over and over.

Although there were still nights of astonishing cold (the trees expanding and flexing, one or two giving up and exploding, the echoes dying quickly in the heavy air) the winter began to wane. The auroras diminished; a wedge of geese appeared in the sky one morning, winging north. Some days the sun rose high enough to melt snow off the roof of the cabin, and icicles formed during the night, pillars between the eaves and the ground. There were even hours now when Winkler could work at his microscope without gloves, could chop wood in only a wool shirt.

The warblers returned, and the juncos. Even a robin — so motionless on the eave Winkler wondered if maybe it had frozen solid and Naaliyah had placed it there as a prank. But when he reached for it, it blinked, and flapped off.

Aircraft started appearing in the southern sky, Beechcraft and Cessnas and even a big Twin Otter, circling a bit before lazing down toward the airstrip at Eagle. Naaliyah looked better each day, her cheeks taking on color, her work accumulating momentum. The winter had been a triumph she would carry with her the rest of her life. Her insects — many of them — were still alive. *She* was still alive. Some afternoons he would walk into the cabin and she'd be laughing on the CB with the ranger. "Really?" she'd say. "He said *that?*"

He could see health in her arms, in the cords of her neck. When she bent she kept her legs straight, like an athlete, her hamstrings long and tight. She washed herself with buckets of hot water and wrapped her hair and midsection in towels and walked around with her bare calves sticking out of her boots, laces trailing behind. Desire flared in him — when she brought a spoon out from between her lips, when she stood in the meadow, eyes closed, chin tilted up at the sun. He hated himself for it, for being an old and lecherous man, for the times she caught his eyes on her body a half second too long.

He sat beside the stove until after midnight and wrote. The snow pecking at the window was almost rain.

A Wednesday in early April: the sky a pale, fabulous blue. Naaliyah stood in the doorway and announced, "Tonight I'm going to town. I'm going into town and I'm going dancing. Anybody who wants to can come along." All afternoon Winkler fumbled with the Stratalab. Naaliyah shaved her legs in the dying light; she brushed her hair; she pulled on a dress he did not even know she had, black printed over with bright red macaws, and zipped her snowsuit over it.

"Do you need me to feed the insects?"

"They'll be fine. I'll be back tonight. You're sure you don't want to come?" He looked around at the meadow; he shook his head. Two minutes later she started the snowmachine and half stood off its bench and throttled off, arcing over the crust frozen on top of the snow.

The daylight slowly left the trees. He could hear the growl of the Skidoo as she guided it down through the trees, and he stood out there a moment longer, watching the light change, snow drifting between branches, and then went in.

★ ★ ★

She started going often — every few
nights, staying in town until past midnight,
once not returning until dawn. Sometimes
he'd walk out into the spruce, toward her
tracks, waiting to see the speck of her
headlight as it turned up the long trail toward the camp, shaking snow from the
overhanging trees, starting animals from
the path. Through gaps in the treetops the
frozen Yukon loomed below him, huge and
wide, here smooth as a runway, there
buckled with heaves.

He'd eat his dinner alone; he'd stare at
the CB and consider switching it on. Certainly it was the park service ranger, the
one with the wind-blasted face and khakis,
but he did not ask her and it was none of
his business anyway.

Silence boomed over the meadow, big
and pale. He fell asleep in the chair by the
stove and when he woke, still in half
dreams, he dragged himself to Naaliyah's
cot and continued sleeping there.

He woke later still to the sound of the
snowmobile roaring into the meadow. The
door opened and closed, and he heard logs
thump into the stove. He opened his eyes.
The heat lamps were all down and the only
light came from embers flaring in the stove

and a candle burning on her desk.

She smelled of beer, and hamburgers, and cigarette smoke. Ice melted from her hair and dripped onto the floor. He found his glasses on the shelf beside him. At the far end of the cabin he could just see her, bending over a cage, lifting a wire lid, taking a spider up in her fingers.

11

We went to the movies on Wednesday nights while you were at hockey games. Only in December did she start going back to my place. She would eat Apple Jacks and look out the window, thinking about you probably. As far as I could tell, she was often thinking about you. I think she had the idea of leaving Alaska before I met her, although I don't say this to deemphasize my role in it. I don't even know if "idea" is the right word, really, just an impulse, a notion — she'd open my road atlas and trace routes away from Anchorage with her finger. She said she wanted to be an airline pilot, or a cop, or a doctor. We'd lay on my mattress and look out the window at the sky. I think she wanted, more than anything, to be a mother.

I have a hole in my life because I know so little about my daughter — my and Sandy's daughter — and I beg you to search your heart and locate whatever kindness is there. Let me know in some way what happened to her. Probably I do not deserve peace but you could give me some.

I know words aren't going to do it. I used to write Sandy and think I could make her understand, but there was no way. We were too far apart.

Call me a jerk, a demon, whatever you will. But if you can, please, answer this letter.

12

One by one the ponds gulped down their ice like big, painful pills. The stars changed, and soon Naaliyah was finding tiny blades standing up from the ground when she shucked aside spruce needles to search for grubs. Everything dripped. Branches unloaded snow like they were finally and completely finished with it. In the shed a first chirring started. When Winkler got up to see, something had gnawed its way out of a stick — it had left a neat, fresh pile of wood dust on the floor of the cage.

The sound of the creek, rushing and bubbling, filled the clearing. Naaliyah dragged him down to the water and held him in it and he stood with her, the water painfully cold against his legs and the graveled bed shifting under his shoes. "Quiet," she said. "Still yourself." He shifted, shrugged, eventually managed to settle in. And for a brief moment, he felt it, a cloud of insects around him, landing and taking off, a thousand points of sense on his skin, nearly weightless. He tried to see them but could make out little more than a spotty cloud, there one second, gone the next.

"What are they?"

"Adult midges. Just emerged. Still working to harden their cuticles." She was waving a hand gently through the air. "A hundred thousand will probably hatch on this stretch alone."

It was a sound, Winkler thought, like the thrumming of the spheres, the mechanisms of the universe made audible. Spring: the sheer vigor of it, the warm and benevolent wind, stirring everything.

Just one more Friday, Naaliyah heading into town for the mail and to use the satellite phone, and check the condition of the roads. It was nearly May and she had been making preparations to leave for more than a week now, preserving insects in jars of alcohol, consolidating others into more portable cages, letting still others go. Five adult mourning cloak butterflies had survived the winter, rolled into the crevices of a stick, and she carried them out into the sun and watched them slowly heat up, opening and closing their wings, finally flapping off.

The snow left the roof, sliding off in big

slabs and collapsing to the ground with a *whump*. Winkler jumped each time.

On this last Friday, Naaliyah buzzed up in the snowmachine, its suspension and cowl lacquered with mud. "David!" she called, shouting, and he walked out into the boggy meadow and splashed through the slush. "A letter." She was breathless, glowing, fumbling through her backpack. Mud was smeared across her goggles. "He wrote back."

She held it out. A single ivory envelope with a First National Bank of Alaska return address embossed in the corner. "He wrote back," she said again.

She might have said more. But there was only that letter, caught between his hands, a bit of ink — Winkler's own name — on a field of white. If he was not careful he would lose himself in those loops of letters, lose himself there and not find his way back. He stumbled backward, making for the cabin.

Naaliyah waited outside, standing at her big warped desk, not working — all of her mind was on Winkler inside, bent on him, every thought leaning toward him, offering him so much hope that Winkler wondered, teetering before the stove, if hope might be visible on some other, still-imperceptible spectrum, coloring the air, like auroras rippling into the sky.

Sparrows moved up the ancient corridors toward Canada; elk stirred in their beds. Somewhere a brown bear stood and stretched and yawned, and three volleyball-sized cubs went tumbling out of the den after her. High on south-facing tundra the first lichens, some of them centuries old, spread their scales across the rocks.

He opened the envelope.

Dear Mr. Winkler —

Thanks for the snowflakes. There is no question they are handsome, another reason to be proud of Alaska.

Yes, yes, Grace is here, alive and well, all of that. I don't know, though, if she'll want to see you. She has a son, you know. She got married early and is already divorced. She never listened much to my advice.

Anyway here's her address. Don't tell her I gave it to you.

> *Grace Ennis*
> *208 East 16th, Apt. C*
> *Anchorage*

I don't think you're a jerk, not anymore. Maybe an asshole. That's a joke. Sorry it took

me so long to respond; I've been out of com-
mission the past few weeks.

Stop by if you're ever in town.

Herman

As with Sandy's box of returned letters, he held this letter in his lap a long time and the light changed around him and the shadows gradually extended their reach.

A sheet of paper, an answered prayer. His mind filled like a pool with a single memory: the morning, before dawn, that his mother died. Winkler was thirteen years old. His father had found her and rushed onto the landing. From his little closet-bedroom, Winkler could hear him hammering on the neighbors' door, yelling about using their telephone. The boy pulled back his mattress and stepped carefully into the parlor. She was still in her chair, her shape rigid already, all wrong, her knees showing beneath the hem of her nightgown, the fingertips of one hand outstretched to touch one of the big windows. The clamor of his father shouting and banging on the landing was improbably distant, and the smells of that furrier's storehouse-turned-apartments — foxes, lynxes, and the tannins that had been used on their coats — were suddenly, impossibly strong. The walls swarmed with ghosts; they drew out from beneath the furniture, from the radiators and the outlets, from the faucets and fissures in the beams, and the keyholes, and chinks in the plaster, the ghosts of minks and caribou, arctic squirrels and bears, marmots, moose, all these animals pouring into the apartment, hundreds of them, silent and invisible, but there nonetheless, walking about — the boy could feel them, he could smell them, he could all but see them. Their breath was on the windows.

They gathered around her in the darkness. She was so still. The animals stamped and fidgeted and flicked their tails. Her throat was stretched and her chin pointed at the ceiling, and her fingers were horribly motionless against the glass, and outside a brand-new quarter inch of snow had collected on the sill and Winkler had been grateful all his life that he had been given that moment with her, maybe one or two complete minutes, he and the animals and his mother, the only person who had really ever understood him, and he imagined he could see the animals taking her with them, solemnly and delicately, escorting the life out of her, something gauzy and illumined, like a jar full of fireflies, or the flame of a candle behind a curtain, her soul, perhaps, or something beyond words, and carrying it with them back into the walls of the building, heading for the roof.

Eventually his father came sprinting back in with the neighbors, and lamps were switched on, and the windows went black, and she was gone.

13

The Ford heaved down the ragged track. Naaliyah worked the brake, easing the truck and the Skidoo on its trailer through long patches of slush. Winkler watched an island of birch on a nearby hill, a slash of brilliance through the darker spruce like a seam of silver.

Several times they had to stop, rear wheels spinning, Winkler out of the cab and leaning into the rear bumper, cold air leaking from shadowy places between trees, the cages of insects stacked in the bed rattling beneath a tarp. But the truck always spun free, the trailer splashing through the ruts, as if their passage out of the valley was inevitable now, determined by gravity and the radiance of the day. As they descended the slush occurred less and less, and willows began to appear, wearing a haze of lime green buds, swaying in the wind.

Winkler rode with his old duffel between his legs and his prints of snow crystals stacked in his lap. Air washed over his face and down the collar of his shirt.

It took only an hour or so to reach the Yukon. Above its vast reaches gulls wheeled and soared. Rays of light dropped from broken clouds. Blocks of ice as big as boxcars littered the banks, and among them were whole trees, stripped of bark and branches, the elaborate knots and elbows of their fiber laid plain. Out in the center, past the breakup ice and a thick line of flotsam, a clear brown channel — wide as a football field — pushed forward, driving great lenses of ice downriver, toward Circle.

It was five hundred miles to Anchorage. To their left, out on the thawed stripe of river, geese were landing, one after another.

Book Six

Book Six

1

He rode the number 2 bus in a new suit holding a cheesecake in a box. A plastic price tag retainer was lost somewhere in the waistband of his pants and its end periodically stabbed his hip. He got off at Fifteenth and dug a torn phone book street map out of his pocket.

Five blocks, southeast. Traffic hissed unseen on A Street. It was afternoon, a gray sky, and the apartment complexes here appeared mostly empty, the residents at work or perhaps departed altogether. Sporadically a house was smart and tended, tulips or lilacs standing out front, but for the most part this was a renters' district: clapboard multiplexes built on fill, or Sears homes plunked here decades before by pipeliners and rail workers, unimproved since conception, some still with horsehair or newspaper insulation visible between missing shakes.

If he had ever been on these sidewalks before, he could not remember it. Nearly everything in the city struck him as new: like mildew, Anchorage had germinated and colonized, crawling up Hillside, clustering around the lakes, roads thickening to highways, industrial lots reaching into muskegs. Dusty vehicles idled in long queues at stoplights; mirrored office towers squatted in vast parking lots. The Fourth Avenue Theater, where he and Sandy used to meet, no longer showed films: the auditorium a tourist buffet, the basement an out-of-favor museum.

But there was that old scent, too, rising in the wake of a delivery truck, or a quiet breeze at midnight, or the drip and gurgle of rainwater in the runnels: a smell of gravel and salt and gasoline, of trees and melting slush, a smell of Alaska in April. It was the place he had grown up in: gulls gliding over downtown streets, the sea boiling up Turnagain Arm.

Two-oh-eight East Sixteenth was one-story, weatherboard, five apartments in a row. Apartment C was in the middle. Other tenants had cacti or jade walruses or potted gardenias on the sills, nylon chairs in the weedy lawns out front, but not Apartment C, just the blinds lowered and the door closed. A simple braided-palm doormat. The stoop was unswept.

There was a child's toy rolled under the hedges: a red plastic baseball bat, inflated cartoonishly along the barrel.

Across the street was a dandelion-choked commons with monkey bars, tandem swings, and a sign: RANEY PLAYGROUND. He retreated with his cheesecake and sat on the swing to the left, which was out of sight of her front door, but offered a view of her hedges, and the doors and windows of the apartments to the west: Apartment A, Apartment B.

The plastic tag jabbed his hip. He fidgeted. The cheesecake in his lap slowly gathered mass until it became a boulder, a bakery box filled with quicksilver. He could not take his eyes off the toy bat lying beneath the hedges. The cheesecake was driving his shoes into the earth.

A *C* on the door. Behind which lived his daughter and grandson. It was incomprehensible.

A dry cleaner's van, rusted at the wheel wells, clattered past. The swing creaked. His mind ticked through the Grace Winklers he had met: New Jersey, Virginia, Tennessee, New Mexico, Boise. The Grace with the Saint Bernards; the Grace with the cockatiels. There are many Grace Winklers and all of them are the real Grace

Winkler. So in that way your journey will never be done. Jed had been right.

Yet across the street, behind that door, were a daughter and grandson he had never met. Couldn't they be an ending of sorts?

In a minute he would do it. He would push himself out of the swing and ring the doorbell. Maybe she'd be disinterested, or baffled; maybe she'd be — more likely — angry. Maybe she'd embrace him; maybe she'd whisper: *Finally.*

The sky inched lower. Honeybees mined dandelions at his ankles. He dragged himself across the street. The swing drifted back and forth behind him.

The cheesecake was impossibly heavy. His shoes left damp prints up the sidewalk. Her rectangle of lawn was lank and unmowed and an urge rose in him to rent a rototiller, tear up the entire lawn and resod it. At least she could come home to that: trim rows of dark green grass.

A kit car turned onto the street, its subwoofer thumping hard. The glass half of Grace's screen door trembled. Adrenaline surged through Winkler's torso. He bent to the stoop and set the cheesecake on the mat. The doorbell was an arm's length away. He would ring it. He could not ring it. The car slowed at the end of the street and then kept on.

His arms hung at his sides, useless. He backed away. When he reached the sidewalk he had to restrain himself from running.

Naaliyah's apartment consisted of four rooms on the second floor of a three-story frame-and-clapboard cube called the Camelot Apartments. Besides her bedroom there was a kitchen, a fungi-splotched bathroom, and a closet-sized main room dominated by an orange corduroy sofa.

She kept most of her insects in a lab at school but there were still twenty or so insectaries stacked on the kitchen counters; she had emptied and repopulated them, leftovers from the Yukon-Charley mingling with new recruits: bark beetles, cabbage weevils, alpine caterpillars in their various instars.

"Save some money," she had told him. "It's no trouble. Wait till you get your feet moving again. I'm never here anyway." Which turned out true: almost immediately she was gone, pedaling off to campus on a rusty blue bicycle, spending days and good portions of nights bent over her data at the library, or meeting with Professor

Houseman, or squatting in front of a bush with her pocket loupe, surveying the fumblings and desperations of springtime insects.

He spent nights on the sofa. He kept his few clothes in a folded pile on top of the radiator. He taped his nineteen extant photographs of snow crystals along the wall above the back of the sofa. His nerite shells rode the molding atop the window. Naaliyah had let him keep the Stratalab — "They won't miss it," she said — and this he kept balanced on the wide lip of wainscoting.

His first nights had been the hardest: headlights traveling Northern Lights Boulevard, the occasional bleating of horns, footfalls crossing the ceiling above. Not since he was a child had he tried to sleep in such a noisy place. Each time the upstairs neighbors flushed their toilet Naaliyah's entire apartment surged with the sound of it, an explosion of water, pipes not two feet from Winkler's head guzzling it all down. He had nightmares that he was back in the bunkroom of the *Agnita*, the orange sofa yawing in the waves, the open ocean pressing at the apartment walls.

A strip mall was going up across the street and before five the workers started their cement mixer, its chain grinding steadily, cement thumping as it churned inside the drum. He'd wake and study the ceiling and listen: a sound like the sound of his own heart, turning over and over.

He shaved off his beard; he showered two and three times a day. Winter lingered in his joints, in his marrow. His eyes leaked fluid and he had to pry his eyelids apart with his fingers. Some mornings it took him two or three minutes to climb off the couch and to his feet.

He ate grapefruits, pears, once an entire half pound of sliced Muenster cheese. The dozen sensations of cold orange juice on his tongue could entertain him for fifteen minutes.

He studied the street map in the ACS Yellow Pages. He peered out through the blinds like a fugitive. She could be there, or there; she could be climbing out of that Plymouth, heaving that red laundry bag out of her trunk; that could be Grace in the sneakers with holes in her stockings; that could be Grace jogging past, in tights and a sports bra, headphones clamped over her ears.

He got a job. He took a bus to the Fifth Avenue Mall to buy proper eyeglasses and while there noticed a sign seeking an assistant lab technician. The store was called LensCrafters. The manager, Dr. Evans — a plump, mop-haired optometrist in silver-rimmed spectacles and a lab coat — frowned at him when she saw the doctorate on his application and hotel maintenance under work history, but said she was desperate and after a few minutes on the telephone with someone at "corporate," hired Winkler then and there.

"But," she said, "you'll have to pick some different eyewear. We need our employees to wear the latest styles. You understand." He acquiesced, opting for Calvin Kleins in black and honey acrylic, retrofitted to allow for his big lenses. Eyedrops, too — he had to squeeze them onto his eyeballs four times a day. Pathologic myopia, she said, which meant Winkler's eyes were continually getting worse, and that it would not be safe for him to drive a car, information he didn't need to pay $243 to learn. The lenses were so thick his eyelashes swept their undersides when he blinked.

Gary, a twenty-three-year-old twelfth-grader, trained him. Thursdays, Fridays, Saturdays, and Sundays, Winkler would ring up customers, inventory frames, bank prescriptions, reorder stock, and haul boxes to the Dumpster out back. (This latter duty would become his favorite, pausing out there after kicking the boxes flat, looking up at the sky, a few cirrus clouds passing above the mall walkway.) For lunches he rode the elevator to the fourth-floor food court and ate Thai Town or Subway at a table tucked among potted tropicals, gazing past milling teenagers to the little penny-choked fountain where a copper salmon spat water into a chlorinated pool.

It was nearly May now and in the afternoons kids were everywhere. School buses sighed past Naaliyah's apartment, their windows jammed with faces.

Twice more he rode the 2 bus in the evening and walked the five blocks to Raney Playground and sat in the swing in a shirt and tie. "Would you ever . . . ?" he'd ask, mumbling. "Do you think you could . . . ? Any chance we . . . ?"

He brought a cherry pie; he brought cream cake decorated with shaved slips of white chocolate. Each time they grew heavy as boulders; each time he left them on her mat without a note, without touching the doorbell.

Then the long ride back down Lake Otis Parkway to Naaliyah's apartment. Then the two quarter-mile blocks in the rain to Baxter beside the unlit framing of the strip-mall-in-progress with plastic sheeting blowing and dripping and the cars of students and nurses and carpools and second-shift parents splashing past. Then passing again beneath the lintel of Camelot, the staircase with its tacked runner of worn carpet, the dust-furred fire extinguisher in the hallway, the wildly veined plaster of the stairwell, the naked bulb far above festooned with cobwebs.

2

Twelve days after arriving in Anchorage he bought a sleeve of daffodils and rode a taxi to the Heavenly Gates Perpetual Care Necropolis fourteen or so miles north of town on the Glenn Highway toward Palmer. A new kind of cemetery, the ad in the phone book said. A dust-to-dust project. Environmentally friendly. No metal vaults, no embalming fluids, plenty of open spaces.

The clouds were so thin that the sky was a searing, painful white. He kept his eyes down. Behind the twin-trailer office, a grizzled, cumulus-haired attendant with dirt under his nails smiled at Winkler and handed him a mimeographed brochure, something about the karmic importance of purchasing a tree to plant atop your loved one. Next to the attendant's ramshackle beach chair was a Seattle Mariners beer cooler and an enormous gray Newfoundland. Winkler stooped to pet her and she doused his palm with saliva.

The directory was a booklet sheathed

and clipped under a plastic cover like a junior high civics report. He found her name easily enough. Sandy Winkler. Plot 242.

The attendant had already circled it on a cartoonish map and Winkler set forth. The shadows of headstones huddled tightly against their bases as if shocked into submission. There were maybe three hundred outdoor graves, scattered across the hillside, and a small columbarium built from peeled logs. Some tombs were marked with stones or crosses; others with totem poles, or spirit houses — waist-high sheds like elongated doghouses, cheerfully painted.

Graves were adorned with American flags or plastic wreaths or nothing at all. New saplings had been planted in the dead midpoint of several plots, aspens, spruce, a few dogwoods. From the branch of one dangled a miniature biplane fashioned from pieces of Budweiser cans, rotating slowly on its tether of monofilament.

Sandy's was simple and clean. Her headstone was granite and offered her name and the years of her life. It was clear from the placement in a high corner of the field, overlooking the gates and office, the small white-and-red taxi waiting for him below, and the highway, and receding hills beyond that, cleaving back all the way into the

Eagle River Valley, that whoever had picked this plot had picked a fair one and Sandy would have been pleased.

Winkler stood over the grave for several minutes. No tears came and his thoughts were surprisingly empty and mundane. Swallows swung to and fro, feasting on gnats.

When he thought of cancer he saw a black throat; he saw ink soaking through a napkin; rot, eating a tree from the inside out. He wanted to ask: Was it hard? Was Grace with you? He wanted to say: I close my eyes and try to see you but it has been too long — the feel of your body and the look of your face is gone. I remember you had an isosceles triangle of freckles on your cheek. I remember you used to wear bulky sweaters to the bank and that your lips moved while you read. I remember how in bed you'd press the soles of your feet against my calves, and I remember the sickening sound of the door closing when you left my apartment on Wednesday nights. But when I close my eyes I see only reds and blues, the undersides of my eyelids.

A ladybug scaled the *D* in her name. Her life represented in a two-inch etched hyphen. A breeze came up and passed over the stones and spirit houses and ascended the hillside into the spruce, and pushed higher still, to the patches of tundra, and the still-melting fields of snow, stirring the tiny new blooms of avens and saxifrage, tucked into the highest rocks, starting their summer yellows and purples.

He propped the daffodils against the stone and wiped his palms on his pants. "Sandy . . . ," he began but did not finish.

It wasn't until he was in the taxi, heading back to the city, that a memory rose. After a matinee, back in his apartment, he and Sandy had impaled marshmallows on forks and roasted them over a burner. She wore his brown corduroy jacket, nothing else. Winkler had been trying to brown his marshmallow evenly, the whole surface area of the cylinder going tan, while Sandy would let hers catch fire and watch it burn, the skin bubbling and charring, beginning to slide off. Then she'd blow it out, chew off the blackened skin, and ignite the white, inner core once more. She had eaten three or four like this already, burning off successively smaller epidermises of marsh-mallow, peeling them down to their cores, and had gobs of marshmallow on her cheeks and in her hair. She was laughing hysterically, her blood swarming with sugar, and she began bumping Winkler's elbow, pretending it was an accident, sabotaging his careful roasting.

In the back of the cab Winkler burst into a smile and the cabbie's eyes rose to the mirror and met his for a moment before returning to the road ahead. Winkler thought: I loved you, Sandy. I love you still.

3

Lilac was a Turnagain subdivision of thirty-six houses, backed against a pond. Each with tightly mown lawns and shrubs edging the front walks and little keypads mounted on the frames of the garage doors. He stood outside Herman's address and studied the windows, the stucco archway, the little gray satellite dish screwed to an eave. How many times had he felt this: Herman inside, himself outside?

Subarus and Volvos and Nissans gleamed in driveways. Two women in gardening gloves chatted over fences and twisted to wave to Winkler and he tried to make his return wave look natural, as if his business were no more pressing than theirs, his life no less composed: an extension of the arm, a snap of the elbow.

He slunk up Herman's walk. He swallowed, he fluttered. A minute passed before he was able to ring the bell.

Within a few seconds Herman opened the door. He was big-faced with small eyes and a complexion that was pocked beneath the cheekbones. His hair was still all gray, buzzed into something like a flattop. An apron hung around his neck, with a sheriff's star and vest silkscreened onto it, and a spatula holstered through a loop sewn on the hip.

Winkler held a shrink-wrapped Craftsman ratchet set he had bought a few hours before. "Herman? Herman Sheeler?"

"Yes."

"I'm David Winkler." He lifted the ratchet set as if to fend off a blow.

Herman's face wrinkled, then opened. He glanced over Winkler's shoulder out into the driveway. Winkler thought: I could have passed you in the street a thousand times.

"Well. My goodness. How did you get here?"

"The bus."

"The People Mover?"

"Number sixty stops at the business park. On Huffman."

"That has to be two miles from here."

Winkler shrugged. He lowered the ratchet set. Behind him a Suburban pulled into a driveway and honked and Herman raised a hand as the truck disappeared behind a descending garage door.

"Well, come in," Herman said, "come in. David Winkler. My goodness."

The entryway emptied into a living room with beige carpet and a high ceiling where a fan turned slowly. French doors opened into a dim room on the left. Stairs rose to the right. Out the back was a screen door through which blew the odor of charcoal and lighter fluid.

Herman stood in the entryway in his apron still inspecting Winkler, and Winkler did his best to hold ground. "After all these years."

Winkler nodded.

"What's that you've got there?"

"Wrenches. They're for you."

Herman took the package and read the label and shook the case. "Sixty-nine pieces. Well. Thank you, David." He carried it into the kitchen, tore off the plastic wrap, and unclasped the box on the breakfast bar beside a foot-high soapstone polar bear. He examined its contents a long time. As if the shiny cylinders might be more than drive sockets and slotted bits. As if in that case might be answers to questions he had chewed over for decades.

In the corner of the family room hockey highlights played on an enormous television. There were watercolors of fish on the walls, salmon and trout, maybe even one of them the same print Winkler had seen in Herman's hallway twenty-five years before.

Herman looked up. "I'm making dinner. There's plenty of food."

Winkler adjusted his glasses. "Oh, I wouldn't . . . I don't need to . . ."

Herman held out his palms. "Stay." He left Winkler clutching a tumbler of skim milk and went out to the patio, where he stood over a smoking grill and flipped what looked like burger patties with his spatula. The kitchen was neat and clean. On the windowsill stood an army of orange pill bottles. A half dozen child's marker drawings were stuck to the refrigerator with poker-chips-turned-magnets and it was to them that Winkler's attention kept slipping, as if the images possessed a gravity independent of the room's.

They were uniformly of tall, multiwindowed buildings with genderless figures standing to the sides among high-stalked flowers. Among them hung a wallet photograph of a five- or six-year-old boy. He had freckles and a bowl haircut and the photographer had posed him against a velvet backdrop with a foot braced on a soccer ball.

Winkler wiped his mouth. "Is this . . . ?"

he began but Herman was still at the grill and would not have been able to hear him. When he did come back in he was asking Winkler if he had been following the Stanley Cup playoffs and if he had any favorites. Winkler shook his head and sipped his milk. In the margins of his vision the photograph of the boy loomed like a black hole.

They sat to veggie burgers on toasted buns and a bowl of grilled asparagus. "I know," Herman said, untying his sheriff's apron, "we ought to be having real burgers. But these are doctor's orders. Antioxidants, soy, all that. And I'll tell you, David, I'm on it, I'm on the program. I emptied the freezer, dumped all my meat. I'll do whatever it takes."

"Doctor?"

Herman knuckled his sternum to the left of the sheriff's badge. "Heart," he said. Then he closed his eyes and joined his palms over his plate and said, "Lord Jesus, thank you for your goodness and bounty, and for watching over me and David here all these years," and raised his milk and drank half of it.

They ate. Winkler chewed and swallowed. As if the intervening years had been nothing; as if his crimes against Herman were negligible. Was this how one person forgave another? Herman talked about San Diego, and a timeshare complex there called Casa de la Jolla, where he spent three weeks each December. Before he ate his asparagus he grimaced at it for a moment, like a child, then closed his eyes and chased it down with a gulp of milk.

When they were finished they sat a moment over their plates. A crow landed in the backyard and began scratching around beneath the grill.

Herman stifled a belch. "Don't say much, do you, David?"

Winkler shrugged. His organs swarmed. Here was Herman, living his life, carrying around his pockmarked face, his mending heart; his hockey skates beneath the coffee table, his health food in the freezer. He had a job, a house — what did Winkler have? Yet they spoke now across a glass-topped dining table as if words were just words, as if their histories were equivalent. The ratchet set open on the counter, the ghost of Sandy traveling the walls. During dinner the child's drawings on the refrigerator had grown to the size of billboards.

Herman unbuttoned his shirt and showed Winkler a thin scar grafted onto his breastbone like a very straight earthworm. "Stenosis. My aortic valve was almost completely blocked. They found it during a physical. Had to cut me open and scrape it out. I lost two months at the bank. I've been trying to work from here, but it's not the same."

With a fork Winkler smeared a puddle of mustard on his plate back and forth. "I'm sorry."

"At least I don't have a pig valve in me," Herman said, and peered over his shoulder and watched the TV for a while. Skaters glided up and down. A truck dealer came on and jabbed a finger at the camera. *Who has the best deals in Alaska? Who?*

They ate frozen yogurt for dessert. Herman piled four scoops into his bowl. Winkler excused himself to the bathroom and shut the door and leaned on the sink. On the tile counter stood a photograph in a varnished wooden frame. It was Sandy. She gazed off to her left. Her hair was short, dyed almost red; her throat was thin and pale, her expression bemused. It was a color print of the photo that had been used in her obituary.

He flushed the toilet and it refilled and silence followed. Outside, in the kitchen, Herman's spoon clinked against his bowl. Winkler's own face was long and thin and as unacceptable as ever in the mirror and he switched off the light and Sandy withdrew into black and he backed out.

Herman was staring into his frozen yogurt. Without looking up he said, "That's Sandy. The picture."

"Yes."

"About four years ago, I guess. At a birthday party. Just before she was diagnosed."

Winkler nodded. The air between them seemed to accumulate energy. "About Sandy . . ."

Herman looked up and the two men studied each other a moment in the kitchen and the objects around them — the pill bottles and the carved polar bear and the boy's drawings and the range and the clusters of wooden spoons in their ceramic container and Herman's sheriff apron hanging from the pantry knob — seemed suddenly to glow, throbbing with their various charges, each dish towel about to incandesce, and then the refrigerator clicked on and the glow subsided and the kitchen returned to normal.

Herman spooned up another mouthful. "Hey," he said. "That was a long time ago."

They would not get closer to the truth

that night. They watched a period of hockey in silence. Winkler insisted on doing the dishes. Herman insisted on driving him to the bus stop.

The truck reeked of stale coffee. Winkler was climbing out of the passenger's seat when Herman said, "You spent the whole winter up there? Off the grid?"

"Yes."

"Was it cold?"

"Maybe not as bad as you'd think."

Herman smiled. "I'll bet it was freezing. Thirty below is what the paper said."

Winkler looked out over the hood. Insects were rising from the lawns and floating toward the lights of the industrial park. Herman watched him.

"She's at my place every weekday at five, you know. To pick up Christopher. I've been watching him while I'm off work. You could come by. To tell you the truth, I could use the help."

Winkler tried to nod. "Christopher," he said. The whole scene seemed ready to twist and rear back and spit him out into the night. The electronic door-ajar chime sounded over and over. Moths hung in the nimbus of streetlight.

Herman said, "You're sure the bus comes down this far?"

Winkler nodded. He shut the door. Herman dropped the transmission into drive. Winkler leaned through the window. "Herman," he said. For a moment in the glow of the dashboard Herman's face was naked and smooth. "I'm sorry."

He reached inside. Herman looked at Winkler's hand maybe a second before taking it. "Heck," he said.

They held the handshake a moment. Then Winkler stood back and wiped his eyes and Herman pulled away into the blue May dusk, his taillights shuttling gently from sight.

4

He returned to Herman's a second time, and a third. They'd eat tofu dogs, or soy pizza, a bowl of microwaved broccoli, Herman shuddering as he swallowed his vegetables, and afterward they'd sit in front of the huge television, Herman in his leather lounger, Winkler on the davenport, and watch the Seattle Mariners. "Get legs!" Herman would shout once in a while, or "Drop!" and Winkler would look over, surprised, realizing a moment too late that on-screen a ball had rolled up against the outfield fence, or the third baseman had made a diving stop.

Every time he showed up, it seemed, a new drawing hung on the refrigerator. Each was a variant of the original: giant flowers — all red one time, a dozen colors the next — below a tall facade cut by hundreds of polygonal windows. There was other evidence, too: a Tonka backhoe on its side on the deck. A two-handled Bob the Builder cup standing in the sink.

In the bathroom Sandy smiled on and on.

Only in the waning minutes, riding to the bus stop, nearing the New Seward Highway overpass, would he and Herman veer toward anything like the truth.

"She didn't stay with me, you know," Herman said once. "I mean, for years she only lived a quarter mile away, but she raised that girl on her own. I helped get her on her feet, found her a job at one of the banks. But she did it on her own. Took Grace to ballet and sent her to camp and washed her clothes and all of it. You know she was still married to you? Far as I know, anyway. Maybe she had boyfriends but I never saw them."

Winkler looked out the window, the trees clocking past. On the next trip, he started it: "I'd like to help pay for the gravesite."

"It's all paid for."

"I'd like to help."

"I didn't do a thing. It was folks at the bank. They loved her there. Absolutely crazy about her. They paid for hospice, the plot at that nature cemetery, just about everything. God bless 'em."

Afterward, each time, they'd lapse into silence, taking a moment to accustom themselves to the minute shifts in their individual burdens, as if with each truth spoken aloud into that truck cab, their bodies became a tiny proportion lighter. Winkler would wave his good-bye; Herman's taillights would glide away.

On the fourth evening they arrived at the business park without speaking. Winkler paused with his hand on the door handle. "The drawings are the boy's, aren't they? Christopher's?"

Herman stared straight ahead and the light of the dashboard was pale on his throat. He nodded.

"And the photo? That's him, too?"

"Right."

From the south, down Old Seward, the last bus was trundling toward them, its marquee glowing palely in the still-light of 11 p.m.

Herman's stare did not leave the dash. "Grace works at Gottschalks," he said. "On Dimond. She manages the shoe department. Nine to five."

5

Early morning. June. Naaliyah picked up the phone. She nodded. She leaned on the sink. Winkler watched from the orange sofa. Felix had collapsed over his sauté pan and burned his chest. The island doctor worried Felix might have bleeding in his spleen and they ferried him to the hospital on St. Vincent, where he was hooked up on dialysis. He was stable now, under control. Soma was with him. The boys were with him. When Naaliyah hung up she stood in the kitchen and her mouth was a wound and her eyes were huge and swimming.

A roofer with a nail gun shot nails into shingles atop the strip mall across the street. On the windowsill sat one of Felix's boats, a red-hulled sloop with a triangular green jib clipped awkwardly to the mast. Winkler said her name and went to her and held her in the kitchen a long time, the little analog arms on the stove clock grinding forward.

After a while she went into her room and

shut the door. An hour passed and another and then, like a glass of water overfilled — the meniscus inverting, going convex, gravity pulling at the edges, the overflow finally giving way — he could no longer suffer his own cowardice.

The outbound Lake Otis bus stopped directly across from Gottschalks and he crossed the parking lot and pushed through the glass doors at 11:45 a.m. It was a Thursday and the store was mostly empty, salesclerks trolling sleepily between the racks, children stomping up the escalator steps, a Japanese couple picking through souvenirs in a sales bin.

A girl behind the cosmetics counter drew color over her lips with a pencil. She pointed toward women's shoes without taking her eyes from the mirror.

Winkler made his way through the warrens of jackets and sweaters. Footwear occupied an entire corner of the store, and glass tables were arrayed here and there with the mouths of expensive-looking loafers angled toward passersby, a display of sandals and another of tall leather boots, one of them bent at the ankle. A woman strolled head-down among the collections, stooped to pick up a stiletto, and turned it over, and set it down. Another sat on a bench in her stockings with a half dozen boxes arrayed in front of her. Sinatra burbled out of ceiling loudspeakers.

A memory, long dormant: infant Grace, basketed in Sandy's arms, the three of them at the family room window staring into a snowfall. Tiny droplets raced down the pane. The baby's eyes were wide and dark. The snow settled onto Shadow Hill Lane and into the tracks of cars that had passed before and along the tops of the hedges. The word had risen that night: *family.*

But what was family? Surely more than genes, eye color, flesh. Family was story: truth and struggle and retribution. Family was time. At the other end of the continent Felix was lying in a hospital bed, asleep, surrounded by kin — Soma and the boys, the ghosts of the Chileans he had known, the disappeared, the still-here. Winkler had a single memory of an infant girl at a window. Faces in a dream, phantoms in the periphery. If he had learned anything it was that family was not so much what you were given as what you were able to maintain.

A portly salesclerk in a dark suit stood behind the shoe counter picking through receipts. Was she Grace? Sinatra kept on.

Winkler thought: I will not even know her when I see her.

Then she came out of a back room. She was carrying three gray shoe boxes. Her hair was black. She was thin, very thin, her hips so fatless he could easily imagine her pelvis riding there on top of her femurs, the knobs of her spine rising up her back and plugging into her skull. Her eyebrows were sudden and dark. It had been twenty-six years but there was no doubt: She was Grace — she was Sandy, but she was Winkler, too, tall and aquiline and slightly gangly and with a look like her flesh was stretched too thin. Just twenty feet now from her father, strung up in his cheap wool suit, and in the nucleus of her every cell twenty-three chromosomes of his DNA.

She knelt and pulled shoes from boxes and paper stuffing from the toes of shoes. The seated woman put on a pair of Mary Janes and took a dozen steps in them and sat down. Grace tugged off the shoes and proffered others. Like some servant girl trapped in a fairy tale.

Winkler took off his glasses and wiped them with his shirt and pushed them back on. The song had changed. The air was sour with perfume. From everywhere came the rasp of hangers shifting and clacking against their metal rods.

The customer appeared to decide. Grace boxed two pairs and toted them to the register and stood beside the portly clerk. She slipped the boxes into a bag. The customer paid, smiled, took her shoes, and made for the escalators.

Grace traded words with the other clerk and the other clerk laughed. Then she left the counter and gathered the boxes and shoes the customer had not purchased and returned them behind the counter into the back room.

Winkler forced an inhalation. The dread that had been rising all morning rose higher in his throat as if by capillary action. He was conscious of neither his feet nor the circles of sweat blooming beneath his arms but only the constriction of his collar around his neck and the incontrovertible fact that his daughter was thirty feet away in a white blouse and navy slacks stacking shoes on shelves.

When she reemerged from the back room, he was still there. She came straight for him. He cowered against a table littered with women's clogs. Her smile was genuine-looking and later he would mull her question over and over in his head until it mushroomed into something larger: "Can I help you?"

He said: "You're Grace. Grace Winkler."

She cocked her head slightly. Her smile hardly wavered. "Grace Ennis."

"Right," he said. "Grace Ennis." But the shoe department had slowly suffused with a clarity that set sparks turning along the fringes of his vision, and the thousands of shoes on their racks appeared ready to catch fire and burn. Her face became a revolution of activity, leaves fluttering around the anchors of her eyes. She was already looking at him differently. Her pupils contracted. Her irises were gray. The whites shot through with tiny red veins.

"Sir?"

He drew a breath. Her voice, her smile — all of it was ghosted with Sandy, haunted and distant and irrefutable. Above him the ceiling tiles seemed to peel away one by one and reveal a sky where stars whirled on and on out toward the arms of the galaxy. "My name is David Winkler," his voice said. "I was married to your mother. Years ago."

She blinked and took a half step back and cocked her head again and looked at him. As if she had been punched but hadn't yet processed the blow. He leaned in. He tried to steady his vision. No tricks now. No predeterminations. Just an old man and a daughter he had never met.

She shook her head. His voice came out of his throat of its own volition — ". . . this isn't . . . imagine what you must be thinking . . . Herman told me . . . if only we could . . ." — a torrent of language, a spring off the near-infinite stream of confessions he had harbored half his life, all of hers.

She faded back against the sandal display, continuing to shake her head. "You are not," she said. Her name tag caught a light and flared and went blank. This ruined father standing before her with his caved-in eyes and big glasses. What memories could she have of him, what knowledge, what expectations after so many failed ones? He had visited her only in dreams and had long since stopped even that but now stood before her in the plain light of the women's shoe section imploring her. She rubbed her eyes until they were spotty.

He said something about time, about how once they had a little more time it might be easier, how she could take all the time she needed. But all around them the physics of time were coming apart, betraying them both. What was a minute? A lifetime? She said, "I hardly even know what you're saying." Then, very quickly, so quickly he could see it, the anger built in her.

". . . we were in Ohio . . . you were born . . . a river . . . we watched the snow . . ."

She brought the side of her hand through the air. He stopped. She said, "You aren't my father." He was her father. His nose, his stature, even the hue of his skin — everything testified to it.

Her upper lip trembled. She glanced into cosmetics, then over at the portly clerk who was examining the back side of a calculator. "The Chevron," Grace said. "The Chevron at Forty-sixth and Lake Otis."

"I —"

"I'll meet you there at four o'clock."

He blinked. "Four o'clock."

"Go," she said.

For a half hour he stood at the fifth-floor railing looking down at the ice rink in the mall basement, a class of little girls practicing toe loops, leaving the front of the line, one after the other, skating past the coach for their jump, landing or falling or backing off altogether, then swirling around the perimeter to the back of the line.

At the Dimond Transit Center a woman with a half dozen shopping bags helped him sort through the tiny print of a time-table. Number 6 intersected Forty-sixth and Lake Otis but to catch it he'd have to wait seventy-two minutes and he worried it might bring him there late so they decided he should take a taxi or walk. He walked. Three and a half miles, along the cindered shoulder of the Old Seward Highway. Vehicles whipped past and it was all he could do to keep his feet tailored to the gravel. Wind tore the sky into shreds. He kept his gaze down.

The Chevron was busy, painters and utility men and deliverers passing in and out of the convenience store, tossing cigarettes at his feet, not much more real to him than the tremulous shadows of gasoline fumes boiling out of the mouths of fuel tanks, and he sat outside on a half pallet of Duraflame logs and watched the vehicles come and go. He took off his right shoe and examined the blister on his heel and laced it up again. Gulls picked through the Dumpsters. For the next hour and a half he would watch traffic along Forty-sixth and wonder which car would be hers.

At four-fifty a Chevrolet Cavalier with a bicycle rack clamped to the roof pulled beside the pumps and Grace got out and put her hands on her hips. He made his way over.

"It's you, isn't it? Who's been leaving all those things at my house?"

He nodded. She pressed her fingers into her forehead and breathed. Her mascara was streaked. She still had her name tag on. "My God," she said.

Winkler stammered. "We just need . . . I only wanted . . ."

"All day long I'm thinking: He's a liar, he's a liar, but I can see myself right there, in your face and in your hands, and still I'm thinking: What does he want? What can he want from me?"

He held up his palms and saw they were shaking and tried holding them against his chest. "Nothing. Only to —"

"You were gone. You were gone my whole life. My whole fucking life and now you're back and what? You think we can pretend everything is great, Mom isn't dead, you didn't leave her?"

"No," Winkler said. "No." He reached for her but a crimping in her face made him pull back. "I only want to get to know you a little. To make it up to you, if that's possible. I'm here now and I know it's late but I —"

"Mom said you went crazy."

Winkler lowered his chin. Cars slugged forward and stopped out on Forty-sixth. Trucks rattled along the highway a mile to the west and the overpass appeared to quake beneath them.

"What is this?" Grace asked the gas pumps, the traffic beyond. "A fucking soap opera?"

"I don't want anything from you. I only want to help."

"I don't need help. I'm doing fine."

"I didn't mean that."

"My father."

Winkler trembled beside the pumps. Someone dropped a quarter into the station's air compressor and it roared to life, ratcheting and chinking.

Grace climbed back into her car. "I *ate* part of those cakes," she said, and shook her head at the steering wheel. He could hardly hear her. "I *ate* them."

Winkler stooped. He placed his hands on the frame of the car door. "The boy," he said. "Could I — ?"

Her head came around. "Do not bring him into this. You do not bring him into this."

"Yes. Okay. I only thought —"

"Thought what? That I could use the

help? A mom on her own? Yeah. Well." She turned the ignition. "It runs in the family."

The compressor howled. There was a feeling in Winkler's chest like a small rockslide had started. A truck had pulled behind Grace's Cavalier and began to honk. She shook her head back and forth. In the bottoms of her eyes tears welled. "Don't come by the store again."

She idled forward with his hands still on the window frame and he stayed with her a couple steps. Then she pressed the accelerator and turned the wheel and he pulled his hands away. The compressor pounded. The big blue rain shelter groaned in the wind. He watched Grace turn right onto Lake Otis, the sight of her leaving like the stacks of a steamship disappearing behind the horizon.

Toward midnight he sat in the Raney Playground swings with his broken, disloyal heart continuing to pump behind his ribs. Maybe fifty feet away his daughter was in her bed, reeling, thinking it out, a thousand betrayals and loves and resentments riding the synapses between brain and heart and back again. Winkler sat on the bench and listened to the occasional traffic. The neighborhood was quiet and impartial; the sunlight nearly gone.

Was Christopher curling against his sheets, winding along a spiral of dream? Would his mother look out at the swings in the morning and sense, somehow, that her father had been there? Would there be a faint imprint of him against the rubber, his palms on the chains, footprints in the gravel, a shadow, a ghost of him?

After so many years of keeping it at bay, finally he was forced to contemplate it: the hours and days of her life. She must have waited; she must always have been waiting. Grace at ballet, scanning parents along the walls; Grace after a camp recital, clipping shut the case of her flute, or violin, or saxophone, wondering if he had been there, among the faces. Her hope carried off bit by bit, as if in the mandibles of an invisible, endless line of ants.

Her father would have left for a very important reason; her father was significant and dashing; if a villain, as her mother claimed, then a misunderstood one. He would return for her in the darkest hours, as she lay awake in her bed, eight years old, nine years old. She'd hear the rich purr of his car in the driveway. She'd hear the soles of his polished, expensive shoes come lightly down the hall.

He'd slip into her room in his dark suit, set his hat on the dresser, sit on the edge of her bed. No lights. Better if we don't wake your mother. On the porch he'd have left an enormous package, wrapped in silver paper, too big to fit through the doorway. Inside something so good, so perfect, she hadn't even known it was the one thing she'd always wanted.

He'd offer a stick of gum from a shiny silver case. He'd smell like a barbershop, or very, very good whiskey, or the flax of his linen suit; he'd smell like the limestone of some ancient and important city. *Tell me what I've missed, Gracie,* he'd say, and push the hair back from her face. *Tell me everything.*

The straining of dreams against the fabric of reality. Growing up meant burying possibilities, one after another. In the LensCrafters display window, stringing up gigantic pairs of cardboard eyeglasses, Gary whispered his riddles: "Hey Dave, what's the difference between a blonde and a pair of sunglasses?"

"I don't know, Gary."

"The sunglasses sit higher on your face."

The 2 bus heaved through its stops, up Lake Otis Parkway, past Tudor. This was June 12, in Anchorage, Alaska. Winkler

566

was sixty years old. He wore oversized glasses; he had liver spots on the backs of his hands. He had been a gardener at a two-star inn for twenty-five years and now he worked at a LensCrafters in the Fifth Avenue Mall, making $7.65 an hour.

6

The hours crawled, each its own prison. When Naaliyah's apartment started feeling too small he stumped down to the basement and sat across from the big coin-operated dryers and watched the clothes of other residents spin. The strip mall was halfway finished. Naaliyah spent an hour each night talking to her father on the telephone: he had fibroids in his liver; he was to stop drinking alcohol altogether, probably for the rest of his life. But: He was going home in a few days; he was beating Nanton at gin rummy every night in the hospital. He was planning his trip back to Chile.

Halfway through the morning of June 19, Winkler rode the bus to Herman's and walked the two miles up Huffman to Lilac and knocked on the door unannounced.

Herman considered him a moment, then smiled. "David," he said. He wore a chamois shirt buttoned all the way to the collar. He kept his body between the door and frame.

"Herman. What do you think of me

watching Christopher? You might be able to get some things done. You could catch up on work."

Herman glanced over his shoulder, into the house. "What does Grace think?"

Winkler tried to give him a look that would explain it, that would make everything clear. Somewhere behind Herman was the boy.

"But you saw her. You went to see her?"

Winkler said nothing. "Oh," Herman said. He rested against the half-open door and whistled. "That Grace is one tough cookie, isn't she?"

"We could tell him I'm a friend. Or a neighbor. A person, someone named David, an associate who helps you out."

"And not tell the truth?"

Winkler shrugged.

"I don't know," Herman said.

Winkler wiped his eyes. "Please. I'd be good with him."

"You probably would be. But . . ." Again he looked back into the house and shook his head. "I just don't know."

Two days later the phone rang at Naaliyah's apartment and it was Herman. "Hey, David. Are you working today?"

"No."

"Do you still want to help with Christopher?"

The bus. The long climb up Huffman. The knock on the door. Herman waved him inside. The boy knelt on the rug and Herman called him over. He approached with his head down. He was five and a half years old. His blond hair was clipped short and his ears stood out as if propped there by small dowels and he looked to Winkler more like Herman than either Sandy or Grace or even himself.

Herman introduced Winkler as David. Christopher executed a solemn handshake, then pivoted on his toe and returned to a cardboard box brimming with segments of orange plastic racetrack. The two men stood in the main room. Herman offered coffee. Winkler tried to hold the cup but had to set it on the hall table.

The boy pieced together sections of track and fixed them in place with little purple tabs. He paused to puzzle through a ramp, tugging a cushion off the couch to serve as a hill. On the table beside him were the remnants of lunch: peanut butter toast, half a glass of orange Kool-Aid.

"He's real good about playing alone. It's only later that he gets tougher. Around naptime."

Winkler attempted a nod.

"She'll be back at five. To pick him up." It was not quite noon.

Winkler was not sure how much longer he'd be able to stand. Christopher's toes were folded beneath him as he knelt by the track and he had not yet turned once to see if he was being watched by the stranger. "Okay," Herman said. "I'll be upstairs. Yesterday I got called in on this re-fi project and I'll be up all night if I don't get to it. You need anything, give a shout." He glanced at Winkler, then went upstairs. The boy did not look up.

Soon enough Christopher's track was built. He had an armada of toy cars in a battered zip-locked bag and took them out one by one and placed them on the coffee table and arrayed them in rows.

Winkler cleared his throat, stepped forward. "Those are all your cars?"

The boy shrugged, as if to say: Whose cars do you think they are? He picked up each one and tried its axles on the coffee table and replaced it in its specific location. Eventually he settled on a green coupe, and opened and closed both its doors and set it on the track and pushed it around shyly. The little wheels hummed against the plastic. When the car reached the makeshift hill, Christopher released it and it rolled down the track and came to a rest a few feet farther on.

He glanced toward the stairs, collected the car, and started it on another lap.

Winkler breathed. He took a few more steps into the room and sat cross-legged with his back against the base of the television. Christopher guided the coupe around the track a few more times. With each pass he released the car at the top of the little hill and let it coast down where it came to a rest just before the turn.

Finally the boy set the car back in its row on the coffee table and sat back on his ankles. The family room was quiet except for the whirring of the ceiling fan overhead and Herman's muted voice speaking into the telephone upstairs.

"What's he doing?" Christopher asked.

"Working. We'll have to let him work for a bit. He'll be back down." The boy picked at his shoes. Winkler's gaze settled on the Kool-Aid on the table. "You want to see something?"

The boy raised his eyes to meet Winkler's and tilted his head. It was a gesture almost exactly like something Sandy would have done, diffident and beautiful, blood undercutting the decades, and Winkler had to fight the urge to take the boy up by his ribs and hug him to his chest.

Instead he went into the kitchen and fumbled through the cupboards for a plastic bowl. This he filled with crushed ice from the refrigerator dispenser, and mixed the ice with several palmfuls of salt. The boy had followed him in and watched with a guarded curiosity.

In another cupboard Winkler found a little Pyrex dish. He brought it and the bowl of ice to the coffee table.

"May I borrow some of your Kool-Aid?"

Christopher nodded. Winkler covered the bottom of the little dish with Kool-Aid and nestled it into the bowl of ice and aligned both bowl and dish so they were in the light. "Now we wait."

"Okay."

They waited. Upstairs they could hear Herman printing something off his computer, the printer churning out pages. The ice in the bowl settled and cracked against the salt. After a minute or so Winkler asked Christopher to poke the Kool-Aid in the dish a few times with the end of a pen and the boy did.

"Now we watch," Winkler said. Christopher set the pen on the table and crowded in to peer into the dish. Before Winkler knew it their heads were touching. The boy didn't move away and Winkler closed his eyes and felt the pressure of the boy's scalp against his. He smelled like peanut butter. Christopher's eyelashes closed, opened.

"What are we looking for?" he whispered.

The Kool-Aid was thickening now, its molecules slowing down, coming almost to a halt. "Poke it one more time," Winkler said. Christopher did. As soon as he withdrew the pen, the film of orange liquid went cloudy, then quickly began to freeze, crystalline shapes running out from its center, ferns and dendrites and prismatic slashes. In half a minute it was a pale orange disc of ice. Winkler retrieved a flashlight from a kitchen drawer and held it under the dish.

The boy's finger poked at the shapes in the ice. Pinwheels and whorled feathers and alluvial plains.

"Do you know why that happened?"

Christopher looked up. He nodded.

"How do you think?"

"Magic."

Winkler looked at him. "Not really."

Christopher said: "Do it again."

Around two Herman came down and

served them cubes of Colby cheese on Triscuits. Before they ate the boy pressed his palms together and Herman did the same and with his eyes closed said, "Lord Jesus, please bless this food and the good men around this table."

"Thank you, Jesus," said Christopher. They ate. The boy chewed with an eye on Winkler. Along the backyard fence a squirrel galloped and checked up and a neighbor's dog let off a chain of barks.

"I think they want me to retire," Herman said.

Christopher took another cracker from the plate.

"I miss two and a half months and now they decide they don't need me."

"Why do you think that?"

"I have to practically wrestle my job back. And the thing is, if I don't get back into the office, I don't know what the heck I'll do."

There were only crumbs left. The boy nodded his head as he chewed, his cheeks bulged out. Someone in a neighboring yard started up a lawnmower. Herman went on: "Grace won't let me leave him at the church daycare. Says it's all about brainwashing."

"You can go back up," Winkler said.

Why were his hands trembling? "I'm happy to stay with him."

"Good," said Herman. "Okay." He pinched Christopher on the ears. "You guys having fun, champ?" The boy nodded. Herman kissed him on the forehead.

They cleared the table. Herman returned upstairs. Christopher pulled open the coat closet and dragged out a child-sized easel that was stowed there and flipped the big pad to a clean sheet and began to draw. He drew a blue circle, five sideways nines he said were fish, then big flowers, then a soaring, multiwindowed house. At four he fell into a trance in front of the television. Cartoon robots assailed enemy trucks. Winkler paced the carpet. The back of the front door loomed at the end of the hall.

He went upstairs at four-thirty. Herman turned from his keyboard and looked at Winkler over the tops of his reading glasses. Winkler said, "Thanks," and, "I should get going."

"I'll tell her you're an old friend. Someone I trust. Someone who helped me out. I'll tell her I was with you the whole time."

Winkler's fingers tapped the door frame. "Okay."

Herman shook his head at papers on his desk. "I have so much work."

On the walk down Huffman, Winkler kept in the ditch, below the shoulder, little blue moths rising from the tall grass in front of him, tumbling in the wake of cars.

7

Dear Soma —

I have a grandson. It is unbelievable — outrageous — to watch him learn the world. He draws pictures. His other grandfather, Herman, who he calls Bumpa, has bought him an easel with giant sheets of paper on it and Christopher makes posters with thirty-four different colors of markers. Houses are very tall, with many small windows. Flowers are tall, too, larger than people, but with tiny petals. All the parks are blooming here and he draws orange tulips in the air around the houses, and small black M's he tells me are bumblebees. He draws Herman standing in the yard, and his mother, of course. I haven't yet made it into a picture but am hoping.

I hope Felix is doing better, able to enjoy being home. Give my best to him. Tell him I think his cooking is terrible.

Summer. Municipal gardeners on stepladders hung baskets of lobelias from every lamppost on Fourth and Fifth avenues. On the solstice the sun stalked the horizon for nineteen hours and twenty-one minutes and at midnight, marathoners passed silently beneath Naaliyah's windows, dragging their long shadows behind them.

Almost immediately he and Herman started pressing their luck. Winkler saw Christopher again, and again. By the second week in July he was going to Herman's every Monday, Tuesday, and Wednesday. Herman fell gratefully into the schedule, disappearing into his upstairs study, working on his phone sometimes all the way through lunch. Grace dropped off the boy at eight-thirty and did not return until five and Winkler was careful, every time, to leave by four-thirty. He found a path through the western woods and subdivisions that kept him away from Huffman and the chance a Chevy Cavalier with a bike rack might go hurtling past. Herman told Grace he was getting more help from his friend and not to worry.

Did she know? At least harbor suspicion? Maybe — miraculously — not. But more likely she did, knew from the first day Christopher piled into the backseat and buckled his seat belt and told her a man named David had spent the afternoon with him. How could she not?

This was what Winkler secretly hoped, that she knew and that it didn't bother her — that indeed it was what she wanted — and she would tolerate it as long as it wasn't brought out in front of her. Maintain ceremony; maintain pretense. Time would adjust her to his presence in her life gradually. And why not start with this?

In the meantime he learned. He learned that Christopher hated mayonnaise, would eat only pizza with the cheese scraped off. He learned that the boy's eyesight was at least three times as good as his own: Christopher could spot a hawk soaring above Herman's deck where Winkler saw only air. He liked the following cartoons, in order of importance: *Arthur*, *The Justice League of America*, *The Jetsons*, and *SpongeBob*. He prayed before eating snacks. He spoke more in the afternoon if he napped from 1 to 2 p.m. His favorite toy cars were Matchboxes, not Hot Wheels, and his favorite action figure was Spider-Man, rubber skin sheathed over a pliant wire frame.

He learned that Grace wore cotton slacks and white blouses to work, and did not go to church with Herman and Christopher on Sundays. She was a fanatic bicyclist; she rode every day at noon, peeling out of her work clothes and into her road-biking gear, eating lunch over the handle-bars, pushing toward the hills. She rode a Trek 5900 made of carbon, black and silver. On weekends she strapped Christopher into a little yellow trailer and pulled him through the streets, Christopher sitting with his hands in his lap, the streets rushing past his plastic windows. Seven years before, she had married a salmon boat captain out of Juneau named Mike Ennis who drove a black van with the bumper sticker "I *am* the man from Nantucket." It had lasted six months. He spent most of the year on his boat, even the off-season. He did not send child support.

Nobody wanted the marriage. Sandy hated Mike. Herman would say only that Mike was "not all that bright." Christopher had met him twice.

He learned that Herman had a girl-friend, an actuary named Misty who lived in San Antonio and telephoned Herman every Monday night. She also owned a timeshare in San Diego at Casa de la Jolla, and spent nine weeks each winter there. Herman had met her inside the swimming pool gates at a vending machine that would not accept her wrinkled dollar but would accept his. Whenever she phoned, Herman would disappear into his upstairs office and emerge an hour later with an insuppressible smile, his ear bright red from the receiver.

He learned that in the back of Herman's pantry were Oreos, three wholesale-sized bags of them.

Naaliyah kept on with her research, although now much of her advisor's attention was on the state's spruce beetle problem, and she had to spend hours in meetings. When she came home, she'd occasionally lie spread-eagled in a trapezoid of sunlight, her eyes closed, her body stretched like a cat's. Her wind-blasted forest ranger from Eagle visited every now and then, slipping past Winkler on the sofa in the shaded purple of midnight and disappearing into Naaliyah's bedroom and slipping out again in the mornings.

Gary told his ophthalmology jokes. "Hey, Dave, why did the gynecologist go to the eye doctor?"

"I don't know, Gary."

"Because things were looking a little fuzzy."

Winkler groaned. Dr. Evans scowled. She, he learned, was a widow, who kept

Gary on as a sort of charity project, a surrogate son, funding his GED with franchise profit. Her hair was curly and her eyes were sweet and she called Winkler David and asked him to call her Sue. But she took her job seriously, grinding lenses nine to five, and as often as not reprimanded Winkler for something: entering prescription information incorrectly, feeding letterhead into the printer backward. Some evenings, closing up, he thought she might ask him to dinner but she never did, just smiled a tight, fluttery smile and made for her station wagon.

The remains of George DelPrete, the salmon merchant from Juneau, resided in the crematorium at Angelus Memorial Park. Winkler brought him lilies. His parents, in the Anchorage Cemetery, got peonies.

He learned that Felix was better. The old cook moved back off St. Vincent; he swallowed vitamin K tablets twice a day. The color was returning to his skin; he walked the perimeter of the yard, wading among the chickens. On the telephone he rasped on and on about the nurses he had flirted with and then Soma would come on and tell him the truth: that Felix had been unnervingly quiet the whole time, that he had cried when they pulled out the catheter.

But it was Christopher that filled Winkler's thoughts. The boy was smart and shy; he was beautiful. He said please when he asked for something; he always put the toilet seat down after he flushed. When he thought hard he pinched his temples like a little philosopher.

To be with him became less and less hazard and more and more imperative. Winkler would have quit his job; he would have leapt in front of a bus.

On the tenth of July, Herman started spending the first three mornings of the week at his office, at the First National Bank of Alaska Home Loan Center on Thirty-sixth. He did not tell Grace. Winkler and Christopher sat on the davenport at Herman's. It was a dazzlingly clear day and light swung up the windows.

"Let's go somewhere," Winkler said.

They rode the bus to Resolution Park and studied the panorama: Susitna, Denali, the big shining reaches of the inlet. A tourist passing with binoculars told them to be on the lookout for belugas, that she had spotted one out in the arm that very morning, and Winkler and the boy peered hard through mounted pay telescopes for fifteen or so minutes, Christopher with almost shocking earnestness, every buoy and whitecap the round white head of a whale rolling, and the outstretched bronze finger of Captain Cook behind them pointing as if he'd spotted one, but before Winkler knew it he was out of quarters, and it was two-thirty, and they had to go.

The boy fell asleep on the bus and his head leaned into Winkler's ribs. Winkler carried him most of the two miles home.

From then on, every Monday, Tuesday, and Wednesday, he and Christopher hardly stayed at Herman's. Together they'd walk into the immature woods behind the Lilac pond, or explore Huffman Park a few hundred yards farther west, or hike the long miles to the business park and ride the bus to the city rose garden or Russian Jack Springs and Winkler would watch the boy as he worked playground obstacles, crawling through tunnels, inching down a slide, surveying other children on the trapeze bar with a hand on his chin before finally deciding it was too risky.

Christopher's favorite place turned out to be Naaliyah's apartment in Camelot. He could sit and watch her insects for hours.

Winkler would help the boy prepare pastes and together they would lower them into the insectaries and watch the little animals eat. He liked the microscope, too, and was happy to examine whatever Winkler put on the stage: a desiccated wasp, moth wings, the corner of a cornflake. Some days Naaliyah would walk in and, reluctantly, frowning at Winkler behind Christopher's back, would show them things: which were carnivores and which were herbivores; her orchid bees, metallic green and gold and blue, pinned to felt in little plastic boxes; three painted lady caterpillars in different instars, one molting before their eyes, slowly and elaborately shrugging out of its skin.

"Butterflies taste with their feet," she'd tell them, and pinch a swallowtail's wings shut and brush the pads of its forelegs with sugar water. Its head would rise; its tongue would extend reflexively. Christopher, peering through a magnifying glass, almost fell off his stool.

He always returned the boy to Herman's by four. Winkler would get back to Camelot, his feet aching, and Naaliyah would accost him at the door: "This is ridiculous. What does the boy tell her?"

"He tells her he's with Herman's friend."

"He tells her he's with you two the whole time. And the boy doesn't even know you're his grandfather!"

"Maybe not."

"He's five, David. You're making a five-year-old tell lies."

"He's almost six. And they're not lies."

"They're not truths."

Winkler groaned. It was wrong and impossible and illicit and yet each minute with the boy was a gift, a scene from a story he could not leave.

He brought Christopher to the Fifth Avenue Mall food court one afternoon and bought him ice cream and Christopher thanked Jesus for the snack and then they sat at the table where Winkler usually ate his lunch, eating spoonfuls of mint chocolate chip among the big ornamental trees and staring out across the rooftops at the distant glittering pan of the Knik Arm.

After a while Christopher said he saw a ship. Winkler squinted.

"There's a big white ship. Right there."

"Like a cruise ship?"

The boy nodded. He looked a while longer and did not touch his ice cream and then began digging in the rear pocket of his pants.

Winkler with his poor eyes could see only the haze of rooftops, the broad plain of ocean beyond. "I hear your grandmother liked cruise ships."

The boy shrugged. He produced an adult-sized wallet from the pocket and unfastened it and withdrew a photo and stared at it a minute, then set it on the table and continued eating.

"Your father," said Winkler, and Christopher, looking out the window, nodded.

8

Every day Christopher seemed to grow more curious, more intelligent. He could hardly walk a block without stopping and going to his knees to watch a beetle traverse a crack in the sidewalk, or a garden spider wrap her prey. His hands were brave and sure, a worm writhing in his palm, an ant crawling up his wrist. "Look at the moon," he'd say, and there it would be, riding white and small in the blue sky above a rooftop. Winkler could not help but think of Naaliyah as a girl, how she climbed through the half-built inn, how each day she transformed her pockets into treasuries.

And indeed Naaliyah and the boy seemed to share a special kinship from the start. She'd pull a chair up to the kitchen counter so the boy could stand on it to see, and with a pocket loupe show him the miracles of her insects: fireflies blinking and reluming; a centipede rearing at them, snapping its mandibles.

"The Irish say butterflies are the souls of

children," she'd tell him. "My papa says they're the Virgin Mary's tears."

The boy's shy leaning. His tender eyes. On the ride back to Herman's he would fall asleep against Winkler's shoulder. If there was time, Winkler would let the bus continue on its course, U-turn in the big Huffman parking lot, churn back up its route, give himself another hour with the small weight of Christopher against him and the city easing past the windows.

Around that time, his dreams began to come back. They were short, quiet things, and in nearly all of them was his mother. He felt her move around him, heard the crack and pop of ice as she chipped it out of the icebox. In some dreams he could feel her thin, cool arms enfold him. It wasn't until later, in the deepest parts of those dreams, that he began to see her, glimpses of flesh, or of a dress pattern he recognized. Once he saw, quite clearly, an image of her hand pressed flat against the glass of a window, the fingers wrinkled and small as though the skin had belonged to a larger person and was strung over a smaller fan of bones. Out the window: cold, constant violet.

In another dream he saw her nurse's uniform, folded on the table next to the bathroom sink. Her big, peach-colored under-wear folded on top. The shower was running and behind the curtain his mother was humming and he could hear the splash and lift as she took the bar of soap from its tray.

In the darkness his legs kicked; he inhaled her smell; he ran to her.

Dreams. LensCrafters. Christopher. There was little else. "I can't tell you how much I appreciate this," Herman would say, tugging at his tie, walking into his house at four-forty, once four fifty-five. Christopher sat on the couch watching *Animal Planet*. Herman would blink his droopy eyes and stand with his hands on his hips or fill a glass of water and swallow his aspirin and anticoagulants at the sink. "You're saving me here, David. I think maybe every human being in the whole city wants to refinance."

"Good-bye, Christopher."

"Good-bye, David."

Winkler slinked out the rear door, made for the trail at the end of the cul-de-sac. Thirty seconds later Grace's Cavalier pulled onto Lilac, her bike clamped to the roof.

They sat in the Fifth Avenue Mall food

court at Winkler's usual table. Christopher was kneeling on his chair, his back to Winkler, rooting through the leaves of a big potted persimmon Winkler had not seen before. Teenagers milled and bickered and clanked their watch chains in the big sun-heated atrium and the odors of fast food drifted from the various stalls and rose to the skylights. Winkler stared out to his left, where the ocean lay glittering, the boy's father out there somewhere, netting salmon, and thought of the great repository of the sea, how the water in us longs to return to it, and how once in the sea, it longs to rise into the clouds, and in the clouds to come to earth once more.

"David," the boy said, into the plant. "Look. A chrisaletter."

"What?"

"What Naaliyah says. Where butterflies come out of?"

"Chrysalides?" He stood, walked to the other side of the tree. "Well, I . . ." There was a little brown and green parcel, the size of the long segment of Winkler's thumb, glommed to the underside of a leaf. The boy poked it: it was flimsy, made of a gray parchment that looked like home-made paper.

Christopher stared at it, unblinking. "Inside there's a caterpillar?"

"I suppose so."

"And butterflies will come out?"

"That's how it usually works. One butterfly. Or maybe a moth. We'll have to ask Naaliyah."

"Can I take it home?"

Winkler glanced over his shoulder. "I don't know, Christopher."

The boy's fingers caressed the cocoon, over and over. Maybe they were brought in with the persimmon. Or mated female lepidoptera flapped through the mall during the night?

Winkler leaned back into the leaves. "Okay," he said. "Let's take it." They broke the leaf off at its stem and the boy carried it all the way back to Herman's in the upturned cup of his palms.

They telephoned Naaliyah, set the chrysalis in an empty water glass with a few twigs, and used a rubber band to strap a square of screen over the mouth. This Christopher gingerly carried out to the deck and set on top of Herman's patio table in the shade.

Dear Soma —

I always figured that as people aged, their dispositions would strengthen. They see more, they get used to more, they grow tougher, more capable of bearing the heavy things. But not me. I'm falling apart. The sight of sunlight on the simplest object — on Naaliyah's keys, say, or on her raincoat on the floor, or on a thousand pairs of eyeglasses in their little niches — can start tears in my eyes. Sunlight, eight and a half minutes old, racing across space, reaching through windows — up here, even in the city, the Alaskan light is so unadulterated it manages to reveal the essence of things, throw them into relief. Everything becomes sublime. Animated movies make me cry. A really good-tasting banana can get me choked up. I have to sit on Naaliyah's sofa in the dark and gather myself.

Even Christopher seems to feel it. We sit outside and look at things under the microscope Naaliyah gave me. We look at whatever he wants — a blade of grass, a sliver of his fingernail. Afterward, he'll get tired, and lean back, and shut his eyes. As if he's drinking in the light. As if already he understands how rare such moments can be.

A field trip: Naaliyah drove Winkler and Christopher into the vast doomed groves of the Kenai to hear the spruce beetles. They passed first through the dead forests, yellow and orange to their crowns, needles carpeting the road, then into still older groves, recently infested, still fighting. "Thirty million trees a year," Naaliyah said and Winkler watched the boy try to absorb this.

They hiked a quarter mile off the road, Naaliyah occasionally stopping to take samples with a handsaw. When they entered the oldest trees, she stopped them at a sizable spruce and pressed listening cones to its trunk. They braced their ears over the narrow ends of the cones. Winkler tried to block out the wind in the branches and the creek below them trickling along and strained only to hear the tree, its hundred minute creaks and shifts.

"I hear it," Christopher said. "I hear it."

Eventually Winkler got it, too: a slow chewing, not unlike a pulse, a sort of sanding-down like the surface of a rough tongue dragged across bone. "They're chewing the tree out from the inside," Naaliyah whispered, and he listened to the beetle larvae locked deep inside the trunk, unseen, spitting up their acids on fibers of phloem, then taking them in their mouths and mincing them, digging their unlit avenues up toward the branches, the whole tree hanging on as the family made its way through it. *Soon,* they seemed to be saying to one another as they chewed. *Soon.*

Herman fended off Grace with three-quarter lies. Yes, he and his friend had taken Christopher to the park Tuesday; yes, they'd driven him down to the Kenai. Yes, he'd noticed that Christopher now refused to step on bugs, didn't even want to see houseflies killed.

"She knows," he'd say afterward, wiping sweat from his palms. "She must. She's just not letting on."

"She must. She has to know my name is David, after all."

"And it's not so bad, is it? To get the boy out? To let me get back to a little work? It's free daycare, isn't it?"

"It's not so bad," Winkler agreed.

Her Cavalier hunkered on Sixteenth Street, outside her apartment. At dusk he sat on the swing, and pushed back with his feet, rocking back and forth. He could just see the doorbell, a single point of light, its faint yellow glow, its incessant flicker.

Naaliyah explained: what they had found was the cocoon of a luna moth, a species her books said did not live in Alaska. She showed them a photo: an adult moth, like a lime-green hang glider, fringed in black, with four spots on its wings and short fuzzy antennae like little feathers. Perhaps, she speculated, the caterpillar was trucked in with the persimmon tree, and pupated there, in the warmth of the mall's atrium.

Inside the empty water glass, Naaliyah said, inside the walls of the chrysalis — if she wasn't parasitized, and dead already — the pupa was lengthening her legs, putting scales on her wings, dusting herself with color. At the base of her brain, no larger than a poppy seed, a tiny vat of hormones was starting to fill. Muscles were thickening along her back. She was reabsorbing her larval eyes, making new and better ones, restructuring half the cells in her head. Her eggs were maturing. She was tasting the air. She was peering through the paper of her cocoon at the sky above Herman's deck.

Winkler took a Thursday off and walked the boy out to the pond to listen to the bullfrogs. He carried his little sleeping body to the couch. He drank sixteen-ouncers of 7-Up with him and watched four consecutive episodes of a television show called *Clifford*, where an enormous red dog and his gang of round-faced kids struggled and eventually overcame various conflicts.

But he and Herman pushed it too far, counted on luck for too long. At 2:30 p.m. on the fifth of August, Winkler and Christopher came in Herman's front door to find Herman standing in his suit and tie in the kitchen. Christopher stopped halfway down the hall, watching them.

The story was breathless and mostly predictable: a client had suggested lunch at O'Brady's. O'Brady's was in the Dimond Center. Herman had thought it wouldn't be a problem. What were the chances? The Dimond Center had sixty-one stores, nineteen restaurants. He had eaten two spoonfuls of soup when he looked up and there was Grace.

"No."

"Yes."

"I thought she rode her bike during lunch hour."

"Not today."

Christopher studied them with his lower lip between his teeth, puzzling through it. Winkler set down the boy's backpack, went to the sink, turned it on.

"I told her how you were with him. I told her you were great."

Water drummed in the sink. Winkler shut his eyes.

"It was like there was nothing in her face. No expression, nothing. She's putting him in daycare at the mall. He'll be in school in a month anyhow. It was a stupid thing to try. We should have told her. C'mon, Christopher," he said and held out his hand. The boy walked over. "Let's go see your mom."

Winkler leaned over the sink. "I thought she knew. I hoped she knew."

"She didn't know."

Herman shepherded the boy into the garage. The garage door churned up. "I was supposed to bring him to her by one," Herman called. "You can stay as long as you want. I'll take the blame, David. I'll try to take the blame."

Then his Explorer was pulling out, and the garage door was descending in its tracks, eclipsing the light, and Winkler was alone, leaning over the sink, water gushing from the faucet and disappearing down the drain.

9

August: days of humidity, dragonflies roving above the ponds. He did not have the stomach to return to Herman's for two weeks. When he did, he went straight to the patio and found the water glass empty, a hole chewed through the retaining mesh, the birch leaves dry, the little deflated bag of the chrysalis empty on the bottom. A tiny slug was coiled inside, sucking it clean. Another desertion.

Was Christopher fighting for him? Was he asking about Winkler at dinner?

No. Christopher was gentle and trusting; he would endure this abandonment quietly, as he had endured other, greater ones: his grandmother, his father.

He started leaving flowers. He'd set them on her doormat — hypericum berries, white daisies, gas station carnations wrapped in green cellophane — and back quickly away as if leaving bombs with unpredictable fuses. Some nights he'd sit in the swing till after dark, her hedges heaving in a wind, the cars on A Street whispering like faraway saws.

Mostly he waited. Customer after customer ambled into LensCrafters and studied their reflections through various frames: Ellen Tracy, Tommy Hilfiger. He typed their orders into his computer, printed them out, handed them to Dr. Evans. So many human beings, none of them seeing clearly.

Rain spattered Naaliyah's windows, and stopped, and started again. The ceiling thumped; water traveled the walls. He sat in the darkened kitchen and listened to her caterpillars consume their various repasts. In the other room his nineteen snow crystals hung over the sofa, half-aglow in the watery light.

In late August, after work, he walked up Spenard to the building where he had grown up, waited for someone to exit, and caught the door before it swung shut. The foyer was completely new, brass mailboxes, a checkerboard floor. The stairwell had been redone, too, and smelled less of memory than of varnish. His footfalls echoed loudly. He limped up four flights — the stairs closer together, the walls more cramped than he remembered. The door to the old apartment was painted white. The roof door was unlocked.

A parking garage blocked a third of the view. A bank sign flashed the temperature, then the time, one after another: 61; 9:15. Each time the bulbs lit, the air filled with the hum of vibrating filaments. Beyond that thousands of city lights shimmered and the color in the sky pooled and the heat of the day drew off toward the inlet.

A bush plane buzzed past, flying low, wing lights blinking. The mountains were huge and pale. The corners of the roof were bare. There were no answers here.

The year swung past the fulcrum of another equinox. Shadows lurked in corners by four o'clock. Everybody but Winkler, it seemed, was doing fine. Business at Nanton's inn was picking up. Felix was improving, back at work. Through Naaliyah's bedroom door he could hear her talking into the phone about Patagonia, lakes and mountains, guanacos standing in roads. "You should just ask her to come with you, Papa," Naaliyah would say. "She'd say yes. I know she would."

Naaliyah, too, was doing as well as ever. She finished the second chapter of her dissertation, taught an undergraduate class. Her students sent e-mails telling her how much they enjoyed it.

Christopher started the first grade. Herman said he carried a Thomas the Tank Engine backpack stuffed full of books. Josh Latham's mother picked him up at three, drove Christopher and Josh to her house, and kept Christopher until five. He loved school, Herman said. Reading, music, maps, kickball, friends — he loved it all.

Herman, for his part, was putting in long hours, his strength reemerging, surprising him. The doctors weaned him off blood thinners. His church was sponsoring a hockey team in the winter city league and had asked Herman to serve as head coach. He spoke of investing in a putt-putt golf course in Del Mar, something Misty clued him into, an "upscale situation," he told Winkler, "and challenging, too, not for the faint of heart. Something that would keep people coming back."

Sometimes Winkler would walk into Herman's living room and see little indentations in the carpet, thin lines, maybe twelve inches long, Herman walking the room in his ice skates.

The back side of Naaliyah's apartment

door. The thousand tiny cracks in the paint. All it took was a breath, a blink of the eyes: Grace could be on the other side, raising her knuckles to knock. He'd pull open the door; she'd lean slightly forward. She'd say it, say, *Dad,* carefully and quietly, as if the word were an egg, a house of cards. Her bicycle helmet dangling from her fist.

How deep did her anger run? Could she keep him out of her life forever? *Don't come back. Don't write. Don't even think of it. You are dead.*

Gerbera daisies. Lilies. Whole spectrums of roses. He laid them on her doormat, stuffed them in her mailbox. Then the swing in Raney Playground, his hands against the chains, his heels grooving the scalloped dust.

In October, two months since Grace had caught Herman having lunch at O'Brady's, Winkler saw her. It was after 8 p.m., and he was riding the bus home from work. She was pedaling hard, and the bus was slow to overtake her, so that for a few moments she was directly beside and beneath his seat, dressed in her sleek gear, pouring herself, like a luger down a track, along Minnesota Drive.

She was one lane over. She was close enough to the streetlight for him to see her face. His breath caught. Her tires clung to the edge stripe as if riding a groove in the pavement. The road climbed as it passed the Westchester Lagoon and Grace stood off the saddle, her bike swinging rhythmically back and forth between her legs. Her shins and ankles were shaved shiny, and beneath the skin the muscles in her calves were like animals in sacks.

The bus overtook her. Winkler pressed his face against the window. The frames of his glasses knocked the glass. At the stoplight on Northern Lights she caught up and was positioned directly beside him. Could she see through the bus window? He slunk lower, peering over the sill. Her bike was like a silver featherweight between her thighs, every line of its sleek architecture promising speed. She unclipped one of her shoes and stood her leg straight in the intersection. She wore black spandex shorts, a reflective shirt, a helmet streaked with orange decals, and clear wraparound sunglasses. A thin line of sweat down her back. His daughter.

She had been in the garage that night, too, on Marilyn Street, twenty-seven years before, curled inside Sandy, the two of them waiting for him in the dark.

Grace pulled a bottle from its carriage on the crossbar and squirted water into her mouth and swished and spat onto the asphalt. The bus rumbled.

That blue-green face from his dreams; hands reaching over the gunwale of a rowboat. The question: *Is she breathing?*

He knocked on the window. He stood up. "Grace," he called. "Grace!" The other passengers swiveled their heads. He fumbled at the window but the only latch was two seats away, and only for emergencies. He smacked his palms against the glass. "Grace!"

But the light turned, bathing her in green, and the driver dropped the bus into gear, and Grace stowed her water bottle and was up, pedaling hard, turning right toward the shadows of Earthquake Park, her legs two lean muscles pistoning the gears, her spokes blurring to haze.

Naaliyah's burgundy towel, still wet, hanging on the bathroom doorknob; five of her hair elastics arrayed on top of the dresser. Felix's ramshackle sloop on the sill. A glass bottle Winkler had not noticed before — his gift to her when she left the Grenadines. Inside, still, were a few milliliters of the eastern Caribbean. He unstoppered it. The water smelled like nothing, no diatomite, no crust of salt.

In her closet hung the puffy blue parka her father had given her, an ember burn on the right sleeve, maybe the size of a dime, the hole circular and black around the edges, the white sworls of stuffing visible beneath. Winkler put it on, the cuffs ending halfway up his forearms, and walked through the apartment.

Had he ever desired Naaliyah? Yes. Had he ever wished he were Felix, surrounded by family, a quick and loyal wife — if a refugee, then a refugee who had made a new home? Yes. Did he sometimes wish he were Herman, in all his literalness, a man he had dismissed so many years ago as little more than obstacle? Yes.

In school Christopher's class made crowns out of construction paper and Christopher had taken to wearing his everywhere. "Like a little prince," Herman said. "Grace fixes it to his hair with hairpins. He wears it to bed. He wears it to church."

At work Gary called across the sales floor: "Dave, your momma's glasses are so thick, she can see into the future!" Dr. Evans scowled.

He dreamed of houses with a thousand windows, flowers tall as people. He dreamed himself older, wrinkles deepening, skeleton collapsing, the water leaving his cells; he was his father, wasting his final hours; he was his mother, dying in her chair, reaching for a windowpane.

Some nights he woke to the sounds of Naaliyah and the ranger having sex in her bedroom. He'd pry open the window, prop it with a textbook, lay a hand over his booming heart, and stare into the midnight, the strip mall empty and silent and nearly finished now, Naaliyah's gentle cries issuing from beneath the door, the sky a pit of violet, edged with black.

10

Every second a million petitions wing past the ear of God. Let it be door number two. Get Janet through this. Make Mom fall in love again, make the pain go away, make this key fit. If I fish this cove, plant this field, step into this darkness, give me the strength to see it through. Help my marriage, my sister, me. What will this fund be worth in thirteen days? In thirteen years? Will I be around in thirteen years? And the most unanswerable of unanswerables: Don't let me die. And: What will happen afterward? Chandeliers and choirs? Flocks of souls like starlings harrying across the sky? Eternity; life again as bacteria, or as sunflowers, or as a leatherback turtle; suffocating blackness; cessation of all cellular function?

We crack open cookies and climb fortunetellers' stairs and peer into the rivers in our palms. We scour the surface of Mars for signs of liquid water. Who hasn't wanted to flip to her last page? Who hasn't asked: *Let me know, just this once, how it will turn out.*

What did it mean that Winkler had dreamed he would meet Sandy in a grocery store as she browsed a rack of magazines? Did it mean their entire interaction and every consequence was prearranged? That armies of his sperm were only months away from her egg, climbing up one another's backs, laying siege to her cytoplasm? Was the seed of Christopher, even then, like DNA torqued and folded and folded again inside the chromatin of a nucleus, planted in that moment?

Maybe it meant nothing. Maybe it meant Sandy was merely one possibility among an infinity of possibilities. Winkler had gone to her in the store and again at the bank; Sandy had phoned him, had carried herself to the movies, then to his bed, Wednesday after Wednesday. Could these things, too, be prefigured? Hadn't the actors acted of their own volition?

Does it matter? In memory, in story, in the end, we can remake our lives any way we need. To be surprised, truly and utterly surprised by what came into your life — this, Winkler was learning, was the true gift.

For the fourth time in his life, he began sleepwalking. He woke wearing his suit, the pants on backward. He woke with a half-eaten mustard-and-bread sandwich on the pillow beside him. He woke standing over Naaliyah and the ranger where they slept on her Salvation Army mattress, the ranger squinting in the sudden light, rising, drawing a sheet around his waist, his expression sliding from shock to anger.

He fed her insects. He worked extra shifts. He did fifty sit-ups every morning with his feet tucked beneath the orange couch.

Every two weeks he was paid $411.60. He'd leave two hundred dollars on the counter for Naaliyah, spend a hundred more on groceries, and most of the rest at Flowers for the Moment on Northern Lights. The groceries went into Naaliyah's cupboards, the flowers onto Grace's porch. Dr. Evans stayed on him about finding an apartment, and he and Herman spent a couple evenings a week watching baseball play-offs or college hockey on television. This was his life.

He wanted more, of course. He wanted to see Grace. He wanted to buy her a fancy dinner, have a waiter pack it in a basket, get a cab to drive the three of them — father, daughter, grandson — up to some cleared lot on Hillside; he wanted to gaze out at the inlet with her and eat halibut and seasoned potatoes and listen to the clink of silverware against plates. His voice would be clean, unwavering. He'd ask important questions. "Did she keep up her sculpture?"

"Not that I saw."

"Did she speak of me?"

"Sometimes."

"Do you remember any of Ohio?"

"I know there was a flood. But Mom wouldn't say more. She'd say things like, 'All that is in the past now.' "

Grace would offer something: "I thought Herman was my father until I was eight. Mom told me. After ballet. She stopped the car a block before the house. I remember I was looking at a button on the cuff of her jacket. I always wanted a jacket like that. With brass buttons on the cuffs. She said Herman wasn't my father, that my father had run off. She said you were somewhere in the south."

"In the south."

"That's what she said."

Christopher would sit quietly, eating french fries, or fish sticks. Grace would wipe his mouth with a big, starched napkin. She'd say, "Mom told me to have him. I was only twenty, but she insisted. She said I should have a child no matter

612

what, no matter how bad the timing. She said being able to give life was not something anyone should take for granted."

He would reach across the tablecloth; she might even let him take her hand. They'd talk about the malleability of time, about relativity, about premonition. He'd tell her that he believed events could be foreseen, that a thousand choices were implicit in a single moment, that he had always loved her, even when he couldn't bear to, and that this, too, was prefigured and inevitable, burned into him, the way the six sides of a snow crystal were honeycombed into its very atoms. His story — his trials and confessions, his dreams, his failings — would well up, would press against the backs of his teeth.

She'd sip her Chardonnay. She'd say: "Tell me about your dreams."

Of course none of this happened, not yet, not ever. Grace was still angry, determined not to need him. She pressed her bicycle up the hills, pouring out toward Girdwood, returning through the drizzle along the New Seward Highway, her hair soaked beneath her helmet, and Winkler would have to wait for her to come around, or for events to bring her around, and maybe he'd be waiting forever, waiting for her to show him whatever part of her heart she could manage to unlock. Maybe it had been too long and she would always be a stranger to him; maybe he'd go into his final hours, his heart laced with regret.

The playground swing groaned beneath his weight. Grace washed and ironed her Gottschalks outfits. She folded Christopher's shorts, rolled his little white socks. Across town, in the break room, Herman folded an entire Danish into his mouth and chased it down with twelve ounces of Pepsi.

"Sometimes," Naaliyah told Winkler, "you look at me and it's like you're looking right through my body. Like you're looking through me and watching something out on the horizon."

In dreams he saw Herman crawl under his desk, his chair upended, the casters spinning. He saw Christopher run through snow, passing beneath streetlights, hurrying from one pool of light to the next, rushing with an earnest, worried gait, in and out of darkness.

11

The party was Herman's idea. "Three months is long enough," he said. "It's time. I'll be there. I'll be your buffer. You'll see. It'll be all right."

Herman would tell Josh Latham's mom that he'd pick Christopher up from school. Grace wouldn't have to know. It was a surprise party, after all. Mrs. Latham would cover for them. Winkler would bring the boy to Naaliyah's from school. Herman would pick them up at five forty-five. Grace would return from her bike ride at six-fifteen. When she came in the door, there they would be, Christopher and Herman and her father, a chorus of "Surprise!"

The fourth of November was a Tuesday. At Fred Meyer, Winkler bought cake mix, canola oil, eggs, frosting, and a packet of silver birthday candles.

All morning the radio predicted snow. A heavy layer of nimbostratus sagged over the inlet, dragging across the islands. At two it began. Winkler watched it from the window, silent and white, the cars below passing like shadows.

At three he stood outside Chugach Elementary School. Snow gathered on the sleeves and shoulders of his coat and atop the school buses and the waiting cars of parents and along the naked branches of trees. Christopher came out with the others, wearing his crown, his Thomas the Tank Engine backpack loaded to the zippers. He looked at the sky and held out his palms. "Snow," he said.

Winkler bent at the waist. "How are you, Christopher?"

"Fine."

"I've missed you."

The boy nodded. His crown was made of construction paper and decorated with cardboard and foil jewels. "I'm not going to Josh's?"

"Not today."

He nodded again, as if this was something he'd suspected all along. Winkler explained: Grace's birthday, the surprise. They started through the first half inch of snow. When they rounded the block, out of sight of the school, the boy reached up with his mitten and took Winkler's hand.

Back in Camelot they kicked snow from

their boots. Winkler cleared insectaries from a corner of countertop, and they worked in the dampness of the kitchen, Christopher standing on a chair to see better. They measured out oil, beat eggs and water into the cake powder. Snow piled up along the sills. The insects were quiet. At four they put a pan of batter in the oven.

Naaliyah came home at four-thirty. She bent and hugged Christopher, swung him in a circle, set him back on the chair once more.

"You're early," said Winkler.

"What are you doing?"

Christopher held up the box. "Making cake."

"You're making a mess."

The boy shrugged. He had batter smeared across his forehead and on his crown. "David says my moth hatched, Naaliyah."

"I heard about that."

"Where did she go?"

Naaliyah looked at Winkler. "Well, she might have gone into the woods and found a birch tree. They like birch trees. Then she probably started looking for a male to fertilize her eggs."

"Do you think she found one?"

"Maybe."

"But probably not," Christopher said. "Because luna moths don't live in Alaska."

Naaliyah reached down and straightened his cardboard crown. "That one did," she said.

Winkler opened the oven and the warm smell of cake washed out. Christopher was sitting on the counter, thinking hard.

"You know," Naaliyah said, "have you ever gone back to the plant where you found her?"

He looked up, shook his head.

"It might be worth a look. There could be other chrysalides, you know. It's perfectly warm in there, and if there are enough leaves on that persimmon tree, maybe the caterpillars will be seasonally independent. Maybe they'll pupate year-round."

The boy stared at her. His face seemed to widen. "What you can do," she said, crouching and tapping one of his kneecaps, "if there are any, is shine a light through them. Usually you can see the outline of what's inside pretty clearly. You can sometimes even see the antennae and figure out what sex it is."

Winkler went into the other room and untaped his prints of snow crystals one by one and stacked them and wrapped them gently in newspaper and knotted a ribbon around the bundle. The daylight had disappeared swiftly, almost immediately, as if the snow had rinsed the light out of the air. They took out the cake and set the pan on a trivet to cool. Herman and the boy took the lid off the frosting and slathered the cake with it and covered the pan with foil.

Christopher's teeth were brown from licking the spatula. "Can we go to the mall, David?"

"Not now, Christopher. Maybe after the party."

He pulled the boy into his coat and pushed mittens over his hands and then they sat on the orange sofa and waited. The boy held the cake in his lap. Condensation clung to the windows. The radio said, *More snow coming.* Winkler thought: All my life, and it's down to this.

Five-forty. Five forty-five. "Is Bumpa Herman coming?" Christopher asked.

"He'll be here."

They sweated on the couch inside their coats. At five-fifty Herman called. "I can't get free." His voice was wrenched, tense.

Winkler groaned. "Can you still come?"

"I'll be there. Hopefully by seven. I just can't get away right now. Soon."

"But Grace —"

"I know, David. I'll get there as soon as I can."

Naaliyah stared at Winkler from across the room. Her mouth said, "You have to go."

He had twenty minutes to get the boy to Grace's. If Grace returned from her ride and her son was not there, she would drive to Mrs. Latham's to pick him up. At which point everything would be ruined.

Both telephone numbers for both taxi companies were busy. He and Christopher set forth down the snowy sidewalk, Christopher with the cake cradled in his arms, Winkler with the bright yellow straps of the Thomas the Tank Engine backpack straining around the shoulders of his coat. Snow blew against the lenses of his glasses and down his collar. Headlights careered past. The boy, bundled thickly into his parka, bore the cake out in front of him like an offering.

The bus was behind schedule. Its grille was pasted with slush. Up Lake Otis, up A Street. "We're going to be late," Winkler said. Christopher drew moths on the steamed-over windows. "Will your mother really have gone riding in this weather?"

"She goes riding in everything. Can we go see the chrysalides right after the party?"

"I'm not sure."

"You said we could."

"I know, Christopher. But first, we'll have to ask your mother. And remember, there might not even be chrysalides."

"There will be."

At each stop passengers got on and mumbled at the driver and snow battered the windshield and the red glow of taillights smeared back and forth beneath the wipers. Slush lay gray and melting in the aisle.

At Fifteenth, Winkler pulled the stop cord. He stood and made his way through the aisle with the backpack and the boy followed him bearing the cake. They stepped off the bus at six twenty-five. "We're too late," Winkler said.

They walked gingerly, their boots sliding in the snow. Twice Christopher refused Winkler's offers to carry the cake.

Five blocks, northeast. Each block seemed longer than the last. The snow seemed to come harder still, an endless procession of flakes, big as quarters, and the mailboxes and fence posts already wore little caps two inches deep. Down Medfra Street a Toyota fishtailed and nearly slid into the ditch before righting itself and keeping on.

When they reached Sixteenth her Cavalier was out front, free of snow, the hood still warm, the jaw of her bike rack unclipped and standing open. Through the window Winkler could see the kitchen light. Maybe she hadn't gone over to Mrs. Latham's yet. Maybe she would still be surprised. He slowed. They slogged up the walk. "She's still here," Christopher said.

At the door they stopped. The boy stood cradling the cake. Winkler leaned the backpack against the siding. "Go on and ring the bell."

Christopher looked up at him.

"Go on then."

"What about the candles?"

Winkler breathed. Snow fell into Christopher's hair and onto the sagging points of his crown. "Okay," Winkler said.

They knelt at the end of the sidewalk with the hedges as a windbreak. Christopher drew back the foil. Winkler pulled the package from his pocket and stood twenty-seven candles in the frosting. The boy bent to one knee and braced the cake on his little thigh. Flakes of snow landed on its surface and cartwheeled across it or melted in the waves of frosting. Winkler bent with a book of matches and made a cup with his hands but still the wind reached the first two match heads and snuffed the flames.

"They won't light."

"Try again," said Christopher. He steadied the cake's wobbling. The third match flared and held, and Winkler touched the flame to each candle and thankfully the wind was still and the flames wavered and then held.

The boy started toward the door. "It's a lot of candles."

"Careful now."

Snow sunk into the flames. The candles lit the boy's throat and face. He carried the cake up the walk as solemnly as if he were bringing offertory to an altar. The flames dragged behind their wicks, bent horizontal. Thomas the Tank Engine beamed from the turquoise pocket on Christopher's backpack. He stopped at the door. Winkler himself rang the bell. He heard it chime inside, a sound like a single churchbell. He retreated down the snowy stoop to the sidewalk.

His heart was a catapult in his chest. Herman was supposed to be here, with apple juice and wine, and a sleeve of plastic cups, a body for Winkler to hide behind, another "Surprise!" to drown out the weak sound of his own voice. A buffer.

Now he wondered: Did Herman set him up for this?

When the door swung open the candle flames ducked toward it, held, and righted themselves. Grace crouched in the gap between door and frame looking over the boy's head. She wore her biking shoes and pants and a hooded sweatshirt and her face was orange in the candlelight.

"Mom," Christopher was saying. "Mom! Happy birthday!"

She peered over his head, out at Winkler.

"Do you see what we made?"

She raised one hand, and held it over her eyes, as though shading out the sun, then placed the other in Christopher's back and took the backpack from the stoop and shepherded the boy and the cake inside. The door fell shut. Winkler stood on the sidewalk a while longer, watching the light in the kitchen above the sash, the snow falling silently, muting everything.

He retreated to the swings. He fingered the package of snow crystals in his pocket. Was she blowing out the candles at least, making a wish? The traffic kept on along Fifteenth, whispering through the snow, and the door stayed closed. He remembered standing outside Sandy's and Herman's house, on Marilyn Street, how he'd watch the lights in the windows go out one by one: living room, kitchen, hallway, bedroom; that ache in him, ice crystals cycling above the street, a gulf of frozen air.

Snow settled on his thighs and shoulders, and on the top of the playground sign. His toes slowly went numb. Finally she came out and stood before him on the other side of the street and he pulled himself out of the swing.

The wind stilled and the flakes fell silently; through the lenses of his glasses each appeared to leave a thin blue thread, as if they sliced through space and revealed, for half a second, a brilliance on the other side.

"Do you want to come in?" she asked. "Is that what you're doing? Every night out here? Like some stalker?"

"No. Yes. I just . . . I thought . . ."

"Then come in. I give up."

He followed her up the walk. At the threshold he beat snow from his jacket and pants. Her bike leaned against the hallway wall, wiped down, a damp towel draped on the handlebars. He swallowed; he stepped inside.

She was still in her cycling shoes and they clicked against the kitchen floor. The cake was on the table, all the candles extinguished. There were no signs of any flowers. Did she throw them all away? Winkler paused beside the little kitchen table. The place smelled like carrots, he thought, boiled carrots. Christopher entered from the other end, where there must have been a common room, and hesitated there.

"Mom? Can we go see the chrysalides? After the party? David said —"

"Not now, Chris." She stood in her kitchen, a butter knife in her hand, eyes on Winkler as if he were a gunslinger about to draw. Her lips — so like Sandy's — parted slightly.

Winkler inhaled slowly. From his pocket he pulled the wrapped stack of snow crystals and held it out. She did not step forward. He set it on the table. "It was supposed to be a surprise. The party, I mean. The cake."

Grace plucked candles, one by one, from the frosting. "This is your grandfather, did you know that, Chris?" She looked at Winkler as she spoke. "This is my dad."

The boy looked at Winkler. Winkler's entire frame shook.

"Go play in your room, Christopher," she said. Her eyes were still on her father.

The boy looked up at her and then at David and took his backpack and retreated down the hall. They could hear his footsteps and then his door close.

Her voice was so low at first he could hardly tell she was speaking. "You think cake is going to do it? Some goddamn chocolate cake? You think that's going to exonerate you? Chocolate fucking cake and flowers?" Her hands were shaking as she dropped the last candle on the table. Winkler moved toward her but thought better of it and instead crossed the kitchen to the window where a failing cactus stood on the counter, half leaning out of its plastic pot.

"No," he said.

"You never came back. You never even thought to come back. And now you do. After all these years. Parading around town with my son. Practically kidnapping him."

He drove his trembling hands into the pockets of his coat. Out the window the dark shapes of hedges moved against a light and the snow blew diagonally a moment and fell straight once more. "I never really believed it," he said. "All those years. That you could still be alive."

Her shoes clicked. Cords in her neck rose and seemed about to break the skin.

Her voice edged toward hysterics: "Do you believe it now? Because here I am. Here I am eating your goddamn chocolate cake." She clawed up a handful of it and threw it past him, into the sink. Then she screamed, a quick, wordless scream, her eyes closed, the sound boiling out of her.

Winkler kept his hands in his pockets, his eyes out the window.

She used the butter knife to scrape cake and frosting off her fingers. She was crying now, quietly, inhaling so vehemently it was as if she were trying to suck the tears back into her eyes. "Was it hard? At least tell me it was hard."

"Of course it was. Each day the sun goes down and you think: I'm a day closer to death. Your mother didn't want to see me. She thought I left you."

"You *did* leave us."

"I did. I know I did."

Grace stood staring down at the cake. Her crying slowed. "Yeah. Well. There's no pardon. A birthday cake is not going to do it."

"I'm not looking for a pardon. I want to help. I want to be here now."

She turned to him and waved the butter knife. "You were gone for my entire life. All of it. Every single day of it. And now you stand here thinking we can pretend there's something between us?"

"No —"

"Damn right. You're not my father, not in any of the important ways. Leaving flowers doesn't make you a father."

In the pauses they could hear the far-off slish of snowy traffic. Winkler gazed down at the toes of his shoes. "I'm sorry."

She pulled a chair from the table and sat down with the cake at her elbow and braced her head in her hands. He waited. The apartment was very quiet. The trembling of his body had subsided. A minute passed. She was no longer crying but she did not move her head from her hands. He considered going to her but instead stepped to his left, down the hall and into the bathroom, and pressed a towel over his mouth.

At the other end of the bathroom a door was open, and through the gap Winkler could see the tip of a pennant on the wall and the corner of a tube-framed bunk bed. Christopher's room. He would have given a year of his life to walk in there and examine everything: the boy's T-shirts, his Legos, his Snoopy pillowcase. What kind of window shade did he have? What pattern on the curtains?

Grace had a room here, too. A laundry basket full of her thin, strappy clothes. A photo of Christopher probably, a photo of her mother maybe. No pictures of the husband. There was a stack of parenting magazines on the toilet tank. A smell like moisturizing lotion, and cotton balls, and a hint of bleach. What sadness to know your daughter has a bedroom somewhere that you are not allowed to see.

Winkler sat on the toilet and tried to gather his breath. He was failing at everything important. A room away his daughter was sitting with her face in her hands and he could not go to her. When she talked, even when she was angry, she moved her hands in the most familiar way, turning her thumbs down; it was a gesture, Winkler realized, he himself made.

She said: You were gone for my entire life. All of it. Every single day of it.

Breathe, he thought. Breathe. Everything was faltering. Where was Herman? Herman should have been there.

On the bathroom sink two toothbrushes shared a filmy Fred Flintstone glass. Christopher's was shorter than Grace's but not patterned with any kid's logos, no dinosaurs or wizards, just a purple, semitranslucent plastic. An adult's toothbrush.

Winkler stood, picked it up, pressed it to his teeth a moment, and returned it to the glass.

Then he felt his eyes go liquid and he leaned against the toilet and flushed it. When he came out of the bathroom Grace was standing in the center of the kitchen. Her face was bloodless. She asked: "Where's Christopher?"

12

A single pattern — two hydrogen atoms, one oxygen — multiplied a billion times, suspended in the air. Rise into it, into the clouds, where those molecules are precipitating around tiny, invisible granules of clay, growing branches, gathering weight — rise through them all, into the great castellated dark above Anchorage, the starlit mesosphere, the deep well of sky, and now head south, soar over the Coast Range, over the great Pacific cloudscapes, to where the weather pulls back and clears, the cities of California below like great shining networks of glitter; leap the dark ranges of Central America, traverse the Caribbean — in a breath — and drop down the chain of the Grenadines toward Venezuela: you are a sinking raindrop, plummeting now, gathering speed, the ocean growing larger by the millisecond; you are dashing on the roof of a cracked, blue house, sliding down the eave, over the soffit, reaching the window. Inside: Felix in bed, in a circle of lantern light, his eyes closed, a sheen of sweat. Soma prays; the laminated Virgin in the kitchen stares benignly, casually, through the wall. Felix's liver, stiff and taut, its architecture ruined, is bypassed by blood; toxic metabolites stream toward his brain. Chunks of kidney drift through his intestines. The sound of his own name passes unheard through the canals of his ears. On Soma's neck the emaciated iron Jesus swings back and forth.

The raindrop glides down the window, falls into the yard.

Felix had already been dead three hours when the phone call went rifling through the miles of undersea fiber, a burst of electrons smashing toward the great vibrating switchboards of the United States, rerouted, rearranged, relaunched across the continent, riding through states, one after another, up the coast and into Anchorage and down the swinging copper wires sizzling with voices, into the apartment at Camelot where Naaliyah sat — had indeed sat all evening — curiously apathetic since David and Christopher had left, the snow settling deeper along her sills, the smell of chocolate cake lingering in the kitchen. She had frosting on a spoon and the can of it in her lap. The phone in her ear: her mother, on the other end.

"Your father . . ." Soma began, but Naaliyah was already gone.

Across town Herman was sitting in his office, finishing the paperwork on one last refinance, the rest of the office dark, the janitors held up by snow, exit lights glowing red above the empty cubicles, when he felt it: a dozen or so cracks in his chest, little fissures that had been quiet all day, shifted. He caught his breath. He banged his palm against the desk to locate the feeling in it.

But the cracks were splitting, finding power, thickening into chasms. Soon his rib cage was splitting asunder. He grabbed the side of his desk and fell, the chair upended, the bottom rotating once, the casters spinning. The mouse of his computer followed him down, swinging back and forth off the lip of the desk like a pendulum. He clawed the carpet, saw — his consciousness narrowing, like the shutter blades in the aperture of a camera — two paper clips against the molding, hidden in the complicated structures of dust.

Grace yelled Christopher's name into the yard. She pushed her bicycle over the curb and mounted it in one smooth mo-

tion and was off, gliding into the snow —
all this in maybe twenty seconds. Winkler
was still in the doorway to the bathroom.
The toilet tank hadn't even refilled. He
stood a moment. She had left the door
open and snow drifted onto the mat.

It was seven-fifteen. He had not even
taken off his coat. He went out and shut
the door behind him and started toward
Cordova Street. Grace's bicycle tires had
cut a thin furrow through the fallen snow.
She had stayed on Sixteenth, heading for A
Street, down the little hill there, and he
worried for her, worried for her tires in the
slush. Already she was far enough away
that he could not hear her calling for
Christopher.

He turned up Cordova, moving in the
opposite direction. The streetlights cast
cones of light down through the snow.
Clumps of flakes melted on his glasses and
in the hair above his ears. He walked
quickly, nearly jogging. It was seventeen
blocks to the mall and he was not sure
what route the boy would take or if he
would know the way. But there was the
dream: Christopher running between
lampposts, darkness to light to darkness.

The doors would not lock until nine and
Winkler pushed inside at eight-thirty. The

entrance mat was soaked and gray with slush. He stamped his feet. The security guard nodded at him. There was the familiar yeasty smell from The Pretzel Factory.

The bottom floor was almost entirely empty. LensCrafters was dark. His boot soles squeaked as he jogged to the elevators.

Cables whirred; the elevator car began its slow rise; the mall fell away beneath the glass walls. Against the huge atrium skylights, snow dashed and slid and the light inside the food court was a muted blue. He stepped out. Christopher was kneeling on a chair by the persimmon tree. He was concentrating hard, not conscious of Winkler's approach, as if he, too, was feeling the electricity of that night, the convergences of it. He had covered just under a mile, by himself, in a blizzard.

Winkler slowed, picked him up, hugged him to his chest. "There's three of them," the boy said, his eyes going back to the tree. "I *heard* them. I could *hear* them in there."

"Come on," Winkler said gently. "We'll go find your mom. We can come back tomorrow."

They walked the snowy blocks. A

snowplow went past, its amber beacon revolving, snow peeling off the blade and soaring in a steady arc over the sidewalk. Out the back spun cinders. Winkler held the hand of the boy and they walked in silence.

They were all the way to Thirteenth when the dream — like a huge, blue mouth — came over him. A man in a green snowsuit scraped his sidewalk with a snow shovel. Big, conglomerate flakes landed in a black puddle. The boy's hand, inside its mitten, tightened against Winkler's fingers.

When they pushed into 208 East Sixteenth, Apartment C, it was empty, as he knew it would be. He was out on the arm of a snowflake, networks of crystal solidifying all around him. The boy poked his head into every room, "Mom? Mom?"

"She's not here," Winkler said. He was still in the doorway. He blinked. "She's looking for you. She's okay."

Christopher stopped and looked at his grandfather. He began to cry. His sobs sounded small and quiet in the kitchen. Winkler pressed a fist to his temple. All the events of his life were compressing to singularity: one night, one hour. Jed with his future machine, its dozen clips and dials. The Datsun at the end of a dusty road.

Water pushing through foundation blocks.

In the infinite permutations of an ice crystal, everything repeats itself, but, really, from another point of view, nothing repeats itself. The arms go out, forming dendrites, sectored plates, the same angle every time, but the final product — because of wind, because of molecular vibration, because of rate of growth and temperature — is never the same. To a certain extent, time *was* malleable, what he did *did* matter. Grace was proof of that. Naaliyah was alive.

What was the dream? Christopher, running. Herman, under the desk, the casters of his chair spinning. His computer's mouse swinging back and forth on its cord.

The boy had tracked in boot prints of snow and they were melting on the linoleum. Grace's car keys were right there on the kitchen table, beside his stack of snow crystal prints. "Get a piece of paper," he told Christopher. "And a pencil."

The boy stared. "Go," Winkler said. He went. Ten seconds later he had a crayon and a sheet of notebook paper. Winkler scrawled a note. He left it on the table. He took the keys, went out to the street, and got into the car. He switched on the headlights. The boy clambered in beside him.

"Can you drive? Are you going to drive?"

"Yes," Winkler said. He started it. He put it into gear.

"I thought your eyes weren't good enough to drive."

"They aren't."

The snow was heavy and Winkler reached out and caught a wiper on its uptick and banged the ice off it.

"But you're going to drive?"

Winkler pressed the accelerator. The little Cavalier started forward. They skidded past the stop sign at A Street well into the intersection but no cars were coming. Winkler turned and the right front tire rode up on the curb and came back off and he straightened the wheel and they were in their lane.

"Oh," the boy said.

Winkler found the headlights and switched them on. They fishtailed down the hill, over Chester Creek, stopped at the light on Fireweed. The defogger roared.

"Your note said hospital," said Christopher. Winkler said nothing. He listened to the boy struggle to rein in his breath. The snow was all over everything.

Herman lay beneath the desk with the

cracks running through his chest and his heart tight in the fist of someone invisible and huge: God? Answers seemed to float through the space around him. It was about love. It was about getting handed at conception a gift that sets you apart from everyone and you spend your whole life drifting through the margins of time, not understanding hours like everyone else seems to: glancing at wristwatches, checking timetables — you hardly know what it is people are trying to accomplish when they go through their days: morning, noon, evening, night. Wake up and sleep and wake up. This was about family, how blood supersedes death; it was about trying your hardest, it was about *snow.*

His fingernails pulled through the fibers of the carpet. It was, he knew — he had always known — about Christopher.

The pads of Grace's brakes squealed against the slush. She pedaled up the Lathams' driveway and unclipped her shoes and dropped the bicycle in the snowy bushes and pounded the front door.

Mrs. Latham was a long time in coming. Grace tried the knob, pounded again. Mrs. Latham pulled it back. "Grace?"

"Chris," she huffed.

"Christopher? He's not here. What about your party?" She put a hand over her mouth.

Grace looked back down the driveway. Mrs. Latham blinked. Snow fell onto the toes of her slippers. "Are you riding your bicycle, Grace?"

"We're going to see Herman," Winkler said. "I need you to help me find his office. Can you remember where it is?"

Christopher looked out the car window, into the snow. The wipers thumped back and forth.

"I mean in the building. Can you find Bumpa Herman's office in the building?"

"Maybe." The boy bit his lower lip. Snow speckled the windshield and drained toward the edges and the wipers swept the drops away. "Put your seat belt on," Winkler said. The light changed. Winkler spun the front wheels, spurted forward, almost put the Cavalier through the side of a minivan.

Grace's rear tire slipped out at the bottom of the Lathams' driveway and she went down and tore her tights, but was back up in a second, leaning into the pedals, heading past Delaney Park, the way she had come. Across town Naaliyah leaned forward in the backseat of a cab, urging the driver forward. Winkler and Christopher passed Benson, passed Thirty-second. If Herman, in his last moments of consciousness, had been able to rise through the roof of his building, and ascend toward the clouds, he might have traced the outlines of their paths, their triangular pursuits, bright lines along the contours of streets, the veins of a leaf, the answer to a riddle, the pattern of family.

Winkler got the Cavalier into the parking lot but was going too fast and when he turned to park, he took the entire vehicle over the curb and into the trunk of an adolescent cherry tree. The sapling groaned and splintered; the car stalled. The headlights shone on, twin beams into the snow. Christopher slowly brought his hands down from where he had braced them over his crown. Herman's Explorer was alone in the parking lot, maybe thirty spaces down, five-inch caps of snow on the hood, bumpers, and roof. Winkler was already at the door by the time Christopher had undone his seat belt.

The main and side doors were locked. Winkler tried the glass stairwell door but it, too, would not budge. The boy joined him and stood looking at Winkler with his bottom lip trembling. "David?"

"It's okay," Winkler said. "Everything is going to be okay." There was a small blue decal in the shape of a police badge at the right edge of the door, but what did that matter? He bent, brushed snow from the landscaping beside the door, and found a rock the size of a softball. This he shot-putted through the glass. It broke with a bang, followed by a little exhalation, a thousand cracks webbing beneath what remained of the protective laminate, and the rock rolled to a stop on the mat inside. He pulled the cuff of his coat over his hand, reached inside, and let them in.

"Which floor, Christopher?" The boy's eyes were huge. "Down here? Or up these steps?" Christopher blinked back tears, pointed to his left.

The elevators were painfully slow. They stood beside each other, grandson and grandfather, each breathing heavy, snow melting on their coats. *Ding* went floor number two. *Ding* went floor number three.

Naaliyah pushed into the terminal, cut to the front of a first-class queue, bartered for an emergency fare. Anchorage to Chicago to Miami to San Juan to Kingstown, St. Vincent. Fifteen hundred dollars. She put it all on her credit card. The Chicago leg departed in thirty-five minutes. "Bags, Miss?" No bags.

Grace pedaled more gingerly now, her side wet and slushy from her fall, snow and grit piled up against the calipers of her brakes. A shape moved beneath the tree of a front yard, and she called, "Christopher?" after it, into the night, into the snow, as her father had once dreamed he would do with her, shouting her name into the stillness of a flooded house.

The boy located Herman's office on the first try. He gazed up at Winkler through wet eyes with a look of minor triumph. Third floor, right next to the elevator. The door was unlocked. Herman's legs stuck out beneath his desk. His computer mouse had stopped swinging. Winkler dialed 911, handed the telephone to Christopher. He crawled under the desk and held his cheek over Herman's mouth. "C'mon," he said. "Oh, come on." He pulled aside Herman's shirt, lowered his ear over the scar on his sternum.

The boy had begun to cry in earnest now, but he held the receiver in both hands and did not shake. "It's ringing," he said. "Someone's picking up."

13

In front of Providence Medical the turn-around was plowed and salted and the driver eased his ambulance beside a set of sliding doors. Already a police officer was running toward them, and an orderly with a gurney behind her.

Christopher was kneeling on the bench inside the ambulance watching them lift Herman out and hook his IV bag onto the gurney's hanger. Winkler's arms were around his shoulders. "They're going to take him in?"

"Yes."

"They're taking him in now?"

"Yes."

Then a waiting room off the main hall, two couches and a handful of chairs and magazines splayed in a rack and a corner television rehashing a bombing in the West Bank. The boy sat very close to Winkler with the points of his soggy crown bent against Winkler's coat and they waited and in Winkler's mind time fell apart.

Diastole. Systole. Somewhere down the hall Herman's skin was pulled back, his ribs gave way. Tubes were installed; light breached his chest a second time. Winkler could hear the thudding of his own heart as clearly as if he had cotton in his ears, a sound like the shoes of a heavy man climbing an interminable staircase. Two miles away Grace was calling her son's name into the night, pedaling down Sixteenth, turning into her apartment. She'd see her car was gone. She'd see the note. She'd get warmer clothes. She'd come.

"David?" Christopher whispered. "Is Bumpa Herman good?"

He pulled the boy closer. The air pulsed — he could feel it. In. Out. "Yes," he said. "Herman is very good."

The television played on. The boy went quiet again at his side. Perhaps he fell asleep. Winkler felt his vision drift, heard the engine of his heart grow louder. Into the seats in the waiting room came the butcher on St. Vincent and Nanton the innkeeper and the captain of the *Agnita* and the nine Grace Winklers and Brent Royster the truck driver, each of them invisible and silent except for the sounds of their hearts, banging on and on, in and out of rhythm with Winkler's own, and with

Herman's down the hall, a sound like the sucking of the sea at Nanton's glass floor, or the clapping of a dozen moths' wings. "Do you hear that, Christopher?" he whispered. "Can you hear that?"

Out in the snow Grace was bearing toward them now, furious and terrified, her heart high in her throat, her rear tire catapulting a stripe of slush up the line of her spine. Crouching low as she glided through intersections. Winkler could hear her heart, too, an echo, a plodding horse tethered to a pole, a sequence of identical numbers whispered into a microphone: *Two. Two. Two. Two . . .*

Inside one of the houses she passed was the widow Dr. Sue Evans, who was carrying a plate past the bedroom and the neatly made queen-size where she'd slept fifteen years with her husband and five more alone. She sat at the coffee table and gazed down into the steam of her lasagna, knife and fork in hand, snow sifting past the windows of her little Midtown bungalow, the head of her husband's elk still above the fireplace. She took up her television remote, paused a moment before pressing the power button, thinking she heard something, a song maybe, a familiar rhythm. She went to the window and opened it, but there was only the sound of the snow touching and touching down everywhere, the silence of it.

And Gary felt it, and Mrs. Latham, and the woman at the flower shop who always ribbed Winkler about how lucky his sweetheart must be. Maybe even Christopher, in his sleep, felt it.

The surgeons converted Herman's heartbeat into light and sound, a blip pinging across a monitor. In the Camelot Apartments, the receiver of Naaliyah's phone, still lying on the kitchen floor, ran once more through its hang-me-up tones. Winkler's invisible chorus in the waiting room leaned forward.

The sensation of a plane lifting — flight, return. The acceleration in Naaliyah's chest. The front tires first, then the rear ones, Anchorage falling away. Her hands on the armrests, her mother's words — *your father* — in her ear like a pair of wasps. The tiny island of St. Vincent a throbbing green disc in the map of her mind.

What was Dr. Evans always telling him? "What we do is important, David. What we do is help people *see*."

His mother's book of Bentley's snow crystals, each of them laid out on their black pages like the image of an individual life, birth to death, each one different but, in the end, each one the same.

Sandy walked out into that motel parking lot and saw Winkler like a zombie with his keys at the Newport door, clutching the baby in the rain. The neon sign flickering in the background. That faraway look in his eyes, that you're-not-here look, that I'm-seeing-horrible-things look. Grace. Sandy would have walked along the bottom of a lake for her daughter, would have found a way to get her safely out of that house. Wouldn't Winkler have done the same? Hadn't he already?

A half hour later Christopher woke. Grace still was not there. The boy pulled his big Velcro wallet out of his pocket, no bills in the billfold but the internal pouch for coins bulging, and from it took the photo of his father. He studied it a minute before holding it up to Winkler.

It was taken at a party in what looked like someone's kitchen. A man — Mike Ennis — had just dunked his head into a kiddie pool full of ice and water and cans of beer and he was rising quickly, his wet hair brought up into a mohawk by the motion, his mouth in a shocked grin, probably from the cold of the water. *Primetime* was scrawled in drunken marker print across his chest.

He was shovel-faced, Winkler thought. His eyesockets set back in his head as though he had two black eyes, peering out beneath a ledge of skull. But handsome in an aggressive sort of way. And who was he to judge deadbeat fathers?

"David?" Christopher's voice was sleepy. Winkler bent.

"Those chrysalides have pupas. I saw them."

Winkler nodded, kept nodding. "That's good," he said. The TV in the corner burbled out a commercial; the boy's mouth trembled with feeling.

Winkler handed back the photograph; Christopher restored it to his wallet.

Later the nurse, Nancy, brought them both meals on plastic trays and held a finger to her lips as if the trays were some great illicit secret, giving healthy people sick people's food, and she winked and Christopher nodded gravely. There were green beans and a sludgy chicken-and-orzo soup and grapes in a dish and an oatmeal cookie in a plastic wrapper. Winkler and Christopher balanced their trays on their laps in the waiting room and Winkler had removed the lid from his soup and was tearing the spoon out of its wrapper when he saw Christopher close his eyes and clamp his hands over his food.

Winkler set down the spoon. He closed his hands and eyes as well.

Christopher said, "Thank you, Jesus, for your goodness and for the bounty of this food. And please look after Bumpa Herman in his bed with all the tubes. And my mom. Amen."

They ate. The thumping continued, slugging in Winkler's ears.

The halls of the hospital were wet and Grace skidded on the heels of her bike shoes, soaked and slushy, blood raging through her. She came into the waiting room, soaking wet, mud and slush up the front of her sweatshirt, skittering in her biking shoes, and picked up her son and held him a long time, crying, sobbing for several minutes, and the boy holding his cookie and looking at it over her shoulder, scared and not sure whether he could go on eating, and she set him down and said, "Thank you," to her father, and then, "Where is he?"

Dawn: the Atlantic showing itself to the sun, the great, ceaseless meridian of shadow pulling back across the hemisphere, touching the eastern edges of the Grenadines, dragging up hillsides, cresting the summit of Mt. Pleasant, Nanton's inn and its outbuildings still crouched in shadow. At the Port Elizabeth pier they loaded Felix's body onto a fishing boat, pushing his box under the thwarts to keep him in the shade. In the island clinic Soma and two of the boys slept in chairs; one of them walked out in the yard, staring at the sky; and Naaliyah leaned forward in the darkness, somewhere over North Dakota, racing against the limitations of atmosphere.

A day later, on St. Vincent, they would load him into the incinerator, and across the channel, stepping into her parents' little blue cracked house for the first time in almost four years, stacked nearly to the ceiling with tiny boats, each of them seeming to tremble and slur in the sunlight, their sails filling with air, Naaliyah would feel it. And waiting in the funeral home, each of the three boys would feel it, a sight like a white horse at dusk, near-glowing, a little flicker, and only a half mile from Naaliyah, in St. Paul's, at that very same moment, the pews starting to fill with friends and the priest lighting candles, the floor braced on its stilts, the whole structure hanging on, Soma would feel it, too: some small part of her flare up, incandesce, give itself up to heat and light. Maybe throughout Chile, too, between the scattered rib bones and in the sockets of broken skulls, in the gaps between the ones who had gone missing, small webs of light fired, tiny serrated bolts running through the soil, a stirring in the forgotten pastures, the bones of friends who had been taken, anticipating the arrival of a long-awaited friend.

Well past midnight in Anchorage and Christopher sat quietly in the waiting room, eyes closed, hands clasped in front of his face. His feet did not reach the floor and he kicked his legs back and forth.

His mother knelt in front of him. "What are you doing, baby?"

His voice was a whisper: "Praying for Bumpa."

In the operating room, one floor up, nurses pulled off gloves, stuffed smocks into hampers. Monitors pulsed, and Herman's eyes were sealed: *stabilized*, they called it.

Stabilized to them, perhaps, but Winkler guessed Herman was moving fast, the room like a train car hauling him through his dreams, through ten thousand dead-tired hours at the bank, all the possible futures in which he and Sandy had children and raised them and ushered them into the world, the morning he realized she really was gone; his faith, his friends, his hockey, his golf, then out through his new life, the life that still could be: San Diego, California, the Pacific-blue California sky, the endlessly clean sea-washed light, that woman down there he liked — Misty! — the two of them driving in a big air-conditioned car to a putt-putt course like you've never seen, David, a classy one, not with plaster dinosaurs and cartoon bears, but with intricate miniature windmills, an entire Swiss village, little window boxes and dwarf trees and lights in the windows and elaborate model trains moving through sidings, through hand-masoned stone tunnels, past saloons with doors that really did swing both ways on tiny springloaded hinges, his simple white golf ball struck well and cleanly, banking off the wall at the perfect angle, finding the right slot, pouring through some unseen piping, dropping out onto the green, green synthetic turf, rolling at an ideal trajectory, making right for the hole . . .

It was three or four in the morning by

now. The emergency ward was dead quiet, no beeping, no footfalls. The television played *Family Feud* reruns without sound. The boy fell asleep again in the waiting room lounger with a *Newsweek* wrinkled beneath his knees and Winkler's coat for a pillow. Grace looked at her father a long time.

She said, "Mom wanted me to write you. Toward the end. She asked me to. She had an old address." She shifted and adjusted the bike helmet in her lap. "She said it was worth a try. Even if you never got it. She said I should tell you she took me to the house, on the day of the flood, and she tried to get the neighbors to help her get her big sculpture out of the basement. But they wouldn't, there were hardly any neighbors who hadn't evacuated, and she said it was all underwater anyway."

She dragged the soles of her bike shoes back and forth across the floor. "Thing was, I couldn't. I couldn't write the letter. I'd look at the blank paper for a minute and get angry and I never sent anything."

Winkler closed his eyes.

"The snowflakes," she said. "Mom told me about that. That that was what you did. They're nice. I've never seen anything like them."

Now she closed her eyes, and outside the snow had stopped. Already it was melting and everywhere the hospital dripped and the respirators in their various rooms wheezed and clicked. She took the time, he thought. She took the time to open them, to see what I'd given her.

He waited until her eyelids fell, and her breathing slowed; then he stood and trod softly down the hall, past the nurses' station and the wastebaskets overflowing with gauze and alcohol wipes and the stacks of blankets on carts and the empty, curtained beds, and past the closed doors behind which people waited in the grips of their various fates, to Herman's room, where the fluorescent bulb in the headboard shone and the heart monitor beeped regularly.

Herman lay very peacefully, six diodes taped across his chest. Three-quarters of his body was wrapped in blankets. His face looked composed, and sentient, and for a moment Winkler thought he might wake, might turn to him and say, *Hey, David. You mind switching the channel?* But his eyes remained shut; his breath was steady.

Winkler stood by the bed a bit longer, then lowered his head, and knelt. He reached up to get his folded hands through the rail and onto the bedside. His thoughts tried to assemble as utterances: *Please. Not again.*

The curtains were still; everywhere in the hospital patients dreamed their dreams and their cells fought on, climbing repair strands, revamping, regenerating, running the seams of their bodies.

He had knelt there maybe ten minutes when Grace tiptoed in behind him and stood to his right. Neither of them said anything. The beeping that was Herman's heart sounded steadily. She shifted and her bicycle shoes clicked against the floor as she knelt beside him. Together, the unlikeliest of penitents, silently, grafting words to air, they sent their prayers into the room.

14

He missed seven days of work but Dr. Evans took one look at him standing in the entrance to the store in his wrinkled suit with his eyeglasses on and took him back.

Felix's body was brought to Kingstown and incinerated and the ashes poured into a white plastic container with a screw top. This Naaliyah held on her lap through the flights from Kingstown to Bridgetown, to Santiago, to Puerto Montt, and finally into Punta Arenas, in Patagonia, at the end of the continent.

Her letter took two weeks to arrive in Anchorage. When it did, Winkler let Christopher open the envelope. They sat on the orange sofa and Winkler read it aloud.

Dear David —
The guidebooks say the reason they paint their houses such bright colors is to contrast the colorless landscape. But to call it colorless is ridiculous. I see color everywhere: lenga leaves touched with red, the

gold of the pampas, a few crimson flowers still on these bushes that I think are called fire bushes. The blue of the sky, too: not indigo like the Caribbean but a sort of pale blue, washed through with white. Even the sea, the Magellan Strait, is a color: like old silver that has been touched with polish in a few places.

It is late spring here and the insects are mating everywhere. Last night during dinner a big brown moth landed on the window and was joined by another and still another. All males — their hair pencils were so heavy with alkaloids and pheromones that after they left I could still see the ghosts of them powdered on the screen.

I took Papa's ashes to San Gregorio. His primo, José, drove me. José is an accountant. We went out in his sports car down this endless gravel road. Several times I thought the axles might break but José kept on driving, banging in and out of potholes. After about an hour we parked on the side of the road. There was nothing but shrubs and lenga trees for miles. With the car shut off, it was very quiet, only the wind. I thought maybe this was a place Papa had once loved but when I asked José he just shrugged and said, "I don't know. It seemed like far enough." Outside it was

660

*very windy and I didn't know how far I
ought to go from the car, so I went maybe
two hundred meters.*

*The wind started taking the ashes before
I could even get the lid all the way off. José
had a couple of bottles of Austral and we
toasted Papa with those and it was a little
anticlimactic but still, I think he would
have liked it. His ashes blowing out across
the pampas and even all the way to the
road and across it. As I watched an ant
came and started tapping a little pebble of
him and took up the clump in its mandibles and carried it away — a little piece of
Papa, back to its nest.*

*I think I will stay here a bit longer.
Could you telephone Professor Houseman
for me? I think he'll understand. Use the
apartment for as long as you'd like, of
course. Keep the caterpillars alive if you
can. Say hello please to Christopher.*

Christopher nodded gravely. "That's
me," he said. "Christopher."
"Yes."
"What is *primo?*"
"I think a cousin. Family of some kind."
"Family." The boy looked at Winkler
and reached up with both hands and ad-
justed his crown.

Winkler kept his hands on the letter and tried to fold it and replace it in its envelope. "Like you and me," he said.

"And Mom," said Christopher. "And Herman."

Upstairs someone flushed the toilet and the walls surged with water and in Naaliyah's tiny kitchen the refrigerator motor clicked on and Winkler said, "Yes. You and me and Mom and Herman."

Herman walked out of the hospital after eight days. He was sixty-six now and this time the bank strung crepe paper from the ceiling tiles and taped balloons to his doorknob and everyone signed a card but he was done, there would be no negotiating. He told Winkler that it took a man to know when to pull himself out of the game and he was trying to be a man.

The following Saturday, Winkler helped him move out of his office, boxing up files, emptying drawers of notepads, carrying binders and hockey trophies down the stairs through the rain to Herman's truck. His files were neat and ordered and the whole extraction took little more than an hour.

On the drive back to his house Herman was quiet and Winkler thought to ask him if he was all right but decided it was best to stay quiet.

But he was all right; he was more than all right. He walked three times a day, a walking stick gripped firmly in his fist, and perhaps he walked a bit slower than before, and more stiffly, holding his chest straight and rigid, as if his heart were in danger of finding a gap in his ribs and tumbling out, but he did not mope. He coaxed moose into the backyard with a salt lick; he bought a birdfeeder and kept it full to the rims. He stowed his skates and goalie pads in one of the upstairs bedrooms and Winkler saw no more of them.

And he extended his timeshare in La Jolla, buying up six additional weeks. "Doctor's orders," he said, smiling a small, guilty smile. Most nights when Winkler was there, the two of them watching the Canucks or the Aces on TV, Misty would telephone and Herman would take the cordless upstairs to his study and when he came back down he'd be smiling and distracted, as if he had lipstick all over his face, sometimes not even noticing if one of the teams put the puck in the net.

On November 24 he left for La Jolla, a little maroon carry-on over his shoulder and his brass putter in his hand. His heart pills made a small cylindrical bulge in his shirt pocket beneath the flannel. He, Winkler, and Christopher sat hip to hip in the back of the cab, all three strapped into their seat belts, the smell of Herman's cologne thick around them. Herman let Christopher hold his putter and the boy held it carefully, across his lap, so that the head cover wouldn't get dirty.

In the departures lane a cop hurried cars in and out. Winkler asked the cab to wait and he and the boy followed Herman to the curb.

"I know Grace would've liked to see you off," Winkler said. Herman waved his hand as if brushing it all away. He picked up Christopher and hugged him and Christopher kissed him on the cheek. "See you in a couple months, champ."

"Okay," said Christopher.

It was cold and snow was brewing in the clouds. "Well," Winkler said. "We'll be here when you come back."

Herman shook his putter in affirmation. "Good-bye, David. Good-bye, Christopher."

They watched the doors slide open and Herman drag his suitcase into the concourse. Then they got back into the cab and the driver started it for home.

At work Dr. Evans kept on Winkler

about getting his own place. She said she knew a woman who had a one-bedroom downtown with good views and wood floors and a deck out back and would rent it for cheap. That evening they closed the shop and she drove Winkler in her station wagon through the hotel district to First Avenue and F Street to a subdivided triplex by Ship Creek. Within an hour he had signed a lease for the top floor.

Thanksgiving loomed. The malls filled with people forced inside by weather: mothers with strollers, gangs of elderly walkers. Winkler and Gary taped cardboard turkeys and pilgrims in the Lens-Crafters windows.

"Okay," Winkler said. "A policeman stops a woman for speeding and asks to see her license. He says, 'Lady, it says here that you should be wearing glasses.' The woman says, 'Well, I have contacts,' and the policeman, he says, 'I don't care who you know! You're still getting a ticket!'"

Gary shook his head. Winkler stood back, grinning.

He fed the caterpillars their leaves and the insatiable beetles their bark paste and they clicked and murmured their gratitude. Each afternoon he met Christopher outside Chugach Elementary and they rode the bus to Naaliyah's, where they watched the insects, or studied various things under the microscope, or walked the streets, stopping to investigate the things they found, until at six or seven Grace came in her Cavalier to collect him.

Some nights, in the darkness, alone in Naaliyah's apartment, he wondered if in the weeks before he died he might dream ahead to what waited for him. Perhaps he would see hedgerows, or poppy fields, or light on a pasture of ocean, or snow crystals maybe, their evanescence, their plurality. Maybe he'd move through a big house and in each room find a person he had lost: Felix, Sandy, his father, his mother. Maybe he'd dream of nothing, the blankness he had glimpsed on that beach so many years ago, a void in which things moved around him undetected and unheard — something like that biological end, beetle larvae chewing determined, hungry labyrinths through him.

Or maybe he would dream himself back into that first apartment, his closet bedroom, his mother's iron sighing over the ironing board, his father turning the pages of a newspaper, the ghosts of animals stepping quietly through the walls.

15

In the backseat of the Cavalier, he and Christopher played the old game, finding shapes in the clouds. Once they were explained, Christopher's choices inevitably surprised him: a sleeping dragon with its tail coiled around its head; a sack of marbles, a thin contrail forming the string around the bag's neck.

It was Thanksgiving and earlier in the day Christopher had presented Winkler with one of his poster-sized drawings. In the background stretched the airport, huge and soaring, its facade broken by a hundred little windows, and the white space around it was peppered with the small T shapes of airplanes. Out front, beside a yellow oval that must have been a taxicab, a man held a golf club. On the curb beside him, a stick boy with yellow hair that Winkler knew to be Christopher held hands with a second man wearing enormous eyeglasses.

"That's Herman?"

"Yes," Christopher answered, madly shy. His fingertip roved to the man with the glasses. "And that's you." Winkler told him it was the greatest picture he had ever seen and that he would keep it forever, or if not forever then as long as he could.

Grace was driving, in a generous mood — even smiling once in a while in the mirror at Winkler. Her bicycle, clamped to the roof rack, cut the wind. Winkler rode in a baseball cap and Christopher wore his orange construction-paper crown, decorated with stickers and newly reinforced with cardboard. In the backseat between them was a brand-new square-bladed Rittenhouse spade.

They drove out the Glenn Highway, past the army base, past Eagle River, and the landfill, mist breaking across the car's grille. By the time they were alongside the Heavenly Gates Perpetual Care Necropolis a light drizzle had started.

Grace parked at the gate. She pulled on her riding shoes and laced them one after the other by placing them on the dash and hauling down on the laces. There was a bruise on her shin, and the skin there was shiny from her having shaved it so close, and when she shifted, the smell of old sweat came off her biking shorts.

Behind her Christopher and Winkler sat as if waiting out the rain. Grace opened her door and threw a heel onto the hood and leaned over her knee to stretch. Through the open door came the wind, damp and cool. Christopher rested his chin on the sill and peered out his window.

"Rain is always worse hearing it on the roof," Winkler said. "But once you're out in it, moving around, it'll feel kind of good. You'll see." The boy's eyes turned up, as if calculating whether or not the rain would feel good.

Grace unclipped her bike from the roof and fit the front wheel's axle into the fork ends. She spun it until the tire was true and clamped the quick-release and affixed the front brake. "You guys have fun," she said, and leaned in and looked at Christopher, still in the backseat, and rested her bike against the car. She climbed into her seat and reached over the back.

"You'll be warm enough?"

He nodded.

She pulled his collar up and brought it around his neck. "Your crown will get wet," she said.

Christopher shook his head. They compromised by pulling up the hood. She tugged on his drawstrings, and looked at

Winkler beside him, holding the boy's fingers with one hand and the spade with the other, and then she shook her head and said, "I love you, Chris," and smiled at them both.

Then she pedaled off, starting on the big hill, her legs moving easily and efficiently on the pedals, her back bowed over the crossbar. They watched until she was nearly at the top of the hill, rounding a bend, and the mist closed over her.

Winkler squeezed Christopher's hand. "You ready?"

The boy shrugged. Winkler walked around the back of the car with the spade and opened the door and took the boy's hand and they set out, climbing toward the cemetery gates with the Cavalier at their backs.

There was a backhoe pulled up behind the office, its arm folded. Inside, the same grizzled attendant pulled back the door, picking his teeth with the cap of a pen.

"We want to buy a tree," Winkler said. The attendant nodded and pulled up the hood of his poncho and the three of them walked out into the rain. There were maybe two dozen saplings leaning against the back of the office, all with their root-balls wrapped in globes of burlap.

From the other side of the house the big old Newfoundland came loping toward them and Christopher reeled back behind Winkler's legs but the dog pushed forward and lacquered the boy's face with drool.

"What kind of tree you guys want?"

Winkler looked down at Christopher. "What kind of tree?"

But the boy was reaching, gently, for the huge wet dog. "What's his name?"

"Her name," the attendant said. "Lucy. Lucy Blue."

Christopher stood for a moment, then reached up and took the big patient dog around the neck, and hugged her. She panted over his shoulder. "Good girl," the boy said, patting her head. "Good Lucy."

"Let's pick the tree, okay, Christopher?"

They walked among the saplings looking at each and Christopher spoke softly to Lucy as if consulting her. At last he pointed to the biggest one, an aspen, maybe half of its leaves lying curled around its base. The remaining hundred or so clung to the branches, bright and yellow, flapping slowly in the rain. "That one?"

The boy nodded, his attention on the tree, a diminutive arborist.

Inside the office the attendant rang it up.

Winkler asked, "You're sure it's not too late in the season?"

"It's fine."

"The ground won't be frozen?"

"Not yet."

"And we can put it anywhere?"

"Anywhere within six feet of the plot."

Winkler paid him and handed the boy the spade and together with the attendant managed to wrestle the big sapling into a wheelbarrow the graveyard loaned out for just such purpose.

"Pails," the attendant said. He disappeared into the office, reemerged with two five-gallon buckets, one stacked inside the other, and hung them on a handle of the wheelbarrow.

Then the two of them started off down the rows, the boy jogging out in front with the big shovel dragging behind him, Winkler driving the barrow over the stones in the makeshift path and the branches of the tree bouncing and the big dog following them both.

Halfway up, Christopher stopped and pulled back his hood. He hugged the dog and took off his crown and pinned it into the fur on the dog's head. "Here," he said, and patted her ribs. "You can wear this a minute. While I help dig."

They wheeled the tree to Sandy's grave. From up there they could see, far off, the rain falling on the high flanks of the Talkeetnas, falling as snow. Winker stood a moment. The boy offered up the spade. Her plot was maybe six by six, the size of a king mattress. Winkler raised the shovel and drove the blade in.

The smell that came up was of turned earth, moss and ferns. Severed worms flailed in the cuts. The soil was pebbly but the digging was not hard and in ten minutes Winkler had made a sizable crater. Once he finished, he heaved the tree out of the wheelbarrow, rolled it to the edge of the hole, and hacked off the burlap. The boy helped him push it over the lip. Winkler grabbed the sapling's trunk. "Is it straight?"

"I think so."

"Put some dirt around it then."

The boy lifted the spade. They filled the hole, and tamped it down. The Newfoundland sat placidly by, the boy's crown cocked between her ears. Rain flecked the lenses of Winkler's glasses. Christopher stood back and appraised their work. "That's it?"

"That's it. Now we water it."

They walked back down through the

graves to a spigot beside the office and filled their buckets. Christopher at first filled his too much and Winkler had to pour some out until he was able to drag it. Water sloshed over the rims and dampened their boots. They hauled up the pails and poured them over the base of the tree and went back again, hauling up the water, pouring it out, watching it soak through the soil, big Lucy following them both.

"What do you think?" Winkler asked, when they were done.

"It's okay," the boy said. His hair was soaked, and his pants were muddy to the knees. The wind came up, and moved the highest branches and sent droplets of rain flying through the air. "I like it. I think it will make it."

"Happy Thanksgiving, Sandy," Winkler said.

"Happy Thanksgiving," Christopher said.

On the way down, moving back toward the gates, toward the car, the boy began to run, his hood down and his boots splashing, calling, "Go, Lucy, go, Lucy!" and the dog ran along beside him, barking with joy, the crown still somehow clinging to her ears, and Winkler turned once to look back at the tree, standing thin and mostly naked beside Sandy's grave, holding its branches up. Then he hurried on, through the headstones, after the boy.

16

On the fifth of December he moved into his new apartment. The view was good: Ship Creek, and the rail yard, and Knik Arm beyond. He brought in his few clothes, his Stratalab, his nerite shells; he taped Christopher's drawing to the center of a large blank wall.

In the mailbox was a letter from Soma, with a Santiago postmark.

Dear David —

I've rented a Honda motoneta. I ride all over the place. Once you learn to be a little aggressive, things are much better. I drove it to the Moneda today. Most of the same offices are still there, with new people in them, of course. I saw where I used to work. They even let me into Felix's kitchen, which is all redone but still very much the same. I have bought each of the boys a little model of the palace, made of plastic, but very accurately done, and I think tomorrow I will wrap them in tissue paper and mail them off.

Naaliyah, we think, will stop here before she returns to the States.

My friend who I am staying with, Violetta, has a balcony on the thirty-third floor. We sit among her ferns and drink Fan-Schops, which are half-Fanta and half-beer. They taste very good, although I'm sure Felix would call them "for women" and say he felt sorry for the beer. I drink one of them and cannot stop. I pour another, and another. . . .

I go jogging with Violetta which is hilarious because we are both very slow and she wears bright orange shorts and hardly any top, and she makes sure we go through the Plaza del Mulato Gil de Castro where all the rich men sit and drink coffee, the two of us huffing and wheezing and stumbling on the cobblestones. Sometimes they whistle at her. I just try to keep my eyes straight ahead and not fall. The thing with running is that it feels so good afterward, when you're in the shower and all the heat is still in your muscles.

But the Honda is the most fun, riding up and down the streets, parking meters ticking by. I love that at any time you can look up and see the sky and the trees and the tops of buildings sliding past.

As he drifted toward sleep he saw Soma on her rented moped, riding the streets of Santiago, meandering in and out of neighborhoods, the city an elaborate version of one of Christopher's drawings: smog on the mountains, planes settling down over the vineyards by the airport, tourists streaming toward the shore, a thousand lamps going on and off in windows high in the buildings.

Did I mention that Violetta has a girlfriend? She calls her her pareja, *like the other shoe in a pair. Her name is Pamela and she grows bougainvillea. She is in charge of it for several huge buildings and she took me to see it today. It crawls probably a hundred meters high up the side of one of her towers downtown. The bricks are thick with it. Pamela said to wait, and we waited as the sun moved, and when it got to the corner of the building, all that bougainvillea, starting at the left, then halfway across, and then, for about twenty seconds, every single flower, caught on fire with the light.*

Sometimes I can't believe I've been allowed to live this long, to see these things. After everything, after all this, I still can't help but think it is so lovely. Isn't it, David? Isn't all of it so damn outrageously beautiful?

17

That night he dreamed of snow. He was in the north, in the Yukon-Charley, in the little cabin at Camp Nowhere, and snow fell in the gaps, weighing down the boughs, filling the valley.

In the dream a figure labored up from the creek, feeling its way through the spruce, a hand going to branches as it pushed its way forward. Despite the snow and distance, he could tell the figure was a woman — he knew this from her gait, the shape of her hips. She was stooped under a load, her face hidden behind a hood. She brought her feet up through the snow. Behind her, faintly, traveled the shadows of animals, accompanying her out of the woods: squirrels and foxes and a pair of ghostly caribou, even a huge, sleek lynx, all of them looking right and left before taking a few more wary steps, insubstantial as shadows. She left the edge of the trees and started across the meadow. The animals followed, gathering behind her, stepping through the starlight, sniffing at the air, and her footprints, the places she had been.

She went not to the door but straight to the window where Winkler stood. She pressed a mitten to the pane and traced the frost there. His own hand went to the glass to meet it. "Naaliyah?" he said, but the figure was smaller than Naaliyah, lighter, and when her face finally turned toward the glass, he knew who it was, what the smile on her face meant.

He woke, and went to the window. The neighboring houses were dark and quiet. A train was easing into the rail yard, a yellow engine with a dozen or so tanker cars pulling in behind it. A gentle snow had begun, its hundred thousand crystals touching down everywhere, on the train cars, and atop the big fuel tanks at the port, and all across the quiet black fields of the harbor. The stars had revolved again, and the Earth was tilting away from the sun.

Snow fell in the city; ice reached across the ponds; the sea groaned as it collapsed, again and again, onto the wharf.

Acknowledgments

I am indebted to the National Endowment for the Arts, the Christopher Isher- wood Foundation, and to Princeton University for its generous Hodder Fellowship — thank you, Mary Hodder. Enormous gratitude to Nan Graham and the incomparable Wendy Weil. Also: Molly Kleinman, Emily Forland, Alexis Gargagliano, Judy Mitchell, and Alan Heathcock. To my brothers, always. To Hal and Jacque Eastman for their unceasing encouragement. To most everyone else: You're in here. For more information on snow crystals, visit the excellent site www.snowcrystals.net.

More than anything, thank you, Shauna, for all your countless graces.

About the Author

Anthony Doerr is the author of *The Shell Collector*, a collection of stories. He has received two O. Henry Prizes, a grant from the National Endowment for the Arts, the Rome Prize from the American Academy of Arts and Letters, and the prestigious Hodder Fellowship from Princeton University. *The Shell Collector* won the 2002 Discover Prize for Fiction and the Ohioana Book Award, and Doerr shared the New York Public Library's 2003 Young Lions Award. He lives with his wife and two sons in Boise, Idaho.

The employees of Thorndike Press hope you have enjoyed this Large Print book. All our Thorndike and Wheeler Large Print titles are designed for easy reading, and all our books are made to last. Other Thorndike Press Large Print books are available at your library, through selected bookstores, or directly from us.

For information about titles, please call:

(800) 223-1244

or visit our Web site at:

www.gale.com/thorndike
www.gale.com/wheeler

To share your comments, please write:

Publisher
Thorndike Press
295 Kennedy Memorial Drive
Waterville, ME   04901